Tante

TANTE

BY
ANNE DOUGLAS SEDGWICK
(MRS. BASIL DE SÉLINCOURT)

AUTHOR OF
THE LITTLE FRENCH GIRL, Etc.

WILDSIDE PRESS

Made in the United States of America

TANTE

TANTE

PART I

CHAPTER I

IT was the evening of Madame Okraska's concert at the old St. James's Hall. London was still the place of the muffled roar and the endearing ugliness. Horse-'buses plied soberly in an unwidened Piccadilly. The private motor was a curiosity. Berlin had not been emulated in an altered Mall nor New York in the façades of giant hotels. The Saturday and Monday pops were still an institution; and the bell of the muffin-man, in such a wintry season, passed frequently along the foggy streets and squares. Already the epoch seems remote.

Madame Okraska was pausing on her way from St. Petersburg to New York and this was the only concert she was to give in London that winter. For many hours the enthusiasts who had come to secure unreserved seats had been sitting on the stone stairs that led to the balcony or gallery, or on the still narrower, darker and colder flight that led to the orchestra from Piccadilly Place. From the adjacent hall they could hear the strains of the Moore & Burgess Minstrels, blatant and innocuously vulgar; and the determined mirth, anatomized by distance, sounded a little melancholy. To those of an imaginative turn of mind it might have seemed that they waited in a tunnel at one far end of which could be perceived the tiny memory of tea at an Aerated Bread shop and at the other the vision of the delights to which they would emerge. For there was no one in the world like Madame Okraska, and to see and hear her was worth cold and weariness and hunger. Not only was she the most famous of living pianists but one of the most beautiful of women; and upon this restoring fact many of the most weary stayed themselves, return-

3

ing again and again to gaze at the pictured face that adorned the outer cover of the programme.

Illuminated by chill gas-jets, armed with books and sand-wiches, the serried and devoted ranks were composed of typical concert-goers, of types, in some cases, becoming as extinct as the muffin-man; young art-students from the suburbs, dressed in Liberty serges and velveteens, and reading ninepenny editions of Browning and Rossetti — though a few, already, were reading Yeats; middle-aged spinsters from Bayswater or South Kensing-ton, who took their weekly concert as they took their daily bath; many earnest young men, soft-hatted and long-haired, studying scores; the usual contingent of the fashionable and economical lady; and the pale-faced business man, bringing an air of duty to the pursuit of pleasure.

Some time before the doors opened a growing urgency began to make itself felt. People got up from their insecurely balanced camp-stools or rose stiffly from the stone steps to turn and stand shoulder to shoulder, subtly transformed from comrades in dis-comfort to combatants for a hazardous reward. The field for personal endeavour was small; the stairs were narrow and their occupants packed like sardines; yet everybody hoped to get a better seat than their positions entitled them to hope for. Hope and fear increased in intensity with the distance from the doors, those mute, mystic doors behind which had not yet been heard a chink or a shuffle and against which leaned, now balefully visible, the earliest comers of all, jaded, pallid, but insufferably assured. The summons came at length in the sound of drawn bolts and chains and a peremptory official voice, blood-tingling as a trumpet-call; and the crowd, shoulder to shoulder and foot to foot, with rigid lips and eyes uplifted, began to mount like one man. Step by step they went, steady and wary, each pressing upon those who went before and presenting a resistant back to those who followed after. The close, emulous contacts bred stealthy strifes and hatreds. A small lady, with short grey hair and thin red face and the conscienceless, smiling eye of a hypno-tized creature, drove her way along the wall and mounted with the agility of a lizard to a place several steps above. Others were infected by the successful outlawry and there were some moments of swaying and striving before the crowd adjusted itself to its self-protective solidity. Emerged upon the broader stairs they ascended panting and scurrying, in a wild stampede, to the sudden quiet and chill and emptiness of the familiar hall, with its high-ranged plaster cupids, whose cheeks and breasts and thighs were thrown comically into relief by a thick coating of dust. Here a permanent fog seemed to hang under the roof; only a few lights twinkled frugally; and the querulous voice of the programme-seller punctuated the monotonous torrent of feet. Row upon row, the seats were filled as if by tumultuous waters entering appointed channels, programmes rustled, sandwiches were drawn from clammy packets, and the thin-faced lady, iniquitously ensconced in the middle of the front row in the gallery, had taken out a strip of knitting and was blandly ready for the evening.

"I always come up here," said one of the ladies from Kensington to a friend. "One hears her pianissimo more perfectly than anywhere else. What a magnificent programme! I shall be glad to hear her give the Schumann Fantaisie in C Major again."

"I think I look forward more to the Bach Fantaisie than to anything," said her companion.

She exposed herself to a pained protest: "Oh surely not; not Bach; I do not come for my Bach to Okraska. She belongs too definitely to the romantics to grasp Bach. Beethoven, if you will; she may give us the Appassionata superbly; but not Bach; she lacks self-effacement."

"Liszt said that no one played Bach as she did."

Authority did not serve her. "Liszt may have said it; Brahms would not have;" was the rejoinder.

Down in the orchestra chairs the audience was roughly to be divided into the technical and the personal devotees; those who chose seats from which they could dwell upon Madame Okraska's full face over the shining surfaces of the piano or upon her profile from the side; and those who, from behind her back, were dedicated to the study of her magical hands.

"I do hope," said a girl in the centre of the front row of chairs, a place of dizzy joy, for one might almost touch the goddess as she sat at the piano, "I do hope she's not getting fat. Someone said they heard she was. I never want to see her again if she gets fat. It would be too awful."

The girl with her conjectured sadly that Madame Okraska must be well over forty.

"I beg your pardon," a massive lady dressed in an embroidered sack-like garment, and wearing many strings of iridescent shells around her throat, leaned forward from behind to say: "She is forty-six; I happen to know; a friend of mine has met Madame Okraska's secretary. Forty-six; but she keeps her beauty wonderfully; her figure is quite beautiful."

An element of personal excitement was evident in the people who sat in these nearest chairs; it constituted a bond, though by no means a friendly one. Emulation, the irrepressible desire to impart knowledge, broke down normal barriers. The massive lady was slightly flushed and her manner almost menacing. Her information was received with a vague, half resentful murmur.

"She looks younger," she continued, while her listeners gave her an unwilling yet alert attention. "It is extraordinary how she retains her youth. But it tells, it tells, the tragic life; one sees it in her eyes and lips."

The first girl now put forward with resolution her pawn of knowledge.

"It has been tragic, hasn't it. The dreadful man she was married to by her relations when she was hardly more than a child, and the death of her second husband. He was the Baron von Marwitz; her real name is von Marwitz; Okraska is her maiden name. He was drowned in saving her life, you know."

"The Baron von Marwitz was drowned no one knows how; he was found drowned; she found his body. She went into a convent after his death."

"A convent? I was reading a life of her in a magazine the other day and nothing was said about a convent."

The massive lady smiled tolerantly: "Nothing would be.

She has a horror of publicity. Yes, she is a mystic as well as an artist; she only resigned the religious life because of what she felt to be her duty to her adopted daughter. One sees the mystical side in her face and hears it in her music."

Madame Okraska was one of those about whose footsteps legends rise, and legend could add little to the romantic facts of her life; — the poverty of her youth; her *début* as a child prodigy at Warsaw and the sudden fame that had followed it; the coronets that had been laid at her feet; her private tragedies, cosmopolitan friendships, her scholarship, caprices and generosities. She had been the Egeria, smiling in mystery, of half a dozen famous men. And it was as satisfactory to the devotee to hear that she always wore white and drank coffee for her breakfast, as that Rubinstein and Liszt had blessed her and Leschetitsky said that she had nothing to learn. Her very origin belonged to the realm of romantic fiction. Her father, a Polish music-master in New Orleans, had run away with his pupil, a beautiful Spanish girl of a good Creole family. Their child had been born in Cracow while the Austrians were bombarding it in 1848.

The lights were now all up and the stalls filling. Ladies and gentlemen from the suburbs, over early, were the first comers; eager schoolgirls marshalled by governesses; scrupulous students with music under their arms, and, finally, the rustling, shining, chattering crowd of fashionable London.

The massive lady had by now her little audience, cowed, if still slightly sulky, well in hand. She pointed out each notability to them, and indirectly, to all her neighbours. The Duchess of Bannister and Lady Champney, the famous beauty; the Prime Minister, whom the girls could have recognized for themselves, and Sir Alliston Compton, the poet. Had they read his sonnet to Madame Okraska, last year, in the "Fortnightly"? They had not. "I wonder who that odd looking girl is with him and the old lady?" one of them ventured.

"A little grand-daughter, a little niece," said the massive lady, who did not know. "Poor Sir Alliston's wife is in a lunatic asylum; isn't it a melancholy head?"

But now one of her listeners, a lady also in the front row,

leaned forward to say hurriedly and deprecatingly, her face suffused with shyness: "That nice young girl is Madame Okraska's adopted daughter. The old lady is Mrs. Forrester, Madame Okraska's great friend; my sister-in-law was for many years a governess in her family, and that is how I come to know."

All those who had heard her turned their eyes upon the young girl, who, in an old-fashioned white cloak, with a collar of swansdown turned up round her fair hair, was taking her place with her companions in the front row of the orchestra-stalls. Even the massive lady was rapt away to silence.

"But I thought the adopted daughter was an Italian," one girl at last commented, having gazed her fill at the being so exalted by fortune. "Her skin is rather dark, but that yellow hair does n't look Italian."

"She is a Norwegian," said the massive lady, keeping however an eye on the relative of Mrs. Forrester's governess; "the child of Norwegian peasants. Don't you know the story? Madame Okraska found the poor little creature lost in a Norwegian forest, leaped from her carriage and took her into her arms; the parents were destitute and she bought the child from them. She is the very soul of generosity."

"She does n't look like a peasant," said the girl, with a flavour of discontent, as though a more apparent rusticity would have lent special magnanimity to Madame Okraska's benevolence. But the massive lady assured her: "Oh yes, it is the true Norse type; their peasantry has its patrician quality. I have been to Norway. Sir Alliston looks very much moved, does n't he? He has been in love with Madame Okraska for years." And she added with a deep sigh of satisfaction: "There has never been a word whispered against her reputation; never a word —'Pure as the foam on midmost ocean tossed.'"

Among the crowds thronging densely to their places, a young man of soldierly aspect, with a dark, narrow face, black hair and square blue eyes, was making his way to a seat in the third row of stalls. His name was Gregory Jardine; he was not a soldier — though he looked one — but a barrister, and he was content to count himself, not altogether incorrectly, a Philistine in all

matters æsthetic. Good music he listened to with, as he put it,
unintelligent and barbarous enjoyment; and since he had, shamefully, never yet heard the great pianist, he had bought the best
stall procurable some weeks before, and now, after a taxing day
in the law courts, had foregone his after-dinner coffee in order
not to miss one note of the opening Appassionata; it was a
sonata he was very fond of. He sometimes picked out the air
of the slow movement on the piano with heavy deliberation; his
musical equipment did not carry him as far as the variations.

When he reached his seat he found it to be by chance next that
of his sister-in-law, his brother Oliver's wife, a pretty, jewelled
and jewel-like young woman, an American of a complicatedly
cosmopolitan type. Gregory liked Betty Jardine, and always
wondered how she had come to marry Oliver, whom he rather
scorned; but he was not altogether pleased to find her near him.
He preferred to take his music in solitude; and Betty was very
talkative.

"Well, this is nice, Gregory!" she said. "You and Captain
Ashton know each other, don't you. No, I couldn't persuade
Oliver to come; he wouldn't give up his whist. Isn't Oliver
dreadful; he moves from the saddle to the whist-table, and back
again; and that is all. Captain Ashton and I have been com-
paring notes; we find that we have missed hardly any of Madame
Okraska's concerts in London. I was only ten when I heard the
first she ever gave here; my governess took me; and actually
Captain Ashton was here on that day, too. Wasn't she a miracle
of loveliness? It was twenty years ago; she had already her
European reputation. It was just after she had divorced that
horrible first husband of hers and married the Baron von Marwitz. This isn't your initiation, of course, Gregory?"

"Actually my initiation," said Gregory, examining the portrait of Madame Okraska on the cover of the programme.

"But you've seen her at Mrs. Forrester's? She always stays
with Mrs. Forrester."

"I know; but I've always missed her, or, at all events, never
been asked to meet her."

"I certainly never have been," said Betty Jardine. "But

Mrs. Forrester thinks of me as frivolity personified, I know, and does n't care to admit anything lower than a cabinet minister or a poet laureate when she has her lion domiciled. She is an old darling; but, between ourselves, she does take her lions a little too seriously, does n't she. Well, prepare for a *coup de foudre*, Gregory. You 'll be sure to fall in love with her. Everybody falls in love with her. Captain Ashton has been in love with her for twenty years. She is extraordinary."

"I 'm ready to be subjugated," said Gregory. "Do people really hang on her hands and kiss them? Shall I want to hang on her hands and kiss them?"

"There is no telling what she will do with us," said Lady Jardine.

Gregory Jardine's face, however, was not framed to express enthusiasm. It was caustic, cold and delicate. His eyes were as clear and as hard as a sky of frosty morning, and his small, firm lips were hard. His chin and lower lip advanced slightly, so that when he smiled his teeth met edge to edge, and the little black moustache, to which he often gave an absent upward twist, lent an ironic quality to this chill, gay smile, at times almost Mephistophelian. He sat twisting the moustache now, leaning his head to listen, amidst the babel of voices, to Betty Jardine's chatter, and the thrills of infectious expectancy that passed over the audience like breezes over a corn-field left him unaffected. His observant, indifferent glance had in it something of the schoolboy's barbarian calm and something of the disabused impersonality of worldly experience.

"Who is the young lady with Mrs. Forrester?" he asked presently. "In white, with yellow hair. Just in front of us. Do you know?"

Betty had leaned forward to look. "Don't you even know her by sight?" she said. "That is Miss Woodruff, the girl who follows Madame Okraska everywhere. She attached herself to her years ago, I believe, in Rome or Paris; — some sort of little art-student she was. What a bore that sort of devotion must be. Is n't she queer?"

"I had heard that she 's an adopted daughter," said Captain

Ashton; "the child of Norwegian peasants, and that Madame Okraska found her in a Norwegian forest — by moonlight; — a most romantic story."

"A fable, I think. Someone was telling me about her the other day. She is only a camp-follower and *protégée;* and a compatriot of mine. She is an orphan and Madame Okraska supports her."

"She does n't look like a *protégée,"* said Gregory Jardine, his eyes on the young person thus described; "she looks like a protector."

"I should think she must be most of all a problem," said Betty. "What a price to pay for celebrity — these hangers-on who make one ridiculous by their infatuation. Madame Okraska is incapable of defending herself against them, I hear. The child's clothes might have come from Norway!"

The *protégée,* protector or problem, who turned to them now and then her oddly blunted, oddly resolute young profile, had tawny hair, and a sun-browned skin. She wore a little white silk frock with flat bows of dull blue upon it. Her evening cloak was bordered with swansdown. Two black bows, one at the crown of her head and one at the nape of her neck, secured the thick plaits of her hair, which was parted and brushed up from her forehead in a bygone school-girlish fashion. She made Gregory think of a picture by Alfred Stevens he had seen somewhere and of an archaic Greek statue, and her appearance and demeanour interested him. He continued to look at her while the unrest and expectancy of the audience rolled into billows of excitement.

A staid, melancholy man, forerunner of the great artist, had appeared and performed his customary and cryptic function. "Why do they always screw up the piano-stool at the last moment!" Betty Jardine murmured. "Is it to pepper our tongues with anguish before the claret? — Oh, she must be coming now! She always keeps one waiting like this!"

The billows had surged to a storm. Signs of frenzy were visible in the faces on the platform. They had caught a glimpse of the approaching divinity.

"Here she is!" cried Betty Jardine. Like everybody else she was clapping frantically, like everybody, that is, except Gregory Jardine; for Gregory, his elbow in his hand, his fingers still neatly twisting the end of his moustache, continued to observe the young girl in the front row, whose face, illuminated and irradiated, was upturned to the figure now mounting to the platform.

CHAPTER II

THE hush that had fallen was like the hush that falls on Alpine watchers in the moment before sunrise, and, with the great musician's slow emerging from below, it was as if the sun had risen.

She came, with her indolent step, the thunder of hands and voices greeting her; and those who gazed at her from the platform saw the pearl-wreathed hair and opulent white shoulders, and those who gazed at her from beneath saw the strange and musing face. Then she stood before them and her dark eyes dwelt, impassive and melancholy, upon the sea of faces, tumultuous and blurred with clapping hands. The sound was like the roaring of the sea and she stood as a goddess might have stood at the brink of the ocean, indifferent and unaware, absorbed in dreams of ancient sorrow. The ovation was so prolonged and she stood there for so long — hardly less the indifferent goddess because, from time to time, she bowed her own famous bow, stately, old-fashioned, formally and sublimely submissive,— that every eye in the great audience could feast upon her in a rapturous assurance of leisure.

She was a woman of forty-eight, of an ample though still beautiful figure. Her flowing dress of white brocade made no attempt to compress, to sustain or to attenuate. No one could say that a woman who stood as she did, with the port of a goddess — the small head majestically poised over such shoulders and such a breast — was getting fat; yet no one could deny that there was redundancy. She was not redundant as other women were; she was not elegant as other women were; she seemed in nothing like others. Her dress was strange; it had folds and amplitudes and dim disks of silver broideries at breast and knee that made it like the dress of some Venetian lady, drawn at random from an ancestral marriage coffer and put on dreamily

13

with no thought of aptness. Her hair was strange; no other woman's hair was massed and folded as was hers, hair dark as night and intertwined and looped with twisted strands of pearl and diamond. Her face was strange, that crowning face, known to all the world. Disparate racial elements mingled in the long Southern oval and the Slavonic modelling of brow and cheek-bone. The lips, serene and passionate, deeply sunken at the corners and shadowed with a pencilling of down, were the lips of Spain; all the mystery of the South was in the grave and tragic eyes. Yet the eyes were cold; and touches of wild ancestral suffering, like the sudden clash of spurs in the languors of a Polonaise, marked the wide nostrils and the heavy eyelids and the broad, black crooked eye-brows that seemed to stammer a little in the perfect sentence of her face.

She subjugated and she appealed. Her adorers were divided between the longing to lie down under her feet and to fold her protectingly in their arms. Calf-love is an undying element in human-nature, a shame-faced derogatory name for the romantic, self-immolating emotion woven from fancy, yearning and the infection of other's ardour. Love of this foam and flame quality, too tender to be mere æsthetic absorption in a beautiful object, too selfless to be sensual, too intense to be only absurd, rose up towards Madame Okraska and encompassed her from hundreds of hearts and eyes. The whole audience was for her one vast heart of adoration, one fixed face of half-hypnotized tenderness. And there she stood before them;—Madame Okraska whom crowned heads delighted to honour; Madame Okraska who got a thousand pounds a night; Madame Okraska who played as no one in the world could play; looking down over them, looking up and around at them, as if, now, a little troubled by the prolonged adulation, patient yet weary, like a mistress assaulted, after long absence, by the violent joy of a great Newfoundland dog; smiling a little, though buffeted, and unwilling to chill the ardent heart by a reprimand. And more than all she was like a great white rose that, fading in the soft, thick, scented air of a hot-house, droops languidly with loosened petals.

They let her go at last and she took her place at the piano.

Her hands fell softly on a group of dreamy ascending chords. Her face, then, in a long pause, took on a rapt expectancy and power. She was the priestess waiting before her altar for the descent of the god, glorious and dreadful. And it was as if with the chill and shudder of a possession that, breathing deeply, drawing her shoulders a little together, she lifted her hands and played. She became the possessed and articulate priestess, her soul, her mind, her passion lent to the message spoken through her. The tumult and insatiable outcry of the Appassionata spread like a river over her listeners. And as she played her face grew more rapt in its brooding concentration, the eyes half-closed, the nostrils wide, the jaw dropping and giving to the mouth an expression at once relaxed and vigilant.

To criticize with the spell of Madame Okraska's personality upon one was hardly possible. Emerged from the glamour, there were those, pretending to professional discriminations, who suggested that she lacked the masculine and classic disciplines of interpretation; that her rendering, though breathed through with noble dignities, was coloured by a capricious and passionate personality; that it was the feeling rather than the thought of the music that she excelled in expressing, its suffering rather than its serenity. Only a rare listener, here and there among her world-wide audiences, was aware of deeper deficiencies and of the slow changes that time had wrought in her art. For it was inspiration no longer; it was the memory of inspiration. The Nemesis of the artist who expresses, not what he feels, but what he is expected to feel, what he has undertaken to feel, had fallen upon the great woman. Her art, too, showed the fragrant taint of an artificial atmosphere. She had played ten times when she should have played once. She lived on her capital of experience, no longer renewing her life, and her renderings had lost that quality of the greatest, the living communication with the experience embodied in the music. It was on the stereotyped memories of such communication that she depended, on the half hypnotic possession by the past; filling in vacancies with temperamental caprice or an emotion no longer the music's but her own.

But to the enchanted ear of the multitude, professional and unprofessional, the essential vitality was there, the vitality embodied to the enchanted eye by the white figure with its drooping, pearl-wreathed head and face sunken in sombre ecstasy. She gave them all they craved: — passion, stormy struggle, the tears of hopeless love, the chill smile of lassitude in accepted defeat, the unappeasable longing for the past. They listened, and their hearts lapsed back from the hallucinated unity of enthusiasm each to its own identity, an identity isolated, intensified, tortured exquisitely by the expression of dim yearnings. All that had been beautiful in the pain and joy that through long ages had gone to the building up of each human consciousness, re-entered and possessed it; the fragrance of blossoming trees, the farewell gaze of dying eyes, the speechless smile of lovers, ancestral memories of Spring-times, loves, and partings, evoked by this poignant lure from dim realms of sub-consciousness, like subterranean rivers rising through creaks and crannies towards the lifted wand of the diviner. It seemed the quintessence of human experience, the ecstasy of perfect and enfranchising sorrow, distilled from the shackling, smirching half-sorrows of actual life. Some of the listening faces smiled; some were sodden, stupefied rather than enlightened; some showed a sensual rudimentary gratification; some, lapped in the tide, yet unaware of its significance, were merely silly. But no Orpheus, wildly harping through the woods, ever led more enthralled and subjugated listeners.

Gregory Jardine's face was neither sodden nor silly nor sensual; but it did not wear the enchanted look of the true votary. Instinctively this young man, though it was emotion that he found in music, resisted any too obvious assault upon his feelings, taking refuge in irony from their force when roused. For the form of music, and its intellectual content, he had little appreciation, and he was thus the more exposed to its emotional appeal; but his intuition of the source and significance of the appeal remained singularly just and accurate. He could not now have analysed his sense of protest and dissatisfaction; yet, while the charm grasped and encircled him, making him, as he said to himself, idiotically grovel or inanely soar, he repelled the poignant sweetness and the thrills that went through him were thrills of a half-unwilling joy.

He sat straightly, his arms folded, his head bent as he twisted the end of his moustache, his eye fixed on the great musician; and he wondered what was the matter with him, or with her. It was as if he couldn't get at the music. Something interfered, something exquisite yet ambiguous, alluring yet never satisfying.

His glance fell presently from the pianist's drooping head to the face of the *protégée,* and the contrast between what was expressed by this young person's gaze and attitude and what he was himself feeling again drew his attention to her. No grovelling and no soaring was here, but an elation almost stern, a brooding concentration almost maternal, a dedicated power. Madame Okraska, he reflected, must be an extraordinary person if she really deserved that gaze. He didn't believe that she quite did. His dissatisfaction with the music extended itself to the musician and, looking from her face to the girl's, he remembered with scepticism Betty's account of their relation.

A group of Chopin Preludes and a Brahms Rhapsodie Hongroise brought the first half of the concert to a close, and Gregory watched with amusement, during the ensuing scene, the vagaries of the intoxicated crowd. People rose to their feet, clapping, shouting, bellowing, screaming. He saw on the platform the face of the massive lady, haggard, fierce, devouring; the face of the shy lady, suffused, the eyes half dazed with adoration like those of a saint in rapture. Old Mrs. Forrester, with her juvenile auburn head, laughed irrepressibly while she clapped, like a happy child. The old poet was nearly moved to tears. Only the *protégée* remained, as it were, outside the infection. She smiled slightly and steadily, as if in a proud contentment, and clapped now and then quite softly, and she turned once and scanned the audience with eyes accustomed to ovations and appraising the significance of this one.

Madame Okraska was recalled six times, but she could not be prevailed upon to give an encore, though for a long time a voice

2

bayed intermittently:—"The Berceuse! Chopin's Berceuse!" The vast harmonies of entreaty and delight died down to sporadic solos, taken up more and more faint-heartedly by weary yet still hopeful hands.

Still smiling slightly, with a preoccupied air, the young girl looked about her, or leaned forward to listen to some kindly bantering addressed to her by Sir Alliston. She hardly spoke, but Gregory perceived that she was by no means shy. She so pleasantly engaged his attention that when Sir Alliston got up from his seat next hers there was another motive than the mere wish to speak to his old friend in his intention of joining Mrs. Forrester for a few moments. The project was not definite and he abandoned it when his relative, Miss Eleanor Scrotton, tense, significant and wearing the sacramental expression customary with her on such occasions, hurried to the empty seat and dropped into it. Eleanor's enthusiasms oppressed him and Betty had told him that Madame Okraska was become the most absorbing of them. His mother and Eleanor's had been cousins. Her father, the late Sir Jonas Scrotton, heavily distinguished in the world of literature and politics, had died only the year before. Gregory remembered him as a vindictive and portentous old man presiding at Miss Scrotton's tea-parties in a black silk skull-cap, and one could but admire in Miss Scrotton the reverence and devotion that had not only borne with but gloried in him. If the amplitude of his mantle had not descended upon her one might metaphorically say that the black skull-cap had. Gregory felt that he might have liked Eleanor better if she had n't been so unintermittently and unilluminatingly intelligent. She wrote scholarly articles in the graver reviews — articles that he invariably skipped — she was always armed with an appreciation and she had the air of thinking the intellectual reputation of London very much her responsibility. Above all she was dowered with an overwhelming power of enthusiasm. Eleanor dressed well and had a handsome, commanding profile with small, compressed lips and large, prominent, melancholy eyes that wickedly reminded Gregory of the eyes of a beetle. Beneath the black feather boa that was thrown round her neck, her thin shoulder-blades, while she talked to Mrs. Forrester and sketched with pouncing fingers the phrasing of certain passages, jerked and vibrated oddly. Mrs. Forrester nodded, smiled, acquiesced. She was rather fond of Eleanor. Their talk was for each other. Miss Woodruff, unheeded, but with nothing of the air of one consciously insignificant, sat looking before her. Beside Eleanor's vehemence and Mrs. Forrester's vivacity she made Gregory think of a tranquil landscape seen at dawn.

He was thus thinking, and looking at her, when, as though sub-consciously aware of his gaze, she suddenly turned her head and looked round at him.

Her eyes, in the long moment while their glances were interchanged, were so clear and deliberate, so unmoved by anything but a certain surprise, that he felt no impulse to pretend politely that he had not been caught staring. They scrutinized each other, gravely, serenely, intently, until a thunder of applause, like a tidal wave surging over the hall, seemed to engulf their gaze. Madame Okraska was once more emerging. Miss Scrotton, catching up her boa, her programme and her fan, scuttled back to her seat with an air of desperate gravity; Sir Alliston returned to his; Mrs. Forrester welcomed him with a smile and a finger at her lips; and as the pianist seated herself and cast a long glance over the still disarranged and cautiously rustling audience, Gregory saw that Miss Woodruff had no further thought for him.

CHAPTER III

MRS. FORRESTER was dispensing tea in her lofty drawing-room which, with its illumined heights and dim recesses, gave to the ceremony an almost ritualistic state. Mrs. Forrester's drawing-room and Mrs. Forrester herself were long-established features of London, and not to have sat beneath the Louis Quinze chandelier nor have drunk tea out of the blue Worcester cups was to have missed something significant of the typical London spectacle.

The drawing-room seemed most characteristic when one came to it from a fog outside, as people had done to-day, and when Mrs. Forrester was found presiding over the blue cups. She was an old lady with auburn hair elaborately dressed and singularly bound in snoods of velvet. She wore flowing silken trains and loose ruffled sacques of a curious bygone cut, and upon each wrist was clasped, mounted on a velvet band, a large square emerald, set in heavily chased gold. The glance of her eyes was as surprisingly youthful as the color of her hair, and her face, though complicatedly wrinkled, had an almost girlish gaiety and vigour. Abrupt and merry, Mrs. Forrester was arresting to the attention and rather alarming. She swept aside bores; she selected the significant; socially she could be rather merciless; but her kindness was without limits when she attached herself, and in private life she suffered fools, if not gladly at all events humorously, in the persons of her three heavy and exemplary sons, who had married wives as unimpeachable and as uninteresting as themselves and provided her with a multitude of grandchildren. Mrs. Forrester fulfilled punctiliously all her duties towards these young folk, and it never occurred to her sons and daughters-in-law that they and their interests were not her chief preoccupation. The energy and variety of her nature were, however, given to her social relations and to her personal friendships, which were many and engrossing. These friendships were always highly flavoured. Mrs. Forrester had a *flair* for genius and needed no popular accrediting to make it manifest to her. And it was n't enough to be merely a genius; there were many of the species, eminent and emblazoned, who were never asked to come under the Louis Quinze chandelier. She asked of her talented friends personal distinction, the power of being interesting in more than their art.

Such a genius, pre-eminently such a one, was Madame von Marwitz. She was more than under the chandelier; Mrs. Forrester's house, when she was in London, was her home. "I am safe with you," she had said to Mrs. Forrester, "with you I am never pursued and never bored." Where Mrs. Forrester evaded and relegated bores, Madame von Marwitz sombrely and helplessly hated them. "What can I do?" she said. "If no one will protect me I am delivered to them. It is a plague of locusts. They devour me. Oh their letters! Oh their flowers! Oh their love and their stupidity! No, the earth is black with them."

Madame von Marwitz was protected from the swarms while she visited her old friend. The habits of the house were altered to suit hers. She stayed in her rooms or came down as she chose. She had complete liberty in everything.

To-day she had not as yet appeared, and everyone had come with the hope of seeing her. There was Lady Campion, the most tactful and discreet of admirers; and Sir Alliston, who would be perhaps asked to go up to her if she did not come down; and Eleanor Scrotton who would certainly go up unasked; and old Miss Harding, a former governess of Mrs. Forrester's sons and a person privileged, who had come leading an evident yet pathetic locust, her brother's widow, little Mrs. Harding, the shy lady of the platform. Miss Harding had told Mrs. Forrester about this sister-in-law and of how, since her husband's death, she had lived for philanthropy, and music in the person of Madame Okraska. She had never met her. She did not ask to meet her now. She would only sit in a corner and gaze. Mrs. Forrester had been moved by the account of such humble faith and had told Miss Harding to bring her sister-in-law.

"I have sent for Karen," Mrs. Forrester said, greeting Gregory Jardine, who came in after Miss and Mrs. Harding; "she will tell us if our chances are good. It was your first time, last night, was n't it, Gregory? I do hope that she may come down."

Gregory Jardine was not a bore, but Mrs. Forrester suspected him to be one of the infatuated. He belonged, she imagined, seeing him appear so promptly after his initiation, to the category of dazzled circlers who fell into her drawing-room in their myriads while Mercedes was with her, like frizzled moths into a candle. Mrs. Forrester had sympathy with moths, and was fond of Gregory, whom she greeted with significant kindliness.

"I never ask her to come down," she went on now to explain to him and to the Hardings. "Never, never. She could not bear that. But she often does come; and she has heard to-day from Karen Woodruff that special friends are hoping to see her. So your chances are good, I think. Ah, here is Karen."

Gregory did not trouble to undeceive his old friend. It was his habit to have tea with her once or twice a month, and his motive in coming to-day had hardly been distinguishable from his usual impulse. If he had come hoping to see anybody, it had been to see the *protégée,* and he watched her now as she advanced down the great room with her cheerful, unembarrassed look, the look of a person serenely accustomed to a publicity in which she had no part.

Seen thus at full length and in full face he found her more than ever like an Alfred Stevens and an archaic Greek statue. Long-limbed, thick-waisted, spare and strong, she wore a straight, grey dress — the dress of a little convent girl coming into the *parloir* on a day of visits — which emphasized the boyish aspect of her figure. Narrow frills of white were at wrist and neck; her shoes were low heeled and square toed; and around her neck a gold locket hung on a black velvet ribbon.

Mrs. Forrester held out her hand to her with the undiscerning kindliness that greets the mere emissary. "Well, my dear, what news of our Tante? Is she coming, do you think?" she inquired. "This is Lady Campion; she has never yet met Tante." The word was pronounced in German fashion.

"I am not sure that she will come," said Miss Woodruff, looking around the assembled circle, while Mrs. Forrester still held her hand. "She is still very tired, so I cannot be sure; I hope so." She smiled calmly at Sir Alliston and Miss Scrotton who were talking together and then lifted her eyes to Gregory who stood near.

"You know Mr. Jardine?" Mrs. Forrester asked, seeing the pleased recognition on the girl's face. "It was his first time last night."

"No, I do not know him," said Miss Woodruff, "but I saw him at the concert. Was it his first time? Think of that."

"Now sit here, child, and tell me about Tante," said Mrs. Forrester, drawing the girl down to a chair beside her. "I saw that she was very tired this morning. She had her massage?" Mrs. Forrester questioned in a lower voice.

"Yes; and fortunately she was able to sleep for two hours after that. Then Mr. Schultz came and she had to see him, and that was tiring."

Mr. Schultz was Madame Okraska's secretary.

"Dear, dear, what a pity that he had to bother her. Did she drink the egg-flip I had sent up to her? Mrs. Jenkins makes them excellently as a rule."

"I did my best to persuade her," said Miss Woodruff, "but she did not seem to care for it."

"Did n't care for it? Was it too sweet? I warned Mrs. Jenkins that her tendency was to put in too much sugar."

"That was it," Miss Woodruff smiled at the other's penetration. "She tasted it and said: '*Trop sucré,*' and put it down. But it was really very nice. I drank it!" said Miss Woodruff.

"But I am so grieved. I shall speak severely to Mrs. Jenkins," Mrs. Forrester murmured, preoccupied. "I am afraid our chances are n't good to-day, Lady Campion," she turned from Miss Woodruff to say. "You must come and dine one night while she is with me. I am always sure of her for dinner."

"She really is n't coming down?" Miss Scrotton leaned over the back of Miss Woodruff's chair to ask with some asperity of manner. "Shall I wait for a little before I go up to her?"

"I can't tell," the young girl replied. "She said she did not know whether she would come or not. She is lying down and reading."

"She does not forget that she comes to me for tea to-morrow?"

"I do not think so, Miss Scrotton."

"Lady Campion wants to talk to you, Karen," Mrs. Forrester now said; "come to this side of the table." And as Sir Alliston was engaged with Miss and Mrs. Harding, Gregory was left to Eleanor Scrotton.

Miss Scrotton felt irritation rather than affection for Gregory Jardine. Yet he was not unimportant to her. Deeper than her pride in old Sir Jonas was her pride in her connection with the Fanshawes, and Gregory's mother had been a Fanshawe. Gregory's very indifference to her and to the standards of the Scrottons had always given to intercourse with him a savour at once acid yet interesting. Though she knew many men of more significance, she remained far more aware of him and his opinions than of theirs. She would have liked Gregory to show more consciousness of her and his relationship, of the fact that she, too, had Fanshawe blood in her veins. She would have liked to impress, or please or, at worst, to displease him. She would very much have liked to secure him more frequently for her dinners and her teas. He vexed and he allured her.

"Do you really mean that last night was the first time you ever heard Mercedes Okraska?" she said, moving to a sofa, to which, somewhat unwillingly, Gregory followed her. "It makes me sorry for you. It's as if a person were to tell you that they'd never before seen the mountains or the sea. If I'd realised that you'd never met her I could have arranged that you should. She often comes to me quite quietly and meets a few friends. She was so devoted to dear father; she called him The Hammer of the Gods. I have the most wonderful letter that she wrote me when he died," Miss Scrotton said, lowering her voice to a reverent pause. "Between ourselves," she went on, "I do sometimes think that our dear Mrs. Forrester cherishes her a little too closely. I confess that I love nothing more than to share my good things. I don't mean that dear Mrs. Forrester does n't; but I should ask more people, frequently and definitely, to meet Mercedes, if I were in her place."

"But if Madame Okraska won't come down and see them?" Gregory inquired.

"Ah, but she will; she will," Miss Scrotton said earnestly; "if it is thought out; arranged for carefully. She does n't, naturally, care to come down on chance, like to-day. She does want to know whom she 's to meet if she makes the effort. She knows of course that Sir Alliston and I are here, and that may bring her; I do hope so for your sake; but of course if she does not come I go up to her. With Mrs. Forrester I am, I think, her nearest friend in England. She has stayed with me in the country; — my tiny flat here would hardly accommodate her. I am going, did you know it, to America with her next week."

"No; really; for a tour?"

"Yes; through the States. We shall be gone till next summer. I know several very charming people in New York and Boston and can help to make it pleasant for Mercedes. Of course for me it is the opportunity of a life-time. Quite apart from her music, she is the most remarkable woman I have ever known."

"She 's clever?"

"Clever is too trivial a word. Her genius goes through everything. We read a great deal together — Dante, Goethe, French essayists, our English poets. To hear her read poetry is almost as wonderful an experience as to hear her play. Is n't it an extraordinary face? One sees it all in her face, I think."

"She is very unusual looking."

"Her face," Miss Scrotton pursued, ignoring her companion's trite comments, "embodies the thoughts and dreams of many races. It makes me always think of Pater's Mona Lisa — you remember: 'Hers is the head upon which all the ends of the world are come and the eyelids are a little weary.' She is, of course, a profoundly tragic person."

"Has she been very unfortunate?"

"Unfortunate indeed. Her youth was passed in bitter poverty; her first marriage was disastrous, and when joy came at last in an ideal second marriage it was shattered by her husband's mysterious death. Yes; he was drowned; found drowned in the lake on their estate in Germany. Mercedes has never been there since. She has never recovered. She is a broken-hearted woman. She sees life as a dark riddle. She counts herself as one of the entombed."

"Dear me," Gregory murmured.

Miss Scrotton glanced at him with some sharpness; but finding his blue eyes fixed abstractedly on Karen Woodruff exonerated him from intending to be disagreeable. "Her childlessness has been a final grief," she added; "a child, as she has often told me, would be a resurrection from the dead."

"And the little girl?" Gregory inquired. "Is she any solace? What is the exact relationship? I hear that she calls her Tante."

"The right to call her Tante is one of Mercedes's gifts to her. She is no relation at all. Mercedes picked her up, literally from the roadside. She is twenty-four, you know; not a child."

"So the story is true, about the Norwegian peasants and the forest?"

"I have to contradict that story at least twice a day," said Miss Scrotton with a smile half indulgent and half weary. "It is true that Karen was found in a forest, but it was the forest of Fontainebleau, *tout simplement;* and it is true that she has Norwegian blood; her mother was a Norwegian; she was the wife of a Norwegian artist in Rome, and there Karen's father, an American, a sculptor of some talent, I believe, met her and ran away with her. They were never married. They lived on chestnuts up among the mountains in Tuscany, I believe, and the mother died when Karen was a little child and the father when she was twelve. Some relatives of the father's put her in a convent school in Paris and she ran away from it and Mercedes found her on the verge of starvation in the forest of Fontainebleau. The Baron von Marwitz had known Mr. Woodruff in Rome and Mercedes persuaded him to take the child into their lives. She had n't a friend or a penny in the world. The father's relatives were delighted to be rid of her and Mercedes has had her on her hands ever since. That is the true story."

"Is n't she fond of her?" Gregory asked.

"Yes, she is fond of her," Miss Scrotton with some impatience replied; "but she is none the less a burden. For a woman like Mercedes, with a life over-full and a strength continually overtaxed, the care and responsibility is an additional weight and weariness."

"Well, but if she misses children so much; this takes the place," Gregory objected.

"Takes the place," Miss Scrotton repeated, "of a child of her own? This little nobody, and an uninteresting nobody, too? Oh, she is a good girl, a very good girl; and she makes herself fairly useful in elementary ways; but how can you imagine that such a tie can satisfy maternal craving?"

"How does she make herself useful?" Gregory asked, waiving the question of maternal cravings. He had vexed Miss Scrotton a good deal, but the theme was one upon which she could not resist enlarging; anything connected with Madame von Marwitz was for her of absorbing interest.

"Well, she is a great deal in Cornwall, at Mercedes's place there," she informed him. "It's a wonderfully lovely place; Les Solitudes; Mercedes built the house. Karen and old Mrs. Talcott look after the little farm and keep things in order."

"Old Mrs. Talcott? Where does she come in?"

"Ah, that is another of Mercedes's romantic benevolences. Mrs. Talcott is a sort of old pensioner; a distant family connection; the funniest old American woman you can conceive of.

She has been with Mercedes since her childhood, and, like everybody else, she is so devotedly attached to her that she regards it as a matter of course that she should be taken care of by her for ever. The way Karen takes her advantages as a matter of course has always vexed me just a little."

"Is Mrs. Talcott interesting?" Gregory pursued his questions with a placid persistence that seemed to indicate real curiosity.

"Good heavens, no!" Miss Scrotton said. "The epitome of the commonplace. She looks like some of the queer old American women one sees in the National Gallery with Baedekers in their hands and bags at their belts; fat, sallow, provincial, with defective grammar and horrible twangs; the kind of American, you know," said Miss Scrotton, warming to her description as she felt that she was amusing Gregory Jardine, "that the other kind always tell you they never by any chance would meet at home."

"And what kind of American is Miss Woodruff? The other kind or Mrs. Talcott's kind?"

"By the other kind I mean Lady Jardine's," said Miss Scrotton; "or — no; she constitutes a further variety; the rarest of all; the kind who would never think about Mrs. Talcott one way or the other. But surely Karen is no kind at all. Could you call her an American? She has never been there. She is a sort of racial waif. The only root, the only nationality she seems to have is Mercedes; her very character is constituted by her relation to Mercedes; her only charm is her devotion — for she is indeed sincerely and wholeheartedly devoted. Mercedes is a sort of fairy-godmother to her, a sun-goddess, who lifted her out of the dust and whirled her away in her chariot. But she isn't interesting," Miss Scrotton again assured him. "She is literal and unemotional, and, in some ways, distinctly dull. I have seen the poor fairy-godmother sigh and shrug sometimes over her inordinately long letters. She writes to her with relentless regularity and I really believe that she imagines that Mercedes quite depends on hearing from her. No; I don't mean that she is conceited; it's not that exactly;

she is only dull; very, very dull; and I don't know how Mercedes endures having her so much with her. She feels that the girl depends on her, of course, and she is helplessly generous."

Gregory Jardine listened to these elucidations, leaning back in the sofa, a hand clasping his ankle, his eyes turning now on Miss Scrotton and now on the subject of their conversation. Miss Scrotton had amused him. She was entertainingly simple if at moments entertainingly intelligent, and he had divined that she was jealous of the crumbs that fell to Miss Woodruff's share from the table of Madame von Marwitz's bounty. A slight malice that had gathered in him during his talk with Eleanor Scrotton found expression in his next remark. "She is certainly charming looking; anyone so charming looking has a right to be dull." But Miss Scrotton did not heed him. She had risen to her feet. "Here she is!" she exclaimed, looking towards the door in radiant satisfaction. "You will meet her after all. I'll do my very best so that you shall have a little talk with her."

The door had been thrown open and Madame Okraska had appeared upon the threshold.

CHAPTER IV

SHE stood for a moment, with her hand resting on the door-frame, and she surveyed an apparently unexpected audience with contemplative melancholy. If she was not pleased to find them so many, she was, at all events unresentful, and Gregory imagined, from Mrs. Forrester's bright flutter in rising, that resentment from the sun-goddess was a peril to be reckoned with. Smiling, though languidly smiling, she advanced up the room, after her graceful and involuntary pause. White fringes rippled softly round her; a white train trailed behind her; on her breast the silken cloak that she wore over a transparent under-robe was clasped with pearls and silver. She was very lovely, very stately, very simple; but she struck her one hyper-critical observer as somewhat prepared; calculated and conscious, as well.

"Thanks, dearest friend," she said to Mrs. Forrester, who, meeting her halfway down the room and taking her hand, asked her solicitously how she did; "I am now a little rested; but it has been a bad night and a busy morning." She spoke with a slightly foreign accent in a voice at once fatigued and sonorous. Her eyes, clear, penetrating and singularly steady, passed over the assembled faces, turned, all of them, towards herself.

She greeted Sir Alliston with a welcoming smile and a lift of the strange crooked eyebrows, and to Miss Scrotton, who, eager and illuminated, was beside her: "Ah, ma chérie," she said, resting her hand affectionately on her shoulder. Mrs. Forrester had her other hand, and, so standing between her two friends, she bowed gravely and graciously to Lady Campion, to Miss Harding, to Mrs. Harding — who, in the stress of this fulfilment had become plum-coloured — and to Gregory Jardine. Then she was seated. Mrs. Forrester poured out her tea, Miss

Harding passed her cake and bread-and-butter, Lady Campion bent to her with frank and graceful compliments, Miss Scrotton sat at her feet on a low settle, and Sir Alliston, leaning on the back of her chair, looked down at her with eyes of antique devotion. Gregory was left on the outskirts of the group and his attention was attracted by the face of little Mrs. Harding, who, all unnoticed and unseated, gazed upon Madame Okraska with the intent liquid eye of a pious dog; the wavering, uncertain smile that played upon her lips was like the humble thudding of the dog's tail. Gregory remembered her face now as one of those, rapt and hypnotized, that he had seen on the platform the night before. In the ovation that Madame Okraska had received at the end of the concert he had noticed this same plum-coloured little lady seizing and kissing the great woman's hand. Shy, by temperament, as he saw, to the point of suffering, he felt sure that only the infection of the crowd had carried her to the act of uncharacteristic daring. He watched her now, finding her piteous and absurd.

But someone beside himself was aware of Mrs. Harding. Miss Woodruff approached her, smiling impersonally, with rather the air of a kindly verger at a church. Yes, she seemed to say, she could find a seat for her. She pointed to the one she had risen from. Mrs. Harding, almost tearful in her gratitude, slid into it with the precaution of the reverent sight-seer who fears to disturb a congregation at prayer, and Miss Woodruff, moving away, went to a table and began to turn over the illustrated papers that lay upon it. Her manner, retired and cheerful, had no humility, none of the poor dependent's unobtrusiveness; rather, Gregory felt, it showed a happy pride, as if, a fortunate priestess in the temple, she had opportunities and felicities denied to mere worshippers. She was interested in her papers. She examined the pictures with something of a child's attentive pleasure.

Gregory came up to her and raising her eyes she smiled at him as though, on the basis of last night's encounter, she took him for granted as potentially a friend.

"What are you looking at?" he asked her, as he might have asked a friendly child.

She turned the paper to him. "The Great Wall of China. They are wonderful pictures."

Gregory stood beside her and looked. The photographs were indeed impressive. The sombre landscape, the pallid sky, and, winding as if for ever over hill and valley, the astonishing structure, like an infinite lonely consciousness. "I should like to see that," said Miss Woodruff.

"Well, you travel a great deal, don't you?" said Gregory. "No doubt Madame Okraska will go to China some day."

Miss Woodruff contemplated the desolate wall. "But this is thousands and thousands of miles from the places where concerts could be given; and I do not know that my guardian has ever thought of China; no, it is not probable that she will ever go there. And then, unfortunately, I do not always go with her. I travel a great deal; but I stop at home a great deal, too. My guardian likes best to be called von Marwitz in private life, by those who know her personally," Miss Woodruff added, smiling again as she presented him with the authorized liturgy.

Gregory was slightly taken aback. He could n't have defined Miss Woodruff's manner as assured, yet it was singularly competent; and no one could have been in less need of benevolent attentions.

"I see," he said. "She looks so much more Polish than German, does n't she? What do you call home?" he added. "Have you lived much in England?"

"By home I mean Cornwall," said Miss Woodruff, who was evidently used to being asked questions. "My guardian has a house there; but it has not been for long. It used to be in Germany, and then for a little in Italy; she has only had Les Solitudes for four years." She looked across at the group under the chandelier. "There is still room for a chair." Her glance indicated a gap in Madame von Marwitz's circle.

This kindly solicitude amused Gregory very much. She had him on her mind as a sight-seer, as she had had Mrs. Harding; and she was full of sympathy for sight-seers. "Oh — thanks

— no," he said, his eyes following hers. "I won't go crowding in."

"She won't mind. She will not even notice;" Miss Woodruff assured him.

"Oh, well, I like to be noticed if I do crowd," Gregory returned smiling.

His slight irony was lost upon her; yet, he was sure of it, she was not dull. Her smile showed him that she congratulated him on an ambitious spirit. "Well, later, then, we will hope," she said. "You would of course rather talk with her. And here is Mr. Drew, so that this chance is gone."

"Who is that singular young man?" Gregory inquired watching with Miss Woodruff the newcomer, who found a place at once in the gap near Madame von Marwitz and was greeted by her with a brighter interest than she had yet shown.

"Mr. Claude Drew?" Miss Woodruff replied with some surprise. "Do you not know? I thought that everybody in London knew him. He is quite a famous writer. He has written poetry and essays. 'Artemis Wedded' is by him — that is poetry; and 'The Bow of Ulysses'— the essay on my guardian comes in that. Oh, he is quite well known."

Mr. Claude Drew was suave and elegant, and his high, stock-like collar and folded satin neck-gear gave him a somewhat recondite appearance. With his dark eyes, pale skin, full, smooth, golden hair, and the vivid red of an advancing Hapsburgian lip, he had the look of a young French dandy drawn by Ingres.

"My guardian is very much interested in him," Miss Woodruff went on. "She believes that he has a great future. She is always interested in promising young men." This, no doubt, was why Miss Woodruff had so kindly encouraged him to take his chances.

"He looks a clever fellow," said Gregory.

"Do you like his face?" Miss Woodruff inquired. Mr. Drew, as if aware of their scrutiny, had turned his eyes upon them for a moment. They were large, jaded eyes, lustrous, yet with the lustre of a surface rather than of depth; dense, velvety and impenetrable.

3

"Well, no, I don't," said Gregory, genially decisive. "He looks unwholesome, I think."

"Oh! Unwholesome?" Miss Woodruff repeated the word thoughtfully rather than interrogatively. "Yes; perhaps it is that. It is a danger of talented modern young men, isn't it. They are not strong enough to be so intelligent; one must be very strong — in character, I mean — if one is to be so intelligent. Perhaps he is not strong in character. Perhaps that is what one feels. Because I do not like his face, either; and I go greatly by faces."

"So do I," said Gregory. After a moment, in which they both continued to look at Mr. Drew, he went on. "I wondered last night what nationality you belonged to. I had been wondering about you for a long while before you looked round at me."

"You had heard about me?" she asked.

He was pleased to be able to say: "Oh, I wondered about you before I heard."

"People are so often interested in me because of my guardian," said Miss Woodruff; "everything about her interests them. But I am an American — if you were not told; that is to say my father was an American — and my mother was a Norwegian; but though I have never been to America I count myself as an American, and with right, I think," she added. "We always spoke English when I was a child, and I remember so many of my father's friends. Some day I hope I may go to America. Have you been there? Do you know New England? My father came from New England."

"No; I've never been there. I'm very insular and untravelled."

"Are you? It is a pity not to travel, isn't it," Miss Woodruff remarked.

"But you like it here in England?"

"Yes, I like it here, with Mrs. Forrester; and in Cornwall. But here with Mrs. Forrester always seems to me more like the life of Europe. English life, as a rule, is, I think, rather like boxes one inside the other." She was perfectly sweet and undogmatic, but her air of cosmopolitan competence amused Gregory, serenely of opinion, for his part, that English was the only life.

"Well, the great thing is that the boxes should fit comfortably into one another, is n't it," he observed; "and I think that on the whole we 've come to fit pretty well in England. And we all come out of our boxes, don't we," he added, pleased with his application of her simile, "for a Madame von Marwitz."

"Yes, I know," said Miss Woodruff, also, evidently, pleased. "That is quite true; you all come out of your boxes for her. But, as a nation, they are not artists, the English, are they? They are kind to the beautiful things; they like to see them; they will take great trouble to see them; but they do not make them. Beauty does not grow here — that is what I mean. It is in its box, too, and it is taken out and passed round from time to time. You do not mind my saying this? You, perhaps, are yourself an artist?"

"Dear me, no; I 'm only a lawyer. I 'm shut up in the tightest of the boxes," said Gregory.

Miss Woodruff scrutinized him with a smile. "I should not think that of you," she said. "You do not look like an artist, it is true; few of us can be artists; but you do not look shut into a box, either. Beauty, to you, is something real; not a pastime, a fashion; no, I cannot think it. When I saw your face last night I thought: Here is one who cares. One counts those faces on one's fingers — even at a great concert. So many think they care who only want to care. To you art is a serious thing and an artist the greatest thing a country can produce. Is not that so?"

Gregory continued to be amused by what he felt to be Miss Woodruff's *naiveté*. He was inclined to think that artists, however admirable in their functions, were undesirable in their persons, and the reverent enthusiasm that Miss Woodruff imagined in him was singularly uncharacteristic. He did n't quite know how to tell her so without seeming rude, so he contented himself with confessing that beauty, in his life, was kept, he feared, very much in its box.

They went on talking, going to an adjacent sofa where Miss Woodruff, while they talked, stroked the deep fur of an immense Persian cat, Hieronimus by name, who established himself between them. Gregory found her very easy to talk to, though they had so few themes in common, and her face he discovered to be even more charming than he had thought it the night before. She was not at all beautiful and he imagined that in her world of artists she would not be particularly appreciated; nor would she be appreciated in his own world of convention — a girl with such a thick waist, such queer clothes, a face so broad, so brown, so abruptly modelled. She was, he felt, a grave and responsible young person, and something in her face suggested that she might have been through a great deal; but she was very cheerful and she laughed with facility at things he said and that she herself said; and when she laughed her eyes nearly closed and the tip of her tongue was caught, with an effect of child-like gaiety, between her teeth. The darkness of her skin made her lips, by contrast, of a pale rose, and her hair, where it grew thickly around her brows and neck, of an almost infantile fairness. Her broad, brown eyebrows lay far apart and her grey eyes were direct, deliberate and limpid.

From where Gregory sat he had Madame von Marwitz in profile and he observed that once or twice, when they laughed, she turned her head and looked at them. Presently she leaned a little to question Mrs. Forrester and then, rather vexed at a sequence, natural but unforeseen, he saw that Mrs. Forrester got up to fetch him.

"Tante has sent for you!" Miss Woodruff exclaimed. "I am so glad."

It really vexed him a little that he should still be supposed to be pining for an introduction; he would so much rather have stayed talking to her. On the sofa she continued to stroke Hieronimus and to keep a congratulatory gaze upon him while he was conducted to a seat beside the great woman.

Madame von Marwitz was very lovely. She was the type of woman with whom, as a boy, he would have fallen desperately in love, seeing her as poetry personified. And she was the type of woman, all indolent and indifferent as she was, who took it for granted that people would fall desperately in love with her. Her long gaze, now, told him that. It seemed to give him time, as it were, to take her in and to arrange with himself how best to adjust himself to a changed life. It was not the glance of a flirt; it held no petty consciousness; it was the gaze of an enchantress aware of her own inevitable power. Gregory met the cold, sweet, melancholy eyes. But as she gazed, as she slowly smiled, he was aware, with a perverse pleasure, that his present seasoned self was completely immune from her magic. He opposed commonplace to enchantment, and in him Madame von Marwitz would find no victim.

"I have never seen you here before, I think," she said. She spoke with a beautiful precision; that of the foreigner perfectly at ease in an alien tongue, yet not loving it sufficiently to take liberties with it.

Gregory said, no, she had never seen him there before.

"Mrs. Forrester is, it seems, a mutual friend," said Madame von Marwitz. "She has known you since boyhood. You have been very fortunate."

Gregory assented.

"She tells me that you are in the law," Madame von Marwitz pursued; "a barrister. I should not have thought that. A diplomat; a soldier, it should have been. Is it not so?"

Gregory had not wanted to be a barrister. It did not please him that Madame von Marwitz should guess so accurately at a disappointment that had made his youth bitter. "I'm a younger son, you see," he said. "And I had to make my living."

When Madame von Marwitz's gaze grew more intent she did not narrow her eyes, but opened them more widely. She opened them more widely now, putting back her head a little. "Ah," she said. "That was hard. That meant suffering. You are caged in a calling you do not care for."

"Oh, no," said Gregory, smiling; "I'm very well off; I'm quite contented."

"Contented?" she raised her crooked eyebrow. "Are you indeed so fortunate? — or so unfortunate?"

To this large question Gregory made no reply, continuing to offer her the non-committal coolness of his smile. He was not liking Madame von Marwitz, and he was becoming aware that if one did n't like her one did not appear to advantage in talking with her. He cast about in his mind for an excuse to get away.

"The law," Madame von Marwitz mused, her eyes dwelling on him. "It is stony; yet with stone one builds. You would not be content, I think, with the journeyman's work of the average lawyer. You shape; you create; you have before you the vision of the strong fortress to be built where the weak may find refuge. You are an architect, not a mason. Only so could you find contentment in your calling."

"I'm afraid that I don't think about it like that," said Gregory. "I should say that the fortress is built already."

There was now a change in her cold sweetness; her smile became a little ambiguous. "You remind me," she said, "that I was speaking in somewhat pretentious similes. I was not asking you what had been done, but what you hoped to do. I was asking — it was that that interested me in you, as it does in all the young men I meet — what was the ideal you brought to your calling."

It was as though, with all her sweetness, she had seen through his critical complacency and were correcting the manners of a conceited boy. Gregory was a good deal taken aback. And it was with a touch of boyish sulkiness that he replied: "I don't think, really, that I can claim ideals."

Definitely, now, the light of mockery shone in her eye. In evading her, in refusing to be drawn within her magic circle, he had aroused an irony that matched his own. She was not the mere phrase-making woman; by no means the mere siren. "How afraid you English are of your ideals," she said. "You live by them, but you will not look at them. I could say to you — as Statius to Virgil in the Purgatorio — that you carry your light behind you so that you light those who follow, but walk yourselves in darkness. You will not claim them; no, and above all, you will not talk about them. Do not be afraid, my young friend; I shall not tamper with your soul." So she spoke, sweetly, deliberately, yet tersely, too, as though to make him feel that she had done all she could for him and that he had proved himself not worth her trouble. Mr. Claude Drew was still on her other hand, carrying on an obviously desultory conversation with Miss Scrotton, and to him Madame von Marwitz turned, saying: "And what is it you wished to tell me of your Carducci? You will send me the proofs? Good. Oh, I shall not be too tired to read what you have written."

Here was a young man, evidently, who was worth her trouble. Gregory sat disposed of and a good deal discomposed, the more so since he had to own that he had opened himself to the rebuff. He rose and moved away, looking about and seeing that Miss Woodruff had left the room; but Mrs. Forrester came to him, her brilliant little face somewhat clouded.

"What is it, my dear Gregory?" she questioned. "She asked to have you brought. Have n't you pleased her?"

Mrs. Forrester, who had known not only himself, but his father in boyhood, was fond of him, but was not disposed to think of him as important. And she expected the unimportant to know, in a sense, their place and to show the important that they did know it. There was a hint, now, of severity, in her countenance.

It would sound, he knew, merely boyish and sulky to say: "She has n't pleased me." But he could n't resist: "I was n't à la hauteur."

Mrs. Forrester, at this, looked at him hard for a moment. She then diagnosed his case as one of bad temper rather than of malice, and could forgive it in one who had failed to interest the great woman and been discarded in consequence; Mercedes, she knew, could discard with decision.

"Well, when you talk to a woman like Madame von Marwitz, you must try to be worthy of your opportunities," she commented, tempering her severity with understanding. "You really had an opportunity. Your face interested her, and your kindness to little Karen. She always likes people who are kind to little Karen."

It was pleasantly open to him now to say: "Little Karen has been kind to me."

"A dear, good child," said Mrs. Forrester. "I am glad that you talked to her. You pleased Mercedes in that."

"She is a delightful girl," said Gregory.

He now took his departure. But he was again to encounter Miss Woodruff. She was in the hall, talking French to a sallow little woman in black, evidently a ladies' maid, who had the oppressed,- anxious countenance and bright, melancholy eyes of a monkey.

"*Allons,*" Miss Woodruff was saying in encouraging tones, while she paused on the first step of the stairs, her hand on the banister; "*ce n'est pas une cause perdue, Louise; nous arrangerons la chose.*"

"*Ah, Mademoiselle, c'est que Madame ne sera pas contente, pas contente du tout quand elle verra la robe,*" was Louise's mournful reply as Gregory came up.

"I hoped we might go on with our talk," he said. He still addressed her somewhat as one addresses a friendly child; "I wanted to hear the end of that story about the Hungarian student."

"He died, in Davos, poor boy," said Miss Woodruff, looking down at him from her slightly higher place, while Louise stood by dejectedly. "He wrote to my guardian and we went to him there and she played to him. It made him so happy. We were with him till he died."

"Shall I see you again?" Gregory asked. "Will you be here for any time? Are you staying in London?"

"My guardian goes to America next week — did you not know? — with Miss Scrotton."

"Oh yes, Eleanor told me. And you're not going too? You're not to see America yet?"

"No; not this time. I go to Cornwall."

"You are to be alone with Mrs. Talcott all the winter?"

"You know Mrs. Talcott?" Miss Woodruff exclaimed in pleased astonishment.

"No; I don't know her; Eleanor told me about her, too."

"It is not being alone," said Miss Woodruff. "She and I have a most happy time together. I thought it strange that you should know Mrs. Talcott. I never met anyone who knew her unless they knew my guardian very well."

"And when are you coming back?"

"From Cornwall? I do not know. I am afraid we shall not see each other — oh, for a very long time," said Miss Woodruff. She smiled. She gave him her hand, leaning down to him from behind the banister. Gregory said that he had friends in Cornwall and that he might run down and see them one day — and then he might see her and Les Solitudes, too. And Miss Woodruff said that that would be very nice.

He heard the last words of the colloquy with Louise as his coat was put on in the hall. "*Alors il ne faut pas renvoyer la robe, Mademoiselle?*"

"*Mais non, mais non; nous nous tirerons d'affaire,*" Miss Woodruff replied, springing gaily up the stairs, her arm, with a sort of dignified familiarity, in which was encouragement and protection, cast round Louise's shoulders.

CHAPTER V.

G REGORY walked at a brisk pace from Mrs. Forrester's house in Wilton Crescent to Hyde Park Corner, and from there, through St. James's Park, to Queen Anne's Mansions where he had a flat. He had moved into it from dismal rooms when prosperity had first come to him, five or six years ago, and was much attached to it. It was high up in the large block of buildings and its windows looked over the greys and greens and silvers of the park, the water shining in the midst, and the dim silhouettes of Whitehall rising in stately significance on the evening sky. Gregory went to the balcony and overhung his view contemplatively for a while. The fog had lifted, and all London was alight.

The drawing-room behind him expressed an accepted convention rather than a personal predilection. It was not the room of a young man of conscious tastes. It was solid, cheerful and somewhat *naif*. There was a great deal of very clean white paint and a great deal of bright wallpaper. There were deep chairs covered with brighter chintz. There were blue and white tiles around the fireplace and heavy, polished brass before. On the tables lay buff and blue reviews and folded evening papers, massive paper-cutters and large silver boxes. Photographs in silver frames also stood there, of female relatives in court dress and of male relatives in uniform. Behind the photographs were pots of growing flowers; and on the walls etchings and engravings after well-known landscapes. It was the room of a young man uninfluenced by Whistler, unaware of Chinese screens and indifferent to the rival claims of Jacobean and Chippendale furniture. It was civilised, not cultivated; and it was thoroughly commonplace.

Gregory thought of himself as the most commonplace of types; — the younger son whose father had n't been able to do anything for him beyond educating him; the younger son who, after years of uncongenial drudgery had emerged, tough, stringy, professional, his boyish dreams dead and his boyish tastes atrophied; a useful hard-working, clear-sighted member of society. And there was truth in this conception of himself. There was truth, too, in Madame von Marwitz's probe. He had more than the normal English sensitiveness where ideals were concerned and more than the normal English instinct for a protective literalness. He did n't intend that anybody should lay their hand on his heart and tell him of lofty aims that it would have made him feel awkward to look at by himself; his fastidiousness was far from commonplace, and so were his disdains; they made cheap successes and cheap ambitions impossible to him. He would never make a fortune out of the law; yet already he was distinguished among the younger men at the bar. With nothing of the air of a paladin he brought into the courts a flavour of classic calm and courtesy. He was punctiliously fair. He never frightened or bullied or confused. His impartiality could become alarming at times to his own clients, and shady cases passed him by. Everybody respected Gregory Jardine and a good many people disliked him. A few old friends, comrades at Eton and Oxford, were devoted to him and looked upon him, in spite of his reputation for almost merciless commonsense, as still potentially Quixotic. As a boy he had been exceptionally tender-hearted; but now he was hard, or thought himself so. He had no vanity and looked upon his own resolution and dignity as the heritage of all men worth their salt; in consequence he was inclined to theoretic severity towards the worsted. The sensitiveness of youth had steeled itself in irony; he was impatient of delusions and exaltations, and scornful of the shambling, shamefaced motives that moved so many of the people who came under his observation.

Yet, leaning on the iron railing, his gaze softening to a grave, peaceful smile as he looked over the vast, vaporous scene, laced with its moving and motionless lines of light, it was this, and its mysteries, its delicacies, its reticent radiance, that expressed him more truly than the commonplaces of the room behind him, accurately as these symbolized the activities of his life. The boy and youth, emotional and poetic, dreamy if also shrewdly humorous, still survived in a sub-conscious region of his nature, an Atlantis sunken beneath the traffic of the surface; and, when he leaned and gazed, as now, at the lovely evocations of the evening, it was like hearing dimly, from far depths, the bells of the buried city ringing.

He was thinking of nothing as he leaned there, though memories, linked in their associated loveliness, floated across his mind — larch-boughs brushed exquisitely against a frosty sky on a winter morning in Northumberland, when, a boy, with gun and dogs, he had paused on the wooded slopes near his home to look round him; or the little well of chill, clear water that he had found one summer day gushing from a mossy source under a canopy of leaves; or the silver sky, and hills folded in greys and purples, that had surrounded him on a day in late autumn when he had walked for miles in loneliness and, again, had paused to look, receiving the scene ineffaceably, so that certain moods always made it rise before him. And linked by some thread of affinity with these pictures, the face of the young girl he had met that afternoon rose before him. Not as he had just seen her, but as he had seen her, for the first time, the night before at the concert. Her face came back to him with the larch-boughs and the spring of water and the lonely hills, while he looked at London beneath him. She touched and interested him, and appealed to something sub-conscious, as music did. But when he passed from picturing her to thinking about her, about her origin and environment and future, it was with much the same lucid and unmoved insight with which he would have examined some unfortunate creature in the witness-box.

Miss Woodruff seemed to him very unfortunate. For her irregular birth he had contempt and for her haphazard upbringing only pity. He saw no place in a well-ordered society for sculptors who ran away with other men's wives and lived on chestnuts and left their illegitimate children to be picked up at the roadside. He was the type of young man who, theoretically, admitted of and indeed admired all independences in women;

practically he preferred them to be sheltered by their male relatives and to read no French novels until they married — if then. Miss Woodruff struck him as at once sheltered and exposed. Her niche under the extended wing of the great woman seemed to him precarious. He saw no real foothold for her in her present *milieu*. She only entered Mrs. Forrester's orbit, that was evident, as a tiny satellite in attendance on the streaming comet. In the wake of the comet she touched, it was true, larger orbits than the artistic; but it was in this accidental and transitory fashion, and his accurate knowledge of the world saw in the nameless and penniless girl the probable bride of some second-rate artist, some wandering, dishevelled musician, or ill-educated, ill-regulated poet. Girls like that, who had the aristocrat's assurance and simplicity and unconsciousness of worldly lore, without the aristocrat's secure standing in the world, were peculiarly in danger of sinking below the level of their own type.

He went in to dress. He was dining with the Armytages and after thinking of Miss Woodruff it was indeed like passing from memories of larch-woods into the chintzes and metals and potted flowers of the drawing-room to think of Constance Armytage. Yet Gregory thought of her very contentedly while he dressed. She was well-dowered, well-educated, well-bred; an extremely nice and extremely pretty young woman with whom he had danced, dined and boated frequently during her first two seasons. The Armytages had a house at Pangbourne and he spent several week-ends with them every summer. Constance liked him and he liked her. He was not in love with her; but he wondered if he might not be. To get married to somebody like Constance seemed the next step in his sensible career. He could see her established most appropriately in the flat. He could see her beautifully burnished chestnut hair, her pretty profile and bright blue eyes above the tea-table; he could see her at the end of the dinner-table presiding charmingly at a dinner. She would be a charming mother, too; the children, when babies, would wear blue sashes and would grow up doing all the proper things at the proper times, from the French *bonne* and the German *Fräulein* to Eton and Oxford and dances and happy marriages. She would continue all the traditions of his outer life, would fulfil it and carry it on peacefully and honourably into the future.

The Armytages lived in a large house in Queen's Gate Gardens. They were not interesting people, but Gregory liked them none the less for that. He approved of the Armytage type — the kind, courageous, intolerant old General who managed to find Gladstone responsible for every misfortune that befell the Empire — blithe, easy-going Lady Armytage, the two sons in the army and the son in the navy and the two unmarried girls, of whom Constance was one and the other still in the school-room. It was a small dinner-party that night; most of the family were there and they had music after it, Constance singing very prettily — she was taking lessons — the last two songs she had learned, one by Widor and one by Tosti.

Yet as he drove home late Gregory was aware that Constance still remained a pleasant possibility to contemplate and that he had come no nearer to being in love with her. It might be easier, he mused, if only she could offer some trivial trick or imperfection, if she had been freckled, say, or had had a stammer, or prominent teeth. He could imagine being married to her so much more easily than being in love with her, and he was a little vexed with himself for his own insusceptibility.

Constance was the last thing that he thought of before going to sleep; yet it was not of her he dreamed. He dreamed, very strangely, of the little cosmopolitan waif whom he had met that afternoon. He was walking down a road in a forest. The sky above was blue, with white clouds heaving above the dark tree-tops, and it was a still, clear day. His mood was the boyish mood of romance and expectancy, touched with a little fear. At a turning of the road he came suddenly upon Karen Woodruff. She was standing at the edge of the forest as if waiting for him, and she held a basket of berries, not wild-strawberry and not bramble, but a fairy-tale fruit that a Hans Andersen heroine might have gathered, and she looked like such a heroine herself, young, and strange, and kind, and wearing the funny little dress of the concert, the white dress with the flat blue bows. She held

out the basket to him as he approached, and, smiling at each
other in silence, they ate the fruit with its wild, sweet savour.
Then, as if he had spoken and she were answering him, she said:
" And I love you."

Gregory woke with this. He lay for some moments still half
dreaming, with no surprise, conscious only of a peaceful wonder.
He had forgotten the dream in the morning; but it returned to
him later in the day, and often afterwards. It persisted in his
memory like a cluster of unforgettable sensations. The taste of
the berries, the scent of the pine-trees, the sweetness of the girl's
smile, these things, rather than any significance that they embodied, remained with him like one of the deep impressions of
his boyhood.

CHAPTER VI

ON the morning that Gregory Jardine had waked from his dream, Madame von Marwitz sat at her writing-table tearing open, with an air of impatient melancholy, note after note and letter after letter, and dropping the envelopes into a wastepaper basket beside her. A cigarette was between her lips; her hair, not dressed, was coiled loosely upon her head; she wore a white silk *peignoir* bordered with white fur and girdled with a sash of silver tissue. She had just come from her bath and her face, though weary, had the freshness of a prolonged toilet.

The room where she sat, with its grand piano and its deep chairs, its sofa and its capacious writing-table, was accurately adjusted to her needs. It, too, was all in white, carpet, curtains and dimity coverings. Madame von Marwitz laughed at her own vagary; but it had had only once to be clearly expressed, and the greens and pinks that had adorned her sitting-room at Mrs. Forrester's were banished as well as the rose-sprigged toilet set and hangings of the bedroom. "I cannot breathe among colours," she had said. "They seem to press upon me. White is like the air; to live among colours, with all their beauty, is like swimming under the water; I can only do it with comfort for a little while."

Madame von Marwitz looked up presently at a wonderful little clock of gold and enamel that stood before her and then struck, not impatiently, but with an intensification of the air of melancholy, an antique silver bell that stood beside the clock. Louise entered.

"Where is Mademoiselle?" Madame von Marwitz asked, speaking in French. Louise answered that Mademoiselle had gone out to take Victor for his walk, Victor being Madame von Marwitz's St. Bernard who remained in England during his mistress's absences.

"You should have taken Victor yourself, Louise," said Madame von Marwitz, not at all unkindly, but with decisive condemnation. "You know that I like Mademoiselle to help me with my letters in the morning."

Louise, her permanent plaintiveness enhanced, murmured that she had a bad headache and that Mademoiselle had kindly offered to take Victor, had said that she would enjoy taking him.

"Moreover," Madame von Marwitz pursued, as though these excuses were not worthy of reply, "I do not care for Mademoiselle to be out alone in such a fog. You should have known that, too. As for the dress, don't fail to send it back this morning — as you should have done last night."

"Mademoiselle thought we might arrange it to please Madame."

"You should have known better, if Mademoiselle did not. Mademoiselle has very little taste in such matters, as you are well aware. Do my feet now; I think that the nails need a little polishing; but very little; I do not wish you to make them look as though they had been varnished; it is a trick of yours."

Madame von Marwitz then resumed her cigarette and her letters while Louise, fetching files and scissors, powders and polishers, mournfully knelt before her mistress, and, drawing the *mule* from a beautifully undeformed white foot, began to bring each nail to a state of perfected art. In the midst of this ceremony Karen Woodruff appeared. She led the great dog by a leash and was still wearing her cap and coat.

"I hope I am not late, Tante," she said, speaking in English and going to kiss her guardian's cheek, while Victor stood by, majestically benignant.

"You are late, my Karen, and you had no business to take out Victor at this hour. If you want to walk with him let it be in the afternoon. *Aïe! aïe!* Louise! what are you doing? Have mercy I beg of you!" Louise had used the file awkwardly. "What is that you have, Karen?" Madame von Marwitz went on. Miss Woodruff held in her hand a large bouquet enveloped in white paper.

4

"An offering, Tante; they just arrived as I came in. Roses, I think."

"I have already sent half a dozen boxes downstairs for Mrs. Forrester to dispose of in the drawing-room. You will take off your things now, child, and help me, please, with all these weary people. *Bon Dieu!* do they really imagine that I am going to answer their inept effusions?"

Miss Woodruff had unwrapped a magnificent bunch of pink roses and laid them beside her guardian. "From that good little dark-faced lady of yesterday, Tante."

Madame von Marwitz, pausing meditatively over a note, glanced at them. "The dark-faced lady?"

"Don't you remember? Mrs. Harding. Here is her card. She sat and gazed at you, so devoutly, while you talked to Mr. Drew and Lady Campion. And she looked very poor. It must mean a great deal for her to buy roses in January — *un suprême effort,*" Miss Woodruff quoted, she and her guardian having a host of such playful allusions.

"I see her now," said Madame von Marwitz. "I see her face; *congestionnée d'émotion, n'est-ce-pas.*" She read the card that Karen presented.

"Silly woman. Take them away, child."

"But no, Tante, it is not silly; it is very touching, I think; and you have liked pink roses sometimes. It makes me sorry for that good little lady that you shouldn't even look at her roses."

"No. I see her. Dark red and very foolish. I do not like her or her flowers. They look stupid flowers — thick and pink, like fat, smiling cheeks. Take them away."

"You have read what she says, Tante, here on the back? I call that very pretty."

"I see it. I see it too often. No. Go now, and take your hat off. Good heavens, child, why did you wear that ancient sealskin cap?"

Karen paused at the door, the rejected roses in her arms. "Why, Tante, it was snowing a little; I didn't want to wear my best hat for a morning walk."

"Have you no other hat beside the best?"

"No, Tante. And I like my little cap. You gave it to me —
years ago — don't you remember; the first time that we went to
Russia together."

"Years ago, indeed, I should imagine from its appearance.
Well; it makes no difference; you will soon be leaving town and
it will do for Cornwall and Tallie."

When Karen returned, Madame von Marwitz, whose feet were
now finished, took her place in an easy chair and said: "Now
to work. Leave the accounts for Schultz. I've glanced at some
of them this morning and, as usual, I seem to be spending twice
as much as I make. How the money runs away I cannot imagine. And Tallie sends me a great batch of bills from Cornwall,
bon Dieu!" *Bon Dieu* was a frequent ejaculation with Madame
von Marwitz, often half sighed, and with the stress laid on the
first word.

"Never mind, you will soon be making a great deal more
money," said Karen.

"It would be more to the point if I could manage to keep a
little of what I make. Schultz tells me that my investments in
the Chinese railroads are going badly, too. Put aside the bills.
We will go through the rest of the letters."

For some time they worked at the pile of correspondence.
Karen would open each letter and read the signature; letters
from those known to Madame von Marwitz, or from her friends,
were handed to her; the letters signed by unknown names Karen
read aloud: — begging letters; letters requesting an autograph;
letters recommending to the great woman's kindly notice some
budding genius, and letters of sheer adulation, listened to, these
last, sometimes with a dreamy indifference to the end, interrupted sometimes with a sudden "*Assez.*"

There were a dozen such letters this morning and when Karen
read the signature of the last: "Your two little adorers Gladys
and Ethel Bocock," Madame von Marwitz remarked: "We
need not have that. Put it into the basket."

"But, Tante," Karen protested, looking round at her with a
smile, "you must hear it; it is so funny and so nice."

"So stupid I call it, my dear. They should not be encouraged."

"But you must be kind, you will be kind, even to the stupid. See, here are two of your photographs, they ask you to sign them. There is a stamped and addressed envelope to return them in. Such love, Tante! such torrents of love! You must listen."

Madame von Marwitz resigned herself, her eyes fixed absently on the smoke curling from her cigarette as if, in its fluctuating evanescence, she saw a symbol of human folly. Gladys and Ethel lived in Clapham and told her that they came in to all her concerts and sat for hours waiting on the stairs. Their letter ended: "Everyone adores you, but no one can adore you like we do. Oh, would you tell us the colour of your eyes? Gladys thinks deep, dark grey, but I think velvety brown; we talk and talk about it and can't decide. We must n't take up any more of your precious time.— Your two little adorers, Gladys and Ethel Bocock."

"Bocock," Madame von Marwitz commented. "No one can adore me like they do. Let us hope not. *Petites sottes.*"

"You will sign the photographs, Tante — and you will say, yes, you must —' To my kind little admirers.' Now be merciful."

"Bocock," Madame von Marwitz mused, holding out an indulgent hand for the pen that Karen gave her and allowing the blotter with the photographs upon it to be placed upon her knee. "And they care for music, *parbleu!* How many of such appreciators are there, do you think, among my adorers? I do this to please you, Karen. It is against my principles to encourage the *schwärmerei* of school-girls. There," she signed quickly across each picture in a large, graceful and illegible hand, adding, with a smile up at Karen,—"To my kind little admirers."

Karen, satisfied, examined the signatures, held them to the fire for a moment to preserve their vivid black in bold relief, and then put them into their envelope, dropping in a small slip of paper upon which she had written: "Her eyes are grey, flecked with black, and are not velvety."

They had now reached the end of the letters.

"A very good, helpful child it is," said Madame von Marwitz. "You are methodical, Karen. You will make a good housewife. That has never been my talent."

"And it is my only one," said Karen.

"Ah, well, no; it is a good, solid little head in other directions, too. And it is no mean musician that the child has become. Yes; there are many well-known artists to whom I would listen less willingly than to my Karen. It is only in the direction of *la toilette*," Madame von Marwitz smiled with a touch of roguishness, "only in the direction of *la toilette* that the taste is rather rudimentary as yet. I was very cross last night, *hein?*"

"It was disappointing not to have pleased you," said Karen, smiling.

"And I was cross. Louise has her *souffre-douleur* expression this morning to an exasperating degree."

"We thought we were going to make the dress quite right," said Karen. "It seemed very simple to arrange the lace around the shoulders; I stood and Louise draped me; and Louise is clever, you know."

"Not clever enough for that. It was all because with your solicitude about Louise you wanted her to escape a scolding. She took the lace to Mrs. Rolley too late and did not explain as I told her to do. And you did not save her, you see. Put those two letters of Mr. Drew's in the portfolio; so. And now come and sit, there. I want to have a serious talk with you, Karen."

Karen obeyed. Madame von Marwitz sat in her deep chair, the window behind her. The fog had lifted and the pale morning sunlight struck softly on the coils of her hair and fell on the face of the young girl sitting before her. With her grey dress and folded hands and serene gaze Karen looked very like the little convent *pensionnaire*. Madame von Marwitz scrutinized her thoughtfully for some moments.

"You are — how old is it, Karen?" she said at last.

"I shall be twenty-four in March," said Karen.

"*Bon Dieu!* I had not realised that it was so much; you are singularly young for your years."

"Am I, Tante? I don't know," Karen reflected, genially. "I often feel, oh far older than the people I talk with."

"Do you, *mon enfant*. Some children, it is true, are far wiser than their elders. You are a wise child; but you are young, Karen, very young for your years, in appearance, in demeanour, in candour of outlook. Tell me; have you ever contemplated your future? asked yourself about it?"

Karen, looking gravely at her, shook her head. "Hardly at all, Tante. Is that very stupid?"

"Not stupid, perhaps; but, again, very child-like. You live in the present."

"The past was so sad, Tante, and since I have been with you I have been so happy. There has seemed no reason for thinking of anything but the present."

"Well, that is right. It is my wish to have you happy. As far as material things go, too, your future shall be assured; I see to that. But, you are twenty-three years old, Karen; you are a woman, and a child no longer. Do you never dream dreams of *un prince charmant;* of a home of your own, and children, and a life to build with one who loves you? If I were to die — and one can count on nothing in life — you would be very desolate."

Karen, for some silent moments, looked at her guardian, intently and with a touch of alarm. "No; I don't dream," she said then. "And perhaps that is because you fill my life so, Tante. If someone came who loved me very much and whom I loved, I should of course be glad to marry; — only not if it would take me from you; I mean that I should want to be often with you. And when I look forward at all I always take it for granted that that will come in time — a husband and children, and a home of my own. But there seems no reason to think of it now. I am quite contented as I am."

The kindly melancholy of Madame von Marwitz's gaze continued to fix her. "But I am not contented for you," she observed. "I wish to see you established. Youth passes, all too quickly, and its opportunities pass, too. I should blame myself if our tie were to cut you off from a wider life. Good husbands are by no means picked up on every bush. One cannot take these things for granted. It is of a possible marriage I wish to speak to you this morning, my Karen. We will talk of it quietly." Madame von Marwitz raised herself in her chair to stretch her hand and take from the mantelpiece a letter lying there. "This came this morning, my Karen," she said. "From our good Lise Lippheim."

Frau Lippheim was a warm-hearted, talented, exuberant Jewess who had been a fellow student of Madame von Marwitz's in girlhood. The eagle-flights of genius had always been beyond her, yet her pinions were wide and, unburdened by domestic solicitudes, she might have gone far. As it was, married to a German musician much her inferior, and immersed in the care and support of a huge family, she ranked only as second or third rate. She gave music-lessons in Leipsig and from time to time, playing in a quintet made up of herself, her eldest son and three eldest girls, gave recitals in Germany, France and England. The Lippheim quintet, in its sober way, held a small but dignified position.

Karen had been deposited by her guardian more than once under the Lippheim's overflowing roof in Leipsig, and it was a vision of Frau Lippheim that came to her as her guardian unfolded the letter — of the near-sighted, pale blue eyes, heavy, benignant features, and crinkled, red-brown hair. So very ugly, almost repulsively so; yet so kind, so valiant, so untiring. The thought of her was touching, and affectionate solicitude almost effaced Karen's personal anxiety; for she could not connect Frau Lippheim with any matrimonial project.

Madame von Marwitz, glancing through her letter, looked up from the last sheet. "I have talked with the good Lise more than once, Karen," she said, "about a hope of hers. She first spoke of it some two years ago; but I told her then that I would say nothing to you till you were older. Now, hearing that I am going away, to leave you for so long, she writes of it again. Did you know that Franz was very much attached to you, Karen?" Franz was Frau Lippheim's eldest son.

The vision that now flashed, luridly, for Karen, was that of an

immense Germanic face with bright, blinking eyes behind
glasses; huge lips; a flattened nose, modelled thickly at the corners, and an enormous laugh that rolled back the lips and revealed suddenly the Semitic element and a boundless energy and
kindliness. She had always felt fond of Franz until this moment. Now, amazed, appalled, a violent repulsion went through
her. She became pale. "No. I had not guessed that," she
said.

Her eyes were averted. Madame von Marwitz glanced at her
and vexation clouded her countenance. She knew that flinty,
unresponsive look. In moments of deep emotion Karen could
almost disconcert her. Her face expressed no hostility; but a
sternness, blind and resisting, like that of a rock. At such
moments she did not look young.

Madame von Marwitz, after her glance, also averted her eyes,
sighing impatiently. "I see that you do not care for the poor
boy. He had hoped, with his mother to back him, that he might
have some chance of winning you; — though it is not Franz who
writes."

She paused; but Karen said nothing. "You know that Franz
has talent and is beginning, now, to make money steadily. Lise
tells me that. And I would give you a little *dot;* enough to
assure your future, and his. I only speak of the material things
because it is part of your childishness never to consider them.
Of him I would not have spoken at all, had I not believed that
you felt friendship and affection for him. He is so good, so
strong, so loyal that I did not think it impossible."

After another silence Karen found something to say. "I have
friendship for him. That is quite different."

"Why so, Karen?" Madame von Marwitz inquired. "Since
you are not a romantic school-girl, let us speak soberly. Friendship, true friendship, for a man whose tastes are yours, whose
pursuits you understand, is the soundest basis upon which to
build a marriage."

"No. Only as a friend, a friend not too near, do I feel affection for Franz. It is repulsive to me — the thought of anything
else. It makes me hate him," said Karen.

"*Tiens!*" Madame von Marwitz opened her eyes in genuine surprise. "I could not have imagined such decisive feeling. I could not have imagined that you despised the good Franz. I need not tell you that I do not agree with you there."

"I do not despise him."

"Ah, there is more than mere negation in your look, your voice, my child. It is pride, wounded pride, that speaks; and it is as if you told me that I had less care for your pride than you had, and thought less of your claims."

"I do not think of my claims."

"You feel them. You feel Franz your inferior."

"I did not think of such things. I thought of his face, near me, and it made me hate him."

Karen continued to look aside with a sombre gaze. And, after examining her for another moment, Madame von Marwitz held out her hand. "Come," she said, "come here, child. I have blundered. I see that I have blundered. Franz shall be sent about his business. Have I hurt you? Do not think of it again."

The girl got up slowly, as if her stress of feeling made her awkward. Stumbling, she knelt down beside her guardian and, taking the hand and holding it against her eyes, she said in a voice heavy with unshed tears: "Am I a burden? Am I an anxiety? Let me go away, then. I can teach. I can teach music and languages. I can do translations, so many things. You have educated me so well. You will always be my dear friend and I shall see you from time to time. But it is as you say, I am a woman now. I would rather go away than have you troubled by me."

Madame von Marwitz's face, as she listened to the heavy voice, that trembled a little over its careful words, darkened. "It is not well what you say, Karen," she replied. "No. You speak to me as you have no right to speak, as though you had a grievance against me. What have I ever done that you should ask me whether you are a burden to me?"

"Only —" said Karen, her voice more noticeably trembling —"only that it seemed to me that I must be in the way if you could think of Franz as a husband for me. I do not know why I feel that. But it hurt me so much that it seemed to me to be true."

"It has always been my joy to care for you," said Madame von Marwitz. "I have always loved you like my own child. I do not admit that to think of Franz as a husband for you was to do you a wrong. I would not listen to an unfitting suitor for my child. It is you who have hurt me — deeply hurt me — by so misunderstanding me." Sorrow and reproach grew in her voice.

"Forgive me," said Karen, who still held the hand before her eyes.

Madame von Marwitz drew her hand gently away and raising Karen's head so that she could look at her, "I forgive you, indeed, Karen," she said. "How could I not forgive you? But, child, do not hurt me so again. Never speak of leaving me again. You must never leave me except to go where a fuller happiness beckons. You do not know how they stabbed — those words of yours. That you could think them, believe them! No, Karen, it was not well. Not only are you dear to me for yourself; there is another bond. You were dear to him. You were beside me in the hour of my supreme agony. You desecrate our sacred memories when you allow small suspicions and fears to enter your thoughts of me. So much has failed me in my life. May I not trust that my child will never fail me?"

Tragic grief gazed from her eyes and Karen's eyes echoed it. "Forgive me, Tante, I have hurt you. I have been stupid," she spoke almost dully; but Madame von Marwitz was looking into the eyes, deep wells of pain and self-reproach.

"Yes, you have hurt me, *ma chérie*," she replied, leaning now her cheek against Karen's head. "And it is not loving to forget that when a cup of suffering brims, a drop the more makes it overflow. You are harsh sometimes, Karen, strangely harsh."

"Forgive me," Karen repeated.

Madame von Marwitz put her arms around her, still leaning her head against hers. "With all my heart, my child, with all my heart," she said. "But do not hurt me so again. Do not forget that I live at the edge of a precipice; an inadvertent foot-

step, and I crash down to the bottom, to lie mangled. Ah, my
child, may life never tear you, burn you, freeze you, as it has
torn and burned and frozen me. Ah, the memories, the cruel
memories!" Great sighs lifted her breast. She murmured,
while Karen knelt enfolding her, "His dead face rises before me.
The face that we saw, Karen. And I know to the full again my
unutterable woe." It was rare with Madame von Marwitz to
allude thus explicitly to the tragedy of her life, the ambiguous,
the dreadful death of her husband. Karen knelt holding her,
pale with the shared memory. They were so for a long time.
Then, sighing softly, *"Bon Dieu! bon Dieu!"* Madame von
Marwitz rose and, gently putting the girl aside, she went into
her bedroom and closed the door.

CHAPTER VII

IT was a hard, chill morning and Gregory, sauntering up and down the platform at Euston beside the open doors of the long steamer-train, felt that the taste and smell of London was, as nowhere else, concentrated, compressed, and presented to one in tabloid form, as it were, at a London station on a winter morning. It was a taste and smell that he, personally, rather liked, singularly compounded as it was, to his fancy, of cold metals and warm sooty surfaces; of the savour of kippers cooking over innumerable London grates and the aroma of mugs of beer served out over innumerable London bars; something at once acrid yet genial, suggesting sordidness and unlimited possibility. The vibration of adventure was in it and the sentiment, oddly intermingled, of human solidarity and personal detachment.

Gregory, as he strolled and waited for his old friend and whilom Oxford tutor, Professor Blackburn, whom he had promised to see off, had often to pause or to deviate in his course; for, though it was still early, and the season not a favourite one for crossing, the platform was quite sufficiently crowded, and crowded, evidently, with homeward-bound Americans, mostly women. Gregory tended to think of America and its people with the kindly lightness common to his type. Their samenesses did n't interest him, and their differences were sometimes vexatious. He had a vague feeling that they 'd really better have been Colonials and be done with it. Professor Blackburn last night had reproved this insular levity. He was going over with an array of discriminations that Gregory had likened to an explorer's charts and instruments. He intended to investigate the most minute and measure the most immense, to lecture continually, to dine out every evening and to write a book of some real appropriateness when he came home. Gregory said that all that he asked of America was that it should keep its institutions to itself and share its pretty girls, and the professor told him that he knew more about the latter than the former. There were not many pretty girls on the platform this morning, though he remarked one rather pleasing young person who sat idly on a pile of luggage and fixed large, speculative, innocently assured eyes upon him when he went by, while near her her mother and a tawny sister disputed bitterly with a porter. Most of the ladies who hastened to and fro seemed, while very energetic, also very jaded. They were packed as tightly with experiences as their boxes with contraband clothing, and they had both, perhaps, rather heavily on their minds, wondering, it was probable, how they were to get them through. Some of them, strenuous, eye-glassed and scholastic, looked, however, as they marshalled their pathetically lean luggage, quite innocent of material trophies.

Among these alien and unfamiliar visages, Gregory caught sight suddenly of one that was alien yet recognizable. He had seen the melancholy, simian features before, and after a moment he placed the neat, black person, walking beside a truck piled high with enormous boxes, as Louise, Madame von Marwitz's maid. To recognise Louise was to think of Miss Woodruff. Gregory looked around the platform with a new interest.

Miss Woodruff was nowhere to be seen, but a new element pervaded the dingy place, and it hardly needed the presence of four or five richly dressed ladies bearing sheaves of flowers, or that of two silk-hatted impresario-looking gentlemen with Jewish noses, to lead Gregory to infer that the element was Madame von Marwitz's, and that he had, inadvertently, fallen upon the very morning of her departure. Already an awareness and an expectancy was abroad that reminded him of that in the concert hall. The contagion of celebrity had made itself felt even before the celebrity herself was visible; but, in another moment, Madame von Marwitz had appeared upon the platform, surrounded by cohorts of friends. Dressed in a long white cloak and flowing in sables, a white lace veil drooping about her shoulders, a sumptuous white feather curving from her brow to her back, she moved amidst the scene like a splendid, dreamy ship entering some grimy Northern harbour.

Mrs. Forrester, on heels as high as a fairy-godmother's and wearing a strange velvet cloak and a stranger velvet bonnet, trotted beside her; Sir Alliston was on the other hand, his delicate Vandyke features nipped with the cold; Mr. Claude Drew walked behind and before went Eleanor Scrotton, smiling a tight, stricken smile of triumph and responsibility. As the group passed Gregory, Miss Scrotton caught sight of him.

"We are in plenty of time, I see," she said. "Dear me! it has been a morning! Mercedes is always late. Could you, I wonder, induce these people to move away. She so detests being stared at."

Eleanor, as usual, roused a mischievous spirit in Gregory. "I'm afraid I'm helpless," he replied. "We're in a public place, and a cat may look at a king. Besides, who could help looking at those marvellous clothes."

"It isn't a question of cats but of impertinent human beings," Miss Scrotton returned with displeasure. "Allow me, Madam," she forged a majestic way through a gazing group.

"Where is Miss Woodruff?" Gregory inquired. He was wondering.

"Tiresome girl," Miss Scrotton said, watching the ladies with the flowers who gathered around her idol. "She will be late, I'm afraid. She had forgotten Victor."

"Victor? Is Victor the courier? Why does Miss Woodruff have to remember him?"

"No, no. Victor is Mercedes's dog, her dearly loved dog," said Miss Scrotton, her impatience with an ignorance that she suspected of wilfulness tempered, as usual, by the satisfaction of giving any and every information about Madame von Marwitz. "It is a sort of superstition with her that he should always be on the platform to see her off. It will be serious, really serious, if Karen doesn't get him here in time. It may depress Mercedes for the whole of the voyage."

"And where has she gone to get him?"

"Oh, she turned back nearly at once. She was with us in the

carriage and we passed Louise in the omnibus with the boxes and
fortunately Karen noticed that Victor was n't with her. It
turned out, when we stopped and asked Louise about him, that
she had given him to the footman to take for a walk and she
thought he had been brought back to Karen. Karen took a
hansom at once and went back. She really ought to have seen
to it before starting. I do hope she will get him here in time.
Madam, if you please; we really can't get by."

A little woman, stout but sprightly, in whom Gregory recognized the agitated mother of the pretty girl, evaded Miss Scrotton's extended hand and darted past her to place herself in front
of Madame von Marwitz. She wore a large, box-like hat from
which a blue veil hung. Her small features, indeterminate in
form and incoherent in assemblage, expressed to an extraordinary
degree determination and strategy. She faced the great woman.

"Baroness," she said, in swift yet deliberate tones; "allow me
to present myself; Mrs. Hamilton K. Slifer. We have mutual
friends; Mrs. Tollman, Mrs. General Tollman of St. Louis, Mis-
souri. She had the pleasure of meeting you in Paris some years
ago. An old family friend of ours. My girls, Baroness; Maude
and Beatrice. They won't forget this day. We 're simply wild
about you, Baroness. We were at your concert the other night."
Maude, the lean and tawny, and Beatrice, the dark and pretty,
had followed deftly in their mother's wake and were smiling,
Maude with steely brightness, Beatrice with nonchalant assurance, at Madame von Marwitz.

"*Bon Dieu!*" the great woman muttered. She gazed away
from the Slifers and about her with helpless consternation.
Then, slightly bowing her head and murmuring: "I thank you,
Madam," she moved on, her friends closing round her. Miss
Scrotton, pale with wrath, put the Slifers aside as she passed
them.

"Well, girls, I knew I could do it!" Mrs. Slifer ejaculated,
drawing a deep breath. They stood near Gregory, and Beatrice,
who had adjusted her camera, was taking a series of snaps of the
retreating celebrity. "We 've met her, anyway, and perhaps if
she ever comes on deck we 'll get another chance. That 's a real

impertinent woman she's got with her. Did you see her try and shove me back?"

"Never mind, mother," said Beatrice, who was evidently easy-going; "I snapped her as she did it and she looked ugly enough to turn milk sour. My! do look at that girl with the queer cap and the big dog. She's a freak and no mistake! Stand back, Maude, and let me have a shot at her."

"Why, I believe it's the adopted daughter!" Maude exclaimed. "Don't you remember. She was in the front row and we heard those people talking about her. I think she's *distinguée* myself. She looks like a Russian countess."

It was indeed Miss Woodruff who had arrived and Gregory, whose eyes followed the Slifers', was aware of a sudden emotion on seeing her. It was the emotion of his dream, touched and startled and sweet, and even more than in his dream she made him think of a Hans Andersen heroine with the little sealskin cap on her fair hair, and a long furred coat reaching to her ankles. She stood holding Victor by a leash, looking about her with a certain anxiety.

Gregory made his way to her and when she saw him she started to meet him, gladly, but without surprise. "Where is Tante?" she said. "Is she already in the train? Did she send you for me?"

"You are in very good time," he reassured her. "She is over there — you see her feather now, don't you. I'll take you to her."

"Thank you so much. It has been a great rush. You have heard of the misfortunes? By good chance I found the quickest cab."

She was walking beside him, her eyes fixed before them on the group where she saw her guardian's plume and veil. "I don't know what Tante would have done if Victor had not been here in time to say good-bye to her."

Madame von Marwitz was holding a parting reception before the open door of her saloon carriage. Flowers and fruits lay on the tables. Louise and Miss Scrotton's maid piled rugs and cushions on the chairs and divans. One of the Jewish gentlemen stood with his hat pushed off his forehead talking in low, important tones to a pallid young newspaper man who made rapid notes.

Madame von Marwitz at once caught sight of Karen and Victor. Past the intervening heads she beckoned Karen to come to her and she and Gregory exchanged salutes. In her swift smile on seeing him he read a mild amusement; she could only think that, like everybody else, he had come to see her off.

The cohorts opened to receive Miss Woodruff and Madame von Marwitz enfolded her and stooped to kiss Victor's head.

Gregory watched the little scene, which was evidently touching to all who witnessed it, and then turned to find Professor Blackburn at his elbow. He, too, it appeared, had been watching Madame von Marwitz. "Yes; I heard her two years ago in Oxford," he said; "and even my antique blood was stirred, as much by her personality as by her music. A most romantic, most pathetic woman. What eyes and what a smile!"

"I see that you are one of the stricken," said Gregory. "Shall I introduce you to my old friend, Mrs. Forrester? She'll no doubt be able to get you a word with Madame Okraska, if you want to hear her speak."

No, the professor said, he preferred to keep his idols remote and vaguely blurred with incense. "Who is the young Norse maiden?" he inquired; "the one you were with. Those singular ladies are accosting her now."

Karen Woodruff, on the outskirts of the group, had been gazing at her guardian with a constrained smile in which Gregory detected self-mastery, and turned her eyes upon the Slifers as the professor asked his question. Mrs. Slifer, marshalling her girls, and stooping to pat Victor, was introducing herself, and while Gregory told the professor that that was Miss Woodruff, Madame Okraska's ward, she bent to expound to the Slifers the inscription on Victor's collar, speaking, it was evident, with kindness. Gregory was touched by the tolerance with which, in the midst of her own sad thoughts, she satisfied the Slifers' curiosity.

"Then she really is Norse," said the professor.

5

"Really half Norse."

"I like her geniality and her reticence," said the professor, watching the humours of the little scene. "Those enterprising ladies won't get much out of her. Ah, they must relinquish her now; her guardian is asking for her. I suppose it's time that I got into my compartment."

The groups were breaking up and the travellers, detaching themselves from their friends, were taking their places. Madame von Marwitz, poised above a sea of upturned faces on the steps of her carriage, bent to enfold Karen Woodruff once more. Doors then slammed, whistles blew, green flags fluttered, and the long train moved slowly out of the station.

Standing at a little distance from the crowd, and holding Victor by his leash, Miss Woodruff looked after the train with a fixed and stiffened smile. She was near tears. The moment was not a propitious one for speaking to her; yet Gregory felt that he could not go without saying good-bye. He approached her and she turned grave eyes upon him.

"And you are going to Cornwall, now?" said Gregory, patting Victor's head.

"Yes; I go to-morrow," said Miss Woodruff in a gentle voice.

"Have you friends there?" Gregory asked, "and books? Things to amuse you?"

"We see the rector and his wife and one or two old ladies now and then. But it is very remote, you know. That is why my guardian loves it so much. She needs the solitude after her rushing life. But books; oh yes; my guardian has an excellent library there; she is a great reader; I could read all day, in every language, if I wanted to. As for amusement, Mrs. Talcott and I are very busy; we see after the garden and the little farm; I practice and take Victor out for walks."

She had quite mastered her emotion and Gregory could look up at her frankly. "Isn't there something I could send you," he said, "to help to pass the time? Magazines? Do you have them? And sweets? Do you like sweets?" His manner was half playful and he smiled at her as he might have smiled at a young school-girl. If only those wide braids under the little cap had been hanging over her shoulders the manner would have been justified. As it was, Gregory felt with some bewilderment that his behaviour was hardly normal. He was not in the habit of offering magazines and sweets to young women. But his solicitude expressed itself in these unconventional forms and luckily she found nothing amiss with them. She was accustomed, no doubt, to a world where such offerings passed freely.

"It is very kind of you," said Miss Woodruff. "I should indeed like to see a review now and then. Mr. Drew is writing another little article on my guardian, in one of this month's reviews, I did not hear which one; and I would like to see that very much. But sweets? No; when I like them I like them too much and eat too many and then I am sorry. Please don't send me sweets." She was smiling.

"What do you like to eat, then, that does n't make you sorry — even when you eat a great deal?"

"Roast-beef!" she said, laughing, and the tip of her tongue was caught between her teeth. He was charmed to feel that, for the moment, at least, he had won her from her sadness.

"But you get roast-beef in Cornwall."

"Oh, excellent. I will not have roast-beef, please."

"Fruit, then? You like fruit?"

"Yes; indeed."

"And you don't get much fruit in Cornwall in winter."

"Only apples," she confessed, "and dried apricots."

He elicited from her that nectarines and grapes were her favourite fruits. But in the midst of their talk she became suddenly grave again.

"I do not believe that you had a single word with her after I came!"

His face betrayed his bewilderment.

"Tante," she enlightened him. "But before then? You did speak with her? She had sent you to look for me?" The depths of her misconception as to his presence were apparent.

"No; it was by chance I saw you," he said. "And I did n't have any talk with Madame von Marwitz." He had no time to undeceive her further if it had been worth while to undeceive her, for Mrs. Forrester, detaching herself from the larger group of bereaved ones, joined them.

"I can't give you a lift, Gregory?" she asked. "You are going citywards? We are all feeling very bleak and despoiled, are n't we? What an awful place a station is when someone has gone away from it."

"Mrs. Forrester," said Karen Woodruff, with wide eyes, "he did not have one single word with her; Mr. Jardine did not get any talk at all with Tante. Oh, that should have been managed."

But Mrs. Forrester, though granting to his supposed plight a glance of sympathetic concern, was in a hurry to get home and he was, again, spared the necessity of a graceless confession. He piloted them through the crowd, saw them — Miss Woodruff, Mrs. Forrester and Victor,— fitted into Mrs. Forrester's brougham, and then himself got into a hansom. It was still the atmosphere of the dream that hovered about him as he decided at what big fruit-shop he should stop to order a box of nectarines. He wanted her to find them waiting for her in Cornwall. And the very box of nectarines, the globes of sombre red fruit nested in cotton-wool, seemed part of the dream. He knew that he was behaving curiously; but she was, after all, the little Hans Andersen heroine and one need n't think of ordinary customs where she was concerned.

CHAPTER VIII

"Les Solitudes,
"February 2nd.

"DEAR Mr. Jardine,— How very, very kind of you. I could hardly believe it when Mrs. Talcott told me that a box was here for me. I could think of nothing to explain it. Then when we opened it and saw, row upon row, those beautiful things like pearls in a casket — it made me feel quite dazed. Nectarines are not things that you expect to have, in rows, all to yourself. Mrs. Talcott and I ate two at once, standing there in the hall where we opened them; we could n't wait for chairs and plates and silver knives; things taste best of all when eaten greedily, I think, and I think that these will all be eaten greedily. It is so kind of you. I thank you very much.— Yours sincerely, Karen Woodruff."

"Les Solitudes,
"February 9th.

"Dear Mr. Jardine,— It is most kind of you to write me this nice note and to send me these reviews. I often have to miss the things that come out in the reviews about my guardian, for the press-cuttings go to her. Mr. Drew says many clever things, does he not; he understands music and he understands — at least almost — what my guardian is to music; but he does not, of course, understand her. He only sees the greatness and sees it made out of great things. When one knows a great person intimately one sees all the little things that make them great; often such very little things; things that Mr. Drew could not know. That is why his article is, to me, rather pretentious; nor will you like it, I think. He fills up with subtleties the

69

gaps in his knowledge, and that makes it all so artificial. But I am most glad to have it.— Sincerely yours,

"Karen Woodruff."

"Les Solitudes,
"February 18th.

"Dear Mr. Jardine,— The beautiful great box of fruit arrived to-day. It is too good and kind of you. I am wondering now whether muscatel grapes are not even more my favourites than nectarines! This is a day of rain and wind, soft rain blowing in gusts and the wind almost warm. Victor and I have come in very wet and now we are both before the large wood fire. London seems so far away that New York hardly seems further. You heard of the great ovation that my guardian had. I had a note from her yesterday and two of the New York papers. If you care to read them I will gladly send them; they tell in full about the first great concert she has given and the criticism is good. I will ask you to let me have them back when you have read them.— With many, many thanks.— Sincerely yours,

"Karen Woodruff."

"Les Solitudes,
"February 28th.

"Dear Mr. Jardine,— I am glad that you liked the box of snowdrops and that they reached you safely, packed in their moss. I got them in a little copse a few miles from here. The primroses will soon be coming now and, if you like, I will send you some of them. I know one gets them early in London; but don't you like best to open yourself a box from the country and see them lying in bunches with their leaves. I like even the slight flatness they have; but mine are very little flattened; I am good at packing flowers! My guardian always tells me so! You are probably right in not caring to see the papers; they are always much alike in what they say. It was only the glimpse of the great enthusiasm they gave that I thought might have interested you. Next week she goes to

Chicago. I am afraid she will be very tired. But Miss Scrotton will take care of her.— Sincerely yours,

"Karen Woodruff."

"Les Solitudes,
"March 17th.

"Dear Mr. Jardine,— I have taken up my pen for only two purposes since I left London — to write my weekly letter to my guardian — and to thank you over and over again. Only now you have quite spoiled Mrs. Talcott and me for our stewed dried fruit that we used to think so nice before we lived on grapes and nectarines. Indeed I have not forgotten the primroses and I shall be so delighted to pick them for you when the time comes, though I suspect it is sheer kindness in you that gives me the pleasure of sending you something. Your nice letter interested me very much. Yes, we have 'Dominique' in the library here, and I will perhaps soon read it; I say perhaps, because I am reading 'Wilhelm Meister '— my guardian was quite horrified with me when she found I had never read it — and must finish that first, and it is very long. Is 'Dominique' indeed your favourite French novel? My guardian places Stendahl and Flaubert first. For myself I do not care much for French novels. I like the Russians best. — Sincerely yours, Karen Woodruff."

"Les Solitudes,
"April 2nd.

"Dear Mr. Jardine,— You make a charming picture of the primroses in the blue and white bowls for me. And of your view over the park. London can be so beautiful; I, too, care for it very much. It is beautiful here now; the hedges all white with blackthorn and the woods full of primroses. My guardian must now be in San Francisco! She is back in New York in May, and is to give three more great concerts there. I am impatiently waiting for my next letter from her. I am so glad you like the primroses. Many, many thanks for the fruit.— Yours sincerely, Karen Woodruff."

"Les Solitudes,
"April 5th.

"Dear Mr. Jardine,— What you say makes me feel quite troubled. I know you write playfully, yet sometimes one can *dire la vérité en riant,* and it is as if you had found my letters very empty and unresponsive. I did not mean them to be that of course; but I am not at all in the habit of writing letters except to people I am very intimate with. Indeed, I am in the habit only of writing to my guardian, and it is difficult for me to think that other people will be interested in the things I am doing. And in one way I do so little here. Nothing that I could believe interesting to you; nothing really but have walks and practise my music and read; and talk sometimes with Mrs. Talcott. About once in two months the vicar's wife has tea with us, and about once in two months we have tea with her; that is all. And I am sure you cannot like descriptions of landscapes. I love to look at landscapes and dislike reading what other people have to say about them; and is not that the same with you? It is quite different that you should write to me of things and people; for you see so many and you do so much and you know that to someone in the depths of the country all this must be very interesting. So do not punish me for my dullness by ceasing to write to me.— Sincerely yours,
"Karen Woodruff."

"Les Solitudes,
"April 10th.

"Dear Mr. Jardine,— Of course I will write you descriptions of landscapes ! — and of all my daily routine, if you really care to hear. No; I am not lonely, though of course I miss my guardian very much. I have the long, long walks with Victor, in wet weather over the inland moors along the roads, and in fine weather along the high cliff paths; sometimes we walk ten miles in an afternoon and come back very tired for tea. In the evenings I sit with Mrs. Talcott over the fire. You ask me to describe Mrs. Talcott to you, and to tell you all about her. She is with me now, and we are in the morning room, where

we always sit; for the great music-room that opens on the
verandah and fronts the sea is shut when my guardian is not
here. This room looks over the sea, too, but from the side of
the house and through an arabesque of trees. The walls are
filled with books and flowering bulbs stand in the windows.
We have had our tea and the sunlight slants in over the white
freesia and white hyacinths. There are primroses everywhere,
too, and they make the room seem more full of sunlight. You
could hardly see a more beautiful room. Mrs. Talcott sits
before the fire with her skirt turned up and her feet in square-
toed shoes on the fender and looks into the fire. She is short
and thick and very old, but she does not seem old; she is
hard; not soft and withered. She has a large, calm face with
very yellow skin, and very light blue eyes set deeply under
white eyebrows. Her hair is white and drawn up tightly to a
knot at the top of her head. She wears no cap and dresses
always in black; very plain, with, in the daytime, a collar of
white lawn turning over a black silk stock and bow, such as
young girls wear, and, in the evening, a little fichu of white
net, very often washed, and thin and starchy. And since her
skirts are always very short, and her figure so square, she makes
one think of a funny little girl as well as of an old woman.
She comes from the State of Maine, and she remembers a striving, rough existence in a little town on the edge of wilder-
nesses. She is a very distant relation of my guardian's. My
guardian's maternal grandparents were Spanish and lived in
New Orleans, and a sister of Señor Bastida's (Bastida was the
name of my guardian's grandfather)—married a New Englander, from Vermont—and that New Englander was an
uncle of Mrs. Talcott's—do you follow!—her uncle married
my guardian's aunt, you see. Mrs. Talcott, in her youth,
stayed sometimes in New Orleans, and dearly loved the beautiful Dolores Bastida who left her home to follow Pavelek
Okraska. Poor Dolores Okraska had many sorrows. Her husband was not a good husband and her parents died. She was
very unhappy and before her baby came—she was in Poland
then,—she sent for Mrs. Talcott. Mrs. Talcott had been mar-

ried, too, and had lost her husband and was very poor. But
she left everything and crossed to Europe in the steerage — and
what it must have been in those days! — imagine! — to join
her unfortunate relative. My guardian has told me of it; she
calls Mrs. Talcott: '*Un coeur d'or dans un corps de bois.*'
She stayed with Dolores Okraska until she died a little time
after. She brought up her child. They were in great want;
my guardian remembers that she had sometimes not enough to
eat. When she was older and had already become famous,
some relatives of the Bastidas heard of her and helped; but
those were years of great struggle for Mrs. Talcott; and it is
so strange to think of that provincial, simple American woman
with her rustic ways and accent, living in Cracow and Warsaw, and Vienna, and steadily doing what she had set herself
to do. She speaks French with a most funny accent even yet,
though she spent so many years abroad, so many in Paris. I
do not know what would have become of my guardian if it had
not been for her. Her father loved her, but was very erratic
and undisciplined. Mrs. Talcott has been with my guardian
for almost all the time ever since. It is a great and silent
devotion. She is very reticent. She never speaks of herself.
She talks to me sometimes in the evenings about her youth in
Maine, and the long white winters and the sleigh-rides; and
the tapping of the maple-trees in Spring; and the nutting
parties in the fall of the year. I think that she likes to remember all this; and I love to hear her, for it reminds me of
what my father used to tell me of his youth; and I love especially to hear of the trailing arbutus, that lovely little flower
that grows beneath the snow; how one brushes back the snow
in early Spring and finds the waxen, sweet, pink flowers and
dark, shining leaves under it. And I always imagine that it
is a doubled nostalgia that I feel and that my mother's Norway
in Spring was like it, with snow and wet woods. There is a
line that brings it all over me: 'In May, when sea-winds
pierced our solitudes.' It is by Emerson. The Spring here is
very lovely, too, but it has not the sweetness that arises from
snow and a long winter. Through the whole winter the fuchsias

keep their green against the white walls of the little village, huddled in between the headlands at the edge of the sea beneath us. You know this country, don't you? The cliffs are so beautiful. I love best the great headlands towards the Lizard, black rock or grey, all spotted with rosettes of orange lichen with sweeps of grey-green sward sloping to them. Victor becomes quite intoxicated with the wind on these heights and goes in circles round and round, like a puppy. Later on, all the slopes are veiled in the delicate little pink thrift, and the stone walls are festooned with white campion.

"Then Mrs. Talcott and I have a great deal to do about the little farm. Mrs. Talcott is so clever at this. She makes it pay besides giving my guardian all the milk and eggs and bacon, too, she needs. There is a farmer and his wife, and a gardener and a boy; but with the beautiful garden we have here it takes most of the day to see to everything. The farmer's wife is a stern looking woman, but really very gentle, and she sings hymns all the day long while she works. She has a very good voice, so that it is sweet to hear her. Yes; I do play. I have a piano here in the morning-room, and I am very fond of my music. And, as I have told you, I read a good deal, too. So there you have all the descriptions and the details. I liked so much what you told me of the home of your boyhood. When I saw you, I knew that you were a person who cared for all these things, even if you were not an artist. What you tell me, too, of the law-courts and the strange people you see there, and the ugly, funny side of human life amused me, though it seems to me more sorrowful than you perhaps feel it. People amuse me very much sometimes, too; but I have not your eye for their foibles. You draw them rather as Forain does; I should do it, I suspect, with more sentimentality. The fruit comes regularly once a week, and punctual thanks seem inappropriate for what has become an institution. But you know how grateful I am. And for the weekly *Punch;* — so *gemütlich* and *bien pensant* and, often, very, very funny, with a funniness that the Continental papers never give one; their jests are never the jests of the *bien pensant.* It is the acrid atmosphere of the café they bring, not that of the dinner party, or, better still, for *Punch,* the picnic. The reviews, too, are very interesting. Mrs. Talcott reads them a good deal, she who seldom reads. She says sometimes very acute and amusing things about politics. My guardian has a horror of politics; but they rather interest Mrs. Talcott. I know nothing of them; but I do not think that my guardian would agree with what you say; I think that she would belong more to your party of freedom and progress. What a long letter I have written to you! I have never written such a long one in my life before, except to my guardian.— Sincerely yours,   Karen Woodruff."

                              " Les Solitudes,
                                   " April 15th.
   " Dear Mr. Jardine,— How very nice to hear that you are coming to Cornwall for Easter and will be near us — at least Falmouth is quite near with a motor. It is beautiful country there, too; I have driven there with my guardian, and it is a beautiful town to see, lying in a wide curve around its blue bay. It is softer and milder than here. A bend of the coast makes so much difference. But why am I telling you all this, when of course you know it! I forget that anyone knows Cornwall but Mrs. Talcott and my guardian and me. But you have not seen this bit of the coast, and it excites me to think that I shall introduce you to our cliffs and to Les Solitudes. If only my guardian were here! It is not itself, this place, without her. It is not to see Les Solitudes if you do not see the great music-room opening its four long windows on the sea and sky; and my guardian sitting in the shade of the verandah looking over the sea. But Mrs. Talcott and I will do the honours as best we may and tell you everything about my guardian that you will wish to know. Let us hear beforehand the day you are coming; for the cook makes excellent cakes, and we will have some baked specially for you. How very nice to see you again.— Sincerely yours,
                              " Karen Woodruff."

CHAPTER IX

ON a chill, sunny morning in April, Gregory Jardine went out on to his balcony before breakfast and stood leaning there as was his wont, looking down over his view. The purpling tree-tops in the park emerged from a light morning mist. The sky, of the palest blue, seemed very high and was streaked with white. Spring was in the air and he could see daffodils shining here and there on the slopes of green.

He had just read Karen Woodruff's last letter, and he was in the mood, charmed, amused and touched, that her letters always brought. Never, he thought, had there been such sweet and such funny letters; so frank and so impersonal; so simple and so mature. During these months of their correspondence the thought of her had been constantly in his mind, mingling now not only with his own deep and distant memories, but, it seemed, with hers, so that while she still walked with him over the hills of his boyhood and stooped to look with him at the spring gushing from under the bracken, they also brushed together the dry, soft snow from the trailing arbutus, or stood above the sea on the Cornish headlands. Never in his life had he so possessed the past and been so aware of it. His youth was with him, even though he still thought of his relation to Karen Woodruff as a paternal and unequal one; imagining a crisis in which his wisdom and knowledge of the world might serve her; a foolish love-affair, perhaps, that he would disentangle; or a disaster connected with the great woman under whose protection she lived; he could so easily imagine disasters befalling Madame von Marwitz and involving everyone around her. And now in a week's time he would be in Cornwall and seeing again the little Hans Andersen heroine. This was the thought that emerged from the sweet vagrancy of his mood;

77

and, as it came, he was pierced suddenly with a strange rapture and fear that had in it the very essence of the spring-time.

Gregory had continued to think of the girl he was to marry in the guise of a Constance Armytage, and although Constance Armytage's engagement to another man found him unmoved, except with relief for the solution of what had really ceased to be a perplexity — since, apparently, he could not manage to fall in love with her — this fact had not been revealing, since he still continued to think of Constance as the type, if she had ceased to be the person. Karen Woodruff was almost the last type he could have fixed upon. She fitted nowhere into his actual life. She only fitted into the life of dreams and memories.

So now, still looking down at the trees and daffodils, he drew a long breath and tried to smile over what had been a trick of the imagination and to relegate Karen to the place of half-humorous dreams. He tried to think calmly of her. He visualized her in her oddity and child-likeness; seeing the flat blue bows of the concert; the old-fashioned gold locket of the tea; the sealskin cap of the station. But still, it was apparent, the infection of the season was working in him; for these trivial bits of her personality had become overwhelmingly sweet and wonderful. The essential Karen infused them. Her limpid grey eyes looked into his. She said, so ridiculously, so adorably: "My guardian likes best to be called von Marwitz by those who know her personally." She laughed, the tip of her tongue caught between her teeth. From the place of dream and memory, the living longing for her actual self emerged indomitably.

Gregory turned from the balcony and went inside. He was dazed. Her primroses stood about the room in the white and blue bowls. He wanted to kiss them. Controlling the impulse, which seemed to him almost insane, he looked at them instead and argued with himself. In love? But one did n't fall in love like that between shaving and breakfast. What possessed him was a transient form of *idée fixe,* and he had behaved very foolishly in playing fairy-godfather to a dear little girl. But at this relegating phrase his sense of humour rose to mock him. He could not relegate Karen Woodruff as a dear little girl. It was he who had behaved like a boy, while she had maintained the calm simplicities of the mature. He had n't the faintest right to hope that she saw anything in his correspondence but what she had herself brought to it. Fear fell more strongly upon him. He sat down to his breakfast, his thoughts in inextricable confusion. And while he drank his coffee and glanced nervously down the columns of his newspaper, a hundred little filaments of memory ran back and linked the beginning to the present. It had not been so sudden. It had been there beside him, in him; and he had not seen it. The meeting of their eyes in the long, grave interchange at the concert had been full of presage. And why had he gone to tea at Mrs. Forrester's? And why, above all why, had he dreamed that dream? It was his real self who had felt no surprise when, at the edge of the forest, she had said: "And I love you." The words had been spoken in answer to his love.

Gregory laid down his paper and stared before him. He was in love. Should he get over it? Did he want to get over it? Was it possible to get over it if he did want to? And, this was the culmination, would she have him? These questions drove him forth.

When Barker, his man, came to clear away the breakfast things he found that the bacon and eggs had not been eaten. Barker was a stone-grey personage who looked like a mid-Victorian Liberal statesman. His gravity often passed into an air of despondent responsibility. "Mr. Jardine has n't eaten his breakfast," he said to his wife, who was Gregory's cook. "It 's this engagement of Miss Armytage's. He was more taken with her than we 'd thought."

Gregory had intended to motor down to Cornwall, still a rare opportunity in those days; a friend who was going abroad had placed his car at his disposal. But he sent the car ahead of him and, on the first day of his freedom, started by train. Next day he motored over to the little village near the Lizard.

It was a pale, crystalline Spring day. From heights, where

the car seemed to poise like a bird in mid-air, one saw the tranquil blue of the sea. The woods were veiled in young green and the hedges thickly starred with blackthorn. Over the great Goonhilly Downs a silvery sheen trembled with impalpable colour and the gorse everywhere was breaking into gold. It was a day of azure, illimitable distances; of exultation and delight. Even if one were not in love one would feel oneself a lover on such a day.

Gregory had told himself that he would be wise; that he would go discreetly and make sure not only that he was really in love, but that there was in his love a basis for life. Marriage must assure and secure his life, not disturb and disintegrate it; and a love resisted and put aside unspoken may soon be relegated to the place of fond and transient dream. Perhaps the little Hans Andersen heroine would settle happily into such a dream. How little he had seen of her. But while he thus schooled himself, while the white roads curved and beckoned and unrolled their long ribbons, the certainties he needed of himself merged more and more into the certainties he needed of her. And he felt his heart, in the singing speed, lift and fly towards the beloved.

He had written to her and told her the hour of his arrival, and at a turning he suddenly saw her standing above the road on one of the stone stiles of the country. Dressed in white and poised against the blue, while she kept watch for his coming, she was like a calm, far-gazing figure-head on a ship, and the ship that bore her seemed to have soared into sight.

She was new, yet unchanged. Her attitude, her smile, as she held up an arresting hand to the chauffeur, filled him with delight and anxiety. It disconcerted him to find how new she was. . He felt that he spoke confusedly to her when she came to shake his hand.

"People often lose their way in coming to see Tante," she said, and it struck him, even in the midst of his preoccupation with her, as too sweetly absurd that the first sentence she spoke to him should sound the familiar chime. "They have gone mistakenly down the lane that leads to the cliff path, that one

there, or the road that leads out to the moors. And one poor
man was quite lost and never found his way to us at all. It
meant, for he had only a day or two to spend in England, that
he did not see her for another year. Tante has had signs put
up since then; but even now people can go wrong."

She mounted beside the chauffeur so that she could guide
him down the last bit of road, sitting sideways, her arm laid
along the back of the seat. From time to time she smiled at
Gregory.

She was a person who accepted the unusual easily and with
no personal conjecture. She was so accustomed, no doubt, to
the sudden appearance of all sorts of people, that she had no
discriminations to apply to his case. There was no shyness and
no surmise in her manner. She smiled at him as composedly
as she had smiled over the Great Wall of China in Mrs. Forrester's drawing-room, and her pleasure in seeing him was
neither less frank nor more intimate.

She wore a broad hat of sun-burnt straw and a white serge
coat and skirt that looked as if they had shrunk in frequent
washings. Her white blouse had the little frills at neck and
wrists and around her throat was the gold locket on its black
ribbon. Her eyes, when she turned them on him and smiled,
seemed to open distances like the limitlessness of the moorland.
Her tawny skin and shining golden hair were like the gorse
and primroses and she in her serenity and gladness like the day
personified.

They did not attempt to talk through the loudly purring
monotones of the car, which picked its way swiftly and delicately
down the turning road and then skimmed lightly on the level
ground between hedges of fuchsia and veronica. As the prospect opened Karen pointed to the golden shoulder of a headland
bathed in sunlight and the horizon line of the sea beyond.
They turned among wind-bitten Cornish elms, leaning inland,
and Gregory saw among them the glimmer of Les Solitudes.

It was a white-walled house with a high-pitched roof of grey
shingles, delicately rippling; a house almost rustic, yet more
nearly noble, very beautiful; simple, yet unobtrusively adapted

6

to luxury. Simplicity reigned within, though one felt luxury there in a chrysalis condition, folded exquisitely and elaborately away and waiting the return of the enchantress.

Karen led him across the shining spaces of the hall and into the morning-room. Books, flowers and sunlight seemed to furnish it, and, with something austere and primitive, to make it the most fitting background for herself. But while her presence perfected it for him, it was her guardian's absence that preoccupied Karen. Again, and comically, she reminded Gregory of the sacristan explaining to the sight-seer that the famous altar-piece had been temporarily removed and that he could not really judge the chapel without its culminating and consecrating object. "If only Tante were here!" she said. "It seems so strange that anyone should see Les Solitudes who has not seen her in it. I do not remember that it has ever happened before. This is the dining-room — yes, I like to show it all to you — she planned it all herself, you know — is it not a beautiful room? You see, though we are Les Solitudes, we can seat a large dinner-party and Tante has sometimes many guests; not often though; this is her place of peace and rest. She collected all this Jacobean furniture; connoisseurs say that it is very beautiful. The music-room, alas, is closed; but I will show you the garden — and Mrs. Talcott in it. I am eager for you and Mrs. Talcott to meet."

He would rather have stayed and talked to her in the morning-room; but she compelled him, rather as a sacristan compels the slightly bewildered sight-seer, to pass on to the next point of interest. She led him out to the upper terrace of the garden, which dropped, ledge by ledge, with low walls and winding hedges, down the cliff-side. She pointed out to him the sea-front of the house, with its wide verandah and clustered trees and the beautiful dip of the roof over the upper windows, far gazing little dormer windows above these. Tante, she told him, had designed the house. "That is her room, the corner one," she said. "She can see the sunrise from her bed."

Gregory was interested neither in Madame von Marwitz's advantages nor in her achievements. He asked Karen where

her own room was. It was at the back of the house, she said;
a dear little room, far up. She, too, had a glimpse of the
Eastern headland and of the sunrise.

They were walking along the paths, their borders starred as
yet frugally with hints of later glories; but already the au-
brietia and arabis made bosses of white or purple on the walls,
and in a little copse daffodils grew thickly.

" There is Mrs. Talcott," said Karen, quickening her pace.
Evidently she considered Mrs. Talcott, in her relation to Tante,
as an important feature of Les Solitudes.

It was her relation to Karen that caused Gregory to look with
interest at the stout old lady, dressed in black alpaca, who was
stooping over a flower-border at a little distance from them.
He had often wondered what this sole companion of Karen's
cloistered life was like. Mrs. Talcott's skirts were short; her
shoes thick-soled and square-toed, fastening with a strap and
button over white stockings at the ankle. She wore a round
straw hat, like a child's, and had a basket of gardening imple-
ments beside her.

" Mrs. Talcott, here is Mr. Jardine," Karen announced, as
they approached her.

Mrs. Talcott raised herself slowly and turned to them, drawing off her gardening gloves. She was a funny looking old
woman, funnier than Karen had prepared him for finding her,
and uglier. Her large face, wallet-shaped and sallow, was
scattered over with white moles, or rather, warts, one of which,
on her eyelid, caused it to droop over her eye and to blink sometimes, suddenly. She had a short, indefinite nose and long,
large lips firmly folded. With its updrawn hair and impassivity
her face recalled that of a Chinese image; but more than of anything else she gave Gregory the impression, vaguely and incon-
gruously tragic, of an old shipwrecked piece of oaken timber,
washed up, finally, out of reach of the waves, on some high,
lonely beach; battered, though still so solid; salted through and
through; crusted with brine, and with odd, bleached excrescences,
like barnacles, adhering to it. Her look of almost inhuman
cleanliness added force to the simile.

"Mr. Jardine heard Tante last winter, you know," said Karen, "and met her at Mrs. Forrester's."

"I'm very happy to make your acquaintance, Sir," said Mrs. Talcott, giving Gregory her hand.

"Mrs. Talcott is a great gardener," Karen went on. "Tante has the ideas and Mrs. Talcott carries them out. And sometimes they are n't easy to carry out, are they, Mrs. Talcott!"

Mrs. Talcott, her hands folded at her waist, contemplated her work.

"Mitchell made a mistake about the campanulas, Karen," she remarked. "He's put the clump of blue over yonder, instead of the white."

"Oh, Mrs. Talcott!" Karen turned to look. "And Tante specially wanted the white there so that they should be against the sea. How very stupid of Mitchell."

"They'll have to come out, I presume," said Mrs. Talcott, but without emotion.

"And where is the *pyramidalis alba?*"

"Well, he's got that up in the flagged garden where she wanted the blue," said Mrs. Talcott.

"And it will be so bad for them to move them again! What a pity! They have been sent for specially," Karen explained to Gregory. "My guardian heard of a particularly beautiful kind, and the white were to be for this corner of the wall, you see that they would look very lovely against the sea, and the blue were to be among the white veronica and white lupins in the flagged garden. And now they are all planted wrong, and so accurately and solidly wrong," she walked ahead of Mrs. Talcott examining the offending plants. "Are you quite sure they're wrong, Mrs. Talcott?"

"Dead sure," Mrs. Talcott made reply. "He did it this morning when I was in the dairy. He did n't understand, or got muddled, or something. I'll commence changing them round as soon as I've done this weeding. It'll be a good two hours' work."

"No, you must not do it till I can help you," said Karen. "To-morrow morning." She had a manner at once deferential

and masterful of addressing the old lady. They were friendly
without being intimate. "Now promise me that you will wait
till I can help you."

"Well, I guess I won't promise. I like to get things off my
mind right away," said Mrs. Talcott. If Karen was masterful,
she was not yielding. "I'll see how the time goes after tea.
Don't you bother about it."

They left her bending again over her beds. "She is very
strong, but I think sometimes she works too hard," said Karen.

By a winding way she led him to the high flagged garden with
its encompassing trees and far blue prospect, and here they sat
for a little while in the sunlight and talked. "How different
all this must be from your home in Northumberland," said
Karen. "I have never been to Northumberland. Is your
brother much there? Is he like you? Have you brothers and
sisters?"

She questioned him with the frank interest with which he
wished to question her. He told her about Oliver and said that
he wasn't like himself. A faint flavour of irony came into his
voice in speaking of his elder brother and finding Karen's calm
eyes dwelling on him he wondered if she thought him unfair.
"We always get on well enough," he said, "but we haven't
much in common. He is a good, dull fellow, half alive."

"And you are very much alive."

"Yes, on the whole, I think so," he answered, smiling, but
sensitively aware of a possible hint of irony in her. But she
had intended none. She continued to look at him calmly.
"You are making use of all of yourself; that is to be alive,
Tante always says; and I feel that it is true of you. And his
wife? the wife of the dull hunting brother? Does she hunt too
and think of foxes most?"

He could assure her that Betty quite made up in the variety
of her activities for Oliver's deficiencies. Karen was interested
in the American Betty and especially in hearing that she had
been at the concert from which their own acquaintance dated.
She asked him, walking back to the house, if he had seen Mrs.
Forrester. "She is an old friend of yours, isn't she?" she said.

"That must be nice. She was so kind to me that last day in London. Tante is very fond of her; very, very fond. I hardly think there is anyone of all her friends she has more feeling for. Here is Victor, come to greet you. You remember Victor, and how he nearly missed the train."

The great, benignant dog came down the path to them and as they walked Karen laid her hand upon his head, telling Gregory that Sir Alliston had given him to Tante when he was quite a tiny puppy. "You saw Sir Alliston, that sad, gentle poet? There is another person that Tante loves." It was with a slight stir of discomfort that Gregory realised more fully from these assessments how final for Karen was the question of Tante's likes and dislikes.

They were on the verandah when she paused. "But I think, though the music-room is closed, that you must see the portrait."

"The portrait? Of you?" Actually, and sincerely, he was off the track.

"Of me? Oh no," said Karen, laughing a little. "Why should it be of me? Of my guardian, of course. Perhaps you know it. It is by Sargent and was in the Royal Academy some years ago."

"I must have missed it. Am I to see it now?"

"Yes. I will ask Mrs. Talcott for the key and we will draw all the blinds and you shall see it." They walked back to the garden in search of Mrs. Talcott.

"Do you like it?" Gregory asked.

Karen reflected for a moment and then said; "He understands her better than Mr. Drew does, or, at all events, does not try to make up for what he does not understand by elaborations. But there are blanks! — oh blanks! — However, it is a very magnificent picture and you shall see. Mrs. Talcott, may I have the key of the music-room? I want to show the Sargent to Mr. Jardine."

They had come to the old woman again, and again she slowly righted herself from her stooping posture. "It's in my room, I'll come and get it," said Mrs. Talcott, and on Karen's protesting against this, she observed that it was about tea-time, anyway. She preceded them to the house.

"But I do beg," Karen stopped her in the hall. "Let me get it. You shall tell me where it is."

Mrs. Talcott yielded. "In my left top drawer on the right hand side under the pile of handkerchiefs," she recited. "Thanks, Karen."

While Karen was gone, Mrs. Talcott in the hall stood in front of Gregory and looked past him in silence into the morning-room. She did not seem to feel it in any sense incumbent upon her to entertain him, though there was nothing forbidding in her manner. But happening presently, while they waited, to glance at the droll old woman, he found her eyes fixed on him in a singularly piercing, if singularly impassive, gaze. She looked away again with no change of expression, shifting her weight from one hip to the other, and something in the attitude suggested to Gregory that she had spent a great part of her life in waiting. She had a capacity, he inferred, for indefinite waiting. Karen came happily running down the stairs, holding the key.

They went into the dim, white room where swathed presences stood as if austerely welcoming them. Karen drew up the blind and Mrs. Talcott, going to the end of the room, mounted a chair and dexterously twitched from its place the sheet that covered the great portrait. Then, standing beside it, and still holding its covering, she looked, not at it, but, meditatively, out at the sea that crossed with its horizon line the four long windows. Karen, also in silence, came and stood beside Gregory.

It was indeed a remarkable picture; white and black; silver and green. To a painter's eye the arresting balance of these colours would have first appealed and the defiant charm with which the angular surfaces of the grand piano and the soft curves of the woman seated at it were combined. The almost impalpable white of an azalea with its flame-green foliage, and a silver statuette, poised high on a slender column of white chalcedony, were the only accessories. But after the first delighted draught of wonder it was the face of Madame Okraska — pre-eminently Madame Okraska in this portrait — that compelled one to con-

centration. She sat, turning from the piano, her knees crossed,
one arm cast over them, the other resting along the edge of the
key-board. The head drooped slightly and the eyes looked out
just below the spectator's eyes, so that in poise and glance it recalled somewhat Michael Angelo's Lorenzo da Medici. And
something that Gregory had felt in her from the first, and that
had roused in him dim hostilities and ironies, was now more fully
revealed. The artist seemed to have looked through the soft mask
of the woman's flesh, through the disturbing and compelling
forces of her own consciousness, to the very structure and anat-
omy of her character. Atavistic, sub-conscious revelations were
in the face. It was to see, in terms of art, a scientific demonstration of race, temperament, and the results of their interplay
with environment. The languors, the feverish indolences, the
caprice of generations of Spanish exiles were there, and the ambiguity, the fierceness of Slav ancestry. And, subtly interwoven,
were the marks of her public life upon her. The face, so
moulded to indifference, was yet so aware of observation, so
adjusted to it, so insatiable of it, that, sitting there, absorbed
and brooding, lovely with her looped pearls and diamonds, her
silver broideries and silken fringes, she was a product of the
public, a creature reared on adulation, breathing it in softly,
peacefully, as the white flowers beside her breathed in light and
air. Her craftsmanship, her genius, though indicated, were sub-
merged in this pervasive quality of an indifference based securely
on the ever present consciousness that none could be indifferent
to her. And more than the passive acceptance and security was
indicated. Strange, sleeping potentialities lurked in the face; as
at the turn of a kaleidoscope, Gregory could fancy it suddenly
transformed, by some hostile touch, some menace, to a savage
violence and rapacity. He was aware, standing between the girl
who worshipped her and the devoted old woman, of the pang of
a curious anxiety.

"Well," said Karen at last, and she looked from the picture to
him. "What do you think of it?"

"It's splendid" said Gregory. "It's very fine. And
beautiful."

"But does it altogether satisfy you?" Her eyes were again on the portrait. "What is lacking, I cannot say; but it seems to me that it is painted with intelligence only, not with love. It is Madame Okraska, the great genius; but it is not Tante; it is not even Madame von Marwitz."

The portrait seemed to Gregory to go so much further and so much deeper than what he had himself seen that it was difficult to believe that hers might be the deepest vision, but he was glad to take refuge in the possibility. "It does seem to me wonderfully like," he said. "But then I don't know 'Tante.'"

Karen now glanced at Mrs. Talcott. "It is a great bone of contention between us," she said, smiling at the old lady, yet smiling, Gregory observed, with a touch of challenge. "She feels it quite complete. That, in someone who does know Tante, I cannot understand."

Mrs. Talcott, making no reply, glanced up at the portrait and then, again, out at the sea.

Gregory looked at her with awakened curiosity. This agreement was an unexpected prop for him. "You, too, think it a perfect likeness?" he asked her. Her old blue eyes, old in the antique tranquillity of their regard, yet still of such a vivid, unfaded turquoise, turned on him and again he had that impression of an impassive piercing.

"It seems to me about as good a picture as anyone's likely to get," said Mrs. Talcott.

"Yes, but, oh Mrs. Talcott"— with controlled impatience Karen took her up —"surely you see,— it is n't Tante. It is a genius, a great woman, a beautiful woman, a beautiful and poetic creature, of course; — he has seen all that — who would n't? but it is almost a woman without a heart. There is something heartless there. I always feel it. And when one thinks of Tante!" And Mrs. Talcott remaining silent, she insisted: "Can you really say you don't see what I mean?"

"Well, I never cared much about pictures anyway," Mrs. Talcott now remarked.

"Well, but you care for this one more than I do!" Karen returned, with a laugh of vexation. "It is n't a question of pictures; it's a question of a likeness. You really think that this does Tante justice? It's that I can't understand."

Mrs. Talcott, thus pursued, again looked up at the portrait, and continued, now, to look at it for several moments. And as she stood there, looking up, she suddenly and comically reminded Gregory of the Frog gardener before the door in "Alice," with his stubborn and deliberate misunderstanding. He could almost have expected to see Mrs. Talcott advance her thumb and rub the portrait, as if to probe the cause of her questioner's persistence. When she finally spoke it was only to vary her former judgment: "It seems to me about as good a picture as Mercedes is likely to get taken," she said. She pronounced the Spanish name: "Mursadees."

Karen, after this, abandoned her attempt to convince Mrs. Talcott. Tea was ready, and they went into the morning-room. Here Mrs. Talcott presided at the tea-table, and for all his dominating preoccupation she continued to engage a large part of Gregory's attention. She sat, leaning back in her chair, slowly eating, her eyes, like tiny, blue stones, immeasurably remote, immeasurably sad, fixed on the sea.

"Is it long since you were in America?" he asked her. He felt drawn to Mrs. Talcott.

"Why, I guess it's getting on for twenty-five years now," she replied, after considering for a moment; "since I've lived there. I've been over three or four times with Mercedes; on tours."

"Twenty-five years since you came over here? That is a long time."

"Oh, it's more than that since I came," said Mrs. Talcott. "Twenty-five years since I lived at home. I came over first nearly fifty years ago. Yes; it's a long time."

"Dear me; you have lived most of your life here, then."

"Yes; you may say I have."

"And don't you ever want to go back to America to stay?"

"I don't know as I do," said Mrs. Talcott.

"You're fonder of it over here, like so many of your compatriots?"

"Well, I don't know as I am," Mrs. Talcott, who had a genius
it seemed for non-committal statements, varied; and then, as
though aware that her answers might seem ungracious, she added:
"All my folks are dead.   There's no reason for my wanting to
go home that I can think of."

"Besides, Mrs. Talcott," Karen now helped her on, "home to
you is where Tante is, isn't it.   Mrs. Talcott has lived with
Tante ever since Tante was born.   No one in the world knows
her as well as she does.   It is rather wonderful to think about."
She had the air, finding Mrs. Talcott appreciated, of putting forward for her her great claim to distinction.

"Yes; I know Mercedes pretty well," Mrs. Talcott conceded.

"How I love to hear about it," said Karen; "about her first
concert, you know, Mrs. Talcott, when you curled her hair —
such long, bright brown hair, she had, and so thick, falling below
her waist, did n't it?"   Mrs. Talcott nodded with a certain complacency.   "And she wore a little white muslin frock and white
shoes and a blue sash; she was only nine years old; it was a great
concert in Warsaw.   And she did n't want her hair curled, and
combed it all out with her fingers just before going on to the
platform — did n't she?"

Mrs. Talcott was slightly smiling over these reminiscences.
"Smart little thing," she commented.   "She did it the last
minute so as it was too late for me to fix it again.   It made me
feel dreadful her going on to the platform with her head all
mussed up like that.   She looked mighty pretty all the same."

"And she was right, too, was n't she?" said Karen, elated,
evidently, at having so successfully drawn Mrs. Talcott out.
"Her hair was never curly, was it.   It looked better straight,
I 'm sure."

"Well, I don't know about that," said Mrs. Talcott.   "I
always like it curled best, when she was little.   But I had to own
to myself she looked mighty pretty, though I was so mad at her."

"Tante has always had her own way, I imagine," said Karen,
"about anything she set her mind on.   She had her way about
being an infant prodigy; though you were so right about that —
she has often said so, has n't she. and how thankful she is that

you were able to stop it before it did her harm. I must show you our photographs of Tante, Mr. Jardine. We have volumes and volumes, and boxes and boxes of them. They are far more like her, I think, many of them, than the portrait. Some of them too dear and quaint — when she was quite tiny."

Tea was over and Karen, rising, looked towards the shelves where, evidently, the volumes and boxes were kept.

" I really think I 'd rather see some more of this lovely place, first," said Gregory. "Do take me further along the cliff. I could see the photographs, you know, the next time I come."

He, too, had risen and was smiling at her with a little constraint.

Karen, arrested on her way to the photographs, looked at him in surprise. " Will you come again? You are to be in Cornwall so long? "

" I 'm to be here about a fortnight and I should like to come often, if I may." She was unaware, disconcertingly unaware; yet her surprise showed the frankest pleasure.

" How very nice," she said. " I did not think that you could come all that way more than once."

While they spoke, Mrs. Talcott's ancient, turquoise eyes were upon them, and in her presence Gregory found it easier to say things than it would have been to say them to Karen alone. Already, he felt sure, Mrs. Talcott understood, and if it was easy to say things in her presence might that not be because he guessed that she sympathised? " But I came down to Cornwall to see you," he said, leaning on his chair back and tilting it a little while he smiled at Karen.

Her pleasure rose in a flush to her cheek. " To see me? "

" Yes; I felt from our letters that we ought to become great friends."

She looked at him, pondering the unlooked-for possibility he put before her. " Great friends? " she repeated. " I have never had a great friend of my own. Friends, of course; the Lippheims and the Belots; and Strepoff; and you, of course, Mrs. Talcott; but never, really, a great friend quite of my own, for they are Tante's friends first and come through Tante. Of course you have come through Tante, too," said Karen, with evident satisfaction; "only not quite in the same way."

"Not at all in the same way," said Gregory. "Don't forget. We met at the concert, and without any introduction! It has nothing to do with Madame von Marwitz this time. It's quite on our own."

"Oh, but I would so much rather have it come through her, if we are to be great friends," Karen returned, smiling, though reflectively. "I think we are to be, for I felt you to be my friend from that first moment. But it was at the concert that we met and it was Tante's concert. So that it was not quite on our own. I want it to be through Tante," she went on, "because it pleases me very much to think that we may be great friends, and my happy things have come to me through Tante, always."

CHAPTER X

HE came next day and every day. They were favoured with the rarely given gift of a perfect spring. They walked along the cliffs and headlands. They sat and talked in the garden. He took her with Mrs. Talcott for long drives to distant parts of the coast which he and Karen would explore, while Mrs. Talcott in the car sat, with apparently interminable patience, waiting for them.

Karen played to him in the morning-room; and this was a new revelation of her. She was not a finished performer and her music was limited by her incapacity; but she had the gift for imparting, with transparent sincerity and unfailing sensitiveness, the very heart of what she played. There were Arias from Schubert Sonatas, and Bach Preludes, and loving little pieces of Schumann, that Gregory thought he had never heard so beautifully played before. Everything they had to say was said, though, it might be, said very softly. He told her that he cared more for her music than for any he had listened to, and Karen laughed, not at all taking him seriously. "But you do care for music, though you are no musician," she said. "I like to play to you; and to someone who does not care it is impossible."

Her acceptances of their bond might give ground for all hope or for none. As for himself there had been, from the moment of seeing her again, of knowing in her presence that fear and that delight, no further doubt as to his own state and its finality. Yet his first perplexities lingered and could at moments become painful.

He felt the beloved creature to be at once inappropriate and inevitable. With all that was deepest and most instinctive in him her nature chimed; the surfaces, the prejudices, the principles of his life she contradicted and confused. She talked to him a great deal, in answer to his questions, about her past life,

94

and what she told him was often disconcerting. The protective
tenderness he had felt for her from the first was troubled by his
realisation of the books she had placidly read — under Tante's
guidance — the people whose queer relationships she placidly
took for granted as in no need of condonation. When he inti-
mated to her that he disapproved of such contacts and customs,
she looked at him, puzzled, and then said, with an air of kindly
maturity at once touching and vexatious: "But that is the
morality of the Philistines."

It was, of course, and Gregory considered it the very best of
moralities; but remembering her mother he could not emphasize
to her how decisively he held by it.

It was in no vulgar or vicious world that her life, as the child
of the unconventional sculptor, as the *protégée* of the great
pianist, had been passed. But it was a world without religion,
without institutions, without order. Gregory, though his was not
the religious temperament, had his reasoned beliefs in the spiritual realities expressed in institutions and he had his inherited
instincts of reverence for the rituals that embodied the spiritual
life of his race. He was impatient with dissent and with facile
scepticisms. He did not expect a woman to have reasoned beliefs, nor did he ask a credulous, uncritical orthodoxy; but he
did want the Christian colouring of mind, the Christian outlook;
he did want his wife to be a woman who would teach her children
to say their prayers at her knees. It was with something like
dismay that he gathered from Karen that her conception of life
was as untouched by any consciousness of creed as that of a noble
young pagan. He was angry at himself for feeling it and when
he found himself applying his rules and measures to her; for
what had it been from the first but her spiritual strength and
loveliness that had drawn him to her? Yet he longed to make
her accept the implications of the formulated faiths that she
lived by. "Oh, no, you 're not," he said to her when, turning
unperturbed eyes upon him, she assured him: "Oh yes, I am
quite, quite a pagan." "I don't think you know what you mean
when you say you 're a pagan," Gregory continued.

"But, yes," she returned. "I have no creed. I was brought

up to think of beauty as the only religion. That is my guardian's religion. It is the religion, she says, of all free souls. And my father thought so, too." It was again the assurance of a wisdom, not her own, yet possessed by her, a wisdom that she did not dream of anybody challenging. Was it not Tante's?

"Well," he remarked, "beauty is a large term. Perhaps 'it includes more than you think."

Karen looked at him with approbation. "That is what Tante says; that it includes everything." And she went on, pleased to reveal to him still more of Tante's treasure, since he had proved himself thus understanding; "Tante, you know, belongs to the Catholic Church; it is the only church of beauty, she says. But she is not *pratiquante;* not *croyante* in any sense. 'Art is her refuge."

"I see," said Gregory. "And what is your refuge?"

Karen, at this, kept silence for a moment, and then said: "It is not that; not art. I do not feel, perhaps, that I need refuges. 'And I am happier than my dear guardian. I believe in immortality; oh yes, indeed." She looked round gravely at him — they were sitting on the turf of a headland above the sea. "I believe, that is, in everything that is beautiful and loving going on for ever."

He felt abashed before her. The most dependent and childlike of creatures where her trust and love were engaged, she was, as well, the most serenely independent. Even Tante, he felt, could not touch her faiths.

"You must n't say that you are a pagan, you see," he said.

"But Plato believed in immortality," Karen returned, smiling. "And you will not tell me that Plato was *pratiquant* or *croyant.*"

He could not claim Plato as a member of the Church of England, though he felt quite ready to demonstrate, before a competent body of listeners, that, as a nineteenth century Englishman, Plato would have been. Karen was not likely to follow such an argument. She would smile at his seeming sophistries.

No; he must accept it, and as a very part of her lovableness, that she could not be made to fit into the plan of his life as he had imagined it. She would not carry on its traditions, for she

would not understand them. To win her would be, in a sense,
to relinquish something of that orderly progression as a professional and social creature that he had mapped out for himself,
though he knew himself to be, through his experience of her,
already a creature more human, a creature enriched. Karen, if
she came to love him, would be, through love, infinitely malleable,
but in the many adjustments that would lie before them it would
be his part to foresee complications and to do the adjusting.
Change in her would be a gradual growth, and never towards
mere conformity.

He felt it to be the first step towards adjustments when he
motored Karen and Mrs. Talcott to Guillian House to lunch with
his friends the Lavingtons. The occasion must mark for him
the subtle altering of an old tie. Karen and the Lavingtons
could never be to each other what he and the Lavingtons had
been. It was part of her breadth that congeniality could never
for her be based on the half automatic affinities of caste and
occupation; and it was part of her narrowness, or, rather, of
her inexperience, that she could see people only as individuals
and would not recognize the real charm of the Lavingtons, which
consisted in their being, like their house and park, part of the
landscape and of an established order of things. Yet, once he
had her there, he watched the metamorphosis that her presence
worked in his old associations with pleasure rather than pain.
It pleased him, intimately, that the Lavingtons should see in
him a lover as yet uncertain of his chances. It pleased him
that they should not find in Karen the type that they must
have expected the future Mrs. Jardine to be, the type of Constance Armytage and the type of Evelyn Lavington, Colonel and
Mrs. Lavington's unmarried daughter, who, but for Karen, might
well have become Mrs. Jardine one day. He observed, with
a lover's fond pride, that Karen, in her shrunken white serge
and white straw hat, Karen, with her pleasant imperturbability,
her mingled simplicity and sophistication, did, most decisively,
make the Lavingtons seem flavourless. Among them, while Mrs.
Lavington walked her round the garden and Evelyn elicited with
kindly concern that she played neither golf, hockey nor tennis,

7

and had never ridden to hounds, her demeanour was that of a little rustic princess benignly doing her social duty. The only reason why she did not appear like this to the Lavingtons was that, immutably unimaginative as they were, they knew that she was n't a princess, was, indeed, only the odd appendage of an odd celebrity with whom their friend had chosen, oddly, to fall in love. They were n't perplexed, because, since he had fallen in love with her, she was placed. But they, in the complete contrast they offered, had little recognition of individual values and judged a dish by the platter it was served on. A princess was a princess, and an appendage an appendage, and a future Mrs. Jardine a very recognizable person; just as, had a subtle *charlotte russe* been brought up to lunch in company with the stewed rhubarb they would have eaten it without comment and hardly been aware that it was n't an everyday milk-pudding.

"Did you and Mrs. Lavington and Evelyn and Mrs. Haverfield find much to talk of after lunch?" Gregory asked, as he motored Mrs. Talcott and Karen back to Les Solitudes.

"Yes; we talked of a good many things," said Karen. "But I know about so few of their things and they about so few of mine. Miss Lavington was very much surprised to think that I had never been to a fox-hunt; and I," Karen smiled, "was very much surprised to think that they had never heard Tante play."

"They hardly ever get up to town, you see," said Gregory. "But surely they knew about her?"

"Not much," said Karen. "Mrs. Lavington asked me about her — for something pleasant to say — and they were such strange questions; as though one should be asked whether Mr. Arthur Balfour were a Russian nihilist or Metchnikoff an Italian poet." Karen spoke quite without grievance or irony.

"And after your Sargent," said Gregory, "you must have been pained by that portrait of Mrs. Haverfield in the drawing-room."

"Mrs. Lavington pointed it out to me specially," said Karen, laughing, "and told me that it had been in the Academy. What a sad thing; with all those eyelashes! And yet opposite to it hung the beautiful Gainsborough of a great-grandmother. Mrs. Lavington saw no difference, I think."

"They have n't been trained to see differences," said Gregory, and he summed up the Lavingtons in the aphorism to himself as well as to Karen; "only to accept samenesses." He hoped indeed, by sacrificing the æsthetic quality of the Lavingtons, to win some approbation of their virtues; but Karen, though not inclined to proffer unasked criticism, found, evidently, no occasion for commendation. Later on, when they were back at Les Solitudes and walking in the garden, she returned to the subject of his friends and said: "I was a little disturbed about Mrs. Talcott; did you notice? no one talked to her at all, hardly. It was as if they thought her my *dame de compagnie*. She is n't my *dame de compagnie;* and if she were, I think that she should have been talked to."

Gregory had observed this fact and had hoped that it might have escaped Karen's notice. To the Lavingtons Mrs. Talcott's platter had been unrecognizable and they had tended to let its contents alone.

"It 's as I said, you know," he put forward a mitigation; " they 've not been trained to see differences; she is very different, is n't she? "

"Well, but so am I," said Karen, "and they talked to me. I don't mean to complain of your friends; that would be very rude when they were so nice and kind; and, besides, are your friends. But people's thoughtlessness displeases me, not that I am not often very thoughtless myself."

Gregory was anxious to exonerate himself. "I hope she did n't feel left out;" he said. "I did notice that she was n't talking. I found her in the garden, alone — she seemed to be enjoying that, too — and she and I went about for quite a long time together."

"I know you did," said Karen. "You are not thoughtless. As for her, one never knows what she feels. I don't think that she does feel things of that sort at all; she has been used to it all her life, one may say; but there 's very little she does n't notice and understand. She understands — oh, perfectly well — that she is a queer old piece of furniture standing in the background, and one has to remember not to treat her like a piece of furniture. It's a part of grace and tact, is n't it, not to take such obvious things for granted. You did n't take them for granted with her, or with me," said Karen, smiling her recognition at him. "For, of course, to most people I am furniture, too; and if Tante is about, there is, of course, nothing to blame in that; everybody becomes furniture when Tante is there."

"Oh no; I can't agree to that," said Gregory. "Not everybody."

"You know what I mean," Karen rejoined. "If you will not agree to it for me, it is because from the first you felt me to be your friend; that is different." They were walking in the flagged garden where the blue campanulas were now safely established in their places and the low afternoon sun slanted in among the trees. Karen still wore her hat and motoring veil and the smoky grey substance flowed softly back about her shoulders. Her face seemed to emerge from a cloud. It had always to Gregory's eyes the air of steadfast advance; the way in which her hair swept back and up from her brows gave it a wind-blown, lifted look. He glanced at her now from time to time, while, in a meditative and communicative mood, she continued to share her reflections with him. Gregory was very happy.

"Even Tante does n't always remember enough about Mrs. Talcott," she went on. "That is of course because Mrs. Talcott is so much a part of her life that she sometimes hardly sees her. She *is*, for her, the dear old restful chair that she sinks back into and forgets about. Besides, some people have a right not to see things. One does n't ask from giants the same sort of perception that one does from pygmies."

This was indeed hard on the Lavingtons; but Gregory was not thinking of the Lavingtons, who could take care of themselves. He was wondering, as he more and more wondered, about Madame von Marwitz, and what she saw and what she permitted herself not to see.

"You are n't invisible to her sometimes?" he inquired.

Her innocence before his ironies made him ashamed always of having spoken them. "It is just that that makes me feel sometimes so badly about Mrs. Talcott," she answered now; "just because she is, in a sense, sometimes invisible, and I'm not. Mrs. Talcott, of course, counts for a great deal more in the way of comfort and confidence than I do; I don't believe that Tante really is as intimate with anybody in the world as with Mrs. Talcott; but she does n't count as much as I do, I am nearly sure, in the way of tenderness. I really think that in the way of tenderness I am nearer than anybody."

They left the flagged garden now, and came down to a lower terrace. Here the sun shone fully; they walked to and fro in the radiance. "Of course," Karen continued to define and confide, "as far as interest goes any one of her real friends counts for more than I do, and you must n't think that I mean to say that I believe myself the most loved; not at all. But I am the tender, home thing in her life; the thing to pet and care for and find waiting. It is that that is so beautiful for me and so tragic for her."

"Why tragic?"

"Oh, but you do not feel it? A woman like that, such a heart, and such a spirit — and no one nearer than I am? That she should have no husband and no child? I am a makeshift for all that she has lost, or never had."

"And Mrs. Talcott?" said Gregory after a moment. "Is it Mrs. Talcott's tragedy to have missed even a makeshift?"

Karen now turned her eyes on him, and her face, as she scrutinized him, showed a slight severity. "Hardly that. She has Tante."

"Has her as the chair has her, you mean?" He could n't for the life of him control the question. It seemed indeed due to their friendship that he should not conceal from her the fact that he found disproportionate elements in her devotion. Yet it was not the right way in which to be frank, and Karen showed him so in her reply. "I mean that Tante is everything to her and that, in the nature of things, she cannot be so much to Tante. You must n't take quite literally what I said of the chair, you know. It can hardly be a makeshift to have somebody like Tante to love and care for. I don't quite know what you mean by speaking like that," Karen said. Her gaze, in meeting his, had become almost stern. She seemed to scan him from a distance.

Gregory, though he felt a pang of disquietude, felt no disposition to retreat. He intended that she should be made to understand what he meant. "I think that what it comes to is that it is you I am thinking of, rather than of Mrs. Talcott," he said. "I don't know your guardian, and I do know you, and it is what she gets rather than what she gives that is most apparent to me."

"Gets? From me? What may that be?" Karen continued to return his gaze almost with haughtiness.

"The most precious thing I can imagine," said Gregory. "Your love. I hope that she is properly grateful for it."

She looked at him and the slow colour mounted to her cheeks; but it was as if in unconscious response to his feeling; it hardly, even yet, signified self-consciousness. She had stood still in asking her last question and she still did not move as she said: "I do not like to hear you speak so. It shows me that you understand nothing."

"Does it? I want to understand everything."

"You care for me," said Karen, standing still, her eyes on his, "and I care for you; but what I most wish in such a friend is that he should see and understand. May I tell you something? Will you wait while I tell you about my life?"

"Please tell me."

"I want you to see and understand Tante," said Karen. "And how much I love her; and why."

They walked on, from the terrace to the cliff-path. Karen stopped when they had gone a little way and leaned her elbows on the stone wall looking out at the sea. "She has been everything to me," she said. "Everything."

He was aware, as he leaned beside her in the mellow evening light, of a great uneasiness mingling with the beautiful gravity of the moment. She was near him as she had never yet been near. She had almost recognized his love. It was there between

them, and it was as if, not turning from it, she yet pointed to
something beyond and above it, something that it was his deep
instinct to evade and hers to show him. He must not take a
step towards her, she seemed to tell him, until he had proved to
her that he had seen what she did. And nothing she could say
would, he felt sure of it, alter his fundamental distrust of
Madame von Marwitz.

"I want to tell you about my life," said Karen, looking out at
the sea from between her hands. "You have heard my story,
of course; people are always told it; but you have never heard it
from my side. You have heard no doubt about my father and
mother, and how she left the man she did not love for him. My
mother died when I was quite little; so, though I remember her
well she does not come into the part of my story that I want to
tell you. But I was thirteen years old when my father died, and
that begins the part that leads to Tante. It was in Rome, in
winter when he died; and I was alone with him; and there was
no money, and I had more to bear than a child's mind and heart
should have. He died. And then there were dreadful days.
Cold, coarse people came and took me and put me in a convent in
Paris. That convent was like hell to me. I was so miserable.
And I had never known restraint or unkindness, and the French
girls, so sly and so small in their thoughts, were hateful to me.
And I did not like the nuns. I was punished and punished —
rightly no doubt. I was fierce and sullen, I remember, and would
not obey. Then I heard, by chance, from a girl whose family
had been to her concert in Paris, that Madame Okraska was with
her husband at Fontainebleau. Of her I knew nothing but the
lovely face in the shop-windows. But her husband's name
brought back distant days to me. He had known my father;
I remembered him — the fair, large, kindly smiling, very sad
man — in my father's studio among the clay and marble. He
bought once a little head my father had done of me when I was a
child. So I ran away from the convent — oh, it was very bad;
I knocked down a nun and escaped the portress, and hid for a
long time in the streets. And I made my way through Paris
and walked for a day and night to Fontainebleau; and there in

the forest, in the evening, I was lost, and almost dead with
hunger and fatigue.   And as I stood by the road I saw the carriage approaching from very far away and saw sitting in it, as
it came nearer, the beautiful woman.   Shall I ever forget it?
The dark forest and the evening sky above and her face looking
at me — looking, looking, full of pity and wonder.   She has told
me that I was the most unhappy thing that she had ever seen.
My father's friend was with her; but though I saw him and
knew that I was safe, I had eyes only for her.   Her face was like
heaven opening.   When the carriage stopped and she leaned to
me, I sprang to her and she put her arms around me.   They
have been round me ever since," said Karen, joining her fingers
over her eyes and leaning her forehead upon them so that her
face was hidden; and for a moment she did not speak.   " Ever
since," she went on presently, " she has been joy and splendour
and beauty.   What she has given me is nothing.   It is what she
is herself that lifts the lives of other people.   Those who do
not know her seem to me to have lives so sad and colourless compared to mine.   You cannot imagine it, anyone so great, yet at
the same time so little and so sweet.   She is merry like no one
else, and witty, and full of cajoleries, like a child.   One cannot
be dull with her, not for one moment.   And there is through it
all her genius, the great flood of wonderful music; can you think
what it is like to live with that?   And under-lying everything
is the great irremediable sorrow.   I was with her when it came;
the terrible thing.   I did not live with them while he was alive,
you know, my Onkel Ernst; he was so good and kind — always
the kindest of friends to me; but he loved her too deeply to be
able to share their life, and how well one understands that in
her husband.   He had me put at a school in Dresden.   I did
not like that much, either.   But, even if I were lonely, I knew
that my wonderful friends — my Tante and my Onkel — were
there, like the sun behind the grey day, and I tried to study and
be dutiful to please them.   And in my holidays I was always
with them, twice it was, at their beautiful estate in Germany.
And it was there that the horror came that wrecked her life;
her husband's death, his death that cannot be explained or under-

stood. He drowned himself. We never say it, but we know it.
That is the fear, the mystery. All his joy with her, his love
and happiness — to leave them; — it was madness; he had always been a sad man; one saw that in his face; the doctors said
it was madness. He disappeared without a word one day. For
three weeks — nothing. Tante was like a creature crying out
on the rack. And it was I who found him by the lake-edge one
morning. She was walking in the park, I knew; she used to
walk and walk fast, fast, quite silent; and with horrible fear I
thought: If I can keep her from seeing. I turned — and she
was beside me. I could not save her. Ah — poor woman! "
Karen closed her hands over her face.

They stood for a long time in silence, Gregory leaning beside
her and looking down at the sea. His thought was not with the
stricken figure she put before him; it dwelt on the girl facing
horror, on the child bearing more than a child should bear. Yet
he was glad to feel, as a background to his thoughts, that
Madame von Marwitz was indeed very pitiful.

"You understand," said Karen, straightening herself at last
and laying her hands on the wall. "You see how it is."

"Yes," said Gregory.

"It is kind of you, and beautiful, to feel me, as your friend,
a person of value," said Karen. "But it does not please me to
have the great fact of my life belittled."

"I have n't meant to do that, really. I see why it means so
much to you. But I see you before I see the facts of your life;
they interest me because of you," said Gregory. "You come
first to me. It 's that I want you to understand."

Karen had at last turned her eyes upon his and they met them
in a long encounter that recalled to Gregory their first. It was
not the moment for explicit recognitions or avowals; the shadow
of the past lay too darkly upon her. But that their relation had
changed her deepened gaze accepted. She took his hand, she
had a fashion almost boyish of taking his rather than giving her
hand, and said: "We shall both understand more and more;
that is so, is it not? And some day you will know her. Until
you know her you cannot really understand."

CHAPTER XI

KAREN and he had walked back to the house in silence, and at the door, where she stood to see him off, it had been arranged that he was to lunch at Les Solitudes next day and that she was to show him a favourite headland, one not far away, but that he had never yet been shown. From the sweetness, yet gravity, of her look and voice he could infer nothing but that she recognized change and a new significance. Her manner had neither the confusion nor the pretended unconsciousness of ordinary girlhood. She was calm, but with a new thoughtfulness. He arrived a little early next day and found Mrs. Talcott alone in the morning-room writing letters. He noticed, as she rose from the bureau, her large, immature, considered writing. "Karen 'll be down in a minute or two, I guess," she said. "Take a chair."

"Don't let me interrupt you," said Gregory, as Mrs. Talcott seated herself before him, her hands folded at her waist. But Mrs. Talcott, remarking briefly, "Don't mention it," did not move back to her former place. She examined him and he examined her and he felt that she probed through his composure to his unrest. "I wanted a little talk," she observed presently. "You 've gotten pretty fond of Karen, have n't you, Mr. Jardine?"

This was to come at once to the point. "Very fond," said Gregory, wondering if she had been diagnosing his fondness in a letter to Madame von Marwitz.

"She has n't got many friends," Mrs. Talcott, after another moment of contemplation, went on. "She 's always been a lonesome sort of child."

"That 's what has struck me, too," said Gregory.

"Sometimes Mercedes takes her along; but sometimes she

106

don't," Mrs. Talcott pursued. "It ain't a particularly lively sort
of life for a young girl, going on in an out-of-the-way place like
this with an old woman like me. She's spent most of her time
with me, when you come to reckon it up." There was no air of
criticism or confidence in Mrs. Talcott. She put forward these
remarks with unbiassed placidity.

"I suppose Madame von Marwitz could n't arrange always to
take her?" Gregory asked after a pause.

"It ain't always convenient toting a young girl round with
you," said Mrs. Talcott. "Sometimes Mercedes feels like it and
sometimes she don't. Karen and I stay at home, now that I 'm
too old to go about with her, and we see her when she's home.
That's the idea. But she ain't much at home. She's mostly
travelling and staying around with folks."

"It is n't a particularly lively time, it seems to me, for either
of you," said Gregory. It was his instinct to blame Madame von
Marwitz for the featureless lives led by her dependents, though
he could but own that it might, perhaps, be difficult to fit them
into the vagabondage of a great pianist's existence.

"Well, it's good enough for me," said Mrs. Talcott. "I 'm
very contented if it comes to that; and so is Karen. She's
known so much that's worse, the same as I have. But she's
known what's better, too; she was a pretty big girl when her
Poppa died and she was a companion to him and I reckon that
without figuring it up much to herself she's lonesome a good
deal."

Gregory for a moment was silent. Then he found it quite
natural to say to Mrs. Talcott: "What I hope is that she will
marry me."

"I hope so, too," said Mrs. Talcott with no alteration of tone.
"I hoped so the moment I set eyes on you. I saw that you were
a good young man and that you 'd make her a good kind
husband."

"Thanks, very much," said Gregory, smiling yet deeply
touched. "I hope I may be. I intend to be if she will have
me."

"The child is mighty fond of you," said Mrs. Talcott. "And

it's not as if she took easy to people. She don't. She's never
seemed to need folks. But I can see that she's mighty fond of
you, and what I want to say is, even if it don't seem to work out
like you want it to right away, you hang on, Mr. Jardine; that's
my advice; an old woman like me understands young girls better
than they understand themselves. Karen is so wrapped up in
Mercedes and thinks such a sight of her that perhaps she'll feel
she don't want to leave her and that sort of thing; but just you
hang on."

"I intend to," said Gregory. "I can't say how much I thank
you for being on my side."

"Yes; I'm on your side, and I'm on Karen's side; and I want
to see this thing put through," said Mrs. Talcott.

Something seemed to hover between them now, a fourth figure
that must be added to the trio they made. He wondered, if he
did hang on successfully and if it did work out as he intended
that it should, how that fourth figure would work in. He
couldn't see a shared life with Karen from which it could be
eliminated, nor did he, of course, wish to see it eliminated; but
he did not see himself, either, as forming one of a band of
satellites, and the main fact about the fourth figure seemed to
be that any relation to it involved one, apparently, in disciple-
ship. There seemed even some disloyalty to Mrs. Talcott in
accepting her sympathy while anxieties and repudiations such as
these were passing through his mind; for she, no doubt, saw in
Karen's relation to Madame von Marwitz the chief asset with
which she could present a husband; and he expected Mrs.
Talcott, now, to make some reference to this asset; but none
came; and if she expected from him some recognition of it, no
expectancy was visible in the old blue eyes fixed on his face.
A silence fell between them, and as it grew longer it grew
the more consoling. Into their compact of understanding she
let him see, he could almost fancy, that the question of Madame
von Marwitz was not to enter.

Karen, when she appeared, was looking preoccupied, and after
shaking his hand and giving him, for a moment, the sweet,
grave smile with which they had parted, she glanced at the

writing-table. "You are writing to Tante, Mrs. Talcott?" she said. "You heard from her this morning?"

"Yes; I heard from her," said Mrs. Talcott. Gregory at once inferred that Madame von Marwitz had been writing for information concerning himself.

She must by now have become aware of his correspondence with Karen and its significant continuity.

"Are there any messages? — any news?" asked Karen, and she could not keep dejection from her voice. She had had no letter.

"It 's only a business note," said Mrs. Talcott. "Has n't Miss Scrotton written?"

"Does my cousin keep you posted as a rule?" Gregory asked, as Karen shook her head.

"No; but Tante asks her to write sometimes, when she is too tired or rushed; and I had a letter from her, giving me their plans, only a few days ago; so that I know that all is well. It is only that I am always greedy for Tante's letters, and this is the day on which they often come."

They went in to lunch. Karen spoke little during the meal. Gregory and Mrs. Talcott carried on a desultory conversation about hotels and the different merits of different countries in this respect. Mrs. Talcott had a vast experience of hotels. From Germany to Australia, from New York to St. Petersburg, they were known to her.

After lunch he and Karen started on their walk. It had been a morning of white fog and the mist still lay thickly over the sea, so that from the high cliff-path, a clear, pale sky above them, they looked down into milky gulfs of space. Then, as the sun shone softly and a gentle breeze arose, a rift of dark, still blue appeared below, as the sky appears behind dissolving clouds, and fold upon fold, slumbrously, the mist rolled back upon itself. The sea lay like a floor of polished sapphire beneath the thick, soft webs. Far below, in a cavern, the sound of lapping water clucked, and a sea-gull, indolently intent, drifted by slowly on dazzling wings.

Karen and Gregory reached their headland and, seating themselves on the short, warm turf, looked out over the sea. During the walk they had hardly spoken, and he had wondered whether her thoughts were with him and with their last words yesterday, or dwelling still on her disappointment. But presently, as if her preoccupation had drifted from her as the fog had drifted from the sea, Karen turned tranquil eyes upon him and said: "I suddenly thought, and the stillness made me think it, and Mrs. Talcott's hotels, too, perhaps, of all that is going on in the world while we sit here so lonely and so peaceful. Frenchmen with fat cheeks and flat-brimmed silk hats sitting at little tin tables in boulevards; is n't it difficult to realize that they exist? and Arabs on camels crossing deserts; they are quite imaginable; and nuns praying in convent cells; and stokers, all stripped and sweating, under the engines of great steamers; and a little Japanese artist carving so carefully the soles of the feet of some tiny image; there they are, all going on; as real to themselves as we are, at the very moment that we sit here and feel that only we, in all the world, are real." She might almost have been confiding her fancies to a husband whose sympathy had been tested by years of fond companionship.

Gregory, wondering at her, loving her, pulled at the short turf as he lay, propped on an elbow, beside her, and said: "What nice thoughts you have."

"You have them, too, I think," said Karen, smiling down at him. "And nicer ones. Mine are usually only amusing, like those; but yours are often beautiful. I see that in your face, you know. It is a face that makes me think always of a cold, clear, steely pool;—that is what it looks like if one does not look down into it but only across it, as it were; but if one bends over and looks down, deep down, one sees the sky and passing white clouds and boughs of trees. I saw deep down at once. That is why," her eyes rested upon him, "we were friends from the first."

"It 's what you bring that you see," said Gregory; "you make me think of all those things."

"Ah, but you think them for yourself, too; when you are alone you think them."

"But when I am alone and think them, without you in the thought of them, it's always with sadness, for something I've lost. You bring them back, with happiness. The thought of you is always happy. I have never known anyone who seemed to me so peacefully happy as you do. You are very happy, are n't you?" Gregory looked down at his little tufts of turf as he asked this question.

"I am glad I seem to you like that," said Karen. "I think I am usually quiet and gay and full of confidence; I sometimes wonder at my confidence. But it is not always so. No, I am not always happy. Sometimes, when I think and remember, it is like feeling a great hole being dug in my heart — as if the iron went down and turned up dark forgotten things. I have that feeling sometimes; and then I wonder that I can ever be happy."

"What things, dear Karen?"

"You know, I think." Karen looked out at the sea. "Tante's face when I found her husband's body. And my father's face when he was dying; he did not know what was to become of me; he was quite weak, like a little child, and he cried on my breast. And my mother's face when she died. I have not told you anything of my mother."

"Will you? I want to hear everything about you; everything," said Gregory.

"This is her locket," Karen said, putting her hand over it. "Her face is in it; would you like to see it?"

He held out his hand, and slipping the ribbon over her head she pressed the little spring and laid the open locket in it.

He saw the tinted photograph of a young girl's head, a girl younger than Karen and with her fair hair and straight brows and square chin; but it was a gentler face and a clumsier, and strange with its alien nationality.

"I always feel as if she were my child and I her mother when I look at that," said Karen. "It was taken before I was born. She had a happy life, and yet my memory of her breaks my heart. She was so very young and it frightened her so much to die; she could not bear to leave us."

Gregory, holding the little locket, looked at it silently. Then he put it to his lips. "You care for me, don't you, Karen?" he said.

"You know, I think," said Karen, repeating her former words.

He laid the locket in her hand, and the moment had for him a sacramental holiness so that the locket was like a wedding-ring; holding it and her hand together he said, lifting his eyes to hers, "I love you. Do you love me?"

Her eyes had filled with tears when he had kissed her mother's face, and there was young awe in her gaze; but no shadow, no surprise.

"Yes," she said, unhesitatingly. "Yes, I love you, dear Gregory."

The simplicity, the inevitableness of his bliss overwhelmed him. He held her hand and looked down at it. All about them was the blue. All her past, its beauty, its dark, forgotten things, she had given to him. She was his for ever. "Oh, my darling Karen," he murmured.

She bent down to look at him now, smiling and unclosing her hand from his gently, so that she could look at her mother's face. "How glad she would be if she could know," she said. "Perhaps she does know. Do you not think so?"

"Dear — I don't know what I think about those hopes. I hope."

"Oh, it is more than hope, my belief that she is there; that she is not lost. Only one cannot tell how or when or where it all may be. For that, yes, it can be only hope. She, too, would love you, I am sure," Karen continued.

"Would she? I'm glad you think so, darling."

"We are so much alike, you see, that it is natural to feel sure that we should think alike. Do you not think that her face is much like mine? What happiness! I am glad it is not a day of rain for our happiness." And she then added, "I hope we may be married."

"Why, we are to be married, dear child," Gregory said,

smiling at her. "There is no 'may' about it, since you love me."

"Only one," said Karen, who still looked at her mother's face. "And perhaps it will be well not to speak much of our love till we can know. But I feel sure that she will say this happiness is for me."

"She?" Gregory repeated. For a moment he imagined that she meant some superstition connected with her mother.

Karen, slipping the ribbon over her head, had returned the locket to its place. "Yes; Tante," she said, still with the locket in her hand.

"Tante?" Gregory repeated.

At his tone, its change, she lifted startled eyes to his.

"What has she to do with it?" Gregory asked after a moment in which she continued to gaze at him.

"What has Tante to do with it?" said Karen in a wondering voice. "Do you think I could marry without Tante's consent?"

"But you love me?"

"I do not understand you. Was it wrong of me to have said so before I had her consent? Was that not right? Not fair to you?"

"Since you love me you ought to be willing to marry me whether you have your guardian's consent or not." His voice strove to control its bitterness; but the day had darkened; all his happiness was blurred. He felt as if a great injury had been done him.

Karen continued to gaze at him in astonishment. "Would you have expected me to marry you without my mother's consent? She is in my mother's place."

"If you loved me I should certainly expect you to say that you would marry me whether your mother consented or not. You are of age. There is nothing against me. Those aren't English ideas at all, Karen."

"But I am not English," said Karen, "my guardian is not English. They are our ideas."

8

"You mean, you seriously mean, that, loving me, you would give me up if she told you to?"

"Yes," said Karen, now with the heaviness of their recognized division. "She would not refuse her consent unless it were right that I should give you up."

For some moments after this Gregory, in silence, looked down at the grass between them, clasping his knees; for he now sat upright. Then, controlling his anger to argumentative rationality, he said, while again wrenching away at the strongly rooted tufts: "If she did refuse, what reason could she give for refusing? As I say, there's absolutely nothing against me."

Karen had kept her troubled eyes on his downcast face. "There might be things she did not like; things she would not believe for my happiness in married life," she replied.

"And you would take her word against mine?"

"You forget, I think," he had lifted his eyes to hers and she looked back at him, steadily, with no entreaty, but with all the perplexity of her deep pain. "She has known me for eleven years. I have only known you for three months."

He could not now control the bitterness or the dismay; for, coldly, cuttingly he knew it, it was quite possible that Madame von Marwitz would not "like things" in him. Their one encounter had not been of a nature to endear him to her. "It simply means," he said, looking into her eyes, "that you haven't any conception of what love is. It means that you don't love me."

They looked at each other for a moment and then Karen said, "That is hard." And after another moment she rose to her feet. Gregory got up and they went down the cliff-path towards Les Solitudes.

He had not spoken recklessly. His words expressed his sense of her remoteness. He could not imagine what sort of love it was that could so composedly be put aside. And making no feminine appeal or protest, she walked steadily, in silence, before him. Only at a turning of the way did he see that her lips were compressed and tears upon her cheeks.

"Karen," he said, looking into her face as he now walked beside her; "won't you talk it over? You astonish me so unspeakably. Can she destroy our friendship, too? Would you give me up as a friend if she did n't like things in me?"

The tears expressed no yielding, for she answered "Yes."

"And how far do you push submission? If she told you to marry someone she chose for you, would you consent, whether you loved him or not?"

"It is not submission," said Karen. "It is our love, hers and mine. She would not wish me to marry a man I did not love. The contrary is true. My guardian before she went away spoke to me of a young man she had chosen for me, someone for whom she had the highest regard and affection; and I, too, am very fond of him. She felt that it would be for my happiness to marry him, and she hoped that I would consent. But I did not love him. I told her that I could never love him; and so it ended immediately. You do her injustice in your thoughts of her; and you do me injustice, too, if you think of me as a person who would marry where I did not love."

He walked beside her, bitterly revolving the sorry comfort of this last speech. "Who was the young man?" he asked. Not that he really cared to know.

"His name is Herr Franz Lippheim," said Karen, gravely. "He is a young musician."

"Herr Franz Lippheim," Gregory repeated, with an irritation glad to wreak itself on this sudden object presented opportunely. "How could you have been imagined as marrying someone called Lippheim?"

"Why not, pray?"

"Is he a German Jew?" Gregory inquired after a moment.

"He is, indeed, of Joachim's nationality," Karen answered, in a voice from which the tears were gone.

They walked on, side by side, the estrangement cutting deep between their new-won nearness. Yet in the estrangement was an intimacy deeper than that of the merely blissful state. They seemed in the last miserable half hour to have advanced by years their knowledge of each other. Mrs. Talcott and tea were waiting for them in the morning-room. The old woman fixed her eyes upon each face in turn and then gave her attention to her tea-pot.

"I am sorry, Mrs. Talcott, that we are so late," Karen said. Her composure was kept only by an effort that gave to her tones a stately conventionality.

"Don't mention it," said Mrs. Talcott. "I'm only just in myself."

"Has it not been a beautiful afternoon?" Karen continued. "What have you been doing in the garden, Mrs. Talcott?"

"I sowed a big bed of mignonette down by the arbour, and Mitchell and I set out a good lot of plants."

Mrs. Talcott made her replies to the questions that Karen continued to ask, in an even voice in which Gregory, who kept his dismal eyes upon her, detected a melancholy patience. Mrs. Talcott must perceive his state to be already one of "hanging on." Of her sympathy he was, at all events, assured. She showed it by rising as soon as he and Karen had drunk their tea. "I've got some more things to do," she said. "Good-bye, Mr. Jardine. Are you coming over to-morrow?"

"No," said Gregory taking Mrs. Talcott's hand. "My holiday is over. I shall be going back to town to-morrow."

Mrs. Talcott looked into his eyes. "Well, that's too bad," she observed.

"Isn't it? I'd far rather stay here, I can assure you," said Gregory.

"We'll miss you, I guess," said Mrs. Talcott. "I'm very glad to have had the pleasure of making your acquaintance."

"And I of making yours."

Mrs. Talcott departed and Gregory turned to Karen. She was standing near the window, looking at him.

"We must say good-bye, too, I suppose," said Gregory, mastering his grief. "You will give me your guardian's address so that I can write to her at once?"

Her face had worn the aspect of a grey, passive sheet of water; a radiant pallor now seemed struck from its dulled surface.

"You are going to write to Tante?" she said.

"Isn't that the next step?" Gregory asked. "You will write, too, won't you? Or is it part of my ordeal that I'm to plead my cause alone?"

Karen had clasped her hands together on her breast and, in the eyes fixed on his, tears gathered. "Do not speak harshly," she said. "I am so sorry there must be the ordeal. But so happy, too — so suddenly. Because I believed that you were going to leave me since you thought me so wrong and so unloving."

"Going to leave you, Karen?" Gregory repeated in amazement. Desperate amusement struggled in his face with self-reproach. "My darling child, what must you think of me? And, actually, you'd have let me go?" He had come to her and taken her hands in his.

"What else could I do?"

"Such an idiot would have deserved it? Could you believe me such an idiot? Darling, you so astonish me. What a strange, indomitable creature you are."

"What else could I do, Gregory?" she repeated, looking into his face and not smiling in answer to his smiling, frowning gaze.

"Love me more; that's what you could have done — a great deal more," said Gregory. "That's what you must do, Karen. I can't bear to think that you wouldn't marry me without her consent. I can't bear to think that you don't love me enough. But leave you because you don't love me as much as I want you to love me! My darling, how little you understand."

"You seemed very angry," said Karen. "I was so unhappy. I don't know how I should have borne it if you had gone away and left me like this. But love should not make one weak, Gregory. There you are wrong, to think it is because I do not love you."

"Ah, you'll find out if I'm wrong!" Gregory exclaimed with tender conviction. "You'll find out how much more you are to love me. Oh, yes, I will kiss you good-bye, Karen. I don't care if all the Tantes in the world forbid it!"

In thinking afterwards of these last moments that they had had together, the discomfitures and dismays of the afternoon tended to resolve themselves for Gregory into the memory of the final yielding. She had let him take her into his arms, and with the joy was the added sweetness of knowing that in permitting and reciprocating his unauthorized kiss she sacrificed some principles, at all events, for his sake.

CHAPTER XII

MADAME VON MARWITZ was sitting on the great terrace of a country-house in Massachusetts, opening and reading her post, as we have already seen her do. Impatient and weary as the occupation often made her, she yet depended upon the morning waves of adulation that lapped in upon her from every quarter of the earth. To miss the fullness of the tide gave her, when by chance there was deficiency, the feeling that badly made *café au lait* gave her at the beginning of the day; something was wrong; the expected stimulant lacked in force or in flavour, and coffee that was not strong and sweet and aromatic was a mishap so unusual that, when it occurred, it became an offence almost gross and unnatural, as did a post that brought few letters of homage and appreciation. To-day the mental coffee was as strong and as perfumed as that of which she had shortly before partaken in her lovely little *Louis Quinze* boudoir, after she had come in from her bath. The bath-room was like that of a Roman Empress, all white marble, with a square of emerald water into which one descended down shallow marble steps. Madame von Marwitz was amused by the complexities of luxury among which she found herself, some of which, even to her, were novel. *"Eh, eh, ma chère,"* she had said to Miss Scrotton, " beautiful if you will, and very beautiful; but its nails are too much polished, its hair too much *ondulé*. I prefer a porcelain to a marble bath-tub." But the ingenuities of hospitality which the Aspreys — earnest and accomplished millionaires — lavished upon their guests made one, she owned, balmily comfortable. And as she sat now in her soft white draperies under a great silken sunshade, raised on a stand above her and looking in the sunlight like a silver bell, the beauty of her surroundings — the splendid Italian gardens, a miracle of achievement even if lacking, as the miraculous may,

an obvious relation with its surroundings; the landscape with
its inlaid lake and wood and hill and great arch of bluest sky;
the tall, transparent, Turneresque trees in the middle distance;
— all this stately serenity seemed to have wrought in her an
answering suavity and gladness. There was almost a latent
gaiety in her glance, as, with her large, white, securely moving
hands, which seemed to express their potential genius in every
deft and delicate gesture, she took up and cut open and unfolded her letters, pausing between them now and then to
tweak off and eat a grape as large as a plum from the bunch
lying on its leaves in a Veronese-like silver platter beside her.

This suavity, this gladness and even gaiety of demeanour
were apparent to Miss Eleanor Scrotton when she presently
emerged from the house and advanced slowly along the terrace,
pausing at intervals beside its balustrade to gaze with a somewhat melancholy eye over the prospect.

Miss Scrotton was struggling with a half formulated sense of
grievance. It was she who had brought Madame von Marwitz
and the Aspreys together. Madame von Marwitz already knew,
of course, most of the people in America who were worth
knowing; if she had n't met them there she had met them in
Europe; but the Aspreys she had, till then, never met, and
they had been, indisputably, Miss Scrotton's possession. Miss
Scrotton had known them slightly for several years; her father
and Mr. Asprey had corresponded on some sociological theme
and the Aspreys had called on him in London in a mood of
proper deference and awe. She had written to the Aspreys before sailing with Mercedes, had found that they were winter-
ing in Egypt, but would be back in Amercia in Spring, ready
to receive Madame von Marwitz and herself with open arms;
and within those arms she had, a week ago, placed her treasure.
No doubt someone else would have done it if she had n't; and
perhaps she had been too eager in her determination that no
one else should do it. Perhaps she was altogether a little too
eager. Madame von Marwitz liked people to care for her and
showed a pretty gratitude for pains endured on her behalf; at
least she usually did so; but it may well have been that the

great woman, at once vaguely aloof and ironically observant,
had become a little irked, or bored, or merely amused at hearing
so continually, as it were, her good Scrotton panting beside her, tense, determined and watchful of opportunity. However that may have been, Miss Scrotton, as Madame von Marwitz's glance now lifted and rested upon herself, detected the
sharper gaiety defined by the French as "*malice,*" lighting,
though ever so mildly, her friend's eyes and lips. Like most
devotees Miss Scrotton had something of the valet in her com-
position, and with the valet's capacity for obsequiousness went
a valet-like shrewdness of perception. She had n't spent four
months travelling about America with Madame von Marwitz
without seeing her in undress. She had long since become uncomfortably aware that when Madame von Marwitz found one
a little ridiculous she could be unkind, and that when one
added plaintiveness to folly she often amused herself by giving
one, to speak metaphorically, soft yet sharp little pinches that
left one nervously uncertain of whether a caress or an aggres-
sion had been intended.

Miss Scrotton was plaintive, and she could not conceal it.
Glory as she might in the *rôle* of second fiddle, she was very
tenaciously aware of what was due to that subservient but by
no means insignificant performer; and the Aspreys had not
shown themselves enough aware, Mercedes had not shown herself aware at all, of what they all owed to her sustaining, discreet and harmonious accompaniment. In the carefully selected
party assembled at Belle Vue for Madame von Marwitz's de-
lectation, she had been made a little to feel that she was but
one of the indistinguishable orchestra that plucked out from
accommodating strings a mellow bass to the one thrilling solo.
Not for one moment did she grudge any of the recognitions
that were her great friend's due; but she did expect to bask
beside her; she did expect to find transmitted to her an important satellite's share of beams; and, it was n't to be denied,
Mercedes had been too much occupied with other people —
and with one other in particular — to shine upon her in any
distinguishing degree. Mercedes had the faculty, chafe against

it as one might — and her very fondness, her very familiarity were a part of the effect — of making one show as an unimportant satellite, as something that would revolve when wanted and be contentedly invisible when that was fitting. "I might almost as well be a paid *dame de compagnie*," Miss Scrotton had more than once murmured to herself with a lip that trembled; and, obscurely, she realised that close association with the great might reveal one as insignificant rather than as glorified. It was therefore with her air of melancholy that she paused in her advance along the terrace to gaze out at the prospect, and with an air of emphasized calm and dignity that she finally came towards her friend; and, as she came, thus armed, the blitheness deepened in the great woman's eyes.

"Well, *ma chèrie*," she remarked, "How goes it?" She spoke in French.

"Very well, *ma bien aimée*," Miss Scrotton replied in the same language. Her French was correct, but Mercedes often made playful sallies at the expense of her accent. She preferred not to talk in French. And when Madame von Marwitz went on to ask her where her fellow *convives* were, it was in English that she answered, "I don't know where they all are — I have been busy writing letters; Mrs. Asprey and Lady Rose are driving, I know, and Mr. Asprey and Mr. Drew I saw in the smoking-room as I passed. The Marquis I don't think is down yet, nor Mrs. Furnivall; the young people are playing tennis, I suppose."

Miss Scrotton looked about the terrace with its rhythmic tubs of flowering trees, its groups of chairs, its white silk parasols, and then wandered to the parapet to turn and glance up at the splendid copy of an Italian villa that rose above it. "It is really very beautiful, Mercedes," she observed. "It becomes the more significant from being so isolated, so divorced from what we are accustomed to find in Europe as a setting for such a place, does n't it? Just as, I always think, the people of the Asprey type, the best this country has to offer, are more significant, too, for being picked out from so much that is indistinguishable. I do flatter myself, darling, that

in this visit, at least, I've been able to offer you something
really worth your while, something that adds to your experience of people and places. You *are* enjoying yourself,"
said Miss Scrotton with a manner of sad satisfaction.

"Yes; truly," Madame von Marwitz made genial reply.
"The more so for finding myself surrounded by so many old
acquaintances. It is a particular pleasure to see again Lady
Rose and the vivacious and intelligent Mrs. Furnivall; it was
in Venice that we last met; her Palazzo there you must one
day see. Monsieur de Hautefeuille and Mr. Drew I counted
already as friends in Europe."

"And Mrs. Asprey you will soon count as one, I hope. She
is really a somewhat remarkable woman. She comes, you
know, of one of their best and oldest families."

"Oh, for that, no; not remarkable. Good, if you will —
bon comme du pain; it strikes me much, that goodness, among
these American rich whom we are accustomed to hear so crudely
caricatured in Europe; — and it is quite a respectable little
aristocracy. They ally themselves, as we see here in our excellent host and hostess, with what there is of old blood in the
country and win tradition to guide their power. They are not
the flaunting, vulgar rich, of whom we hear so much from
those who do not know them, but the anxious, thoughtful, vir-
tuous rich, oppressed by their responsibilities and all studying
so hard, poor dears, at stiff, deep books, in order to fulfil them
worthily. They all go to *conférences,* these ladies, it seems,
and study sociology. They take life with a seriousness that I
have never seen equalled. Mrs. Asprey is like them all; good,
oh, but yes. And I am pleased to know her, too. Mrs. Furnivall had promised her long since, she tells me, that it should
be. She and Mrs. Furnivall are old school-mates."

Miss Scrotton, all her merit thus mildly withdrawn from her,
stood silent for some moments looking away at the lake and the
Turneresque trees.

"It was so very kind of you, Mercedes, to have had Mr. Drew
asked here," she observed at last, very casually. "It is a real
opportunity for a young bohemian of that type; you are a true

fairy-godmother to him; first Mrs. Forrester and now the Aspreys. Curious, was n't it, his appearing over here so suddenly?"

"Curious? It did not strike me so," said Madame von Marwitz, showing no consciousness of the thrust her friend had ventured to essay. "People come to America a great deal, do they not; and often suddenly. It is the country of suddenness. His books are much read here, it seems, and he had business with his publishers. He knew, too, that I was here; and that to him was also an attraction. Why curious, my Scrotton?"

Miss Scrotton disliked intensely being called "my Scrotton;" but she had never yet found the necessary courage to protest against the appellation. "Oh, only because I had had no hint of it until he appeared," she returned. "And I wondered if you had had. Yes; I suppose he would be a good deal read over here. It is a very derivative and artificial talent, don't you think, darling?"

"Rather derivative; rather artificial," Madame von Marwitz replied serenely.

"He does n't look well, does he?" Miss Scrotton pursued, after a little pause. "I don't like that puffiness about the eyelids and chin. It will be fatal for him to become fat."

"No," said Madame von Marwitz, as serenely as before, her eyes now on a letter that she held. "Ah, no; he could rise above fat, that young man. I can see him fat with impunity. Would it become, then, somewhat the Talleyrand type? How many distinguished men have been fat. Napoleon, Renan, Gibbon, Dr. Johnson —" she turned her sheet as she mildly brought out the desultory list. "And all seem to end in n, do they not? I am glad that I asked Mr. Drew. He flavours the dish like an aromatic herb; and what a success he has been; *hein?* But he is the type of personal success. He is independent, indifferent, individual."

"Ah, my dear, you are too generous to that young man," Miss Scrotton mused. "It's beautiful, it's wonderful to watch; but you are, indeed, too kind to him." She mused, she was

absent, yet she knew, and knew that Mercedes knew, that never
before in all their intercourse had she ventured on such a speech.
It implied watchfulness; it implied criticism; it implied, even,
anxiety; it implied all manner of things that it was not permitted for a satellite to say.

The Baroness's eyes were on her letter, and though she did
not raise them her dark brows lifted. "*Tiens,*" she continued,
"you find that I am too kind to him?"

Miss Scrotton, to keep up the appearance of ingenuousness,
was forced to further definition. "I don't think, darling, that in
your sympathy, your solicitude, where young talent is concerned,
you quite realize how much you give, how much you can be
made use of. The man admires you, of course, and has, of
course, talent of a sort. Yet, when I see you together, I
confess that I receive sometimes the impression of a scattering
of pearls."

Madame von Marwitz laid down her letter. "Ah! ah! — oh!
oh! — *ma bonne,*" she said. She laughed out. Her eyes were
lit with dancing sparks. "Do you know you speak as if you
were very, very jealous of this young man who is found so
charming?"

"Jealous, my dear Mercedes?" Miss Scrotton's emotion
showed itself in a dark flush.

"*Mais oui; mais oui;* you tell me that my friend is a swine.
Does that not mean that you, of late, have received too few
pearls?"

"My dear Mercedes! Who called him a swine?"

"One does n't speak of scattered pearls without rousing these
associations." Her tone was beaming.

Was it possible to swallow such an affront? Was it possible
not to? And she had brought it upon herself. There was
comfort and a certain restoration of dignity in this thought.
Miss Scrotton, struggling inwardly, feigned lightness. "So few
of us are worthy of your pearls, dear. Unworthiness does n't,
I hope, consign us to the porcine category. Perhaps it is that
being, like him, a little person, I 'm able to see Mr. Drew's merits
and demerits more impartially than you do. That is all. I

really ought to know a good deal about Mr. Drew," Miss Scrotton pursued, regaining more self-control, now that she had steered her way out of the dreadful shoals where her friend's words had threatened to sink her; "I've known him since the days when he was at Oxford and I used to stay there with my uncle the Dean. He was sitting, then, at the feet of Pater. It's a derivative, a *parvenu* talent, and, I do feel it, I confess I do, a derivative personality altogether, like that of so many of these clever young men nowadays. He is, you know, of anything but distinguished antecedents, and his reaction from his own *milieu* has been, perhaps, from the first, a little marked. Unfortunately his marriage is there to remind people of it, and I never see Mr. Drew *dans le monde* without, irrepressibly, thinking of the dismal little wife in Surbiton whom I once called upon, and his swarms — but swarms, my dear — of large-mouthed children."

Miss Scrotton wondered, as she proceeded, whether she had again too far abandoned discretion.

The Baroness examined her next letter for a moment before opening it and if she, too, had received her sting, she abandoned nothing.

She answered with complete, though perhaps ominous, mildness: "He is rather like Shelley, I always think, a sophisticated Shelley who had sat at the feet of Pater. Shelley, too, had swarms of children, and it is possible that they were large-mouthed. The plebeian origin that you tell me of rather attracts me. I care, especially, for the fine flame that mounts from darkness; and I, too, on one side, as you will remember, *ma bonne,* am *du peuple.*"

"My dear Mercedes! Your father was an artist, a man of genius; and if your parents had risen from the gutter, you, by your own genius, transcend the question of rank as completely as a Shakespeare."

The continued mildness was alarming Miss Scrotton; an eagerness to make amends was in her eye.

"Ah — but did he, poor man!" Madame von Marwitz mused, rather irrelevantly, her eyes on her letter. "One hears now, not. But thank you, my Scrotton, you mean to be consoling. I have, however, no dread of the gutter. *Tiens,*" she turned a page, " here is news indeed."

Miss Scrotton had now taken a chair beside her and her fingers tapped a little impatiently as the Baroness's eye — far from the thought of pearls and swine — went over the letter.

"*Tiens, tiens,*" Madame von Marwitz repeated; " the little Karen is sought in marriage."

" Really," said Miss Scrotton, " how very fortunate for the poor little thing. Who is the young man, and how, in heaven's name, has she secured a young man in the wilds of Cornwall ? "

Madame von Marwitz made no reply. She was absorbed in another letter. And Miss Scrotton now perceived, with amazement and indignation, that the one laid down was written in the hand of Gregory Jardine.

" You don't mean to tell me," Miss Scrotton said, after some moments of hardly held patience, " that it 's Gregory ? "

Madame von Marwitz, having finished her second letter, was gazing before her with a somewhat ambiguous expression.

" Tallie speaks well of him," she remarked at last. " He has made a very good impression on Tallie."

" Are you speaking of Gregory Jardine, Mercedes ? " Miss Scrotton repeated.

Madame von Marwitz now looked at her and as she looked the tricksy light of malice again grew in her eye. " *Mais oui; mais oui.* You have guessed correctly, my Scrotton," she said. " And you may read his letter. It is pleasant to me to see that stiff, self-satisfied young man brought to his knees. Read it, *ma chère,* read it. It is an excellent letter."

Miss Scrotton read, and, while she read, Madame von Marwitz's cold, deep eyes rested on her, still vaguely smiling.

" How very extraordinary," said Miss Scrotton. She handed back the letter.

" Extraordinary ? Now, why, *ma bonne ?* " her friend inquired, all limpid frankness. " He looked indeed, a stockish, chill young man, of the cold-nosed type — *ah, que je n'aime pas ça!* — but he is a good young man; a most unimpeachable young man; and our little Karen has melted him; how much his letter shows."

"Gregory Jardine is a very able and a very distinguished person," said Miss Scrotton, "and of an excellent county family. His mother and mine were cousins, as you know, and I have always taken the greatest interest in him. One can't but wonder how the child managed it." Mercedes, she knew, was drawing a peculiar satisfaction from her displeasure; but she could n't control it.

"Ah, the child is not a manager. She is so far from managing it, you see, that she leaves it to me to manage. It touches and surprises me, I confess, to find that her devotion to me rules her even at a moment like this. Yes; Karen has pleased me very much."

"Of course that old-fashioned formality would in itself charm Gregory. He is very conventional. But I do hope, my dear Mercedes, that you will think it over a little before giving your consent. It is really a most unsuitable match. Karen's feelings are, evidently, not at all deeply engaged and with Gregory it must be a momentary infatuation. He will get over it in time and thank you for saving him; and Karen will marry Herr Lippheim, as you hoped she would."

"Now upon my word, my Scrotton," said Madame von Marwitz in a manner as near insolence as its grace permitted, "I do not follow you. A barrister, a dingy little London barrister, to marry my ward? You call that an unsuitable marriage? I protest that I do not follow you and I assert, to the contrary, that he has played his cards well. Who is he? A nobody. You speak of your county families; what do they signify outside their county? Karen in herself is, I grant you, also a nobody; but she stands to me in a relation almost filial — if I chose to call it so; and I signify more than the families of many counties put together. Let us be frank. He opens no doors to Karen. She opens doors to him."

Miss Scrotton, addressed in these measured and determined tones, changed colour. "My dear Mercedes, of course you are right there. Of course in one sense, if you take Gregory in as you have taken Karen in, you open doors to him. I only meant that a young man in his position, with his way to make in the world, ought to marry some well-born woman with a little money. He must have money if he is to get on. He ought to be in Parliament one day; and Karen is without a penny, you have often told me so, as well as illegitimate. Of course if you intend to make her a large allowance, that is a different matter; but can you really afford to do that, darling?"

"I consider your young man very fortunate to get Karen without one penny," Madame von Marwitz pursued, in the same measured tones, "and I shall certainly make him no present of my hard-earned money. Let him earn the money for Karen, now, as I have done for so many years. Had she married my good Franz, it would have been a very different thing. This young man is well able to support her in comfort. No; it all comes most opportunely. I wanted Karen to settle and to settle soon. I shall cable my consent and my blessings to them at once. Will you kindly find me a servant, *ma chère.*"

Miss Scrotton, as she rose automatically to carry out this request, was feeling that it is possible almost to hate one's idols. She had transgressed, and she knew it, and Mercedes had been aware of what she had done and had punished her for it. She even wondered if the quick determination to accept Gregory as Karen's suitor had n't been part of the punishment. Mercedes knew that she had a pride in her cousin and had determined to humble it. She had perhaps herself to thank for having riveted this most disastrous match upon him. It was with a bitter heart that she walked on into the house.

As she went in Mr. Claude Drew came out and Miss Scrotton gave him a chill greeting. She certainly hated Mr. Claude Drew.

Claude Drew blinked a little in the bright sunlight and had somewhat the air of a graceful, nocturnal bird emerging into the day. He was dressed with an appropriateness to the circumstances of stately *villégiature* so exquisite as to have a touch of the fantastic.

Madame von Marwitz sat with her back to him in the limpid shadow of the great white parasol and was again looking, not at Karen's, but at Gregory Jardine's, letter. One hand hung over the arm of her chair.

9

Mr. Drew approached with quiet paces and, taking this hand, before Madame von Marwitz could see him, he bowed over it and kissed it. The manner of the salutation made of it at once a formality and a caress.

Madame von Marwitz looked up quickly and withdrew her hand. "You startled me, my young friend," she said. In her gaze was a 'mingled severity and softness and she smiled as if irrepressibly.

Mr. Drew smiled back. "I 've been wearying to escape from our host and come to you," he said. "He will talk to me about the reform of American politics. Why reform them? They are much more amusing unreformed, are n't they? And why talk to me about them. I think he wants me to write about them. If I were to write a book for the Americans, I would tell them that it is their mission to be amusing. Democracies must be either absurd or uninteresting. America began by being uninteresting; and now it has quite taken its place as absurd. I love to hear about their fat, bribed, clean-shaven senators; just as I love to read the advertisements of tooth-brushes and breakfast foods and underwear in their magazines, written in the language of persuasive, familiar fraternity. It was difficult not to confess this to Mr. Asprey; but I do not think he would have understood me." Mr. Drew spoke in a soft, slightly sibilant voice, with little smiling pauses between sentences that all seemed vaguely shuffled together. He paused now, smiling, and looking down at Madame von Marwitz.

"You speak foolishly," said Madame von Marwitz. "But he would have thought you wicked."

"Because I like beauty and don't like democracy. I suppose so." Still smiling at her he added, "One forgets democracies when one looks at you. You are very beautiful this morning."

"I am not, this morning, in a mood for unconventionalities," Madame von Marwitz returned, meeting his gaze with her mingled severity and softness.

And again, with composure, he ignored her severity and returned her smile. It would have been unfair to say that there was effrontery in Mr. Drew's gaze; it merely had its way with you and, if you did n't like its way, passed from you unperturbed. With all his rather sickly grace and ambiguous placidity, Mr. Drew was not lacking in character. He had risen superior to a good many things, the dismal wife at Surbiton and the large-mouthed children perhaps among them, and he had won his detachment. The homage he offered was not unalloyed by humour. To a person of Madame von Marwitz's calibre, he seemed to say, he would not pretend to raptures or reverences they had both long since seen through. It would bore him to be rapturous or reverent, and if you did n't like him, so his whole demeanour mildly demonstrated, you could leave him, or, rather, he could leave you. So that when Madame von Marwitz sought to quell him she found herself met with a gentle unawareness, even a gentle indifference. Cogitation and a certain disquiet were often in her eye when it rested on this devotee.

"Does one make conventional speeches to the moon?" he now remarked, taking a chair beside her and turning the brim of his white hat over his eyes so that of his face only the sensual, delicate mouth and chin were in sunlight. "I should n't want to make speeches to you if you were conventional. You are done with your letters? I may talk to you?"

"Yes, I have done. You may talk, as foolishly as you please, but not unconventionally; whether I am or am not conventional is not a matter that concerns you. I have had good news to-day. My little Karen is to marry."

"Your little Karen? Which of all the myriads is this adorer?"

"The child you saw with me in London. The one who stays in Cornwall."

"You mean the fair, square girl who calls you Tante? I only remember of her that she was fair and square and called you Tante."

"That is she. She is to marry an excellent young man, a young man," said Madame von Marwitz, slightly smiling at him, "who would never wish to make speeches to the moon, who is, indeed, not aware of the moon. But he is very much aware of Karen; so much so," and she continued to smile, as if over an amusing if still slightly perplexing memory, "that when she is there he is not aware of me. What do you say to that?"

"I say," Mr. Drew replied, "that the barbarians will always be many and the civilized few. Who is this barbarian?"

"A Mr. Gregory Jardine."

"Jardine? *Connais-pas,*" said Mr. Drew.

"He is a cousin of our Scrotton's," said Madame von Marwitz, "and a man of law. Very stiff and clean like a roll of expensive paper. He has asked me very nicely if he may inscribe the name of Mrs. Jardine upon a page of it. He is the sort of young man of law, I think I distinguish," Madame von Marwitz mused, her eyes on the landscape, "who does not smoke a briar wood pipe and ride on an omnibus, but who keeps good cigars in a silver box and always takes a hansom. He will make Karen comfortable and, I gather from her letter, happy. It will be a strange change of *milieu* for the child, but I have, I think, made her independent of *milieus.* She will write more than Mrs. Jardine on his scroll. It is a child of character."

"And she will no longer be in Cornwall," Mr. Drew observed. "I am glad of that."

"Why, pray? I am not glad of it. I shall miss my Karen at Les Solitudes."

"But I, you see, don't want to have other worshippers there when I go to stay with you," said Mr. Drew; "for, you know, you are going to let me stay a great deal with you in Cornwall. You will play to me, and I will write something that you will, perhaps, care to read. And the moon will be very kind and listen to many speeches. You know," he added, with a change of tone, "that I am in love with you. I must be alone with you at Les Solitudes."

"Let us have none of that, if you please," said Madame von Marwitz. She looked away from him along the sunny stretches of the terrace and she frowned slightly, though smiling on, as if with tolerant affection. And in her look was something half dazed and half resentful like the look of a fierce wild bird, subdued by the warmth and firmness of an enclosing hand.

CHAPTER XIII

GREGORY went down to Cornwall again only nine days after he had left it. He and Karen met as if under an arch of infinite blessings. He had his cable to show her and she hers to show him, and, although Gregory did not see them as the exquisite documents that Karen felt them to be, they did for him all that he asked Madame von Marwitz to do.

"I give her to you. Be worthy of my trust. Mercedes von Marwitz"— his read. And Karen's: "I could only yield you to a greater joy than you can find with me — but it could not be to a greater love. Do not forget me in your happiness. You are mine, my beloved child, not less but more than ever.— Tante."

Karen's joy was unshadowed. It made him think of primroses and crystal springs. She was not shy; he was shyer than she, made a little dumb, a little helpless, by his man's reverence, his man's awed sense of the beloved's dawn-like wonder. She was not changed; any change in Karen would come as quiet growth, not as transformation. Gregory's gladness had not this simplicity. It revealed to him a new world, a world newly beautiful but newly perilous, and a changed self,— the self of boyhood, renewed yet transformed, through whose joy ran the reactionary melancholy that, in a happiness attained, glances at fear, and at a climax of life, is aware of gulfs of sorrow as yet unsounded. More than his lover's passion was a tenderness for her and for her unquestioning acceptances that seemed near tears. Karen was in character so wrought and in nature so simple. Her subtleties were all objective, subtleties of sympathy, of recognition, of adaptation to the requirements of devoted action; her simplicity was that of a whole-heartedness unaware at high moments of all but the essential.

She had to tell him fully, holding his hand and looking into his eyes, all about her side of it; what she had thought when she

133

saw him at the concert — certain assumptions there gave Gregory his stir of uneasiness —" You were caring just as much as I was — in the same way — for her music "; what she had thought at Mrs. Forrester's, and at the railway station, and when the letters went on and on. She had of course seen what was coming that evening after they had been to the Lavington's; " When you did n't understand about me and Tante, you know; and I made you understand." And then he had made her understand how much he cared for her and she for him; only it had all come so quietly; " I did not think a great deal about it, or wonder; it sank into me — like stars one sees in a still lake, so that next day it was no surprise at all, when you told me; it was like looking up and seeing all the real stars in the sky. Afterwards it was dreadful for a little while, was n't it? " Karen held his hand for a moment to her cheek.

When all the past had been looked at together, Gregory asked her if she would not marry him quite soon; he hoped, indeed, that it might be within the month. " You see, why not? " he said. " I miss you so dreadfully and I can't be here; and why should you be? Let me come down and marry you in that nice little church on the other side of the village as soon as our banns can be called."

But, for the first time, a slight anxiety showed in her eyes. " I miss you dreadfully, too," she said. " But you forget, Tante will not be back till July. We must wait for Tante, Gregory. We are in May now, it is not so far to July. You will not mind too much? "

He felt, sitting under the arch of blessings as he was, that it would be most ungrateful and inappropriate to mind. But then, he said, if they must put it off like that, Karen would have to come to London. She must come and stay with Betty. " And get your trousseau "; this was a brilliant idea. " You 'll have to get your trousseau, you know, and Betty is an authority on clothes."

" Oh, but clothes. I never have clothes in that sense," said Karen. " A little seamstress down here makes most of them and Louise helps her sometimes if she has time. Tante gave me

twenty pounds before she went away; would twenty pounds do
for a trousseau?"

"Betty would think twenty pounds just about enough for your
gloves and stockings, I imagine," said Gregory.

"And will you expect me to be so luxurious? You are not
rich? We shall not live richly?"

"I'm not at all rich; but I want you to have pretty things —
layers and layers of the nice, white, soft things brides always
have, and a great many new hats and dresses. Could n't I give
you a little tip — to begin the trousseau?"

"Ah, it can wait, can't it?" said Karen easily. "No; you
can't give me a tip. Tante, I am sure, will see that I have a
nice trousseau. She may even give me a little *dot* when I marry.
I have no money at all; not one penny, you know. Do you
mind?"

"I'd far rather have you without a penny because I want to
give you everything. If Tante does n't give you the little *dot*,
I shall."

Karen was pondering a little seriously. "I don't know what
Tante will feel since you have enough for us both. It was when
she wished me to marry Franz that she spoke of a *dot*. And
Franz is of course very poor and has a great family of brothers
and sisters to help support. You will know Franz one day.
You did not speak very nicely of Franz that time, you know;
that was another reason why I thought you were so angry. And
it made me angry, too," said Karen, smiling at him.

"Was n't I nice? I am sure Franz is."

"Oh, so good and kind and true. And very talented. And
his mother would be a wonderful musician if she had not so
many children to take care of; that has harmed her music. And
she, too, is a golden-hearted person; she used often to help me
with my dresses. Do you remember that little white silk dress
of mine? perhaps so; I wore it at the concert, such a pretty
dress, I think. Frau Lippheim helped me with that — she and
a little German seamstress in Leipsig. I see us now, all bending
over the rustling silk, round the table with the lamp on it. We
had to make it so quickly. Tante had sent for me to come to

her in Vienna and I had nothing to wear at the great concert she was to give. We sat up till twelve to finish it. Franz and Lotta cooked our supper for us and we only stopped long enough to eat. Dear Frau Lippheim. Some day you will know all the Lippheims."

He listened to her with dreamy, amused delight, seeing her bending in the ugly German room over the little white silk dress and only vaguely aware of the queer figures she put before him. He had no inclination to know Franz and his mother, and no curiosity about them. But Karen continued. "That is the one, the only thing I can give you," she said, reflecting. "You know so few artists, don't you; so few people of talent. As to people, your life is narrow, is n't it so? I have met so many great people in my life, first through my father and then through Tante. Painters, poets, musicians. You will probably know them now, too; some of them certainly, for some are also friends of mine. Strepoff, for example; oh — how I shall like you to meet him. You have read him, of course, and about his escape from Siberia and his long exile."

"Strepoff? Yes, I think so. A dismal sort of fellow, is n't he?"

Gregory's delight was merging now in a more definite amusement, tinged, it may be confessed, with alarm. He remembered to have seen a photograph of this celebrity, very turbulently haired and very fixed and fiery of eye. He remembered a large bare throat and a defiant necktie. He had no wish to make Strepoff's acquaintance. It was quite enough to read about him in the magazines and admire his exploits from a distance.

"Dismal?" Karen had repeated, with a touch of severity. "Who would not be after such a life? Yes, he is a sad man, and the thought of Russia never leaves him. But he is full of gaiety, too. He spent some months with us two years ago at the Italian lakes and I grew so fond of him. We had great jokes together, he and I. And he sometimes writes to me now, such teasing, funny letters. The last was from San Francisco. He is giving lectures out there, raising money; for he never ceases the struggle. He calls me Liebchen. He is very fond of me."

" What do you call him? " Gregory inquired.

" Just Strepoff; everybody calls him that. Dear Belot, too," Karen pursued. " He could not fail to interest you. Perhaps you have already met him. He has been in London."

" Belot? Does he write poetry? "

" Poetry? No. Belot is a painter; a great painter. Surely you have heard of Belot? "

" Well, I'm afraid that if I have I've forgotten. You see, as you say, I live so out of the world of art."

" Did you not see his portrait of Susanne Mauret — the great French actress? It has been exhibited through all the world."

" Of course I have. Belot of course. The impressionist painter. It looked to me, I confess, awfully queer; but I could see that it was very clever."

" Impressionist? No; Belot would not rank himself among the impressionists. And he would not like to hear his work called clever; I warn you of that. He has a horror of cleverness. It was not a clever picture, but sober, strange, beautiful. Well, I know Belot and his wife quite intimately. They are great friends of the Lippheims, too, and call themselves the Franco-Prussian alliance. Madame Belot is a dear little woman. You must have often seen his pictures of her and the children. He has numbers of children and adores them. *La petite* Margot is my special pet and she always sends me a little present on my birthday. Madame Belot was once his model," Karen added, " and is quite *du peuple,* and I believe that some of his friends were sorry that he married her; but she makes him very happy. That beautiful nude in the Luxembourg by Chantefoy is of her — long before she married, of course. She does not sit for the *ensemble* now, and indeed I fear it has lost all its beauty, for she is very fat. It would be nice to go to Paris on our wedding-tour and see the Belots," said Karen.

Gregory made an evasive answer. He reflected that once he had married her it would probably be easy to detach Karen from these most undesirable associates. He hoped that she would take to Betty. Betty would be an excellent antidote. " And you think your sister-in-law will want me?" said Karen, when he brought her from the Belots back to Betty. "She does n't know me."

"She must begin to know you as soon as possible. You will have Mrs. Forrester at hand, you see, if my family should oppress you too much. Barring Betty, who hardly counts as one of them, they are n't interesting, I warn you."

"I may oppress them," said Karen, with the shrewdness that often surprised him. "Who will they take refuge with?"

"Oh, they have all London to fall back upon. They do nothing when they 're up but go out. That 's my plan; that they should leave you a good deal when they go out, and leave you to me."

"That will be nice," said Karen. "But Mrs. Forrester, you know," she went on, "is not exactly an intimate of mine that I could fall back upon. I am, in her eyes, only a little appendage of Tante's."

"Ah, but you have ceased, now, to be an appendage of Tante's. And Mrs. Forrester is an intimate, an old one, of mine."

"She 'll take me in as your appendage," Karen smiled.

"Not at all. It 's you, now, who are the person to whom the appendage belongs. I 'm your appendage. That quite alters the situation. You will have to stand in the foreground and do all the conventional things."

"Shall I?" smiled Karen, unperturbed. She was, as he knew, not to be disconcerted by any novel social situation. She had witnessed so many situations and such complicated ones that the merely conventional were, in her eyes, relatively insignificant and irrevelant. There would be for her none of the débutante's sense of awkwardness or insufficiency. Again she reminded him of the rustic little princess, unaware of alien customs, and ready to learn and to laugh at her own blunders.

It was arranged, Mrs. Talcott's appearance helping to decisions, that as soon as Karen heard from her guardian, who might have plans to suggest, she should come up to London and stay with Lady Jardine.

Mrs. Talcott, on entering, had grasped Gregory's hand and

shaken it vigorously, remarking: "I'm very pleased to see you back again."

"I didn't tell Mrs. Talcott anything, Gregory," said Karen. "But I am sure she guessed."

"Mrs. Talcott and I had our understandings," said Gregory, "but I'm sure she guessed from the moment she saw me down here. She was much quicker than you, Karen."

"I've seen a good many young folks in my time," Mrs. Talcott conceded.

Gregory's sense of the deepened significance in all things lent a special pathos to his conjectures to-day about Mrs. Talcott. He did not know how far her affection for Karen went and whether it were more than the mere kindly solicitude of the aged for the young; but the girl's presence in her life must give at least interest and colour, and after Mrs. Talcott had spoken her congratulations and declared that she believed they'd be real happy together, he said, the idea striking him as an apt one, "And Mrs. Talcott, you must come up and stay with us in London sometimes, won't you?"

"Oh, Mrs. Talcott — yes, yes;" said Karen, delighted. He had never seen her kiss Mrs. Talcott, but she now clasped her arm, standing beside her. Mrs. Talcott did not smile; but, after a moment, the aspect of her face changed; it always took some moments for Mrs. Talcott's expression to change. Now it was like seeing the briny old piece of shipwrecked oak mildly illuminated with sunlight on its lonely beach.

"That's real kind of you; real kind," said Mrs. Talcott reflectively. "I don't expect I'll get up there. I'm not much of a traveller these days. But it's real kind of you to have thought of it."

"But it must be," Karen declared. "Only think; I should pour out your coffee for you in the morning, after all these years when you've poured out mine; and we would walk in the park — Gregory's flat overlooks the park you know — and we would drive in hansoms — don't you like hansoms — and go to the play in the evening. But yes, indeed, you shall come."

Mrs. Talcott listened to these projects, still with her mild illumination, remarking when Karen had done, "I guess not, Karen; I guess I'll stay here. I've been moving round considerable all my life long and now I expect I'll just stay put. There's no one to look after things here but me and they'd get pretty muddled if I was away, I expect. Mitchell isn't a very bright man."

"The real difficulty is," said Karen, holding Mrs. Talcott's arm and looking at her with affectionate exasperation, "that she doesn't like to leave Les Solitudes lest she should miss a moment of Tante. Tante sometimes turns up almost at a moment's notice. We shall have to get Tante safely away to Russia, or America again, before we can ask you; isn't that the truth, Mrs. Talcott?"

"Well, I don't know. Perhaps there's something in it," Mrs. Talcott admitted. "Mercedes likes to know I'm here seeing to things. She mightn't feel easy in her mind if I was away."

"We'll lay it before her, then," said Karen. "I know she will say that you must come."

CHAPTER XIV.

IT was not until some three weeks after that Karen paid her visit to London. Tante had not written at once and Gregory had to control his discontent and impatience as best he might. He and Karen wrote to each other every day and he was aware of a fretful anxiety in his letters which contrasted strangely with the serenity of hers. Once more she made him feel that she was the more mature. In his brooding imaginativeness he was like the most youthful of lovers, seeing his treasure menaced on every hand by the hazards of life. He warned Karen against cliff-edges; he warned her, now that motors were every day becoming more common, against their sudden eruption in " cornery " lanes; he begged her repeatedly to keep safe and sound until he could himself take care of her. Karen replied with sober reassurances and promises and showed no corresponding alarms on his behalf. She had, evidently, more confidence in the law of probability.

She wired at last to say that she had heard from Tante and would come up next day if Lady Jardine could have her at such short notice. Gregory had made his arrangements with Betty, who showed a most charming sympathy for his situation, and when, at the station, he saw Karen's face smiling at him from a window, when he seized her arm and drew her forth, it was with a sense of relief and triumph as great as though she were restored to him after actual perils.

" Darling, it has seemed such ages," he said.

He was conscious, delightedly, absorbedly, of everything about her. She wore her little straw hat with the black bow and a long hooded cape of thin grey cloth. In her hand she held a small basket containing her knitting — she was knitting him a pair of golf stockings — and a book.

He piloted her to the cab he had in waiting. Her one small shabby box was put on the top and a very large dressing-case,

141

curiously contrasting in its battered and discoloured magnifi-
cence with the box, placed inside; it was a discarded one of
Madame von Marwitz's, as its tarnished initials told him. It
was only as the cab rolled out of the station, after he had kissed
Karen and was holding her hand, that he realized that she was
far less aware of him than he of her. Not that she was not
glad; she sighed deeply with content, smiling at him, holding
his hand closely; but there was a shadow of preoccupation on her.

"Tell me, darling, is everything all right?" he asked. "You
have had good news from your guardian?"

She said nothing for a moment, looking out of the window,
and then back at him. Then she said: "She is beautiful to
me. But I have made her sad."

"Made her sad? Why have you made her sad?" Gregory
suppressed — only just suppressed — an indignant note.

"I did not think of it myself," said Karen. "I did n't think
of her side at all, I'm afraid, because I did not realise how much
I was to her. But you remember what I told you I was, the
little home thing; I am that even more deeply than I had
thought; and she feels — dear, dear one — that that is gone
from her, that it can never be the same again." She turned her
eyes from him and the tears gathered thickly in them.

"But, dearest," said Gregory, "she can't want to make you
sad, can she? She must really be glad to have you happy.
She herself wanted you to get married, and had found Franz
Lippheim for you, you know." Instinct warned him to go
carefully.

Karen shook her head with a little impatience. "One may
be glad to have someone happy, yet sad for oneself. She is sad.
Very, very sad."

"May I see her letter?" Gregory asked after a moment, and
Karen, hesitating, then drew it from the pocket of her cloak,
saying, as she handed it to him, and as if to atone for the impatience, "It does n't make me love you any less — you understand that, dear Gregory — because she is sad. It only makes
me feel, in my own happiness, how much I love her."

Gregory read. The address was "Belle Vue."

"My Darling Child,— A week has passed since I had your letter and now the second has come and I must write to you. My Karen knows that when in pain it is my instinct to shut myself away, to be quite still, quite silent, and so to let the waves go over me. That is why, she will understand, I have not written yet. I have waited for the strength and courage to come back to me so that I might look my sorrow in the face. For though it is joy for you, and I rejoice in it, it is sorrow, could it be otherwise, for me. So the years go on and so our cherished flowers drop from us; so we feel our roots of life chilling and growing old; and the marriage-veil that we wrap round a beloved child becomes the symbol of the shroud that is to fold us from her. I knew that I should one day have to give up my Karen; I wished it; she knows that; but now that it has come and that the torch is in her hand, I can only feel the darkness in which her going leaves me. Not to find my little Karen there, in my life, part of my life; — that is the thought that pierces me. In how many places have I found her, for years and years; do you remember them all, Karen? I know that in heart we are not to be severed; I know that, as I cabled to you, you are not less but more mine than ever; but the body cries out for the dear presence; for the warm little hand in my tired hand, the loving eyes in my sad eyes, the loving heart to lean my stricken heart upon. How shall I bear the loneliness and the silence of my life without you?

"Do not forget me, my Karen. Ah, I know you will not, yet the cry arises. Do not let this new love that has come to you in your youth and gladness shut me out more than it must. Do not forget the old, the lonely Tante. Ah, these poor tears, they fall and fall. I am sad, sad to death, my Karen. Great darknesses are behind me, and before me I see the darkness to which I go.

"Farewell, my darling.— *Lebewohl.*— Tell Mr. Jardine that he must make my child happy indeed if I am to forgive him for my loss.

"Yes; it shall be in July, when I return. I send you a little gift that my Karen may make herself the fine lady, ready for all

the gaieties of the new life.   He will wish it to be a joyful one,
I know; he will wish her to drink deep of all that the world has
to offer of splendid, and rare, and noble.   My child is worthy
of a great life, I have equipped her for it.   Go forward, my
Karen, with your husband, into the light.   My heart is with you
always.   Tante."

Gregory read, and instinctively, while he read, he glanced at
Karen, steadying his face lest she should guess from its tremor
of contempt how latent antagonisms hardened to a more ironic
dislike.   But Karen gazed from the window — grave, preoccupied.   Such suspicions were far indeed from her.   Gregory
could give himself to the letter and its intimations undiscovered.
Suffering?   Perhaps Madame von Marwitz was suffering; but
she had no business to say it.   Forgive him indeed; well, if
those were the terms of forgiveness, he promised himself that
he should deserve it.   Meanwhile he must conceal his resentment.

"I'm so sorry, darling," he said, giving the letter back to
Karen.   "We shall have to cheer her up, shan't we?   When she
sees how very happy you are with me I am sure she'll feel
happier."   He wasn't at all sure.

"I don't know, Gregory.   I am afraid that my happiness
cannot make her less lonely."

Karen's griefs were not to be lightly dispersed.   But she was
not a person to enlarge upon them.   After another moment she
pointed out something from the window and laughed; but the
unshadowed gladness that he had imagined for their meeting was
overcast.

Betty awaited them with tea in her Pont Street drawing-room,
a room of polished, glittering, softly lustrous surfaces.   Precious
objects stood grouped on little Empire tables or ranged in Empire cabinets.   Flat, firm cushions of rose-coloured satin stood
against the backs of Empire chairs and sofas.   On the walls
were French engravings and a delicate portrait of Betty done
at the time of her marriage by Boutet de Monvel.   The room,
like Betty herself, combined elegance and cordiality.

I was there, you know, at the very beginning," she said, taking Karen's hands and scanning her with her jewel-like eyes. "It was love at first sight. He asked who you were at once and I'm pleased to think that it was I who gave him his first information. Now that I look back upon it," said Betty, taking her place at the tea-table and holding Karen still with her bright and friendly gaze, "I remember that he was far more interested in you than in anything else that evening. I don't believe that Madame Okraska existed for him." Betty was drawing on her imagination in a manner that she took for granted to be pleasing.

"I should be sorry to think that," Karen observed and Gregory was relieved to see that she did not take Betty's supposition seriously. She watched her pretty hands move among the teacups with an air of pleased interest.

"Would you really? You would want him to retain all his æsthetic faculties even while he was falling in love? Do you think one could?" Betty asked her questions smiling. "Or perhaps you think that one would fall in love the more securely from listening to Madame Okraska at the same time. I think perhaps I should. I do admire her so much. I hope now that some day I shall know her. She must be, I am sure, as lovely as she looks."

"Yes, indeed," said Karen. "And you will meet her very soon, you see, for she comes back in July."

Gregory sat and listened to their talk, satisfied that they were to get on, yet with a slight discomfort. Betty questioned and Karen replied, unaware that she revealed aspects of her past that Betty might not interpret as she would feel it natural that they should be interpreted, supremely unaware that any criticism could attach itself to her guardian as a result of these revelations. Yes; she had met so-and-so and this and that, in Rome, in Paris, in London or St. Petersburg; but no, evidently, she could hardly say that she knew any of these people, friends of Tante's though they were. The ambiguity of her status as little camp-follower became defined for Betty's penetrating and appraising eyes and the inappropriateness of the letter, with its broken-hearted maternal tone, returned to Gregory with re-

newed irony. He did n't want to share with Betty his hidden
animosities and once or twice, when her eye glanced past Karen
and rested reflectively upon himself, he knew that Betty was
wondering how much he saw and how he liked it. The Lippheims again made their socially unillustrious appearance;
Karen had so often stayed with them before Les Solitudes had
been built and while Tante travelled with Mrs. Talcott; she
had never stayed — Gregory was thankful for small mercies —
with the Belots; Tante, after all, had her own definite discriminations; she would not have placed Karen in the charge
of Chantefoy's lady of the Luxembourg, however reputable her
present position; but Gregory was uneasy lest Karen should
disclose how simply she took Madame Belot's past. The fact
that Karen's opportunities in regard to dress were so obviously
haphazard, coming up with the question of the trousseau, was
somewhat atoned for by the sum that Madame von Marwitz
now sent — Gregory had forgotten to ask the amount. "A
hundred pounds"; said Betty cheerfully; "Oh, yes; we can
get you very nicely started on that."

"Tante seems to think," said Karen, "that I shall have to
be very gay and have a great many dresses; but I hope it will
not have to be so very much. I am fond of quiet things."

"Well, especially at first, I suppose you will have a good many
dinners and dances; Gregory is fond of dancing, you know.
But I don't think you lead such a taxing social life, do you,
Gregory? You are a rather sober person, are n't you?"

"That is what I thought," said Karen. "For I am sober,
too, and I want to read so many things, in the evening, you
know, Gregory. I want to read Political Economy and understand about politics; Tante does not care for politics, but she
always finds me too ignorant of the large social questions. You
will teach me all that, won't you? And we must hear so much
music; and travel, too, in your holidays; I do not see how we
can have much time for many dinners. As for dances, I do
not know how to dance; would that make any difference, when
you went? I could sit and look on, could n't I?"

"No, indeed; you can't sit and look on; you 'll have to dance

with me," said Gregory. "I will teach you dancing as well
as Political Economy. She must have lessons, must n't she,
Betty? Of course you must learn to dance."

"I do not think I shall learn easily," Karen said, smiling
from him to Betty. "I do not think I should do you credit in
a ballroom. But I will try, of course."

Gregory was quite prepared for Betty's probes when Karen
went upstairs to her room. "What a dear she is, Gregory,"
she said; "and how clever it was of you to find her, hidden
away as she has been. I suppose the life of a great musician
does n't admit of formalities. She never had time to introduce, as it were, her adopted daughter."

"Well, no; a great musician could hardly take an adopted
or a real daughter around to dances; and Karen is n't exactly
adopted."

"No, I see." Betty's eyes sounded him. "She is really
very nice I suppose, Madame von Marwitz? You like her very
much? Mrs. Forrester dotes upon her, of course; but Mrs.
Forrester is an enthusiast."

"And I 'm not, as you know," Gregory returned, he flattered
himself, with skill. "I don't think that I shall ever dote on
Madame von Marwitz. When I know her I hope to like her
very much. At present I hardly know her better than you
do."

"Ah — but you must know a great deal about her from
Karen," said Betty, who could combine tact with pertinacity;
"but she, too, in that respect, is an enthusiast, I suppose."

"Well, naturally. It 's been a wonderful relationship. You
remember you felt that so much in telling me about Karen at
the very first."

"Of course; and it 's all true, is n't it; the forest and all the
rest of it. Only, not having met Karen, one did n't realize how
much Madame von Marwitz was in luck." Betty, it was evident, had already begun to wonder whether Tante was as lovely
as she looked.

CHAPTER XV

"DEAR Mrs. Forrester, you know that I worship the ground she treads on," said Miss Scrotton; "but it can't be denied — can you deny it? — that Mercedes is capricious."

It was one day only after Miss Scrotton's return from America and she had returned alone, and it was to this fact that she alluded rather than to the more general results of Madame von Marwitz's sudden postponement. Owing to the postponement, Karen to-day was being married in Cornwall without her guardian's presence. Miss Scrotton had touched on that. She had said that she did n't think Mercedes would like it, she had added that she could n't herself, however inconvenient delay might have been, understand how Karen and Gregory could have done it. But she had not at first much conjecture to give to the bridal pair. It was upon the fact that Mercedes, at the last moment, had thrown all plans overboard, that she dwelt, with a nipped and tightened utterance and a gaze, fixed on the wall above the tea-table, almost tragic. Mrs. Forrester was the one person in whom she could confide. It was through Mrs. Forrester that she had met Mercedes; her devotion to Mercedes constituted to Mrs. Forrester, as she was aware, her chief merit. Not that Mrs. Forrester was n't fond of her; she had been fond of her ever since, as a relative of the Jardines' and a precociously intelligent little girl who had published a book on Port-Royal at the age of eighteen, she had first attracted her attention at a literary tea-party. But Mrs. Forrester would not have sat so long or listened so patiently to any other theme than the one that so absorbed them both and that so united them in their absorption. Miss Scrotton even suspected that a tinge of bland and kindly pity coloured Mrs. Forrester's readiness to sympathize. She must know Mercedes

well enough to know that she could give her devotees bad half
hours, though the galling thing was to suspect that Mrs. Forrester was one of the few people to whom she would n't give
them.   Mrs. Forrester might worship as devoutly as anybody,
yet her devotion never let her in for so much forbearance and
sacrifice.   Perhaps, poor Miss Scrotton worked it out, the reason was that to Mrs. Forrester Mercedes was but one among
many, whereas to herself Mercedes was the central prize and
treasure.   Mrs. Forrester was incapable of a pang of jealousy
or emulation; she was always delighted yet never eager.   When,
in the first flow of intimacy with Mercedes, Miss Scrotton had
actually imagined, for an ecstatic and solemn fortnight, that
she stood first with her, Mrs. Forrester had met her air of
irrepressible triumph with a geniality in which was no trace of
grievance or humiliation.   The downfall had been swift; Mercedes had snubbed her one day, delicately and accurately, in
Mrs. Forrester's presence, and Miss Scrotton's cheek still burned
when she remembered it.   There were thus all sorts of unspoken things between her and Mrs. Forrester, and not the
least of them was that her folly should have endeared her.   Miss
Scrotton at once chafed against and relied upon her old friend's
magnanimity.   Her intercourse with her was largely made up
of a gloomy demand for sympathy and a stately evasion of it.

Mrs. Forrester now poured her out a second cup of tea, answering, soothingly, "Yes, she is capricious.   But what do you
expect, my dear Eleanor?   She is a force of nature, above our
little solidarities and laws.   What do you expect?   When one
worships a force of nature, *il faut subir son sort.*"   It was kind
of Mrs. Forrester to include herself in these submissions.

"I had really built all my summer about the plans that we
had made," Miss Scrotton said.   "Mercedes was to have come
back with me, I was to have stopped in Cornwall for Karen's
marriage and after my month here in London I was to have
joined her at Les Solitudes for August.   Now August is empty
and I had refused more than one very pleasant invitation in
order to go to Mercedes.   She is n't coming back for another
three months."

"You did n't care to go with the Aspreys to the Adirondacks?"

"How could I go, dear Mrs. Forrester, when I was full of engagements here in London for July? And, moreover, they did n't ask me. It is rather curious when one comes to think of it. I brought the Aspreys and Mercedes together, I gave her to them, one may say, but, I am afraid I must own it, they seized her and looked upon me as a useful rung in the ladder that reached her. It has been a disillusionizing experience, I can't deny it; but *passons* for the Aspreys and their kind. The fact is," said Miss Scrotton, dropping her voice a little, "the real fact is, dear Mrs. Forrester, that the Aspreys are n't responsible. It was n't for them she 'd have stayed, and I think they must realize it. No, it is all Claude Drew. He is at the bottom of everything that I feel as strange and altered in Mercedes. He has an unholy influence over her, oh, yes, I mean it, Mrs. Forrester. I have never seen Mercedes so swayed before."

"Swayed?" Mrs. Forrester questioned.

"Oh, but yes, indeed. He managed the whole thing — and when I think that he would in all probability never have seen the Aspreys if it had not been for me! — Mercedes had him asked there, you know; they are very, but very, very fashionable people, they know everybody worth knowing all over the world. I need n't tell you that, of course. But it was all arranged, he and Mercedes, and Lady Rose and the Marquis de Hautefeuille, and a young American couple — with the Aspreys in the background as universal providers — it made a little group where I was plainly *de trop*. Mr. Drew planned everything with her. She is to have her piano and he is to write a book under her aegis. And they are to live in the pinewoods with the most elaborate simplicity. However, I am sure the Adirondacks will soon bore her."

"And how soon will Mr. Drew bore her?" asked Mrs. Forrester, who had listened to these rather pitiful revelations with, now and then, a slight elevation of her intelligent eyebrows.

The question gave Miss Scrotton an opportunity for almost

ominous emphasis; she paused over it, holding Mrs. Forrester with a brooding eye.

"He won't bore her," she then brought out.

"What, never? never?" Mrs. Forrester questioned gaily.

"Never, never," Miss Scrotton repeated. "He is too clever. He will keep her interested — and uncertain."

"Well," Mrs. Forrester returned, as if this were all to the good, "it is a comfort to think that the poor darling has found a distraction."

"You feel it that? I wish I could. I wish I could feel it anything but an infatuation. If only he were n't so much the type of a great woman's folly; if only he were n't so of the region of whispers. It is n't like our wonderful Sir Alliston; one sees her there standing high on a mountain peak with the winds of heaven about her. To see her with Mr. Drew is like seeing her through some ambiguous, sticky fog. Oh, I can't deny that it has all made me very, very unhappy." Tears blinked in Miss Scrotton's eyes.

Mrs. Forrester was kind, she leaned forward and patted Miss Scrotton's hand, she smiled reassuringly, and she refused, for a moment, to share her anxiety. "No, no, no," she said, "you are troubling yourself quite needlessly, my dear Eleanor. Mercedes is amusing herself and the young man is an interesting young man; she has talked to me and written to me about him. And I think she needed distraction just now, I think this marriage of little Karen's has affected her a good deal. The child is of course connected in her mind with so much that is dear and tragic in the past."

"Oh, Karen!" said Miss Scrotton, who, drying her eyes, had accepted Mrs. Forrester's consolations with a slight sulkiness, "she has n't given a thought to Karen, I can assure you."

"No; you can't assure me, Eleanor," Mrs. Forrester returned, now with a touch of severity. "I don't think you quite understand how deep a bond of that sort can be for Mercedes — even if she seldom speaks of it. She has written to me very affectingly about it. I only hope she will not take it to heart that they could not wait for her. I could not blame them.

Everything was arranged; a house in the Highlands lent to them
for the honeymoon."

"Take it to heart? Dear me no; she won't like it, probably;
but that is a different matter."

"Gregory is radiant, you know."

"Is he?" said Miss Scrotton gloomily. "I wish I could feel
radiant about that match; but I can't. I did hope that Gregory
would marry well."

"It isn't perhaps quite what one would have expected for
him," Mrs. Forrester conceded; "but she is a dear girl. She
behaved very prettily while she was here with Lady Jardine."

"Did she? It is a very different marriage, isn't it, from
the one that Mercedes had thought suitable. She told you, I
suppose, about Franz Lippheim."

"Yes; I heard about that. Mercedes was a good deal dis-
appointed. She is very much attached to the young man and
thought that Karen was, too. I have never seen him."

"From what I've heard he seemed to me as eminently suit-
able a husband for Karen as my poor Gregory is unsuitable.
What he can have discovered in the girl, I can't imagine. But
I remember now how much interested in her he was on that
day that he met her here at tea. She is such a dull girl," said
Miss Scrotton sadly. "Such a heavy, clumsy person. And
Gregory has so much wit and irony. It is very curious."

"These things always are. Well, they are married now, and
I wish them joy."

"No one is at the wedding, I suppose, but old Mrs. Talcott.
The next thing we shall hear will be that Sir Alliston has fallen
in love with Mrs. Talcott," said Miss Scrotton, indulging her
gloomy humour.

"Oh, yes; the Jardines went down, and Mrs. Morton;"—
Mrs. Morton was a married sister of Gregory's. "Lady Jardine has very much taken to the child you know. They have
given her a lovely little tiara."

"Dear me," said Miss Scrotton; "it is a case of Cinderella.
No; I can't rejoice over it, though, of course I wish them joy;

I wired to them this morning and I'm sending them a very handsome paper-cutter of dear father's. Gregory will appreciate that, I think. But no; I shall always be sorry that she did n't marry Franz Lippheim."

CHAPTER XVI

THE Jardines did not come back to London till October. They had spent a month in Scotland and a month in Italy and two weeks in France, returning by way of Paris, where Gregory passed through the ordeal of the Belots. He saw Madame Belot clasp Karen to her breast and the long line of little Belots swarm up to be kissed successively, Monsieur Belot, a short, stout, ruddy man, with outstanding grey hair and a square grey beard, watching the scene benignantly, his palette on his thumb. Madame Belot did n't any longer suggest Chantefoy's picture; she suggested nothing artistic and everything domestic. From a wistful Burne-Jones type with large eyes and a drooping mouth she had relapsed to her plebeian origins and now, fat, kind, cheerful, she was nothing but wife and mother, with a figure like a sack and cheap tortoise-shell combs stuck, apparently at random, in the untidy *bandeaux* of her hair.

Following Karen and Monsieur Belot about the big studio, among canvases on easels and canvases leaned against the walls, Gregory felt himself rather bewildered, and not quite as he had expected to be bewildered. They might be impossible, Madame Belot of course was impossible; but they were not vulgar and they were extremely intelligent, and their intelligence displayed itself in realms to which he was almost disconcertingly a stranger. Even Madame Belot, holding a stalwart, brown-fisted baby on her arm, could comment on her husband's work with a discerning aptness of phrase which made his own appreciation seem very trite and tentative. He might be putting up with the Belots, but it was quite as likely, he perceived, that they might be putting up with him. He realized, in this world of the Belots, the significance, the laboriousness, the high level

154

of vitality, and he realized that to the Belots his own world
was probably seen as a dull, half useful, half obstructive fact,
significant mainly for its purchasing power. For its power of
appreciation they had no respect at all. *" Il radote, ma chèrie,"*
Monsieur Belot said to Karen of a famous person, now, after
years of neglect, loudly acclaimed in London at the moment
when, by fellow-artists, he was seen as defunct. "He no longer
lives; he repeats himself. Ah, it is the peril," Monsieur Belot
turned kindly including eyes on Gregory; "if one is not born
anew, continually, the artist dies; it becomes machinery."

Karen was at home among the Belot's standards. She talked
with Belot, of processes, methods, technique, the talk of artists,
not artistic talk. *" Et la grande Tante? "* he asked her, when
they were all seated at a nondescript meal about a long table
of uncovered oak, the children unpleasantly clamorous and
Madame Belot dispensing, from one end, strange, tepid tea,
but excellent chocolate, while Belot, from the other, sent round
plates of fruit and buttered rolls. Karen was laughing with
la petite Margot, whom she held in her lap.

"She is coming," said Karen. "At last. In three weeks I
shall see her now. She has been spending the summer in
America, you know; among the mountains."

One of the boys inquired whether there were not danger to
Madame von Marwitz from *les Peaux-Rouges,* and when he was
reassured and the question of buffaloes disposed of Madame
Belot was able to make herself heard, informing Karen that the
Lippheims, Franz, Frau Lippheim, Lotta, Minna and Elizabeth,
were to give three concerts in Paris that winter. "You have
not seen them yet, Karen?" she asked. "They have not yet
met Monsieur Jardine?" And when Karen said no, not yet;
but that she had heard from Frau Lippheim that they were
to come to London after Paris, Madame Belot suggested that
the young couple might have time now to travel up to Leipsig
and take the Lippheims by surprise. *" Voilà de braves gens et
de bons artistes,"* said Monsieur Belot.

"You did like my dear Belots," Karen said, as she and
Gregory drove away. She had, since her marriage, grown in

perception; Gregory would have found it difficult, now, to hide ironies and antipathies from her. Even retrospectively she saw things which at the time she had not seen, saw, for instance, that the idea of the Belots had not been alluring to him. He knew, too, that she would have considered dislike of the Belots as showing defect in him not in them, but cheerfully, if with a touch of her severity. She had an infinite tolerance for the defects and foibles of those she loved. He was glad to be able to reply with full sincerity: *"Ils sont de braves gens et de bons artistes."*

"But," Karen said, looking closely at him, and with a smile, "you would not care to pass your life with them. And you were quite disturbed lest I should say that I wanted to go and take the Lippheims by surprise at Leipsig. You like *les gens du monde* better than artists, Gregory."

"What are you?" Gregory smiled back at her. "I like you better."

"I? I am *gens du monde manqué* and *artiste manqué*. I am neither fish, flesh nor fowl," said Karen. "I'm only — positively — my husband's wife and Tante's ward. And that quite satisfies me."

He knew that it did. Their happiness was flawless; flawless as far as her husband's wife was concerned. It was in regard to Tante's ward that Gregory was more and more conscious of keeping something from Karen, while more and more it grew difficult to keep anything from her. Already, if sub-consciously, she must have become aware that her guardian's unabated mournfulness did not affect her husband as it did herself. She had showed him no more of Tante's letters, and they had been quite frequent. She had told him while they were in Scotland that it had hurt Tante very much that they should not have waited till her return; but she did not enlarge on the theme; and Gregory knew why; to enlarge would have been to reproach him. Karen had yielded, against her own wishes, to his entreaties. She had agreed that their marriage should not be so postponed at the last minute. In his vehemence Gregory had been skilful; he had said not one word of reproach against

Madame von Marwitz for her disconcerting change of plan.
It was not surprising to him; it was what he had expected of
Madame von Marwitz, that she would put Karen aside for a
whim. Karen would not see her guardian's action in this
light; yet she must know that her beloved was vulnerable to
the charge, at all events, of inconsiderateness, and she had been
grateful to him, no doubt, for showing no consciousness of it.
She had consented, perhaps, partly through gratitude, though
she had felt her pledged word, too, as binding. Once she had
consented, whatever the results, Gregory knew that she would
not visit them on him. It was of her own responsibility that
she was thinking when, with a grave face, she had told him of
Tante's hurt. "After all, dearest," Gregory had ventured,
"we did want her, did n't we? It was really she who chose
not to come, was n't it?"

"I am sure that Tante wanted to see me married," said
Karen, touching on her own hidden wound.

He helped her there, knowing, in his guile, that to exonerate
Tante was to help not only Karen but himself. "Of course;
but she does n't think things out, does she? She is accustomed
to having things arranged for her. I suppose she did n't a bit
realise all that had been settled over here, nor what an impatient
lover it was who held you to your word."

Her face cleared as he showed her that he recognised Tante's
case as so explicable. "I 'm so glad that you see it all," she
said. "For you do. She is oh! so unpractical, poor darling;
she would forget everything, you know, unless I or Mrs. Talcott
were there to keep reminding her — except her music, of course;
but that is like breathing to her. And I am so sorry, so dreadfully sorry; because, of course, to know that she hurt me by
not coming must hurt her more. But we will make it up to
her. And oh! Gregory, only think, she says she may come and
stay with us."

One of her first exclamations on going over his flat with him
was that they could put up Tante, if she would come. The
drawing-room could be devoted to her music; for there was
ample room for the grand piano — which accompanied Madame

von Marwitz as invariably as her tooth-brush; and the spare-bedroom had a dressing-room attached that would do nicely for Louise. Now there seemed hope of this dream being realised.

Karen had not yet received a wedding-present from her guardian, but in Paris, on the homeward way, she heard that it had been dispatched from New York and would be awaiting her in London, and it was of this gift that she had been talking as she and Gregory drove from the station to St. James's on a warm October evening. Tante had not told her what the present was, but had written that Karen would care for it very much. "To find her present waiting for us is like having Tante to welcome us," Karen said. After her surmise about the present she relapsed into happy musings and Gregory, too, was silent, able only to give a side-glance of gratitude, as it were, at the thought that Tante was to welcome them by proxy.

His mood was one of almost tremulous elation. He was bringing her home after bridal wanderings that had never lost their element of dream-like unreality. There had always been the feeling that he might wake any day to find Italy and Karen both equally illusory. But to see Karen in his home, taking her place in his accustomed life, would be to feel his joy linking itself securely with reality.

The look of London at this sunny hour of late afternoon and at this autumnal season matched his consciousness of a tranquil metamorphosis. Idle still and empty of its more vivid significance, one yet felt in it the soft stirrings of a re-entering tide of life. Cabs passed, piled with brightly badged luggage; the drowsily reminiscent shop-windows showed here and there an adventurous forecast, and a house or two, among the rows of dumb, sleeping faces, opened wide eyes at the leisurely streets. The pale, high pinks of the sky drooped and melted into the greys and whites and buffs below, and blurred the heavy greens of the park with falling veils of rose. The scene seemed drawn in flat delicate tones of pastel.

Karen sat beside him in the cab and, while she gazed before her, she had slipped her hand into his. She had preserved much of the look of the unmarried Karen in her dress. The difference was in the achievement of an ideal rather than in a change. The line of her little grey travelling hat above her brows was still unusual; with her grey gloves and long grey silken coat she had an air, cool, competent, prepared for any emergency of travel. She would have looked equally appropriate dozing under the hooded light in a railway carriage, taking her place at a *table d'hôte* in a provincial French town, or walking in the wind and sun along a foreign *plage*. After looking at the London to which he brought her, Gregory looked at her. Marriage had worked none of its even superficial disenchantments in him. After three months of intimacy, Karen still constantly arrested him with a sense of the undiscovered, the unforeseen. What it consisted in he could not have defined; she was simple, even guileless, still; she had no reticences; yet she seemed to express so much of which she was unaware that he felt himself to be continually making her acquaintance. That quiet slipping now of her hand into his, while her gaze maintained its calm detachment, the charm of her mingled tenderness and independence, had its vague sting for Gregory. She accepted him and whatever he might mean with something of the happy matter-of-fact with which she accepted all that was hers. She loved him with a completeness and selflessness that had made the world suddenly close round him with gentle arms; but Gregory often wondered if she were in love with him. Rapture, restlessness and fear all seemed alien to her, and to turn from thoughts of her and of their love to Karen herself was like passing from dreams of poignant, starry ecstasy to a clear, white dawn, with dew on the grass and a lark rising and the waking sweetness of a world at once poetical and practical about one. She strengthened and stilled his passion for her. And she seemed unaware of passion.

They arrived at the great, hive-like mansion and in the lift, which took them almost to the top, Karen, standing near him, again put her hand in his and smiled at him. She was not feeling his tremor, but she was limpidly happy and as conscious as he of an epoch-making moment.

Barker opened the door to them, murmuring a decorous welcome and they went down the passage towards the drawing-room. They must at once inaugurate their home-coming, Gregory said, by going out on the balcony and looking at the view together.

"I beg your pardon, sir," said Barker, who followed after them, "but I hope you and Mrs. Jardine will think it best what I've done with the large case, sir, that has come. I didn't know where you'd like it put, and it was a job getting it in anywhere. There wasn't room to leave it standing here."

"Tante's present!" Karen exclaimed. "Oh, where is it?"

"I had it put in the drawing-room, Ma'am," said Barker. "It made a hole in the wall and knocked down two prints, sir; I'm very sorry, but there was no handling it conveniently."

They turned down the next passage; the drawing-room was at the end. Gregory threw open the door and he and Karen paused upon the threshold. Standing in the middle of the room, high and dark against the half-obliterated windows, was a huge packing-case, an incredibly huge packing-case. At a first glance it had blotted out the room. The furniture, huddled in the corners, seemed to have drawn back from the apparition, scared and startled, and Gregory, in confronting it, felt an actual twinge of fear. The vast, unexpected form loomed to his imagination, for a moment, like a tidal-wave rising terrifically in familiar surroundings and poised in menace above him and his wife. He controlled an exclamation of dismay, and the ominous simile receded before a familiar indignation; that, too, he controlled; he could not say: "How stupid!"

"Is it a piano?" Karen, after their long pause, asked in a hushed, tentative voice.

"It's too high for a piano, darling," said Gregory, who had her arm in his—"and I have my little upright, you see. I can't imagine."

"Shall I get the porter, sir, to help open it while you and Mrs. Jardine have tea?" Barker asked. "I laid tea in the dining-room, Ma'am."

"Yes; let us have it opened at once," said Karen. "But I

must be here when it is opened." She drew her arm from Gregory's and made the tour of the case. "It is probably something very fragile and that is why it is packed in such a great box; it cannot itself be so big."

"Barker will begin peeling off the outer husks while we get ready for tea; we shall have plenty of time," said Gregory. "Get the porter up at once, Barker. I'm afraid your guardian has an exaggerated idea of the size of our domain, darling. The present looks as if only baronial halls could accommodate it."

She glanced up at him while he led her to their room and he knew that something in his voice struck her; he had n't been able to control it and it sounded like ill-temper. Perhaps it was ill-temper. It was with a feeling of relief, and almost of escape, that he shut the door of the room upon tidal-waves and put his arms around his wife. "Darling," he said, "this is really it — at last — our home-coming."

She returned his clasp and kiss with her frank, sweet fervour, though he saw in her eyes a slight bewilderment. He insisted — he had often during their travels been her maid — on taking off her hat and shoes for her before going into his adjoining dressing-room. Karen always protested. "It is so dear and foolish; I am so used to waiting on myself; I am so unused to being the fine idle lady." And she protested now, adding, as he knelt before her, and putting her hand on his head: "And besides, I believe that in some ways I am stronger than you. It should not be you to take care of me."

"Stronger? In what ways? Upon my word, Madam!" Gregory exclaimed smiling up at her, "Do you know that I was one of the best men of my time at Oxford?"

"I don't mean in body, I mean in feelings, in nerves," said Karen. "It is more like Tante."

He wondered, while in his little dressing-room he splashed restoringly in hot water, what she quite did mean. Did she guess at the queer, morbid moment that had struck at his blissful mood? It was indeed disconcerting to have her find him like Tante.

11

"Do you mind," said Karen, when he joined her again, smiling at him and clasping her hands in playful entreaty, "seeing at once what the present is before we have tea? I do not know how I could eat tea while I had not seen it."

"Mind? I'm eager to see it, too," said Gregory, with a pang of self-reproach. "Of course we must wait tea."

The porter, in the passage, was carrying away the outer boards of the packing-case and in the drawing-room they found Barker, knee deep in straw, ripping the heavy sacking covering that enveloped a much diminished but still enormous parcel.

Gregory came to his aid. They drew forth fine shavings and unwrapped layers of paper, neatly secured; slowly the core of the mystery disclosed itself in a temple-like form with a roof of dull black lacquer and dimly gilded inner walls, a thickly swathed figure wedged between them. The gift was, they now perceived, a Chinese Bouddha in his shrine, and, as Gregory and Barker disengaged the figure and laid it upon the ground, amusement, though still of an acrid sort, overcame Gregory's vexation. "A Bouddha, upon my word!" he said. "This is a gorgeous gift."

Karen stooped to help unroll as if from a mummy, the multitudinous bandages of fine paper; the passive bronze visage of the idol was revealed, and by degrees, the seated figure, ludicrously prone. They moved the temple to the end of the room, where two pictures were taken down and a sofa pushed away to make room for it; the Bouddha was hoisted, with difficulty, on to its lotus, and there, dark on its glimmering background of gold, it sat and ambiguously blessed them.

Karen had worked with them neatly and expeditiously, and in silence, and Gregory, glancing at her face from time to time, felt sure that she was adjusting herself to a mingled bewilderment and disappointment; to the wish also, that she might be worthy of her new possession. She stood now before the Bouddha and gazed at it.

They had turned up the electric lights, but the curtains were not drawn and the scent, and light, and vague, diffused roar of London at this evening hour came in at the open windows. Barker, the porter and the housemaid were carrying away the litter of paper and straw. The bright cheerful room with its lovable banality and familiar comfort smiled its welcome; and there, in the midst, the majestic and alien presence sat, overpowering, and grotesque in its inappropriateness.

Karen now turned her eyes on her husband and slightly smiled. "It is very wonderful," she said, "but I feel as if Tante expected a great deal of me in giving it to me — a great deal more than is in me. It ought to be a very deep and mystic person to have that Bouddha."

"Yes, it's a wonderful thing; quite awesome. Perhaps she expects you to become deep and mystic," said Gregory. "Please don't."

"There is no danger of that," said Karen. "Of course it is the beauty of it and the strangeness, that made Tante care for it. It is the sort of thing she would love to have herself."

"Where on earth is he to go?" Gregory surmised. "Yes, he might look well in that big music-room at Les Solitudes, or in some vast hall where he would be more of an episode and less of a white elephant. I hardly thing he'll fit anywhere into the passage," he ventured.

Karen had been looking from him to the Bouddha. "But Gregory, of course he must stay here," she said, "in the room we live in. Tante, I am sure, meant that." Her voice had a tremor. "I am sure it would hurt her dreadfully if we put him out of the way."

Barker was now gone and Gregory put his arm around her. "But it makes all the room wrong, does n't it? It will make us all wrong — that's what I rather feel. We are n't à la hauteur." He remembered, after speaking them, that these were the words he had used of his one colloquy with Madame von Marwitz.

"I don't think," said Karen after a moment, "that you are quite kind."

"Darling — I'm only teasing you," said Gregory. "I'll like the thing if you want me to, and make offerings to him every morning — he looks in need of sacrifices and offerings, does n't he? And what a queer Oriental scent is in the air. Rather nice, that."

"Please don't call it the 'thing,'" said Karen. He saw into her divided loyalty. And his comfort was to know that she did n't like the Bouddha either.

"I won't," he promised. "It is n't a thing, but a duty, a privilege, a responsibility. He shall stay here, where he is. He really won't crowd us too impossibly, and that sofa can go."

"You see," said Karen, and tears now came to her eyes, "it would hurt her so dreadfully if she could dream that we did not love it very, very much."

"I know," said Gregory, kissing her. "I perfectly understand. We will love it very, very much. Come now, you must be hungry; let us have our tea."

CHAPTER XVII

MADAME VON MARWITZ sat in the deep chintz sofa with Karen beside her, and while she talked to the young couple, Karen's hand in hers, her eyes continually went about the room with an expression that did not seem to match her alert, if rather mechanical, conversation. Karen had already seen her, the day before, when she had gone to the station to meet her and had driven with her to Mrs. Forrester's. But Miss Scrotton had been there, too, almost tearful in her welcoming back of her great friend, and there had been little opportunity for talk in the carriage. Tante had smiled upon her, deeply, had held her hand, closely, and had asked, with the playful air which forestalls gratitude, how she liked her present. "You will see it, my Scrotton; a Bouddha in his shrine — of the best period; a thing really rare and beautiful. Mr. Asprey told me of it, at a sale in New York; and I was able to secure it. *Hein, ma petite;* you were pleased? "

" Oh, Tante, my letter told you that," said Karen.

" And your husband? He was pleased? "

" He thought that it was gorgeous," said Karen, but after a momentary hesitation not lost upon her guardian.

" I was sorely tempted to keep it myself," said Madame von Marwitz. " I could see it in the music-room at Les Solitudes. But at once I felt — it is Karen's. My only anxiety was for its background. I have never seen Mr. Jardine's flat. But I knew that I could trust the man my child had chosen to have beauty about him."

" It is n't exactly a beautiful room," Karen confessed, smiling. " It is n't like the music-room; you won't expect that from a London flat — or from us. But it is very bright and comfortable and, yes, pretty. I hope that you will like my home."

Miss Scrotton, Karen felt, while she made these preparatory statements, had eyed her in a somewhat gaunt manner; but she was accustomed to a gaunt manner from Miss Scrotton, and Miss Scrotton's drawing-room, certainly, was not as nice as Gregory's. Karen had not cared at all for its quality of earnest effort. Miss Scrotton, not many years ago, had been surrounded with art-tinted hangings and photographs from Rossetti, and the austerity of her eighteenth-century reaction was now almost defiant. Her drawing-room, in its arid chastity, challenged you, as it were, to dare remember the æsthetics of South Kensington.

Karen did not feel that Gregory's drawing-room required apologies and Tante had been so mild and sweet, if also a little absent, that she trusted her to show leniency.

She had, as yet, to-day, said nothing about the Bouddha or the background on which she found him. She talked to Gregory, while they waited for tea, asking him a great many questions, not seeming, always, to listen to his answers. "Ah, yes. Well done. Bravo," she said at intervals, as he told her about their wedding-trip and how he and Karen had enjoyed this or that. When Barker brought in the tea-tray and set it on a little table before Karen, she took up one of the cups — they were of an old English ware with a wreath of roses inside and lines of half obliterated gilt — and said — it was her first comment on the background —"*Tiens, c'est joli.* Is this one of your presents, Karen?"

Karen told her that the tea-set was not a present; it had belonged to a great-grandmother of Gregory's.

Madame von Marwitz continued to examine the cup and, as she set it down among the others, with the deliberate nicety of gesture that gave at once power and grace to her slightest movement, she said: "You were fortunate in your great-grandmother, Mr. Jardine."

Her voice, her glance, her gestures, were already affecting Gregory unpleasantly. There was in them a quality of considered control, as though she recognised difficulty and were gently and warily evading it. Seated on his chintz sofa in the

bright, burnished room, all in white, with a white lace head-
dress, half veil, half turban, binding her hair and falling on
her shoulders, she made him think, in her inappropriateness
and splendour, of her own Bouddha, who, in his glimmering
shrine, lifted his hand as if in a gesture of bland exorcism before which the mirage of a vulgar and trivial age must presently
fade away. The Bouddha looked permanent and the room
looked transient; the only thing in it that could stand up
against him, as it were, was Karen. To her husband's eye,
newly aware of æsthetic discriminations, Karen seemed to interpret and justify her surroundings, to show their commonplace as part of their charm and to make the Bouddha and
Madame von Marwitz herself, in all their portentous distinction,
look like incidental ornaments.

Madame von Marwitz's silence in regard to the Bouddha had
already become a blight, but it was, perhaps, the growing crisp
decision in Gregory's manner that made Karen first aware of
constraint. Her eyes then turned from Tante to the shrine
at the end of the room, and she said: "You don't care for the
way it looks here, Tante, do you — your present?"

Madame von Marwitz had finished her tea and she turned in
the sofa so that she could consider the Bouddha no longer
incidentally but decisively. "I am glad that it is yours, *ma
chérie*," she said, after the pause of her contemplation. "Some
day you must place it more happily. You don't intend, do
you, Mr. Jardine, to live for any length of time in these
rooms?"

"Oh, but I like it here so much, Tante," Karen took upon
herself the reply. "I want to go on living where Gregory has
lived for so long. We have such a view, you see; and such air."

Madame von Marwitz mused upon her for a moment and
then giving her chin a little pinch, half meditative, half caress-
ing, she inquired, with Continental frankness: "A very pretty
sentiment, *ma petite*, but what will you do when the babies
come?"

Karen was not disconcerted. "I rather hope we may not
have babies for a year or two, Tante; and when they do come

there will be room, quite happily, for several. You don't know how big the flat is; you will see. Gregory has always been able to put up his married sister and her husband; that gives us one quite big room over and a small one."

"But then you can have no friends if your rooms are full of babies," Madame von Marwitz objected, still with mild playfulness.

"No," Karen had to admit it; "but while they were very small I do not think I should have much time for friends in the house, should I. And we think, Gregory and I, of soon taking a tiny cottage in the country, too."

"Then, while you remain here, and unless my Bouddha is to look very foolish," said Madame von Marwitz, "you must, I think, change your drawing-room. It can be changed," she gazed about her with a touch of wildness. "Something could be done. It could be darkened; quieted; it talks too much and too loudly now, does it not? But you could move these so large chairs and couches away and have sober furniture, of a good period; one can still pick up good things if one is clever; a Chinese screen here and there; a fine old mirror; a touch of splendour; a flavour of dignity. The shape of the room is not impossible; the outlook, as you say, gives space and breathing; something could be done."

Karen's gaze followed hers, cogitating but not acquiescent. "But you see, Tante," she remarked, "these are things that Gregory has lived with. And I like them so, too. I should not like them changed."

"But they are not things that you have lived with, *parbleu!*" said Madame von Marwitz laughing gently. "It is a pretty sentiment, *ma petite,* it does you honour; you are — but oh! so deeply — the wife, already, are you not, my Karen? but I am sure that your husband will not wish you to sacrifice your taste to your devotion. Young men, many of them do not care for these domestic matters; do not see them. My Karen must not pretend to me that she does not care and see. I am right, am I not, Mr. Jardine? you would not wish to deprive Karen of the bride's distinctive pleasure — the furnishing of her own nest."

Gregory's eyes met hers; — it seemed to be their second long encounter; — eyes like jewels, these of Madame von Marwitz; full of intense life, intense colour, still, bright and cold, tragically cold. He seemed to see suddenly that all the face — the long eyebrows, with the plaintive ripple of irregularity bending their line, the languid lips, the mournful eyelids, the soft contours of cheek and throat,— were a veil for the coldness of her eyes. To look into them was like coming suddenly through dusky woods to a lonely mountain tarn, lying fathomless and icy beneath a moonlit sky. Gregory was aware, as if newly and more strongly than before, of how ambiguous was her beauty, how sinister her coldness.

Above the depths where these impressions were received was his consciousness that he must be careful if Karen were not to guess how much he was disliking her guardian. It was not difficult for him to smile at a person he disliked, but it was difficult not to smile sardonically. This was an apparently trivial occasion on which to feel that it was a contest that she had inaugurated between them; but he did feel it. "Karen knows that she can burn everything in the room as far as I'm concerned," he said. "Even your Bouddha," he added, smiling a little more nonchalantly, "I'd gladly sacrifice if it gave her pleasure."

Nothing was lost upon Madame von Marwitz, of that he was convinced. She saw, perhaps, further than he did; for he did not see, nor wish to, beyond the moment of guarded hostility. And it was with the utmost gentleness and precaution, with, indeed, the air of one who draws softly aside from a sleeping viper found upon the path, that she answered: "I trust, indeed, that it may never be my Karen's pleasure, or yours, Mr. Jardine, to destroy what is precious; that would hurt me very much. And now, child, may I not see the rest of this beloved domain?" She turned from him to Karen.

Gregory rose; he had told Karen that he would leave them alone after tea; he had letters to write and he would see Madame von Marwitz before she went. He had the sense, as he closed the door, of flying before temptation. What might he not say to Madame von Marwitz if he saw too much of her?

When she and Karen were left alone, Madame von Marwitz's expression changed. The veils of lightness fell away; her face became profoundly melancholy; she gazed in silence at Karen and then held out her arms to her; Karen came closer and was enfolded in their embrace.

"My child, my child," said Madame von Marwitz, leaning, as was her wont at these moments, her forehead against Karen's cheek.

"Dear Tante," said Karen. "You are not sad?" she murmured.

"Sad?" her guardian repeated after a moment. "Am I ever anything but sad? But it is not of my sadness that I wish to speak. It is of you. Are you happy, my dear one?"

"Oh, Tante — so happy, so very happy; more than I can say."

"Is it so?" Madame von Marwitz lifted her head and stroked back the girl's hair. "Is it so indeed? He loves you very much, Karen?"

"Oh, yes, Tante."

"It is a great love? selfless? passionate? It is a love worthy of my child?"

"Yes, indeed." A slight austerity was now apparent in Karen's tone. Silence fell between them for a moment, and then, stroking again the golden head, Madame von Marwitz continued, with great tenderness; "It is well. It is what I have prayed for — for my child. And let me not cast one shadow, even of memory, upon your happiness. Yet ah — ah Karen — if you could have let me share in the sunshine a little. If you could have remembered how dark was my way, how lonely. That my child should have married without me. It hurts. It hurts —"

She did not wish to cast a shadow, yet she was weeping, the silent, undisfigured weeping that Karen knew so well, showing only in the slow welling of tears from darkened eyes.

"Oh, Tante," Karen now leaned her head to her guardian's shoulder, "I did not dream you would mind so much. It was so difficult to know what to do."

"Have I shown myself so indifferent to you in the past, my Karen, that you should have thought I would not mind?"

"I do not mean that, Tante. I thought that you would feel that it was what it was best for me to do. I had given my word. All the plans were made."

"You had given your word? Would he not have let you put me before your word? For once? For that one time in all our lives?"

"It was not that, Tante. Gregory would have done what I wished. You must not think that I was forced in any way." Karen now had raised her head. "But we had waited for you. We thought that you were coming. It was only at the last moment that you let us know, Tante, and you did not even say when you were coming back."

Madame von Marwitz kept silence for some moments after this, savouring perhaps in the words — though Karen's eyes, in speaking them, had also filled with tears — some hint of resistance. She looked away from the girl, keeping her hand in hers, as she said: "I could not come. I could not tell you when I was to come. There were reasons that bound me; ties; claims; a tangle of troubled human lives — the threads passing through my fingers. No; I was not free; and there I would have had you trust me. No, no, my Karen, we will speak of it no farther. I understand young hearts — they are forgetful; they cannot dwell on the shadowed places. Let us put it aside, the great grief. What surprises me is to find that the littlest, littlest ones cling so closely. I am foolish, Karen. I have had much to bear lately, and I cannot shake off the little griefs. That others than myself should have chosen my child's trousseau; oh, it is small — so very small a thing; yet it hurts; it hurts. That the joy of seeking all the pretty clothes together — that, that, too, should have been taken from me. Do not weep, child."

"Tante, you could not come, and the things had to be made ready. They all — Mrs. Forrester — Betty — seemed to feel there was no time to lose. And I have always chosen my own clothes; I did not know that you would feel this so."

"Betty? Who is Betty?" Madame von Marwitz mournfully yet alertly inquired.

"Lady Jardine, Gregory's sister-in-law. You remember, Tante, I have written of her. She has been so kind."

"Betty," Madame von Marwitz repeated, sadly. "Yes, I remember; she was at your wedding, I think. There, dry your eyes, child. I understand. It is a loving heart, but it forgot. The sad old Tante was crowded out by new friends — new joys."

"No, you must not say that, Tante. It is not true."

The hardness that Madame von Marwitz knew how to interpret was showing itself on Karen's face, despite the tears. Her guardian rose, passing her arm around her shoulders. "It is not true, then, *chérie*. When one is very sad one is foolish. Ah, I know it; one imagines too quickly things that are not true. They float and then they cling, like the tiny barbed down of the thistle, and then, behold, one's brain is choked with thorny weeds. That is how it comes, my Karen. Forgive me. There; kiss me."

"Darling Tante," Karen murmured, clasping her closely. "Nothing, nothing crowded you out. Nothing could ever crowd you out. Say that you believe me. Say that all the thistles are rooted up and thrown away."

"Rooted up and burned — burned root and branch, my child. I promise it. I trust my child; she is mine; my loving one. *Ainsi soit-il.* And now," Madame von Marwitz spoke with sudden gaiety, "and now show me your home, my Karen, show me all over this home of yours to which already you are so attached. Ah — it is a child in love!"

They went from room to room, their arms around each other's waists. Madame von Marwitz cast her spell over Mrs. Barker in the kitchen, and smiled a long smile upon Rose, the housemaid. "Yes, yes, very nice, very pretty," she said, in the spareroom, the little dressing-room, the dining-room and kitchen. In Karen's room, with its rose-budded chintz and many photographs of herself, of Gregory, she paused and looked about. "Very, very pretty," she repeated. "You like bedsteads of brass, my Karen?"

"Yes, Tante. They look so clean and bright."

"So clean and bright. I do not think that I could sleep in brass," Madame von Marwitz mused. "But it is a simple child."

"Yes, that is just it, Tante," said Karen, smiling. "And I wanted to explain to you about the drawing-room. You see it is that; I am simple; not a sea-anemone of taste, like you. I quite well see things. I see that Les Solitudes is beautiful, and that this is not like Les Solitudes. Yet I like it here just as it is."

"Because it is his, is it not so, my child-in-love? Ah, she must not be teased. You can be happy, then, among so much brass? — so many things that glitter and are highly coloured?"

"Yes, indeed. And it is a pretty bedroom, Tante. You must say that it is a pretty bedroom?"

"Is it? Must I? Pretty? Yes, no doubt it is pretty. Yet I could have wished that my Karen's nest had more distinction, expressed a finer sense of personality. I imagine that every young woman in this vast beehive of homes has just such a bedroom."

"You think so, Tante? I am afraid that if you think this like everybody's room you will find Gregory's library even worse. You must see that now; it is all that you have not seen." Karen took her last bull by the horns, leading her out.

"Has it red wall-paper, sealing-wax red; with racing prints on the walls and a very large photograph over the mantelpiece of a rowing-crew at Oxford?" Madame von Marwitz questioned with a mixture of roguishness and resignation.

"Yes, yes, you wicked Tante. How did you know?"

"I know; I see it," said Madame von Marwitz. "But a man's room expresses a man's past. One cannot complain of that."

They went to the library. Madame von Marwitz had described it with singular accuracy. Gregory rose from his letters and his eyes went from her face to Karen's, both showing their traces of tears.

"It is *au revoir,* then," said Madame von Marwitz, standing before him, her arm round Karen's shoulders. "I am happy in my child's happiness, Mr. Jardine. You have made her happy, and I thank you. You will lend her to me, sometimes? You will be generous with me and let me see her?"

"Of course; whenever you want to; whenever she wants to," said Gregory, leaning his hands on the back of his chair and tilting it a little while he smiled the fullest acquiescence.

Madame von Marwitz's eyes brooded on him. "That is kind," she said gently.

"Oh no, it isn't," Gregory returned.

"I think," said Madame von Marwitz, becoming even more gentle, "that you misunderstand my meaning. When people love, it is hard sometimes not to be selfish in the joy of love, and the lesser claims tend to be forgotten. I only ask that you should make it easy for Karen to come to me."

To this Gregory did not reply. He continued to tilt his chair and to smile at Madame von Marwitz.

"This husband of yours, Karen," said Madame von Marwitz, "does not understand me yet. You must interpret me to him. Adieu, Mr. Jardine. Will you come with me alone to the door, Karen. It is our first farewell in a home I do not give you."

She gave Gregory her hand. They left him and went down the passage together. Madame von Marwitz kept her arm round the girl's shoulders, but its grasp had tightened.

"My child! my own child!" she murmured, as, at the door, she turned and clasped her. Her voice strove with deep emotion.

"Dear, dear Tante," said Karen, also with a faltering voice.

Madame von Marwitz achieved an uncertain smile. "Farewell, my dear one. I bless you. My blessing be upon you." Then, on the threshold she paused. "Try to make your husband like me a little, my Karen," she said.

Karen did not come back to him in the smoking-room and Gregory presently got up and went to look for her. He found her in the drawing-room, sitting in the twilight, her elbow on her knee, her chin in her hand. He did not know what she could be feeling; the fact that dominated in his own mind was that her guardian had made her weep.

"Well, darling," he said. He stooped over her and put his hand on her shoulder.

The face she lifted to him was ambiguous. She had not wept again; on the contrary, he felt sure that she had been intently thinking. The result of her thought, now, was a look of resolute serenity. But he was sure that she did not feel serene. For the first time, Karen was hiding her feeling from him. " Well, darling," she replied.

She got up and put her arms around his neck; she looked at him, smiling calmly; then, as if struck by a sudden memory, she said: " It is the night of the dance, Gregory."

They were to dine at Edith Morton's and go on to Karen's first dance. Under Betty's supervision she had already made progress through half-a-dozen lessons, though she had not, she confessed to Gregory, greatly distinguished herself at them. " *I'll* get you round all right," he had promised her. They looked forward to the dance.

" So it is," said Gregory. " It's not time to dress yet, is it?"

" It's only half-past six. Shall I wear my white silk, Gregory, with the little white rose wreath?"

" Yes, and the nice little square-toed white silk shoes — like a Reynolds lady's — and like nobody else's. I do so like your square toes."

" I cannot bear pinched toes," said Karen. " My father gave me a horror of that; and Tante. Her feet are as perfect as her hands. She has all her shoes made for her by a wonderful old man in Vienna who is an artist in shoes. She was looking well, wasn't she, Tante?" Karen added, in even tones. Gregory and she were sitting now on the sofa together, their arms linked and hand-in-hand.

" Beautiful," said Gregory with sincerity. " How well that odd head-dress became her."

" Didn't it? It was nice that she liked those pretty tea-cups, wasn't it. And appreciated our view; even though," Karen smiled, taking now another bull by the horns, " she was so hard on our flat. I'm afraid she feels her Bouddha *en travestie* here."

" Well, he is, of course. I do hope," said Gregory, also seizing his bull, " that she didn't think me rude in my joke about being willing to burn him. And you will change everything — burn anything — barring the Bouddha and the tea-cups — that you want to, won't you, dear?"

"No; I wouldn't, even if I wanted to; and I don't want to. Perhaps Tante did not quite understand. I think it may take a little time for her to understand your jokes or you her outspokenness. She is like a child in her candour about the things she likes or dislikes." A fuller ease had come to her voice. By her brave pretence that all was well she was persuading herself that all could be made well.

Perhaps it might be, thought Gregory, if only he could go on keeping his temper with Madame von Marwitz and if Karen, wise and courageous darling, could accept the unspoken between them, and spare him definitions and declarations. A situation undefined is so often a situation saved. Life grows over and around it. It becomes a mere mummied fly, preserved in amber; unsightly perhaps; but unpernicious. After all, he told himself — and he went on thinking over the incidents of the afternoon while he dressed — after all, Madame von Marwitz might not be much in London; she was a comet and her course would lead her streaming all over the world for the greater part of her time. And above all and mercifully, Madame von Marwitz was not a person upon whose affections one would have to count. He seemed to have found out all sorts of things about her this afternoon: he could have given Sargent points. The main strength of her feeling for anyone, deep instinct told him, was an insatiable demand that they should feel sufficiently for her. And the chief difficulty — he refused to dignify it by the name of danger — was that Madame von Marwitz had her deep instincts, too, and had, no doubt, found out all sorts of things about him. He did not like her; he had not liked her from the first; and she could hardly fail to feel that he liked her less and less. He was able to do Madame von Marwitz justice. Even a selflessly devoted mother could hardly rejoice wholeheartedly in the marriage of a daughter to a man who disliked herself; and how much less could Madame von Marwitz, who was not a mother and not selflessly devoted to anybody, rejoice in Karen's marriage. She was right in feeling that it menaced her own

position.   He did her justice; he made every allowance for her;
he intended to be straight with her; but the fact that stood out
for Gregory was that, already, she was not straight with him.
Already she was picking surreptitiously, craftily, at his life; and
this was to pick at Karen's.

He would give her a long string and make every allowance for
the vexations of her situation; but if she began seriously to
tarnish Karen's happiness he would have to pull the string
smartly.   The difficulty — he refused to see this as danger either
— was that he could not pull the string upon Madame von
Marwitz without, by the same gesture, upsetting himself as well.

CHAPTER XVIII

THE unspoken, for the first month or so of Madame von Marwitz's return, remained accepted. There were no declarations and no definitions, and Gregory's immunity was founded on something more reassuring than the mere fact that Madame von Marwitz frequently went away. When she was in London, it became apparent, he was to see very little of her, and as long as they did not meet too often he felt that he was, in so far, safe. Madame von Marwitz was tremendously busy. She paid many week-end visits; she sat to Belot — who had come to London to paint it — for a great portrait; she was to give three concerts in London during the winter and two in Paris, and it was natural enough that she had not found time to come to the flat again.

But although Gregory saw so little of her, although she was not in his life as a presence, he felt her in it as an influence. She might have been the invisible but portentous comet moving majestically on the far confines of his solar system; and one accounted for oddities of behaviour in the visible planets by inferring that the comet was the cause of them. If he saw very little of Madame von Marwitz, he saw, too, much less of his twin planet, Karen. It was not so much that Karen's course was odd as that it was altered. If Madame von Marwitz sent for her very intermittently, she had, all the same, in all her life, as she told Gregory, never seen so much of her guardian. She frankly displayed to him the radiance of her state, wishing him, as he guessed, to share to the full every detail of her privileges, and to realise to the full her gratitude to him for proving so conclusively to Tante that there was none of the selfishness of love in him. Tante must see that he made it very easy for her to go to her, and Gregory derived his own secret satisfaction from the thought that Karen's radiance was the best of retorts to Madame

von Marwitz's veiled intimations. As long as she made Karen
happy and let him alone, he seemed to himself to tell her, he
would get on very well; and he suspected that her clutch of
Karen would soon loosen when she found it unchallenged. In
the meantime there was not much satisfaction for him elsewhere.
Karen's altered course left him often lonely. Not only had the
readings of Political Economy, begun with so much ardour in
in their spare evenings, almost lapsed for lack of consecutive-
ness; but he frequently found on coming home tired for his tea,
and eager for the sight of his wife, a little note from her telling
him that she had been summoned to Mrs. Forrester's as Tante
was "with Fafner in his cave" and wanted her.

Fafner was the name that Madame von Marwitz gave to her
moods of sometimes tragic and sometimes petulant melancholy.
Karen had told him all about Fafner and how, in the cave, Tante
would lie sometimes for long hours, silent, her eyes closed, holding her hand; sometimes asking her to read to her, English,
French, German or Italian poetry; their range of reading always
astonished Gregory.

He gathered, too, from Karen's confidences, how little, until
now, he had gauged the variety of the great woman's resources,
how little done justice to her capacity for being merely delightful. She could be whimsically gay in the midst of melancholy,
and her jests and merriment were the more touching, the more
exquisite, from the fact that they flowered upon the dark background of the cave. It was, he saw, with a richer flavour that
Karen tasted again the charm of old days, when, after some great
musical or social event, in which the girl had played her part
of contented observer, they had laughed together over follies and
appreciated qualities, in the familiar language of allusion evolved
from long community in experience.

Karen repeated to him Tante's sallies at the expense of this
or that person and the phrase with which she introduced these
transformations of human foolishness to the service of comedy.
" Come, let us make *méringues* of them."

The dull or ludicrous creatures, so to be whipped up and baked
crisp, revealed, in the light of the analogy, the tempting vacuity

of a bowl of white of egg. When Tante introduced her wit into
the colourless substance she frothed it to a sparkling work of art.

Gregory was aware sometimes of a pang as he listened. He
and Karen had, indeed, their many little jokes, and their stock
of common association was growing; but there was nothing like
the range of reference, nothing like the variety of experience,
that her life with Madame von Marwitz had given her to draw
upon. It was to her companionship, intermittent as it had been,
with the world-wandering genius that she owed the security of
judgment that often amused yet often disconcerted him, the
catholicity of taste beside which, though he would not acknowl-
edge its final validity, he felt his own taste to be sometimes
narrow and sometimes guileless. He saw that Karen had every
ground for feeling her own point of view a larger one than his.
It was no personal complacency that her assurance expressed,
but the modest recognition of privilege. Beyond their personal
tie, so her whole demeanour showed him, he had nothing to add
to her highly dowered life.

Gregory had known that his world would mean nothing to
Karen; yet when, under Betty's guidance, she fulfilled her social
duties, dined out, gave dinners, received and returned visits, the
very compliance of her indifference, while always amusing, vexed
him a little, and a little alarmed him, too. He had known that
he would have to make all the adjustments, but how adjust oneself to a permanent separation between one's private and one's
social life? Old ties, lacking new elements of growth, tended to
become formalities. When Karen was not there, he did not care
to go without her to see people, and when she was with him the
very charm of her personality was a barrier between him and
them. His life became narrower as well as lonelier. There was
nothing much to be done with people to whom one's wife was
indifferent.

It was very obvious to him that she found the sober, conventional people who were his friends very flavourless, especially
when she came to them from Fafner's cave. He had always
taken his friends for granted, as part of the pleasant routine of
life, like one's breakfast or one's bath; but now, seeing them

anew, through Karen's eyes, he was inclined more and more to
believe that they were n't as dull as she found them. She lacked
the fundamental experience of a rooted life. She was yet to
learn — he hoped, he determined, she should learn — that a
social system of harmonious people, significant perhaps more because of their places in the system than as units, and bound together by a highly evolved code, was, when all was said and done,
a more satisfactory place in which to spend one's life than an
anarchic world of erratic, undisciplined, independent individuals.
Karen, however, did not understand the use of the system and
she saw its members with eyes as clear to their defects as were
Gregory's to the defects of Madame von Marwitz.

Gregory's friends belonged to that orderly and efficient section
of the nation that moves contentedly between the simply professional and the ultra fashionable. They had a great many
duties, social, political and domestic, which they took with a
pleasant seriousness, and a great many pleasures which they took
seriously, too. They " came up " from the quiet responsibilities
of the country-side for a season and " did " the concerts and
exhibitions as they " did " their shopping and their balls.   Art,
to most of them, was a thing accepted on authority, like the
latest cut for sleeves or the latest fashion for dressing the hair.
A few of them, like the Cornish Lavingtons, had never heard
Madame Okraska; a great many of them had never heard of
Belot.   The Madame Okraskas and the Belots of the world were
to them a queer, alien people, regarded with only a mild, derivative interest.   They recognized the artist as a decorative appur-
tenance of civilized life, very much as they recognized the dentist
or the undertaker as its convenient appurtenances.   It still
struck them as rather strange that one should meet artists socially and, perhaps, as rather regrettable, their traditional
standard of good faith requiring that the people one met socially
should, on the whole, be people whom one wouldn't mind one's
sons and daughters marrying; and they did n't conceive of artists
as entering that category.

Gregory, with all his acuteness, did not gauge the astonishment with which Karen came to realize these standards of his

world. Her cheerful evenness of demeanour was a cloak, sometimes for indignation and sometimes for mirth. She could only
face the fact that this world must, in a sense, be hers, by relegating it and all that it meant to the merest background in their
lives. Her real life consisted in Gregory; in Tante. All that
she had to do with these people — oh, so nice and kind they were,
she saw that well, but oh so stupid, most of them, so inconceivably blind to everything of value in life — all that she had to
do was, from time to time, to open their box, their well-padded,
well-provendered box, and look at them pleasantly. She felt
sure that for Gregory's sake, if not for theirs, she should always
be able to look pleasantly; unless — she had been afraid of this
sometimes — they should say or do things that in their blindness
struck at Tante and at the realities that Tante stood for. But
all had gone so well, so Karen believed, that she felt no mis-
givings when Tante expressed a wish to look into the box with
her and said, " You must give a little dinner-party for me, my
Karen, so that I may see your new *milieu.*"

Gregory controlled a dry little grimace when Karen reported
this speech to him. He couldn't but suspect Tante's motives in
wanting them to give a little dinner-party for her. But he
feigned the most genial interest in the plan and agreed with
Karen that they must ask their very nicest to meet Tante.

Betty had helped Karen with all her dinners; she had seen
as yet very little of the great woman, and entered fully into
Karen's eagerness that everything should be very nice.

" Gregory will take her in," said Betty; " and we'll put
Bertram Fraser on her other side. He's always delightful.
And we'll have the Canning-Thompsons and the Overtons and
the Byngs; the Byngs are so decorative! " Constance Armytage
was now Mrs. Byng.

" And my dear old General," said Karen, sitting at her desk
with a paper on her knee and an obedient pencil in her hand;
" I forget his name, but we met him at the dinner that you gave
after we married; you know, Betty, with the thin russet face and
the little blue eyes. May he take me in? "

" General Montgomery. Yes; that is a good idea; glorious

old man. Though Lady Montgomery is rather a stodge," said
Betty; " but Oliver can have her."

"I remember, a sleek, small head—like a turtle—with
salmon-pink feathers on it. Poor Oliver. Will he mind?"

"Not a bit. He never minds anything but the dinner; and
with Mrs. Barker we can trust to that."

"Tante often likes soldiers," said Karen, pleased with her
good idea. " Our flags, she says, they are, and that the world
would be drab-coloured without them."

So it was arranged. Bertram Fraser was an old family friend
of the Jardines'. His father was still the rector of their Northumberland parish, and he and Gregory and Oliver had hunted
and fished and shot and gone to Oxford together. Bertram had
been a traveller in strange countries since those days, had written one or two clever books and was now in Parliament. The
Overtons, also country neighbours, were fond of music as well
as of hunting, and Mr. Canning-Thompson was an eminent, if
rather ponderous, Q.C., for whose wife, the gentle and emaciated
Lady Mary, Gregory had a special affection. She was a great
philanthropist and a patient student of early Italian art, and
he and she talked gardens and pictures together.

Betty and Oliver were the first to arrive on the festal night,
Betty's efficiency, expressed by all her diamonds and a dress of
rose-coloured velvet, making up for whatever there might be of
inefficiency in Karen's appearance and deportment. Karen was
still, touchingly so to her husband's eyes, the little Hans Andersen heroine in appearance. She wore to-night the white silk
dress and the wreath of little white roses.

Oliver and Gregory chatted desultorily until the Byngs arrived.
Oliver was fair and ruddy and his air of dozing contentment
was always vexatious to his younger brother. He had every
reason for contentment. Betty's money had securely buttressed
the family fortunes and he had three delightful little boys to
buttress Betty's money. Gregory grew a little out of temper
after talking for five minutes to Oliver and this was not a fortunate mood in which to realise, as the Montgomerys, the Overtons
and the Canning-Thompsons followed the Byngs, at eight-fifteen,

that Madame von Marwitz was probably going to be late. At eight-thirty, Karen, looking at him with some anxiety expressed in her raised brows, silently conveyed to him her fear that the soup, at the very least, would be spoiled. At eight-forty Betty murmured to Karen that they had perhaps better begin without Madame von Marwitz — had n't they? She must, for some reason, be unable to come. Dinner was for eight. " Oh, but we must wait longer," said Karen. " She would have telephoned — or Mrs. Forrester would — if she had not been coming. Tante is always late; but always, always," she added, without condemnation if with anxiety. " And there is the bell now. Yes, I heard it."

It was a quarter to nine when Madame von Marwitz, with Karen, who had hastened out to meet her, following behind, appeared at last, benign and unperturbed as a moon sliding from clouds. In the doorway she made her accustomed pause, the pause of one not surveying her audience but indulgently allowing her audience to survey her. It was the attitude in which Belot was painting his great portrait of her. But it was not met to-night by the eyes to which she was accustomed. The hungry guests looked at Madame von Marwitz with austere relief and looked only long enough to satisfy themselves that her appearance really meant dinner.

Gregory led the way with her into the dining-room and suspected in her air of absent musing a certain discomfiture.

She was, as usual, strangely and beautifully attired, as though for the operatic stage rather than for a dinner-party. Strings of pearls fell from either side of her head to her shoulders and a wide tiara of pearls banded her forehead in a manner recalling a Russian head-dress. She looked, though so lovely, also so conspicuous that there was a certain ludicrousness in her appearance. It apparently displeased or surprised Lady Montgomery, who, on Gregory's other hand, her head adorned with the salmon-pink, ostrich feathers, raised a long tortoiseshell lorgnette and fixed Madame von Marwitz through it for a mute, resentful moment. Madame von Marwitz, erect and sublime as a goddess in a shrine,

looked back. It was a look lifted far above the region of Lady
Montgomery's formal, and after all only tentative, disapproba-
tions; divine impertinence, sóvereign disdain informed it. Lady
Montgomery dropped her lorgnette with a little clatter and,
adjusting her heavy diamond bracelets, turned her sleek mid-
Victorian head to her neighbour. Gregory did not know whether
to be amused or vexed.

It was now his part to carry on a conversation with the great
woman: and he found the task difficult. She was not silent, nor
unresponsive. She listened to his remarks with the almost disconcerting closeness of attention that he had observed in her on
their meeting of the other day, seeming to seek in them some
savour that still escaped her good-will. She answered him
alertly, swiftly, and often at random, as though by her intelligence and competence to cover his ineptitude. Her smile was
brightly mechanical; her voice at once insistent and monotonous.
She had an air, which Gregory felt more and more to be almost
insolent, of doing her duty.

Bertram Fraser's turn came and he rose to it with his usual
buoyancy. He was interested in meeting Madame von Marwitz;
but he was a young man who had made his way in the world and
perhaps exaggerated his achievement. He expected people to be
interested also in meeting him. He expected from the great
genius a reciprocal buoyancy. Madame von Marwitz bent her
brows upon him. Irony grew in her smile, a staccato crispness
in her utterance. Cool and competent as he was, Bertram presently looked disconcerted; he did not easily forgive those who
disconcerted him, and, making no further effort to carry on the
conversation, he sat silent, smiling a little, and waited for his
partner to turn to him again. Had Gregory not taken up his
talk, lamely and coldly, with Madame von Marwitz, she would
have been left in an awkward isolation.

She answered him now in a voice of lassitude and melancholy.
Leaning back in her chair, strange and almost stupefying object
that she was, her eyes moved slowly round the table with a wintry
desolation of glance, until, meeting Karen's eyes, they beamed

forth a brave warmth of cherishing, encouraging sweetness.
"Yes, *ma chérie*," they seemed to say; "Bear up, I am bearing
up. I will make *méringues* of them for you."

She could make *méringues* of them; Gregory did n't doubt it.
Yet, and here was the glow of malicious satisfaction that atoned
to him for the discomforts he endured, they were, every one of
them, making *méringues* of her.

In their narrowness, in their defects, ran an instinct, as shrewd
as it was unconscious, that was a match for Madame von Marwitz's intelligence. They were so unperceiving that no one of
them, except perhaps Betty and Karen — who of course did n't
count among them at all — was aware of the wintry wind of
Madame von Marwitz's boredom; yet if it had been recognised
it would have been felt as insignificant. They knew that she
was a genius, and that she was very odd looking and that, as
Mrs. Jardine's guardian, she had not come in a professional
capacity and might therefore not play to them after dinner.
So defined, she was seen, with all her splendour of association,
as incidental.

Only perhaps in this particular section of the British people
could this particular effect of cheerful imperviousness have been
achieved. They were not of the voracious, cultured hordes who
make their way by their well-trained appreciations, nor of the
fashionable lion-collecting tribe who do not need to make their
way but who need to have their way made amusing. Well-bred,
securely stationed, untouched by boredom or anxiety, they were
at once too dull and too intelligent to be fluttered by the presence of a celebrity. They wanted nothing of her, except, perhaps,
that after their coffee she should give them some music, and they
did not want this at all eagerly.

If Madame von Marwitz had come to crush, to subjugate or
to enchant, she had failed in every respect and Gregory saw that
her failure was not lost upon her. Her manner, as the consciousness grew, became more frankly that of the vain, ill-
tempered child, ignored. She ceased to speak; her eyes, fixed on
the wall over Sir Oliver's head, enlarged in a sullen despondency.

Lady Montgomery was making her way through a bunch of

grapes and Lady Mary had only peeled her peach, when, suddenly, taking upon herself the prerogative of a hostess, Madame von Marwitz caught up her fan and gloves with a gesture of open impatience, and swept to the door almost before Gregory had time to reach it or the startled guests to rise from their places.

CHAPTER XIX

WHEN the time came for going to the drawing-room, Gregory found Betty entertaining the company there, while Karen, on a distant sofa, was apparently engaged in showing her guardian a book of photographs. He took in the situation at a glance, and, as he took it in, he was aware that part of its significance lay in the fact that it obliged him to a swift interchange with Betty, an interchange that irked him, defining as it did a community of understanding from which Karen, in her simplicity, was shut out.

He went across to the couple on the sofa. Only sudden illness could have excused Madame von Marwitz's departure from the dining-room, yet he determined to ask no questions, and to leave any explanations to her.

Karen's eyes, in looking at him, were grave and a little anxious; but the anxiety, he saw, was not on his account. "Tante wanted to see our kodaks," she said. "Do sit here with us, Gregory. Betty is talking to everybody so beautifully."

"But you must go and talk to everybody beautifully, too, now, darling," said Gregory. He put his hand on her shoulder and looked down at her smiling. The gesture, with its marital assurance, the smile that was almost a caress, were involuntary; yet they expressed more than his tender pride and solicitude, they defined his possession of her, and they excluded Tante. "It's been a nice little dinner, has n't it," he went on, continuing to look at her and not at Madame von Marwitz. "I saw that the General was enjoying you immensely. There he is, looking over at you now; he wants to go on talking about Garibaldi with you. He said he'd never met a young woman so well up in modern history."

Madame von Marwitz's brooding eyes were on him while he thus spoke. He ignored them.

Karen looked a little perplexed. "Did you think it went so well, then, Gregory?"

"Why, did n't you?"

"I am not sure. I don't think I shall ever much like dinners, when I give them," she addressed herself to her guardian as well as to her husband. "They make one feel so responsible."

"Well, as far as you were responsible for this one you were responsible for its being very nice. Everybody enjoyed themselves. Now go and talk to the General."

"I did enjoy him," said Karen, half closing her book. "But Tante has rather a headache — I am afraid she is tired. You saw at dinner that she was tired."

"Yes, oh yes, indeed, I thought that you must be feeling a little ill, perhaps," Gregory observed blandly, turning his eyes now on Madame von Marwitz. "Well, you see, Karen, I will take your place here, and it will give me a chance for a quiet talk with your guardian."

"People must not bother her," Karen rose, pleased, he could see, with this arrangement, and hoping, he knew, that the opportunity was a propitious one, and that in it her dear ones might draw together. "You will see that they don't bother her, Gregory, and go on showing her these."

"They won't bother a bit, I promise," said Gregory, taking her place as she rose. "They are all very happily engaged, and Madame von Marwitz and I will look at the photographs in perfect peace."

Something in these words and in the manner with which her guardian received them, with a deepening of her long, steady glance, arrested Karen's departure. She stood above them, half confident, yet half hesitating.

"Go, *mon enfant*," said Madame von Marwitz, turning the steady glance on her. "Go. Nobody here, as your husband truly says, is thinking of me. I shall be quite untroubled."

Still with her look of preoccupation Karen moved away.

Cheerfully and deliberately Gregory now proceeded to turn the pages of the kodak album, and to point out with painstaking geniality the charms and associations of each view. "*Tu l'as voulu, Georges Dandin,"* expressed his thought, for he did n't believe that Madame von Marwitz, more than any person not completely self-abnegating, could tolerate looking at other people's kodaks. But since it was her chosen occupation, the best she could find to do with their dinner-party, she should be gratified; should be shown Karen standing on a peak in the Tyrol; Karen feeding the pigeons before St. Mark's; Karen, again — was n't it rather'nice of her? — in a gondola. Madame von Marwitz bent her head with its swinging pearls above the pictures, proffering now and then a low murmur of assent.

But in the midst of the Paris pictures she lifted her head and looked at him. It was again the steady, penetrating look, and now it seemed, with the smile that veiled it, to claim some common understanding rather than seek it. "Enough," she said. She dismissed the kodaks with a tap of her fan. "I wish to talk with you. I wish to talk with you of our Karen."

Gregory closed the volume. Madame von Marwitz's attitude as she leaned back, her arms lightly folded, affected him in its deliberate grace and power as newly significant. Keeping his frosty, observant eyes upon her, Gregory waited for what she had to say. "I am glad, very glad, that you have given me this opportunity for a quiet conversation," so she took up the threads of her intention. "I have wanted, for long, to consult with you about various matters concerning Karen, and, in especial, about her future life. Tell me — this is what I wish in particular to ask you — you are going, are you not, in time, when she has learned more skill in social arts, to take my Karen into the world — *dans le monde*," Madame von Marwitz repeated, as though to make her meaning genially clear. "Skill she is as yet too young to have mastered — or cared to master. But she had always been at ease on the largest stage, and she will do you credit, I assure you."

It was rather, to Gregory's imagination — always quick at similes — as though she had struck a well-aimed blow right in the centre of a huge gong hanging between them. There she was, the blow said. It was this she meant. No open avowal of hostility could have been more reverberating or purposeful, and

no open avowal of hostility would have been so sinister. But
Gregory, though his ears seemed to ring with the clang of it, was
ready for her. He, too, with folded arms, sat leaning back and
he, too, smiled genially. "That's rather crushing, you know,"
he made reply, "or did n't you? Karen is in my world. This
is my world."

Madame von Marwitz gazed at him for a moment as if to
gauge his seriousness. And then she turned her eyes on his
world and gazed at that. It was mildly chatting. It was placid,
cheerful, unaware of deficiency. It thought that it was enjoying
itself. It was, indeed, enjoying itself, if with the slightest of
materials. Betty and Bertram Fraser laughed together; Lady
Mary and Oliver ever so slowly conversed. Constance Byng and
Mr. Overton discussed the latest opera, young Byng had joined
Karen and the General, and a comfortable drone of politics came
from Mrs. Overton and Mr. Canning-Thompson. Removed a
little from these groups Lady Montgomery, very much like a
turtle, sat with her head erect and her eyes half closed, evidently
sleepy. It was upon Lady Montgomery that Madame von Marwitz's gaze dwelt longest.

"You are contented," she then said to Gregory, "with these
good people; for yourself and for your wife?"

"Perfectly," said Gregory. "You see, Karen has married a
commonplace person."

Madame von Marwitz paused again, and again her eyes dwelt
on Lady Montgomery, whose pink feathers had given a sudden
nod and then serenely righted themselves. "I see," she then
remarked. "But she is not contented."

"Ah, come," said Gregory. "You can't shatter the conceit of
a happy husband so easily, Madame von Marwitz. You ask too
much of me if you ask me to believe that Karen makes confidences to you that she does n't to me. I can't take it on, you
know," he continued to smile.

He had already felt that the loveliness of Madame von Marwitz's face was a veil for its coldness, and hints had come to him
that it masked, also, some more sinister quality. And now,
for a moment, as if a primeval creature peeped at him from

among delicate woodlands, a racial savagery crossed her face
with a strange, distorting tremor. The blood mounted to her
brow; her skin darkened curiously, and her eyes became hot
and heavy as though the very irises felt the glow.

"You do not accept my word, Mr. Jardine?" she said. Her
voice was controlled, but he had a disagreeable sensation of
scorching, as though a hot iron had been passed slowly before
his face.

Gregory shook his foot a little, clasping his ankle. "I don't
say that, of course. But I'm glad to think you're mistaken."

"Let me tell you, Mr. Jardine," she returned, still with the
curbed elemental fury colouring her face and voice, "that
even a happy husband's conceit is no match for a mother's intuition. Karen is like my child to me; and to its mother a
child makes confidences that it is unaware of making. Karen
finds your world narrow; borné; it does not afford her the wide
life she has known."

"You mean," said Gregory, "the life she led with Mrs. Talcott?"

He had not meant to say it. If he had paused to think it
over he would have seen that it exposed him to her as consciously hostile and also as almost feminine in his malice. And,
as if this recognition of his false move restored to her her full
self-mastery, she met his irony with a masculine sincerity, putting him, as on the occasion of their first encounter, lamentably
in the wrong. "Ah," she commented, her eyes dwelling on
him. "Ah, I see. You have wondered. You have criticized.
You have, I think, Mr. Jardine, misunderstood my life and its
capacities. Allow me to explain. Your wife is the creature
dearest to me in the world, and if you misread my devotion to
her you endanger our relation. You would not, I am sure, wish
to do that; is it not so? Allow me therefore to exculpate myself. I am a woman who, since childhood, has had to labour
for my livelihood and for that of those I love. You can know
nothing of what that labour of the artist's life entails,— interminable   journeys,   suffocating   ennui,   the   unwholesome
monotony and publicity of a life passed in hotels and trains.

It was not fit that a young and growing girl should share that life. As much as has been possible I have guarded Karen from its dust and weariness. I have had, of necessity, to leave her much alone, and she has needed protection, stability, peace. I could have placed her in no lovelier spot than my Cornish home, nor in safer hands than those of the guardian and companion of my own youth. Do you not feel it a little unworthy, Mr. Jardine, when you have all the present and all the future, to grudge me even my past with my child?"

She spoke slowly, with a noble dignity, all hint of sultry menace passed; willing, for Karen's sake, to stoop to this self-justification before Karen's husband. And, for Karen's sake, she had the air of holding in steady hands their relation, hers and his, assailed so gracelessly by his taunting words. Gregory, for the first time in his knowledge of her, felt a little bewildered. It was she who had opened hostilities, yet she almost made him forget it; she almost made him feel that he alone had been graceless. "I do beg your pardon," he said. "Yes; I had wondered a little about it; and I understand better now." But he gathered his wits together sufficiently to add, on a fairer foothold: "I am sure you gave Karen all you could. What I meant was, I think, that you should be generous enough to believe that I am giving her all I can."

Madame von Marwitz rose as he said this and he also got up. It was not so much, Gregory was aware, that they had fought to a truce as that they had openly crossed swords. Her eyes still dwelt on him, and now as if in a sad wonder. "But you are young. You are a man. You have ambition. You wish to give more to the loved woman."

"I don't really quite know what you mean by more, Madame von Marwitz," said Gregory. "If it applies to my world, I don't expect, or wish, to give Karen a better one."

They stood and confronted each other for a moment of silence.

"*Bien,*" Madame von Marwitz then said, unemphatically, mildly. "*Bien.* I must see what I can do." She turned her eyes on Karen, who, immediately aware of her glance, hastened

to her. Madame von Marwitz laid an arm about her neck.
"I must bid you good-night, *ma chérie*. I am very tired."

"Tante, dear, I saw that you were so tired, I am so sorry.
It has all been a weariness to you," Karen murmured.

"No, my child; no," Madame von Marwitz smiled down into
her eyes, passing her hand lightly over the little white-rose
wreath. "I have seen you, and seen you happy; that is happiness enough for me. Good-night, Mr. Jardine. Karen will
come with me."

Pausing for no further farewells, Madame von Marwitz
passed from the room with a majestic, generalized bending of
the head.

Betty joined her brother-in-law. "Dear me, Gregory," she
said. "We've had the tragic muse to supper, have n't we.
What is the matter, what has been the matter with Madame von
Marwitz? Is she ill?"

"She says she's tired," said Gregory.

"It was disconcerting, was n't it, her trailing suddenly out
of the dining-room in that singular fashion," said Betty. "Do
you know, Gregory, that I 'm getting quite vexed with Madame
von Marwitz."

"Really? Why, Betty?"

"Well, it has been accumulating. I 'm a very easy-going
person, you know; but I 've been noticing that whenever I
want Karen, Madame von Marwitz always nips in and cuts me
out, so that I have hardly seen her at all since her guardian
came to London. And then it did rather rile me, I confess, to
find that the one hat in Karen's trousseau that I specially chose
for her is the one — the only one — that Madame von Marwitz
objects to. Karen never wears it now. She certainly behaved
very absurdly to-night, Gregory. I suppose she expected us to
sit round in a circle and stare."

"Perhaps she did," Gregory acquiesced. "Perhaps we should
have."

He was anxious to maintain the appearance of bland lightness before Betty. Karen had re-entered as they spoke and

Betty called her to them. "Tell me, Karen dear, is Madame von Marwitz ill? She did n't give me a chance to say goodnight to her." Betty had the air of wishing to exonerate herself.

"She is n't ill," said Karen, whose face was grave. "But very tired."

"Now what made her tired, I wonder?" Betty mused. "She looks such a robust person."

It was bad of Betty, and as Karen stood before them, looking from one to the other, Gregory saw that she suspected them. Her face hardened. "A great artist needs to be robust," she said. "My guardian works every day at her piano for five or six hours."

"Dear me," Betty murmured. "How splendid. I'd no idea the big ones had to keep it up like that."

"There is great ignorance about an artist's life," Karen continued coldly to inform her. "Do you not know what von Bulow said: If I miss my practising for one day I notice it; if for two days my friends notice it; if I miss it for three days the public notices it. The artist is like an acrobat, juggling always, intent always on his three golden balls kept flying in the air. That is what it is like. Every atom of their strength is used. People, like my guardian, literally give their lives for the world."

"Oh, yes, it is wonderful, of course," Betty assented. "But of course they must enjoy it; it can hardly be called a sacrifice."

"Enjoy is a very small word to apply to such a great thing," said Karen. "You may say also, if you like, that the saint enjoys his life of suffering for others. It is his life to give himself to goodness; it is the artist's life to give himself to beauty. But it is beauty and goodness they seek, not enjoyment; we must not try to measure these great people by our standards."

Before this arraignment Betty showed a tact for which Gregory was grateful to her. He, as so often, found Karen, in her innocent sententiousness, at once absurd and adorable, but he could grant that to Betty she might seem absurd only.

"Don't be cross with me, Karen," she said. "I suppose I am feeling sore at being snubbed by Madame von Marwitz."

"But indeed she did not mean to snub you, Betty," said Karen earnestly. "And I am not cross; please do not think that. Only I cannot bear to hear some of the things that are said of artists."

"Well, prove that you're not cross," said Betty, smiling, "by at last giving me an afternoon when we can do something together. Will you come and see the pictures at Burlington House with me to-morrow and have tea with me afterwards? I've really seen nothing of you for so long."

"To-morrow is promised to Tante, Betty. I'm so sorry. Her great concert is to be on Friday, you know; and till then, and on the Saturday, I have said that I will be with her. She gets so very tired. And I know how to take care of her when she is tired like that."

"Oh, dear!" Betty sighed. "There is no hope for us poor little people, is there, while Madame von Marwitz is in London. Well, on Monday, then, Karen. Will you promise me Monday afternoon?"

"Monday is free, and I shall like so very much to come, Betty," Karen replied.

When Gregory and his wife were left alone together, they stood for some moments without speaking on either side of the fire, and, as Karen's eyes were on the flames, Gregory, looking at her carefully, read on her face the signs of stress and self-command. The irony, the irritation and the oppression that Madame von Marwitz had aroused in him this evening merged suddenly, as he looked at Karen into intense anger. What had she not done to them already, sinister woman? It was because of her that constraint, reticence and uncertainty were rising again between him and Karen.

"Darling," he said, putting out his hand and drawing her to him; "you look very tired."

She came, he fancied, with at first a little reluctance, but, as

he put his arm around her, she leaned her head against his
shoulder with a sigh. "I am tired, Gregory."

They stood thus for some moments and then, as if the confident tenderness their attitude expressed forced her to face
with him their difficulty, she said carefully: "Gregory, dear,
did you say anything to depress Tante this evening?"

"Why do you ask, darling?" Gregory, after a slight pause,
also carefully inquired.

"Only that she seemed depressed, very much depressed. I
thought, I hoped that you and she were talking so nicely, so
happily."

There was another little pause and then Gregory said: "She
rather depressed me, I think."

"Depressed you? But how, Gregory?"

He must indeed be very careful. It was far too late, now, for
simple frankness; simple frankness had, perhaps, from the beginning been impossible and in that fact lay the insecurity of
his position, and the immense advantage of Madame von Marwitz's. And as he paused and sought his words it was as if, in
the image of the Bouddha, looking down upon him and Karen,
Madame von Marwitz were with them now, a tranquil and
ironic witness of his discomfiture. "Well," he said, "she made
me feel that I had only a very dingy sort of life to offer you
and that my friends were all very tiresome — *borné* was the
word she used. That did rather — well — dash my spirits."

Standing there within his arm, of her face, seen from above,
only the brow, the eyelashes, the cheek visible, she was very still
for a long moment. Then, gently, she said — and in the gentleness he felt that she put aside the too natural suspicion that he
was complaining of Tante behind her back: "She doesn't
realise that I don't care at all about people. And they are
rather *bornés,* aren't they, Gregory."

"I don't find them so," said Gregory, reasonably. "They
aren't geniuses, of course, or acrobats, or saints, or anything of
that sort; but they seem to me, on the whole, a very nice lot of
people."

"Very nice indeed, Gregory. But I don't think it is saints

and geniuses that Tante misses here; she misses minds that are able to recognise genius." Her quick ear had caught the involuntary irony of his quotation.

"Ah, but, dear, you must n't expect to find the average nice person able to pay homage at a dinner-party. There is a time and a place for everything, is n't there."

"It was not that I meant, Gregory, or that Tante meant. There is always a place for intelligence. It was n't an interesting dinner, you must have felt that as well as I, not the sort of dinner Tante would naturally expect. They were only interested in their own things, were n't they? And quite apart from homage, there is such a thing as realisation. Mr. Fraser talked to Tante — I saw it all quite well — as he might have talked to the next dowager he met. Tante is n't used to being talked to as if she were *toute comme une autre;* she is n't *toute comme une autre.*"

"But one must pretend to be, at a dinner-party," Gregory returned. To have to defend his friends when it was Tante who stood so lamentably in need of defence had begun to work upon his nerves. "And some dowagers are as interesting as anybody. There are all sorts of ways of being interesting. Dowagers are as intelligent as geniuses sometimes." His lightness was not unprovocative.

"It is n't funny, Gregory, to see Tante put into a false position."

"But, my dear, we did the best we could for her."

"I know that we did; and our best is n't good enough for her. That is all that I ask you to realise," said Karen.

She was angry, and from the depths of his anger against Madame von Marwitz Gregory felt a little gush of anger against Karen rise. "You are telling me what she told me," he said; "that my best is n't good enough for her. You may say it and think it, of course; but it's a thing that Madame von Marwitz has no right to say."

Karen moved away from his arm. Something more than the old girlish sternness was in the look with which she faced him, though that flashed at him, a shield rather than a weapon. He

recognised the hidden pain and astonishment and his anger faded
in tenderness. How could she but resent and repell any hint
that belittled Tante's claims and justifications? how could she
hear but with dismay the half threat of his last words, the intimation that from her he would accept what he would not accept
from Tante? The sudden compunction of his comprehension
almost brought the tears to his eyes. Karen saw that his resistance melted and the sternness fell from her look. "But
Gregory," she said, her voice a little trembling, "Tante did not
say that. Please don't make mistakes. It is so dreadful to misunderstand; nothing frightens me so much. I say it; that our
best isn't good enough, and I am thinking of Tante; only of
Tante; but she — too sweetly and mistakenly — was thinking
of me. Tante does n't care, for herself, about our world; why
should she? And she is mistaken to care about it for me; because it makes no difference, none at all, to me, if it is *borné*.
All that I care about, you know that, Gregory, is you and
Tante."

Gregory had his arms around her. "Do forgive me, darling,"
he said.

"But was I horrid?" Karen asked.

"No. It was I who was stupid," he said. "Do you know,
I believe we were almost quarrelling, Karen."

"And we can quarrel safely — you and I, Gregory, can't we?"
Karen said, her voice still trembling.

He leaned his head against her hair. "Of course we can.
Only — don't let us quarrel — ever. It is so dreadful."

"Isn't it dreadful, Gregory. But we must not let it frighten
us, ever, because of course we must quarrel now and then. And
we often have already, have n't we," she went on, reassuring him,
and herself. "Do you remember, in the Tyrol, about the black
bread! — And I was right that time.— And the terrible conflict
in Paris, about *La Gaine d'Or;* when I said you were a Philistine."

"Well, you owned afterwards, after you read about the beastly
thing, that you were glad we had n't gone."

"Yes; I was glad. You were right there. Sometimes it is

you and sometimes I," Karen declared, as if that were the happy solution.

So, in their mutual love, they put aside the menacing differ- · ence. Something had happened, they could but be aware of that; but their love tided them over. They did not argue further as to who was right and who wrong that evening.

CHAPTER XX

THE first of Madame von Marwitz's great concerts was given on Friday, and Karen spent the whole of that day and of Saturday with her, summoned by an urgent telephone message early in the morning. On Sunday she was still secluded in her rooms, and Miss Scrotton, breaking in determinedly upon her, found her lying prone upon the sofa, Karen beside her.

"I cannot see you, my Scrotton," said Madame von Marwitz, with kindly yet listless decision. "Did they not tell you below that I was seeing nobody? Karen is with me to watch over my ill-temper. She is a soothing little milk-poultice and I can bear nothing else. I am worn out."

Before poor Miss Scrotton's brow of gloom Karen suggested that she should herself go down to Mrs. Forrester for tea and leave her place to Miss Scrotton, but, with a weary shake of the head, Madame von Marwitz rejected the proposal. "No; Scrotton is too intelligent for me to-day," she said. "You will go down to Mrs. Forrester for your tea, my Scrotton, and wait for another day to see me."

Miss Scrotton went down nearly in tears.

"She refused to see Sir Alliston," Mrs. Forrester said, soothingly. "She really is fit for nothing. I have never seen her so exhausted."

"Yet Karen Jardine always manages to force her way in," said Miss Scrotton, controlling the tears with difficulty. "She has absolutely taken possession of Mercedes. It really is almost absurd, such devotion, and in a married woman. Gregory doesn't like it at all. Oh, I know it. Betty Jardine gave me a hint only yesterday of how matters stand."

"Lady Jardine has always seemed to me a rather trivial little person. I should not accept her impression of a situation," said Mrs. Forrester. "Mercedes sends for Karen constantly. And I

201

am sure that Gregory is glad to think that she can be of use to Mercedes."

" Oh, Betty Jardine thinks, too, that it is Mercedes who takes Karen from her husband. But I really can't agree with her, or with you, dear Mrs. Forrester, there. Mercedes is simply too indolent and kind-hearted to defend herself from the sort of habit the girl has imposed upon her. As for Gregory being grateful I can only assure you that you are entirely mistaken. My own impression is that he is beginning to dislike Mercedes. Oh, he is a very jealous temperament; I have always felt it in him. He is one of those cold, passionate men who become the most infatuated and tyrannical of husbands."

" My dear Eleanor," Mrs. Forrester raised her eyebrows. " I see no sign of tyranny. He allows Karen to come here constantly."

" Yes; because he knows that to refuse would be to endanger his relation to her. Mercedes is angelic to him of course, and does n't give him a chance for making things difficult for Karen. But it is quite obvious to me that he hates the whole situation."

" I hope not," said Mrs. Forrester, gravely now. " I hope not. It would be tragical indeed if this last close relation in Mercedes's life were to be spoiled for her. I could not forgive Gregory if he made it difficult in any way for Karen to be with her guardian."

" Well, as long as he can conceal his jealousy, Mercedes will manage, I suppose, to keep things smooth. But I can't see it as you do, Mrs. Forrester. I can't believe for a moment that Mercedes needs Karen or that the tie is such a close one. She only likes to see her now because she is bored and impatient and unhappy, and Karen is — she said it just now, before the girl — a poultice for her nerves. And the reason for her nerves is n't far to seek. I must be frank with you, dear Mrs. Forrester; you know I always have been, and I 'm distressed, deeply distressed about Mercedes. She expected Claude Drew to be back from America by now and I heard yesterday from that horrid young friend of his, Algernon Bently, that he has again postponed his return. It 's that that agonizes and infuriates Mercedes, it 's that that makes her unwilling to be alone with me. I 've seen too much; I know too much; she fears me, Mrs. Forrester. She knows that I know that Claude Drew is punishing her now for having snubbed him in America."

"My dear Eleanor," Mrs. Forrester murmured distressfully. "You exaggerate that young man's significance."

"Dear Mrs. Forrester," Miss Scrotton returned, almost now with a solemn exasperation, "I wish it were possible to exaggerate it. I watched it grow. His very effrontery fascinates her. We know, you and I, what Mercedes expects in devotion from a man who cares for her. They must adore her on their knees. Now Mr. Drew adored standing nonchalantly on his feet and looking coolly into her eyes. She resented it; she had constantly to put him in his place. But she would rather have him out of his place than not have him there at all. That is what she is feeling now. That is why she is so worn out. She is wishing that Claude Drew would come back from America, and she is wanting to write one letter to his ten and finding that she writes five. He writes to her constantly, I suppose?"

"I believe he does," Mrs. Forrester conceded. "Mercedes is quite open about the frequency of his letters. I am sure that you exaggerate, Eleanor. He interests her, and he charms her if you will. Like every woman, she is aware of devotion and pleased by it. I don't believe it's anything more."

"I believe," said Miss Scrotton, after a moment, and with resolution, "that it's a great passion; the last great passion of her life."

"Oh, my dear!"

"A great passion," Miss Scrotton persisted, "and for a man whom she knows not to be in any way her equal. It is that that exasperates her."

Mrs. Forrester meditated for a little while and then, owning to a certain mutual recognition of facts, she said: "I don't believe that it's a great passion; but I think that a woman like Mercedes, a genius of that scope, needs always to feel in her life the elements of a 'situation'—and life always provides such women with a choice of situations. They are stimulants. Mr. Drew and his like, with whatever unrest and emotion they may cause her, nourish her art. Even a great passion would be a tempest that filled her sails and drove her on; in the midst of it she would never lose the power of steering. She has essentially the strength and detachment of genius. She watches her own emotions and makes use of them. Did you ever hear her play more magnificently than on Friday? If Mr. Drew *y était pour quelque chose,* it was in the sense that she made mincemeat of him and presented us in consequence with a magnificent sausage."

Miss Scrotton, who had somewhat forgotten her personal grievance in the exhilaration of these analyses, granted the sausage and granted that Mercedes made mincemeat of Mr. Drew — and of her friends into the bargain. "But my contention and my fear is," she said, "that he will make mincemeat of her before he is done with her."

Miss Scrotton did not rank highly for wisdom in Mrs. Forrester's estimation; but for her perspicacity and intelligence she had more regard than she cared to admit. Echoes of Eleanor's distrusts and fears remained with her, and, though it was but a minor one, such an echo vibrated loudly on Monday afternoon when Betty Jardine appeared at tea-time with Karen.

It was the afternoon that Karen had promised to Betty, and when this fact had been made known to Tante it was no grievance and no protest that she showed, only a slight hesitation, a slight gravity, and then, as if with cheerful courage in the face of an old sadness: "*Eh bien,*" she said. "Bring her back here to tea, *ma chérie.* So I shall come to know this new friend of my Karen's better."

Betty was not at all pleased at being brought back to tea. But Karen asked her so gravely and prettily and said so urgently that Tante wanted especially to know her better, and asked, moreover, if Betty would let her come to lunch with her instead of tea, so that they should have their full time together, that Betty once more pocketed her suspicions of a design on Madame von Marwitz's part. The suspicion was there, however, in her pocket, and she kept her hand on it rather as if it were a small but efficacious pistol which she carried about in case of an emergency. Betty was one who could aim steadily and shoot

straight when occasion demanded. It was a latent antagonist
who entered Mrs. Forrester's drawing-room on that Monday
afternoon, Karen, all guileless, following after. Mrs. Forrester
and the Baroness were alone and, in a deep Chesterfield near the
tea-table, Madame von Marwitz leaned an arm, bared to the
elbow, in cushions and rested a meditative head on her hand.
She half rose to greet Betty. " This is kind of you, Lady Jardine," she said. " I feared that I had lost my Karen for the
afternoon. *Elle me manque toujours;* she knows that." Smiling up at Karen she drew her down beside her, studying her
with eyes of fond, maternal solicitude. " My child looks well,
does she not, Mrs. Forrester? And the pretty hat! I am glad
not to see the foolish green one."

" Oh, I like the green one very much, Tante," said Karen.
" But you shall not see it again."

" I hope I'm to see it again," said Betty, turning over her
pistol. " I chose it, you know."

Madame von Marwitz turned startled eyes upon her. " Ah —
but I did not know. Did you tell me this, Karen? " the eyes of
distress now turned to Karen. " Have I forgotten? Was the
green hat, the little green hat with the wing, indeed of Lady
Jardine's choosing? Have I been so very rude? "

" Betty will understand, Tante," said Karen — while Mrs.
Forrester, softly chinking among her blue Worcester teacups,
kept a cogitating eye on Betty Jardine —" that I have so many
new hats now that you must easily forget which is which."

" All I ask," said Betty, laughing over her mishap, " is that I,
sometimes, may see Karen in the green hat, for I think it
charming."

" Indeed, Betty, so do I," said Karen, smiling.

" And I must be forgiven for not liking the green hat,"
Madame von Marwitz returned.

Betty and Karen were supplied with tea, and after they had
selected their cakes, and a few inconsequent remarks had been
exchanged, Madame von Marwitz said:

" And now, my Karen, I have a little plan to tell you of; a
little treat that I have arranged for you. We are to go together,

on this next Saturday, to stay at Thole Castle with my friends
the Duke and Duchess of Bannister. I have told them that I
wish to bring my child."

"But how delightful, Tante. It is to be in the country? We
shall be there, you and I and Gregory, till Monday?"

"I thought that I should please you. Yes; till Monday.
And in beautiful country. But it is to be our own small treat;
yours and mine. Your husband will lend you to me for those
two days." Holding the girl's hand Madame von Marwitz smiled
indulgently at her, with eyes only for her. Betty, however, was
listening.

"But cannot Gregory come, too, Tante?" Karen questioned,
her pleasure dashed.

"These friends of mine, my Karen," said Madame von Marwitz, "have heard of you as mine only. It is as my child that
you will come with me; just as it is as your husband's wife that
you see his friends. That is quite clear, quite happy, quite
understood."

Karen's eyes now turned on Betty. They did not seek counsel,
they asked no question of Betty; but they gave her, in their
slight bewilderment, her opportunity.

"But Karen, I think you are right," so she took up the gage
that Madame von Marwitz had flung. "I don't think that you
must accept this invitation without, at least, consulting
Gregory."

Madame von Marwitz did not look at her. She continued to
gaze as serenely at Karen as though Betty were a dog that
had barked irrelevantly from the hearth-rug. But Karen fixed
widened eyes upon her.

"I do not need to consult Gregory, Betty," she said. "We
have, I know, no engagements for this Saturday to Monday, and
he will be delighted for me that I am to go with Tante."

"That may be, my dear," Betty returned with a manner as
imperturbable as Madame von Marwitz's; "but I think that you
should give him an opportunity of saying so. He may not care
for his wife to go to strangers without him."

" They are not strangers. They are friends of Tante's."

" Gregory may not care for you to make — as Madame von Marwitz suggests — a different set of friends from his own."

" If they become my friends they will become his," said Karen.

During this little altercation, Madame von Marwitz, large and white, her profile turned to Betty, sat holding Karen's hand and gazing at her with an almost slumbrous melancholy.

Mrs. Forrester, controlling her displeasure with some difficulty, interposed. " I don't think Lady Jardine really quite understands the position, Karen," she said. " It is n't the normal one, Lady Jardine. Madame von Marwitz stands, really, to Karen in a mother's place."

" Oh, but I can't agree with you, Mrs. Forrester," Betty replied. " Madame von Marwitz does n't strike me as being in the least like Karen's mother. And she is n't Karen's mother. And Karen's husband, now, should certainly stand first in her life."

A silence followed the sharp report. Mrs. Forrester's and Karen's eyes had turned on the Baroness who sat still, as though her breast had received the shot. With tragic eyes she gazed out above Karen's head; then: " It is true," she said in a low voice, as though communing with herself; " I am indeed alone." She rose. With the slow step of a Niobe she moved down the room and disappeared.

" I do not forgive you for this, Betty," said Karen, following her guardian. Betty, like a naughty school-girl, was left confronting Mrs. Forrester across the tea-table.

" Lady Jardine," said the old lady, fixing her bright eyes on her guest, " I don't think you can have realised what you were saying. Madame von Marwitz's isolation is one of the many tragedies of her life, and you have made it clear to her."

" I 'm very sorry," said Betty. " But I feel what Madame von Marwitz is doing to be so mistaken, so wrong."

" These formalities don't obtain nowadays, especially if a wife is so singularly related to a woman like Madame von Marwitz. And Mercedes is quite above all such little consciousnesses, I assure you. She is not aware of sets, in that petty way. It is merely a treat she is giving the child, for she knows how much Karen loves to be with her. And it is only in her train that Karen goes."

"Precisely." Betty had risen and stood smoothing her muff and not feigning to smile. "In her train. I don't think that Gregory's wife should go in anybody's train."

"It was markedly in Mercedes's train that he found her."

"All the more reason for wishing now to withdraw her from it. Karen has become something more than Madame von Marwitz's *panache.*"

Mrs. Forrester at this fixed Betty very hard and echoes of Miss Scrotton rang loudly. "You must let me warn you, Lady Jardine," she said, "that you are making a position, difficult already for Mercedes, more difficult still. It would be a grievous thing if Karen were to recognize her husband's jealousy. I'm afraid I can't avoid seeing what you have made so plain to-day, that Gregory is trying to undermine Karen's relation to her guardian."

At this Betty had actually to laugh. "But don't you see that it is simply the other way round?" she said. "It is Madame von Marwitz who is trying to undermine Karen's relation to Gregory. It is she who is jealous. It's that I can't avoid seeing."

"I don't think we have anything to gain by continuing this conversation," Mrs. Forrester replied. "May I give you some more tea before you go?"

"No, thanks. Is Karen coming with me, I wonder? We had arranged that I was to take her home."

Mrs. Forrester rang the bell and she and Betty stood in an uneasy silence until the man returned to say that Mrs. Jardine was to spend the evening with Madame von Marwitz who had suddenly been taken very ill.

"Oh, dear! Oh, dear!" Mrs. Forrester almost moaned. "This means one of her terrible headaches and we were to have dined out. I must telephone excuses at once."

"I wish I hadn't had to make you think me such a pig," said Betty.

"I don't think you a pig," said Mrs. Forrester, "but I do think you a very mistaken and a very unwise woman. And I do beg you, for Gregory and for Karen's sake, to be careful what you do."

CHAPTER XXI

"I'M afraid you think that I've made a dreadful mess of things, Gregory. I simply could n't help myself," said Betty, half an hour later. "If only she had n't gone on gazing at Karen in that aggressive way I might have curbed my tongue, and if only, afterwards, Mrs. Forrester had n't shown herself such an infatuated partisan. But I'm afraid she was right in saying that I was an unwise woman. Certainly I have n't made things easier for you, unless you want a *situation nette*. It's there to your hand if you do want it, and in your place I should. It was a challenge she gave, you know, to you through me. After the other night there was no mistaking it. I should forbid Karen to go on Saturday."

Gregory stood before her still wearing his overcoat, for they had driven up simultaneously to the door below, his hands in his pockets and eyes of deep cogitation fixed on his sister-in-law. He was inclined to think that she had made a dreadful mess of things; yet, at the same time, he was feeling a certain elation in the chaos thus created.

"You advise me to declare war on Madame von Marwitz?" he inquired. "Come; the situation is hardly *nette* enough to warrant that; what?"

"Ah; you do see it then!" Betty from the sofa where she sat erect, her hands in her muff, almost joyfully declared. "You do see, then, what she is after!"

He did n't intend to let Betty see what he saw, if that were now possible. "She's after Karen, of course; but why not? It's a jealous and exacting affection, that is evident; but as long as Karen cares to satisfy it I'm quite pleased that she should. I can't declare war on Madame von Marwitz, Betty, even if I wanted to. Because, if she is fond of Karen, Karen is ten times fonder of her."

"Expose her to Karen!" Betty magnificently urged. "You can, I'm sure. You've been seeing things more and more clearly, just as I have; you've been seeing that Madame von Marwitz, as far as her character goes, is a fraud. Trip her up. Have things out. Gregory, I warn you, she's a dangerous woman, and Karen is a very simple one."

"But that's just it, my dear Betty. If Karen is too simple to see, now, that she's dangerous, how shall I make her look so? It's I who'll look the jealous idiot Mrs. Forrester thinks me," Gregory half mused to himself. "And, besides, I really don't know that I should want to trip her up. I don't know that I should like to have Karen disillusioned. She's a fraud if you like, and Karen, as I say, is ten times fonder of her than she is of Karen; but she is fond of Karen; I do believe that. And she has been a fairy-godmother to her. And they have been through all sorts of things together. No; their relationship is one that has its rights. I see it, and I intend to make Madame von Marwitz feel that I see it. So that my only plan is to go on being suave and acquiescent."

"Well; you may have to sacrifice me, then. Karen is indignant with me, I warn you."

"I'm a resourceful person, Betty. I shan't sacrifice you. And you must be patient with Karen."

Betty, who had risen, stood for a moment looking at the Bouddha. "Patient? I should think so. She is the one I'm sorriest for. Are you going to keep that ridiculous thing in here permanently, Gregory?"

"It's symbolic, isn't it?" said Gregory. "It will stay here, I suppose, as long as Madame von Marwitz and Karen go on caring for each other. With all my griefs and suspicions I hope that the Bouddha is a fixture."

He felt, after Betty had gone, that he had burned a good many of his boats in thus making her, to some extent, his confidant. He had confessed that he had griefs and suspicions, and that, in itself, was to involve still further his relation to his wife. But he had kept from Betty how grave were his grounds for suspicion. The bearing away of Karen to the ducal week-end

was n't really, in itself, so alarming an incident; but, as a sequel
to Madame von Marwitz's parting declaration of the other evening, her supremely insolent, " I must see what I can do," it
became sinister and affected him like the sound of a second,
more prolonged, more reverberating clash upon the gong. To
submit was to show himself in Madame von Marwitz's eyes as
contemptibly supine; to protest was to appear in Karen's as
meanly petty.

His reflections were interrupted by the ringing of the telephone and when he went to it Karen's voice told him that she
was spending the evening with Tante, who was ill, and that she
would not be back till ten. Something chill and authoritative
in the tones affected him unpleasantly. Karen considered that
she had a grievance and perhaps suspected him of being its cause.
After all, he thought, hanging up the receiver with some abrupt-
ness, there was such a thing as being too simple. One had,
indeed, to be very patient with her. And one thing he promised himself whatever came of it; he was n't going to sacrifice
Betty by one jot or tittle to his duel with Madame von
Marwitz.

It was past ten when Karen returned and his mood of latent
hostility melted when he saw how tired she looked and how
unhappy. She, too, had steeled herself in advance against something that she expected to find in him and he was thankful to
feel that she would n't find it. She was to find him suave and
acquiescent; he would consent without a murmur to Madame von
Marwitz's plan for the week-end.

" Darling, I 'm so sorry that she 's ill, your guardian," he said,
taking her hat and coat from her as she sank wearily on the sofa.
" How is she now? "

She looked up at him in the rosy light of the electric lamps
and her face showed no temporizing recognitions or gratitudes.
" Gregory," she said abruptly, " do you mind — does it displease
you — if I go with Tante next Saturday to stay with some
friends of hers? "

" Mind? Why should I? " said Gregory, standing before her
with his hands in his pockets. " I 'd rather have you here, of

course. I've been feeling a little deserted lately. But I want you to do anything that gives you pleasure."

She studied him. "Betty thought it a wrong thing for me to do. She hurt Tante's feelings deeply this afternoon. She spoke as if she had some authority to come between you and me and between me and Tante. I am very much displeased with her," said Karen, with her strangely mature decision.

The moment had come, decisively, not to sacrifice Betty. "Betty sees things more conventionally and perhaps more wisely," he said, "than you or I — or Madame von Marwitz, even, perhaps. She feels a sense of responsibility towards you — and towards me. Anything she said she meant kindly, I'm sure."

Karen listened carefully as though mastering herself. "Responsibility towards me? Why should she? I feel none towards her."

"But, my dear child, that wouldn't be in your place," he could not control the ironic note. "You are a younger woman and a much more inexperienced one. It's merely as if you'd married into a family where there was an elder sister to look after you."

Karen's eyes dwelt on him and her face was cold, rocky. "Do you forget, as she does, that I have still with me a person who, for years, has looked after me, a person older still and more experienced still than the little Betty? I don't need any guidance from your sister; for I have my guardian to tell me, as she always has, what is best for me to do. It is impertinent of Betty to imagine that she has any right to interfere. And she was more than impertinent. I had not wished to tell you; but you must understand that Betty has been insolent."

"Come, Karen; don't use such unsuitable words. Hasty perhaps; not insolent. Betty herself has told me all about it."

A steely penetration came to Karen's eyes. "She has told you? She has been here?"

"Yes."

"She complained of Tante to you?"

"She thinks her wrong."

" And you; you think her wrong? "

Gregory paused and looked at the young girl on the sofa, his wife. There was that in her attitude, exhausted yet unappealing, in her face, weary yet implacable, which, while it made her seem pitiful to him, made her also almost a stranger; this armed hostility towards himself, who loved her, this quickness of resentment, this cold assurance of right. He could understand and pity; but he, too, was tired and overwrought. What had he done to deserve such a look and such a tone from her except endure, with unexampled patience, the pressure upon his life, soft, unremitting, sinister, of something hateful to him and menacing to their happiness? What, above all, was his place in this deep but narrow young heart? It seemed filled with but one absorbing preoccupation, one passion of devotion.

He turned from her and went to the mantelpiece, and shifting the vases upon it as he spoke, remembering with a bitter upper layer of consciousness how Madame von Marwitz's blighting gaze had rested upon these ornaments in her first visit; —" I 'm not going to discuss your guardian with you, Karen," he said; " I have n't said that I thought her wrong. I 've consented that you should do as she wishes. You have no right to ask anything more of me. I certainly am not going to be forced by you into saying that I think Betty wrong. If you are not unfair to Betty you are certainly most unfair to me and it seems to me that it is your tendency to be fair to one person only. I 'm in no danger of forgetting her control and guidance of your life, I assure you. If you were to let me forget it, she would n't. She is showing me now — after telling me the other night what she thought of my *monde* — how she controls you. It 's very natural of her, no doubt, and very natural of you to feel her right; and I submit. So that you have no ground of grievance against me." He turned to her again. " And now I think you had better go to bed. You look very tired. I 've some work to get through, so I 'll say good-night to you, Karen dear."

She rose with a curious automatic obedience, and, coming to him, lifted her forehead, like a child, for his kiss. Her face showed, perhaps, a bleak wonder, but it showed no softness. She

might be bewildered by this sudden change in their relation, but
she was not weakened. She went away, softly closing the door
behind her.

In their room, Karen stood for a moment before undressing
and looked about her. Something had happened, and though
she could not clearly see what it was it seemed to have altered
the aspect of everything, so that this pretty room, full of light
and comfort, was strange to her. She felt an alien in it; and
as she looked round it she thought of how her little room at Les
Solitudes where, with such an untroubled heart, she had slept
and waked for so many years.

Three large photographs of Tante hung on the walls, and their
eyes met hers as if with an unfaltering love and comprehension.
And on the dressing-table was a photograph of Gregory; the new
thing in her life; the thing that menaced the old. She went and
took it up, and Gregory's face, too, was suddenly strange to her;
cold, hard, sardonic. She wondered, gazing at it, that she had
never seen before how cold and hard it was. Quickly undressing she lay down and closed her eyes. A succession of images
passed with processional steadiness before her mind; the carriage
in the Forest of Fontainebleau and Tante in it looking at her;
Tante in the hotel at Fontainebleau, her arm around the little
waif, saying: " But it is a Norse child; her name and her hair
and her eyes;" Tante's dreadful face as she tottered back to
Karen's arms from the sight at the lake-edge; Tante that evening lying white and sombre on her pillows with eyelids pressed
down as if on tears, saying: " Do they wish to take my child,
too, from me? "

Then came the other face, the new face; like a sword; thrusting among the sacred visions. Consciously she saw her husband's face now, as she had often, with a half wilful unconsciousness, seen it, looking at Tante — ah, a fierce resentment flamed
up in her at last with the unavoidable clearness of her vision —
looking at Tante with a courteous blankness that cloaked hostility; with cold curiosity; with mastered irony, suspicion, dislike.
He was, then, a man not generous, not large and wise of heart,
a man without the loving humour that would have enabled him

to see past the defects and flaws of greatness, nor with the heart and mind to recognize and love it when he saw it. He was petty, too, and narrow, and arrogantly sure of his own small measures. Her memories heaped themselves into the overwhelming realisation. She was married to a man who was hostile to what — until he had come — had been the dearest thing in her life. She had taken to her heart something that killed its very pulse. How could she love a man who looked such things at Tante — who thought such things of Tante? How love him without disloyalty to the older tie? Already her forbearance, her hiding from him of her fear, had been disloyalty, a cowardly acquiescence in something that, from the first hint of it, she should openly have rebelled against. Slow flames of shame and anger burned her. How could she not hate him? But how could she not love him? He was part of her life, as unquestionably, as indissolubly, as Tante.

Then, the visions crumbling, the flames falling, a chaos of mere feeling overwhelmed her. It was as though her blood were running backward, knotting itself in clots of darkness and agony. He had sent her away unlovingly — punishing her for her fidelity. Her love for Tante destroyed his love for her. He must have known her pain; yet he could speak like that to her; look like that. The tears rose to her eyes and rolled down her cheeks as she lay straightly in the bed, on her back, the clothes drawn to her throat, her hands clasped tightly on her breast. Hours had passed and here she lay alone.

Hours had passed and she heard at last his careful step along the passage, and the shock of it tingled through her with a renewal of fear and irrepressible joy. He opened, carefully, the dressing-room door. She listened, stilling her breaths.

He would come to her. They would speak together. He would not leave her when she was so unhappy. Even the thought of Tante's wrongs was effaced by the fear and yearning, and, as the bedroom door opened and Gregory came in, her heart seemed to lift and dissolve in a throb of relief and blissfulness.

But, with her joy, the thought of Tante hovered like a heavy darkness above her eyes, keeping them closed. She lay still, ashamed of so much gladness, yet knowing that if he took her in his arms her arms could but close about him.

The stillness deceived Gregory. In the dim light from the dressing-room he saw her, as he thought, sleeping placidly, her broad braids lying along the sheet.

He looked at her for a moment. Then, not stooping to her, he turned away.

CHAPTER XXII

IF only, Gregory often felt, in thinking it over and over in the days of outer unity and inner estrangement that followed, she had not been able to go to sleep so placidly.

All resentment had faded from his heart when he went in to her. He had longed for reconciliation and for reassurance. But as he had looked at the seeming calm of Karen's face his tenderness and compunction passed into a bitter consciousness of frustrated love. Her calm was like a repulse. Their personal estrangement and misunderstanding left her unmoved. She had said what she had to say to him; she had vindicated her guardian; and now she slept, unmindful of him. He asked himself, and for the first time clearly and steadily, as he lay awake for hours afterwards in the little dressing-room bed, whether Karen's feelings for him passed beyond a faithful, sober affection that took him for granted, unhesitatingly and uncritically, as a new asset in a life dedicated elsewhere. Romance for her was personified in Tante, and her husband was a creature of mere kindly domesticity. It was to think too bitterly of Karen's love for him to see it thus, he knew, even while the torment grasped him; but the pressure of his own love for her, the loveliness, the romance that she so supremely personified for him, surged too strongly against the barrier of her mute, unanswering face, for him to feel temperately and weigh fairly. There was a lack in her, and because of it she hurt him thus cruelly.

They met next morning over a mutual misinterpretation, and, with a sense of mingled discord and relief, found themselves kissing and smiling as if nothing had happened. Pride sustained them; the hope that, since the other seemed so unconscious, a hurt dealt so unconsciously need not, for pride's sake, be resented; the fear that explanation or protest might empha-

sise estrangement. The easiest thing to do was to go on acting
as if nothing had happened. Karen poured out his coffee and
questioned him about the latest political news. He helped her
to eggs and bacon and took an interest in her letters.

And since it was easiest to begin so, it was easiest so to go on.
The routine of their shared life blurred for them the sharp realisations of the night. But while the fact that such suffering
had come to them was one that could, perhaps, be lived down,
the fact that they did not speak of it spread through all their
life with a strange, new savour.

Karen went to her ducal week-end; but she did not, when
she came back from it, regale her husband with her usual wealth
of detailed description. She could no longer assume the air
of happy confidence where Tante and her doings with Tante
were concerned. That air of determined cheerfulness, that
pretence that nothing was really the matter and that Tante
and Gregory were bound to get on together if she took it for
granted that they would, had broken down. There was relief
for Gregory, though relief of a chill, grey order, in seeing
that Karen had accepted the fact that he and Tante were not
to get on. Yet he smarted from the new sense of being shut
out from her life.

It was he who assumed the air; he who pretended that nothing was the matter. He questioned her genially about the visit,
and Karen answered all his questions as genially. Yes; it had
been very nice; the great house sometimes very beautiful and
sometimes very ugly; the beauty seemed, in a funny way, almost
as accidental as the ugliness. The people had been very interesting to look at; so many slender pretty women; there were
no fat women and no ugly women at all, or, if they were, they
contrived not to look it. It all seemed perfectly arranged.

Had she talked to many of them? Gregory asked. Had she
come across anybody she liked? Karen shook her head. She
had liked them all — to look at — but it had gone no further
than that; she had talked very little with any of them; and,
soberly, unemphatically, she had added: "They were all too
much occupied with Tante — or with each other — to think

much of me. I was the only one not slender and not beautiful!"

Gregory asked who had taken her in to dinner on the two nights, and masked ironic inner comments when he heard that on Saturday it had been a young actor who, she thought, had been a little cross at having her as his portion. "He did n't try to talk to me; nor I to him, when I found that he was cross," she said. "I did n't like him at all. He had fat cheeks and very shrewd black eyes." On Sunday it had been a young son of the house, a boy at Eton. "Very, very dear and nice. We had a great talk about climbing Swiss mountains, which I have done a good deal, you know."

Tante, it appeared, had had the ambassador on Saturday and the Duke himself on Sunday. And she and Tante, as usual, had had great fun in their own rooms every night, talking everybody over when the day was done. Karen said nothing to emphasise the contrast between the duke's friends and Gregory's, but she could n't have failed to draw her comparison. Here was a *monde* where Tante was fully appreciated. That she herself had not been was not a matter to engage her thoughts. But it engaged Gregory's. The position in which she had been placed was a further proof to him of Tante's lack of consideration. Where Karen was placed depended, precisely, he felt sure of it, on where Madame von Marwitz wished her to be placed. It was as the little camp-follower that she had taken her.

After this event came a pause in the fortunes of our young couple. Madame von Marwitz, with Mrs. Forrester, went to Paris to give her two concerts there and was gone for a fortnight. In this fortnight he and Karen resumed, though warily, as it were, some old customs. They read their political economy again in the evenings when they did not go out, and he found her at tea-time waiting for him as she had used to do. She shared his life; she was gentle and thoughtful; yet she had never been less near. He felt that she guarded herself against admissions. To come near now would be to grant that it had been Tante's presence that had parted them.

She wrote to Madame von Marwitz, and heard from her, con-

stantly. Madame von Marwitz sent her presents from Paris;
a wonderful white silk dressing-gown; a box of chocolate; a
charming bit of old enamel picked up in a *rive gauche* curiosity
shop. Then one day she wrote to say that Tallie had been quite
ill — *povera vecchia* — and would Karen be a kind, kind child
and run down and see her at Les Solitudes.

Gregory had not forgotten the plan for having Mrs. Talcott
with them that winter and had reminded Karen of it, but it
appeared then that she had not forgotten, either; had indeed,
spoken to Tante of it; but that Tante had not seemed to think
it a good plan. Tante said that Mrs. Talcott did not like leaving Les Solitudes; and, moreover, that she herself, might be
going down there for the inside of a week at any moment and
Karen knew how Tallie would hate the idea of not being on
the spot to prepare for her. Let them postpone the idea of a
visit; at all events until she was no longer in England.

Gregory now suggested that Karen might bring Mrs. Talcott
back with her. There was some guile in the suggestion. Encircling this little oasis of peace where he and Karen could, at
all events, draw their breaths, were storms and arid wastes.
Madame von Marwitz would soon be back. She might even be
thinking of redeeming her promise of coming to stay with
them. If old Mrs. Talcott, slightly invalided, could be installed
before the great woman's return, she might keep her out for
the rest of her stay in London, and must, certainly, keep Karen
in to a greater extent than when she had no guest to entertain.

Karen could not suspect his motive; he saw that from her
frank look of pleasure. She promised to do her best. It was
worth while, he reflected, to lose her for a few days if she were
to bring back such a bulwark as Mrs. Talcott might prove herself to be. And, besides, he would be sincerely glad to see the
old woman. The thought of her gave him a sense of comfort
and security.

He saw Karen off next morning. She was to be at Les Solitudes for three or four days, and on the second day of her
stay he had his first letter from her. It was strange to hear
from her again, from Cornwall. It was the first letter he had

had from Karen since their marriage and, with all its odd
recalling of the girlish formality of tone, it was a sweet one.
She had found Mrs. Talcott much better, but still quite weak
and jaded, and very glad indeed to see her. And Mrs. Talcott
really seemed to think that she would like to get away. Karen
believed that Mrs. Talcott had actually been feeling lonely, uncharacteristic as that seemed. She would probably bring her
back on Saturday. The letter ended: "My dear husband,
your loving Karen."

Mrs. Talcott, therefore, was expected, and Mrs. Barker was
told to make ready for her.

But on Saturday morning, when Karen was starting, he had
a wire from her telling him that plans were altered and that
she was coming back alone.

He went to meet her at Paddington, remembering the meeting when she had come up after their engagement. It was
a different Karen, a Karen furred and finished and nearly elegant, who stepped from the train; but she had, as then, her
little basket with the knitting and the book; and the girlish
face was scarcely altered; there was even a preoccupation on
it that recalled still more vividly the former meeting at Paddington. "Well, dearest, and why is n't Mrs. Talcott here,
too?" were his first words.

Karen took his arm as he steered her towards the luggage.
"It is only put off, I hope, that visit," she said, "because I
heard this morning, Gregory, and wired to you then, that Tante
asks if she may come to us next week." Her voice was not
artificial; it expressed determination as well as gentleness and
seemed to warn him that he must not show her if he were not
pleased. Yet duplicity, in his unpleasant surprise, was difficult to assume.

"Really. At last. How nice," he said; and his voice rang
oddly. "But poor old Mrs. Talcott. Madame von Marwitz
did n't know, I suppose," he went on, "that we 'd just been
planning to have her?"

Karen, her arm still in his, stood looking over the heaped up luggage and now pointed out her box to the porter. Then, as they turned away and went towards their cab, she said, more gently and more determinedly: "Yes; she did know we had planned it. I wrote and told her so, and that is why she wrote back so quickly to ask if we could not put off Mrs. Talcott for her; because she will be leaving London very soon and it will be, this next week, her only chance of being with us. Mrs. Talcott did not mind at all. I don't think she really wanted to come so much, Gregory. It is as Tante says, you know," Karen settled herself in a corner of the hansom, "she really does not like leaving Les Solitudes."

Gregory had the feeling of being enmeshed. Why had Madame von Marwitz thrown this web? Had she really divined in a flash his hope and his intention? Was there any truth in her sudden statement that this was the only week she could give them? "Oh! Really," was all that he found to say to Karen's explanations, and then, "Where is Madame von Marwitz going when she leaves us then?"

"To the Riviera, with the Duchess of Bannister, I think it is arranged. I may wire to her, then, Gregory, at once, and say that she is to come?"

"Of course. How long are we to have the pleasure of entertaining her?"

"She did not say; for a week at least, I hope. Perhaps, even, for a fortnight if that will be convenient for you. It will be a great joy to me," Karen went on, "if only"— she was speaking with that determined steadiness, looking before her as they drove; now, suddenly, she turned her eyes on him —"if only you will try to enjoy it, too, Gregory."

It was, in a sense, a challenge, yet it was, too, almost an appeal, and it brought them nearer than they had been for weeks.

Gregory's hand caught hers and, holding it tightly, smiling at her rather tremulously, he said: "I enjoy anything, darling, that makes you happy."

"Ah, but," said Karen, her voice keeping its earnest con-

trol, " I cannot be happy with you and Tante unless you can
enjoy her for yourself. Try to know Tante, Gregory," she
went on, now with a little breathlessness; " she wants that so
much. One of the first things she asked me when she came
back was that I should try to make you care for her. She felt
at once — and oh! so did I, Gregory — that something was not
happy between you."

Her hand holding his tightly, her earnest eyes on his, Gregory
felt his blood turn a little cold as he recognized once more the
soft, unremitting pressure. It had begun, then, so early. She
had asked Karen that when she first came back. " But you
see, dearest," he said, trying to keep his head between realizations of Madame von Marwitz's craft and Karen's candour,
" I 've never been able to feel that Madame von Marwitz wanted
me to care for her or to come in at all, as it were. I don't
mean anything unkind; only that I imagined that what she
did ask of me was to keep outside and leave your relation and
hers alone. And that 's what I 've tried to do."

" Oh, you mistake Tante, Gregory, you mistake her."
Karen's hand grasped his more tightly in the urgency of her
opportunity. " She cared for me too much — yes, it is there
that you do not understand — to feel what you think. For
she knows that I cannot be happy while you shut yourself away
from her."

" Then it 's not she who shuts me out? " he tried to smile.

" No; no; oh, no, Gregory."

" I must push in, even when I seem to feel I 'm not wanted? "

She would not yield to his attempted lightness. " You
must n't push in; you must be in; with us, with Tante and
me."

" Do you mean literally? I 'm to be a third at your tête-à-
têtes? "

" No, Gregory, I do not mean that; but in thought, in sympathy. You will try to know Tante. You will make her feel
that you and I are not parted when she is there."

She saw it all, all Tante's side, with a dreadful clearness.
And it was impossible that she should see what he did. He

must submit to seeming blurred and dull, to pretending not to
see anything.   At all events her hand was in his.   He felt able
to face the duel at close quarters with Madame von Marwitz as
long as Karen let him keep her hand.

CHAPTER XXIII

TANTE arrived on Monday afternoon and the arrival reminded Gregory of the Bouddha's installation; but, whereas the Bouddha had overflowed the drawing-room only, Madame von Marwitz overflowed the flat.

A multitude of boxes were borne into the passages where, end to end, like a good's train on a main line, they stood impeding traffic.

Louise, harassed and sallow, hurried from room to room, expostulating, explaining, replying in shrill tones to Madame von Marwitz's sonorous orders. Victor, led by Mrs. Forrester's footman, made his appearance shortly after his mistress, and, set at large, penetrated unerringly to the kitchen where he lapped up a dish of custard; while Mrs. Barker, in the drawing-room, already with signs of resentment on her face, was receiving minute directions from Madame von Marwitz in regard to a cup of chocolate. In the dining-room, Gregory found two strange-looking men, to whom Barker, also clouded, had served whisky and soda; one of these was Madame von Marwitz's secretary, Schultz; the other a concert impresario. They greeted Gregory with a disconcerting affability.

In the midst of the confusion Madame von Marwitz moved, weary and benignant, her arm around Karen's shoulders, or seated herself at the piano to run her fingers appraisingly over it in a majestic surge of arpeggios. Gregory found her hat and veil tossed on the bed in his and Karen's room, and when he went into his dressing-room he stumbled over three bandboxes, just arrived from a modiste's, and hastily thrust there by Louise.

Victor bounded to greet him as he sought refuge in the library, and overturned a table that stood in the hall with two

226

fine pieces of oriental china upon it. The splintering crash of crockery filled the flat. Mrs. Barker had taken the chocolate to the drawing-room some time since, and Madame von Marwitz, the cup in her hand, appeared upon the threshold with Karen. " Alas ! The bad dog ! " she said, surveying the wreckage while she sipped her chocolate.

Rose was summoned to sweep up the pieces and Karen stooped over them with murmured regret.

" Were they wedding-presents, my Karen? " Madame von Marwitz asked. " Console yourself; they were not of a good period — I noticed them. I will give you better."

The vases had belonged to Gregory's mother. He was aware that he stood rather blankly looking at the fragments, as Rose collected them. " Oh, Gregory, I am so sorry," said Karen, taking upon herself the responsibility for Victor's mischance. " I am afraid they are broken to bits. See, this is the largest piece of all. They can't be mended. No, Tante, they were not wedding-presents; they belonged to Gregory and we were very fond of them."

" Alas ! " said Madame von Marwitz above her chocolate, and on a deeper note.

Gregory was convinced that she had known they were not wedding-presents. But her manner was flawless and he saw that she intended to keep it so. She dined with them alone and at the table addressed her talk to him, fixing, as ill-luck would have it, on the theatre as her theme, and on *La Gaine d'Or* as the piece which, in Paris, had particularly interested her. " You and Karen, of course, saw it when you were there," she said.

It was the piece of sinister fame to which he had refused to take Karen. He owned that they had not seen it.

" Ah, but that is a pity, truly a pity," said Madame von Marwitz. " How did it happen? You cannot have failed to hear of it."

Unable to plead Karen as the cause for his abstention since Madame von Marwitz regretted that Karen had missed the piece, Gregory said that he had heard too much perhaps. " I don't believe I should care for anything the man wrote," he confessed.

"*Tiens!*" said Madame von Marwitz, opening her eyes. "You know him?"

"Heaven forbid!" Gregory ejaculated, smiling with some tartness.

"But why this rigour? What have you against M. Saumier?"

It was difficult for a young Englishman of conventional tastes to formulate what he had against M. Saumier. Gregory took refuge in evasions. "Oh, I've glanced at reviews of his plays; seen his face in illustrated papers. One gets an idea of a man's personality and the kind of thing he's likely to write."

"A great artist," Madame von Marwitz mildly suggested. "One of our greatest."

"Is he really? I'd hardly grasped that. I had an idea that he was merely one of the clever lot. But I never can see why one should put oneself, through a man's art, into contact with the sort of person one would avoid having anything to do with in life."

Madame von Marwitz listened attentively. "Do you refuse to look at a Cellini bronze?"

"Literature is different, isn't it? It's more personal. There's more life in it. If a man's a low fellow I don't interest myself in his interpretation of life. He's seen nothing that I'm likely to want to see."

Madame von Marwitz smiled, now with a touch of irony. "But you frighten me. How am I to tell you that I know M. Saumier?"

Gregory was decidedly taken back. "That's a penalty you have to pay for being a celebrity, no doubt," he said. "All celebrities know each other, I suppose."

"By no means. I allow no one to be thrust upon me, I assure you. And I have the greatest admiration for M. Saumier's talent. A great artist cannot be a low fellow; if he were one he would be so much more than that that the social defect would be negligible. Few great artists, I imagine, have been of such a character as would win the approval of a garden

party at Lambeth Palace. I am sorry, indeed sorry, that you
and Karen missed *La Gaine d'Or*. It is not a play for the
jeune fille; no; though, holding as I do that nothing so fortifies
and arms the taste as liberty, I should have allowed Karen to
see it even before her marriage. It is a play cruel and acrid
and beautiful. Yes; there is great beauty, and it flowers, as
so often, on a bitter root. Ah, well, you will waive your
scruples now, I trust. I will take Karen with me to see it
when we are next in Paris together, and that must be soon.
We will go for a night or two. You would like to see Paris
with me again; *pas vrai, chérie?* "

Gregory had been uncomfortably aware of Karen's contemplation while he defended his prejudices, and he was prepared for
an open espousal of her guardian's point of view; it was, he
knew, her own. But he received once more, as he had received
already on several occasions, an unexpected and gratifying proof
of Karen's recognition of marital responsibility. "I should
like to be in Paris with you again, Tante," she said, "but not
to go to that play. I agreed not to go to it when Gregory and
I were there. I should not care to go when he so much dislikes it." Her eyes met her guardian's while she spoke. They
were gentle and non-committal; they gave Gregory no cause for
triumph, nor Tante for humiliation; they expressed merely her
own recognition of a bond.

Madame von Marwitz rose to the occasion, but — oh, it was
there, the soft pressure, never more present to Gregory's consciousness than when it seemed most absent — she rose too em-
phatically, as if to a need. Her eyes mused on the girl's face,
tenderly brooded and understood. And Karen's voice and look
had asked her not to understand.

"Ah, that is right; that is a wife," she murmured.
"Though, believe me, *chérie,* I did not know that I was so trans-
gressing." And turning her glance on Gregory, "*Je vous fais
mes compliments,*" she added.

Karen said that he must bring his cigar into the drawing-
room, for Tante would smoke her cigarette with him, and there,
until bedtime, things went as well as they had at dinner — or

as badly; for part of their badness, Gregory more and more resentfully became aware, was that they were made to seem to go well, from her side, not from his.

She had a genius, veritably uncanny for, with all sweetness and hesitancy, revealing him as stiff and unresponsively complacent. It was impossible for him to talk freely with a person uncongenial to him of the things he felt deeply; and, pertinaciously, over her coffee and cigarettes, it was the deep things that she softly wooed him to share with her.

He might be stiff and stupid, but he flattered himself that he was n't once short or sharp — as he would have been over and over again with any other woman who so bothered him. And he was sincerely unaware that his courtesy, in its dry evasiveness, was more repudiating than rudeness.

When Karen went with her guardian to her room that night, the little room that looked so choked and overcrowded with the great woman's multiplied necessities, Madame von Marwitz, sinking on the sofa, drew her to her and looked closely at her, with an intentness almost tragic, tenderly smoothing back her hair.

Karen looked back at her very firmly.

" Tell me, my child," Madame von Marwitz said, as if, suddenly, taking refuge in the inessential from the pressure of her own thoughts, " how did you find our Tallie? I have not heard of that from you yet."

" She is looking rather pale and thin, Tante; but she is quite well again; already she will go out into the garden," Karen answered, with, perhaps, an evident relief.

" That is well," said Madame von Marwitz with quiet satisfaction. " That is well. I cannot think of Tallie as ill. She is never ill. It is perhaps the peaceful, happy life she leads — *povera* — that preserves her. And the air, the wonderful air of our Cornwall. I fixed on Cornwall for the sake of Tallie, in great part; I sought for a truly halcyon spot where that faithful one might end her days in joy. You knew that, Karen? "

" No, Tante; you never told me that."

" It is so," Madame von Marwitz continued to muse, her

eyes on the fire, "It is so. I have given great thought to my Tallie's happiness. She has earned it." And after a moment, in the same quiet tone, she went on. "This idea of yours, my Karen, of bringing Tallie up to town; was it wise, do you think?"

Karen, also, had been looking at the flames. She brought her eyes now back to her guardian. "Was n't it wise, Tante? We had asked her to come and stay — long ago, you know."

"Had she seemed eager?"

"Eager? No; I can't imagine Mrs. Talcott eager about anything. We hoped we could persuade her, that was all. Why not wise, Tante?"

"Only, my child, that after the quiet life there, the solitude that she loves and that I chose for her sake, the pure sea air and the life among her flowers, London, I fear, would much weary and fatigue her. Tallie is getting old. We must not forget that Tallie is very old. This illness warns us. It does not seem to me a good plan. It was your plan, Karen?"

Karen was listening, with a little bewilderment. "It seemed to me very good. I had not thought of Mrs. Talcott as so old as that. I always think of her as old, but so strong and tough. It was Gregory who suggested it, in the first place, and this time, too. When I told him that I was going he thought of our plan at once and told me that now I must persuade her to come to us for a good long visit. He is really very fond of Mrs. Talcott, Tante, and she of him, I think. It would please you to see them together."

Karen spoke on innocently; but, as she spoke, she became aware from a new steadiness in her guardian's look, that her words had conveyed some significance of which she was herself unconscious.

Madame von Marwitz's hand had tightened on hers. "Ah," she said after a moment. She looked away.

"What is it, Tante?" Karen asked.

Madame von Marwitz had begun to draw deep, slow breaths. Karen knew the sound; it meant a painful control. "Tante, what is it?" she repeated.

"Nothing. Nothing, my child." Madame von Marwitz laid her arm around Karen's shoulders and continued to look away from her.

"But it is n't nothing," said Karen, after a little pause. "Something that I have said troubles or hurts you."

"Is it so? Perhaps you say the truth, my child. Hurts are not new to me. No, my Karen, no. It is nothing for us to speak of. I understand. But your husband, Karen, he must have found it thoughtless in me, indelicate, to force myself in when he had hoped so strongly for another guest."

A slow flush mounted to Karen's cheek. She kept silence for a moment, then in a careful voice she said: "No, Tante; I do not believe that."

"No?" said Madame von Marwitz. "No, my Karen?"

"He knew, on the contrary, that I hoped to have you soon — at any time that you could come," said Karen, in slightly trembling tones.

Madame von Marwitz nodded. "He knew that, as you tell me; and, knowing it, he asked Tallie; hoping that with her installed — for a long visit — my stay might be prevented. Do not let us hide from each other, my Karen. We have hidden too long and it is the beginning of the end if we may not say to each other what we see."

Sitting with downcast eyes, Karen was silent, struggling perhaps with new realisations.

Madame von Marwitz bent to kiss her forehead and then, resuming the tender stroking of her hair, she went on: "Your husband dislikes me. Let us look the ugly thing full in the face. You know it, and I know it, and — *parbleu!* — he knows it well. There; the truth is out. Ah, the brave little heart; it sought to hide its sorrow from me. But Tante is not so dull a person. The loneliness of heart must cease for you. And the sorrow, too, may pass away. Be patient, Karen. You will see. He may come to feel more kindly towards the woman who so loves his wife. Strange, is it not, and a chastisement for my egotism, if I have still any of that frothy element lingering in my nature, that I should find, suddenly, at the end of

my life — so near me, bound to me by such ties — one who is
unwilling to trust me, oh, for the least little bit; so unwilling to
accept me at merely my face value. Most people," she added,
" have loved me easily."

Karen sat on in silence. Her guardian knew this apathetic
silence, and that it was symptomatic in her of deep emotion.
And, the contagion of the suffering beside her gaining upon
her, her own fictitious calm wavered. She bent again to look
into the girl's averted face. " Karen, *chérie*," she said, and
now with a quicker utterance; " it is not worse than I yet
realise? You do not hide something that I have not yet seen.
It is dislike; I accept it. It is aversion, even. But his love
for you; that is strong, sincere? He will not make it too difficult for me? I am not wrong in coming here to be with my
child? "

Karen at length turned her eyes on her guardian with a
heavy look. " What would you find too difficult? " she asked.

Madame von Marwitz hesitated slightly, taken aback. But
she grasped in an instant her advantage. " That by being here
I should feel that I came between you and your husband. That
by being here I made it more difficult for you."

" I should not be happier if you were away — if what you
think is true, should I? " said Karen.

" Yes, my child," Madame von Marwitz returned, and now
almost with severity. " You would. You would not so sharply
feel your husband's aversion for me if I were not here. You
would not have it in your ears; before your eyes."

" I thought that you talked together quite easily to-night,"
Karen continued. " I saw, of course, that you did not understand each other; but with time that might be. I thought
that if you were here he would by degrees come to know you,
for he does not know you yet."

" We talked easily, did we not, my child, to shield you, and
you were not more deceived by the ease than he or I. He does
not understand me? I hope so indeed. But to say that I do
not understand him shows already your wish to shield him, and
at my expense. I do understand him; too well. And if there

is this repugnance in him now, may it not grow with the enforced intimacy? That is my fear, my dread."

"He has never said that he disliked you."

"Said it? To you? I should imagine not, *parbleu!*"

"He has only said," Karen pursued with a curious doggedness, "that he did not feel that you cared for him to care."

"Ah! Is it so? You have talked of it, then? And he has said that? And did you believe it? Of me?"

But the growing passion and urgency of her voice seemed to shut Karen more closely in upon herself rather than sweep her into impulsive confidence. There was a hot exasperation in Madame von Marwitz's eye as it studied the averted, stubborn head. "No," was the reply she received.

"No, no, indeed. It was not the truth that he said to you and you know that it was not the truth. Oh, I make no accusation against your husband; he believed it the truth; but you cannot believe that I would rest satisfied with what must make you unhappy. And how can you be happy if your husband does not care for me? How can you be happy if he feels repugnance for me? You cannot be. Is it not so? Or am I wrong?"

"No," Karen again repeated.

"Then," said Madame von Marwitz, and a sob now lifted her voice, "then do not let him put it upon me. Not that! Oh promise me, my Karen! For that would be the end."

Karen turned to her suddenly, and passed her arms around her. "Tante — Tante," she said; "what are you saying? The end? There could not be an end for us! Do not speak so. Do not. Do not." She was trembling.

"Ah — could there not! Could there not!" With the words Madame von Marwitz broke into violent sobs. "Has it not been my doom, always — always to have what I love taken from me! You love this man who hates me! You defend him! He will part you from me! I foresee it! From the first it has been my dread!"

"No one can ever part us, Tante. No one. Ever." Karen whispered, holding her tightly, and her face, bending above the sobbing woman, was suddenly old and stricken in its tormented and almost maternal love. "Tante; remember your own words. You gave me courage. Will you not be patient? For my sake? Be patient, Tante. Be patient. He does not know you yet."

CHAPTER XXIV

GREGORY heard no word of the revealing talk; yet, when he and Karen were alone, he was aware of a new chill, or a new discretion, in the atmosphere. It was as if a veil of ice, invisible yet impassable, hung between them, and he could only infer that she had something to hide, he could only suspect, with a bitterer resentment, that Madame von Marwitz had been more directly exerting her pressure.

The pressure, whatever it had been, had the effect of making Karen, when they were all three confronted, more calm, more mildly cheerful than before, more than ever the fond wife who did not even suspect that a flaw might be imagined in her happiness.

Gregory had an idea — his only comfort in this sorry maze where he found himself so involved — that this attitude of Karen's, combined with his own undeviating consideration, had a disconcerting effect upon Madame von Marwitz and at moments induced her to show her weapon too openly in their wary duel. If he ever betrayed his dislike Karen must see that it was Tante who would n't allow him to conceal it, who, sorrowfully and gently, turned herself about in the light she elicited and displayed herself to Karen as rejected and uncomplaining. He hoped that Karen saw it. But he could be sure of nothing that Karen saw. The flawless loyalty of her outward bearing might be but the shield for a deepening hurt. All that he could do was what, in former days and in different conditions, Mrs. Talcott had advised him to do; "hang on," and parry Madame von Marwitz's thrusts. She had come, he more and more felt sure of it, urged by her itching jealousy, for the purpose of making mischief; and if it was not a motive of which she was conscious, that made her but the more dangerous with her deep, instinctive craft.

Meanwhile if there were fundamental anxieties to fret one's heart, there were superficial irritations that abraded one's nerves.

Karen was accustomed to the turmoil that surrounded the guarded shrine where genius slept or worked, too much accustomed, without doubt, to realise its effect upon her husband.

The electric bells were never silent. Seated figures, bearing band-boxes or rolls of music, filled the hall at all hours of the day and night. Alert interviewers button-holed him on his way in and out and asked for a few details about Mrs. Jardine's youth, and her relationship to Madame Okraska.

Madame von Marwitz rose capriciously and ate capriciously; trays with strange meals upon them were carried at strange hours to her rooms, and Barker, Mrs. Barker and Rose all quarrelled with Louise.

Madame von Marwitz also showed oddities of temper which, with all her determination to appear at her best, it did not occur to her to control, oddities that met, from Karen, with a fond tolerance.

It startled Gregory when they saw Madame von Marwitz, emerging from her room, administer two smart boxes upon Louise's ears, remarking as she did so, with gravity rather than anger: "*Voilà pour toi, ma fille.*"

"Is Madame von Marwitz in the habit of slapping her servants?" he asked Karen in their room, aware that his frigid mien required justification.

She looked at him through the veil of ice. "Tante's servants adore her."

"Well, it seems a pity to take such an advantage of their adoration."

"Louise is sometimes very clumsy and impertinent."

"I can't help thinking that that sort of treatment makes servants impertinent."

"I do not care to hear your criticism of my guardian, Gregory."

"I beg your pardon," said Gregory.

Betty Jardine met him on a windy April evening in Queen Anne's Gate. "I see that you had to sacrifice me, Gregory," she said. She smiled; she bore no grudge; but her smile was tinged with a shrewd pity.

He felt that he flushed. "You mean that you 've not been to see us since the occasion."

"I 've not been asked!" Betty laughed.

"Madame von Marwitz is with us, you know," Gregory proffered rather lamely.

"Yes; I do know. How do you like having a genius domiciled? I hear that she is introducing Karen into a very artistic set. After the Bannisters, Mr. Claude Drew. He is back from America at last, it seems, and is an assiduous adorer. You have seen a good deal of him?"

"I have n't seen him at all. Has he been back for long?"

"Four or five days only, I believe; but I don't know how often he and Madame von Marwitz and Karen have been seen together. Don't think me a cat, Gregory; but if she is engaged in a flirtation with that most unpleasant young man I hope you will see to it that Karen is n't used as a screen. There have been some really horrid stories about him, you know."

Gregory parted from his sister-in-law, perturbed. Indiscreet and naughty she might be, but Betty was not a cat. The veil of ice was so impenetrable that no sound of Karen's daily life came to him through it. He had not an idea of what she did with herself when he was n't there, or, rather, of what Madame von Marwitz did with her.

"You 've been seeing something of Mr. Claude Drew, I hear," he said to Karen that evening. "Do you like him better than you used to do?" They were in the drawing-room before dinner and dinner had been, as usual, waiting for half an hour for Madame von Marwitz.

Gregory's voice betrayed more than a kindly interest, and Karen answered coldly, if without suspicion; "No; I do not like him better. But Tante likes him. It is not I who see him, it is Tante. I am only with them sometimes."

"And I? Am I to be with them sometimes?" Gregory inquired with an air of gaiety.

"If you will come back to tea to-morrow, Gregory," she answered gravely, " you will meet him. He comes to tea then."

For the last few days Gregory had fallen into the habit of only getting back in time for dinner. " You know it's only because I usually find that you've gone out with your guardian that I haven't come back in time for tea," he observed.

" I know," Karen returned, without aggressiveness. " And so, to-morrow, you will find us if you come."

He got back at tea-time next day, expecting to make a fourth only of the small group; but, on his way to the drawing-room, he paused, arrested, in the hall, where a collection of the oddest looking hats and coats he had ever seen were piled and hung.

One of the hats was a large, discoloured, cream-coloured felt, much battered, with its brown band awry; one was of the type of flat-brimmed silk, known in Paris as the *Latin Quartier;* another was an enormous sombrero. Gregory stood frowning at these strange signs somewhat as if they had been a drove of cockroaches. He had, as never yet before, the sense of an alien and offensive invasion of his home, and an old, almost forgotten disquiet smote upon him in the thought that what to him was strange was to Karen normal. This was her life and she had never really entered his.

In the drawing-room, he paused again at the door, and looked over the company assembled under the Bouddha's smile. Madame von Marwitz was its centre; pearl-wreathed, silken and silver, she leaned opulently on the cushions of the sofa where she sat, and Karen at the tea-table seemed curiously to have relapsed into the background place where he had first found her. She was watching, with her old contented placidity, a scene in which she had little part. No, mercifully, though in it she was not of it. This was Gregory's relieving thought as his eye ran over them, the women with powdered faces and extravagant clothes and the men with the oddest collars and boots and hair. " Shoddy Bohemians," was his terse definition of them; an inaccurate definition; for though, in the main, Bohemians, they were not, in the main, shoddy.

Belot was there, with his massive head and sagacious eyes; and a famous actress, ugly, thin, with a long, slightly crooked face, tinted hair, and the melancholy, mysterious eyes of a llama. Claude Drew, at a little table behind Madame von Marwitz, negligently turned the leaves of a book. Lady Rose Harding, the only one of the company with whom Gregory felt an affinity, though a dubious one, talked to the French actress and to Madame von Marwitz. Lady Rose had ridden across deserts on camels, and sketched strange Asiatic mountains, and paid a pilgrimage to Tolstoi, and written books on all these exploits; and she had been to the Adirondacks that summer with the Aspreys and Madame von Marwitz, and was now writing a book on that. In a corner a vast, though youthful, German Jew, with finely crisped red-gold hair, large lips and small, kind eyes blinking near-sightedly behind gold-rimmed spectacles, sat with another young man, his hands on his widely parted knees, in an attitude suggesting a capacity to cope with the most unwieldy instruments of an orchestra; his companion, black and emaciated, talked in German, with violent gestures and a strange accent, jerking constantly a lock of hair out of his eyes. A squat, fat little woman, bundled up, clasping her knees with her joined hands, sat on a footstool at Madame von Marwitz's feet, gazing at her and listening to her with a smile of obsequious attention, and now and then, suddenly, and as if irrelevantly, breaking into a jubilant laugh. Her dusty hair looked as though, like the White Queen's, a comb and brush might be entangled in its masses; the low cut neck of her bodice displayed a ruddy throat wreathed in many strings of dirty seed-pearls, and her grey satin dress was garnished with dirty lace.

Gregory had stood for an appreciable moment at the door surveying the scene, before either Karen or her guardian saw him, and it was then the latter who did the honours of the occasion, naming him to the bundled lady, who was an English poetess, and to Mlle. Suzanne Mauret, the French actress. The inky-locked youth turned out to be a famous Russian violinist, and the vast young German Jew none other than Herr Franz Lippheim, to whom — this was the fact that at once, violently, engaged Gregory's attention — Madame von Marwitz had destined Karen.

Franz Lippheim, after Gregory had spoken to everybody and when he at last was introduced, sprang to his feet and came forward, beaming so intently from behind his spectacles that Gregory, fearing that he might, conceivably, be about to kiss him, made an involuntary gesture of withdrawal. But Herr Lippheim, all unaware, grasped his hand the more vigorously. "Our little Karen's husband!" "Unserer kleinen Karen's Mann!" he uttered in a deeply moved German.

In the driest of tones Gregory asked Karen for some tea, and while he stood above her Herr Lippheim's beam continued to include them both.

"Sit down here, Franz, near me," said Karen. She, too, had smiled joyously as Herr Lippheim greeted her husband. The expression of her face now had changed.

Herr Lippheim obeyed, placing, as before, his hands on his knees, the elbows turned outward, and contemplating Karen's husband with a gaze that might have softened a heart less steeled than Gregory's.

This, then, was Madame von Marwitz's next move; her next experiment in seeing what she could "do." Was not Herr Lippheim a taunt? And with what did he so unpleasantly associate the name of the French actress? The link clicked suddenly. *La Gaine d'Or,* in its veiling French, was about to be produced in London, and it was Mlle. Mauret who had created the heroine's rôle in Paris. These were the people by means of whom Madame von Marwitz displayed her power over Karen's life; — a depraved woman (he knew and cared nothing about Mlle. Mauret's private morality; she was the more repulsive to him if her morals weren't bad; only a woman of no morals should be capable of acting in *La Gaine d'Or;*) that impudent puppy Drew, and this preposterous young man who addressed Karen by her Christian name and included himself in his inappropriate enthusiasm.

He drank his tea, standing in silence by Karen's side, and avoiding all encounter with Herr Lippheim's genial eyes.

"It is like old times, isn't it, Franz?" said Karen, ignoring her husband and addressing her former suitor. "It has been —

16

oh, years — since I have heard such talk. Tante needs all of you, really, to draw her out. She has been wonderful this afternoon, has n't she?"

"*Ah, kolossal!*" said Herr Lippheim, making no gesture, but expressing the depths of his appreciation by an emphasized solemnity of gaze.

"You are right, I think, and so does Tante, evidently," Karen continued, "about the *tempo rubato* in the Mozart. It is strange that Monsieur Ivanowski does n't feel it."

"Ah! but that is it, he does feel it; it is only that he does not think it," said Herr Lippheim, now running his fingers through his hair. "Hear him play the Mozart. He then contradicts in his music all that his words have said."

But though Karen talked so pointedly to him, Herr Lippheim could not keep his eyes or his thoughts from Gregory. "You are a musician, too, Mr. Jardine?" he smiled, bending forward, blinking up through his glasses and laboriously carving out his excellent English. "You do not express, but you have the soul of an artist? Or perhaps you, too, play, like our Karen here."

"No," Gregory returned, with a chill utterance. "I know nothing about music."

"Is it so, Karen?" Herr Lippheim questioned, his guileless warmth hardly tempered.

"My husband is no artist," Karen answered.

It was from her tone rather than from Gregory's that Herr Lippheim seemed to receive his intimation; he was a little disconcerted; he could interpret Karen's tones. "Ach so! Ach so!" he said; but, his goodwill still seeking to find its way to the polished and ambiguous person who had gained Karen's heart,—"But now you will live amongst artists, Mr. Jardine, and you will hear music, great music, played to you by the greatest. So you will come to feel it in the heart." And as Gregory, to this, made no reply, "You will educate him, Karen; is it not so? With you and the great Tante, how could it be otherwise?"

"I am afraid that one cannot create the love of art when it is not there, Franz," Karen returned. She was neither plaintive

nor confiding; yet there was an edge in her voice which Gregory
felt and which, he knew, he was intended to feel. Karen was
angry with him.

"Have you seen Belot's portrait of Tante, yet, Franz?"— she
again excluded her husband; —"It is just finished."

Herr Lippheim had seen it only that morning and he repeated,
but now in preoccupied tones, "*Kolossal!*"

They talked, and Gregory stood above them, aloof from their
conversation frigidly gazing over the company, his elbow in his
hand, his neat fingers twisting his moustache. If he was giving
Madame von Marwitz a handle against him he couldn't help
it. Over the heads of Karen and Herr Lippheim his eyes for
a moment encountered hers. They looked at each other steadily
and neither feigned a smile.

Eleanor Scrotton arrived at six, flushed and flustered.

"Thank heaven, I haven't missed her!" she said to Gregory,
to whom, to-day, Eleanor was an almost welcome sight. Her
eyes had fixed themselves on Mlle. Mauret. "Have you had
a talk with her yet?"

"I haven't had a talk and I yield my claim to you," said
Gregory. "Are you very eager to meet the lady?"

"Who wouldn't be, my dear Gregory! What a wonderful
face! What thought and suffering! Oh, it has been the most
extraordinary of stories. You don't know? Well, I will tell you
about her some time. She is, doubtless, one of the greatest
living actresses. And she is still quite young. Barely forty."

He watched Eleanor make her way to the actress's side, reflecting sardonically upon the modern growths of British tolerance.
Half the respectable matrons in London would, no doubt, take
their girls to see *La Gaine d'Or;* mercifully, they would in all
probability not understand it; but if they did, was there anything that inartistic London would not swallow in its terror
of being accused of philistinism?

The company was dispersing. Herr Lippheim stood holding
Karen's hands saying, as she shook them, that he would bring
das Mütterchen and *die Schwesterchen* to-morrow. Belot came
for a last cup of tea and drank it in sonorous draughts, exchang-

ing a few words with Gregory. He had nothing against Belot. Mr. Drew leaned on Madame von Marwitz's sofa and spoke to her in a low voice while she looked at him inscrutably, her eyes half closed.

"Lucky man," said Lady Rose to Gregory, on her way out, "to have her under your roof. I hope you are a scrupulous Boswell and taking notes." In the hall Barker was assorting the sombrero, the *Latin Quartier* and the cream-coloured felt; the last belonged to Herr Lippheim, who was putting it on when Gregory escorted Lady Rose to the door.

Gregory gave the young man a listless hand. He could n't forgive Herr Lippheim. That he should ever, under whatever encouragements from Karen's guardian, have dared to aspire to her, was a monstrous fact.

He watched the thick rims of Herr Lippheim's ears, under the cream-coloured felt, descending in the lift and wondered if the sight was to be often inflicted upon him.

When he went back to the drawing-room, Karen was alone. Madame von Marwitz had taken Miss Scrotton to her own room. Karen was standing by the tea-table, looking down at it, her hands on the back of the chair from which she had risen to say good-bye to her guardian's guests. She raised her eyes as her husband came in and they rested on him with a strange expression.

CHAPTER XXV

"WILL you shut the door, Gregory?" Karen said. "I want to speak to you." The feeling with which he looked at her was that with which he had faced her sleeping, as he thought, after their former dispute. The sense of failure and disillusion was upon him. As before, it was only of her guardian that she was thinking. He knew that he had given Madame von Marwitz a handle against him.

He obeyed her and when he came and stood before her she went on. "Before we all meet at dinner again, I must ask you something. Do not make your contempt of Tante's guests — and of mine — more plain to her than you have already done this afternoon."

"Did I make it plain?" Gregory asked, after a moment.

"I think that if I felt it so strongly, Tante must have felt it," said Karen, and to this, after another pause, Gregory found nothing further to say than "I'm sorry."

"I hardly think," said Karen, holding the back of her chair tightly and looking down again while she spoke, "that you can have realized that Herr Lippheim is not only Tante's friend, but mine. I don't think you can have realized how you treated him. I know that he is very simple and unworldly; but he is good and kind and faithful; he is a true artist — almost a great one, and he has the heart of a child. And beside him, while you were hurting and bewildering him so to-day, you looked to me — how shall I say it — petty, yes, and foolish, yes, and full of self-conceit."

The emotion with which Gregory heard her speak these words, deliberately, if in a hardened and controlled voice, expressed itself, as emotion did with him, in a slight, fixed smile. He could not pause to examine Karen's possible justice; that she should speak so, to him, was the overpowering fact.

"I imagined that I behaved with courtesy," he said.

245

"Yes, you were courteous," Karen replied. "You made me think of a painted piece of wood while he was like a growing tree."

"Your simile is certainly very mortifying," said Gregory, continuing to smile. But he was not mortified. He was cruelly hurt.

"I do not wish to mortify you. I have not mortified you, because you think yourself above it all. But I would like, if I could," said Karen, "to make you see the truth. I would like to make you see that in behaving as you have you show yourself not above it but below it."

"And I would like to make you see the truth, too," Gregory returned, in the voice of his bitter hurt; "and I ask you, if your prejudice will permit of it, to make some allowance for my feeling when I found you surrounded by — this rabble."

"Rabble? My guardian's friends?" Karen had grown ashen.

"I hope they're not; but I'm not concerned with her friends; I'm concerned with you. She can take people in, on the artistic plane, whom it's not fit that you should meet. That horrible actress,— I wouldn't have her come within sight of you if I could help it. Your guardian knows my feeling about the parts she plays. She had no business to ask her here. As for Herr Lippheim, I have no doubt that he is an admirable person in his own walk of life, but he is a preposterous person, and it is preposterous that your guardian should have thought of him as a possible husband for you." Gregory imagined that he was speaking carefully and choosing his words, but he was aware that his anger coloured his voice. He had also been aware, some little time before, in a lower layer of consciousness, of the stir and rustle of steps and dresses in the passage outside — Madame von Marwitz conducting Eleanor Scrotton to the door. And now — had she actually been listening, or did his words coincide with the sudden opening of the door? — Madame von Marwitz herself appeared upon the threshold.

Her face made the catastrophe all too evident. She had heard him. She had, he felt convinced, crept quietly back and stood to listen before entering. His memory reconstructed the long pause between the departing rustle and this apparition.

Madame von Marwitz's face had its curious look of smothered heat. The whites of her eyes were suffused though her cheeks were pale.

"I must apologise," she said. "I overheard you as I entered, Mr. Jardine, and what I heard I cannot ignore. What is it that you say to Karen? What is it that you say of the man I thought of as a possible husband for her?"

She advanced into the room and laying her arm round Karen's shoulders she stood confronting him.

"I don't think I can discuss this with you," said Gregory. "I am very sorry that you overheard me." The slight smile of his pain had gone. He looked at Madame von Marwitz with a flinty eye.

"Ah, but you must discuss it; you shall," said Madame von Marwitz. "You say things to my child that I am not to overhear. You seek to poison her mind against me. You take her from me and then blacken me in her eyes. A possible husband! Would to God," said Madame von Marwitz, with sombre fury, "that the possibility had been fulfilled! Would to God that it were my brave, deep-hearted Franz who were her husband — not you, most ungrateful, most ungenerous of men."

"Tante," said Karen, who still stood looking down, grasping her chair-back and encircled by her guardian's arm, "he did not mean you to hear him. Forgive him."

"I beg your pardon, Karen," said Gregory, "I am very sorry that Madame von Marwitz overheard me; but I have said nothing for which I wish to apologize."

"Ah! You hear him!" cried Madame von Marwitz, and the inner conflagration now glittered in her eyes like flames behind the windows of a burning house. "You hear him, Karen? Forgive him! How can I forgive him when he has made you wretched! How can I ever forgive him when he tears your life by thrusting me forth from it — me — and everything I am and mean! You have witnessed it, Karen — you have seen my efforts to win your husband. You have seen his contempt for me, his rancour, his half-hidden insolence. Never — ah, never in my life have I faced such humiliation as has been offered to me beneath his roof — humiliations, endured for your sake, Karen — for yours only! Ah " — releasing Karen suddenly, she advanced a step towards Gregory, with a startling cry, stretching out her arm —" ungrateful and ungenerous indeed! And you find yourself one to scorn my Franz! You find yourself one to sneer at my friends, to stand and look at them and me as if we were vermin infesting your room! Did I not see it! You! *justes cieux!* with your bourgeois little world; your little — little world — so small — so small! your people like dull beasts pacing in a cage, believing that in the meat thrust in between their bars and the number of steps to be taken from side to side lies all the meaning of life; people who survey with their heavy eyes of surfeit the free souls of the world! Hypocrites! Pharisees! And to this cage you have consigned my child! and you would make of her, too, a creature of counted paces and of unearned meat! You would shut her in from the life of beauty and freedom that she has known! Ah never! never! there you do not triumph! You have taken her from me; you have won her love; but her mind is not yours; she sees the cage as I do; you do not share the deep things of the soul with her. And in her loyal heart — ah, I know it — will be the cry, undying, for one whose heart you have trod upon and broken! "

With these last words, gasped forth on rising sobs, Madame von Marwitz sank into the chair where Karen still leaned and broke into passionate tears.

Gregory again was smiling, with the smile now of decorum at bay, of embarrassment rather than contempt; but to Karen's eyes it was the smile of supercilious arrogance. She looked at him sternly over her guardian's bowed and oddly rolling head. " Speak, Gregory! Speak! " she commanded.

" My dear," said Gregory — their voices seemed to pass above the clash and uproar of stormy waters, Madame von Marwitz had abandoned herself to an elemental grief —" I have nothing to say to your guardian."

" To me, then," Karen clenched her hands on the back of the

chair; "to me, then, you have something to say. Is it not true? Have you not repulsed her efforts to come near you? Have you not, behind her back, permitted yourself to speak with scorn of the man she hoped I would marry?"

Gregory paused, and in the pause, as he observed, Madame von Marwitz was able to withhold for a moment her strange groans and gaspings while she listened. "I don't think there has been any such effort," he said. "We were both keeping up appearances, your guardian and I; and I think that I kept them up best. As for Herr Lippheim, it was only when you accused me of rudeness to him that I confessed how much it astonished me to find that he was the man your guardian had wished you to marry. It does astonish me. Herr Lippheim is n't even a gentleman."

"Enough!" cried Madame von Marwitz. She sprang to her feet. "Enough!" she said, half suffocated. "It is the voice of the cage! We will not stay to hear its standards applied. Come with me, Karen, that I may say farewell to you."

She caught Karen by the arm. Her face was strange, savage, suffused. Gregory went to open the door for them. "Base one!" she said to him. "Ignominious one!"

She drew Karen swiftly along the passage and, still keeping her sharp clasp of her wrist while she opened and closed the door of her room, she sank, encircling her with her arms, upon the sofa, and wept loudly over her.

Karen, too, was now weeping; heavy, shaking sobs.

"My child! My poor child!" Madame von Marwitz murmured brokenly after a little time had gone. "I would have spared you this. It has come. We have both seen it. And now, so that your life may not be ruined, I must leave it."

"But Tante — my Tante —" sobbed Karen — Madame von Marwitz did not remember that Karen had ever so sobbed before —"you cannot mean those words. What shall I do if you say this? What is left for me?"

"My child, your life is left you," said Madame von Marwitz, holding her close and speaking with her lips in the girl's hair. "Your husband's love is left; the happiness that you chose and that I shall shatter if I stay; ah, yes, my Karen, how deny it now? I see my path. It is plain before me. To-night I go to Mrs. Forrester and to-morrow I breathe the air of Cornwall."

"But Tante — wait — wait. You will see Gregory again? You will let him explain? Oh, let me first talk with him! He says bitter things, but so do you, Tante; and he does not mean to offend as much as you think."

At this, after a little pause, Madame von Marwitz drew herself slightly away and put her handkerchief to her eyes and cheeks. The violence of her grief was over. "Does he still so blind you, Karen?" she then asked. "Do you still not see that your husband hates me — and has hated me from the beginning?"

"Not hate! — Not hate!" Karen sobbed. "He does not understand you — that is all. Only wait — till to-morrow. Only let me talk to him!"

"No. He does not understand. That is evident," said Madame von Marwitz with a bitter smile. "Nor will he ever understand. Will you talk to him, Karen, so that he shall explain why he smirches my love and my sincerity? You know as well as I what was the meaning of those words of his. Can you, loving me, ask me to sue further for the favour of a man who has so insulted me? No. It cannot be. I cannot see him again. You and I are still to meet, I trust; but it cannot again be under this roof."

Karen now sobbed helplessly, leaning forward, her face in her hands, and Madame von Marwitz, again laying an arm around her shoulders, gazed with majestic sorrow into the fire. "Even so," she said at last, when Karen's sobs had sunken to long, broken breaths; "even so. It is the law of life. Sacrifice: sacrifice: to the very end. Life, to the artist, must be this altar where he lays his joys. We are destined to be alone, Karen. We are driven forth into the wilderness for the sins of the people. So I have often seen it, and cried out against it in my tortured youth, and struggled against it in my strength and in my folly. But now, with another strength, I am enabled to

stand upright and to face the vision of my destiny. I am to
be alone. So be it."

No answer came from Karen and Madame von Marwitz, after
a pause, continued, in gentler, if no less solemn tones: "And
my child, too, is brave. She, too, will stand upright. She, too,
has her destiny to fulfil — in the world — not in the wilderness.
And if the burden should ever grow too heavy, and the road cut
her feet too sharply, and the joy turn to dust, she will remember
— always — that Tante's arms and heart are open to her — at
all times, in all places, and to the end of life. And now," this,
with a sigh of fatigue, came on a more matter-of-fact note —
"let a cab be called for me. Louise will follow with my boxes."

Karen's tears had ceased. She made no further protest or
appeal.

Rising, she dried her eyes, rang and ordered the cab to be called
and found her guardian's white cloak and veiled hat.

And while she shrouded her in these, Madame von Marwitz,
still gazing, as if at visions, in the fire, lifted her arms and bent
her head with almost the passivity of a dead thing. Once or
twice she murmured broken phrases: "My ewe-lamb; —
taken; — I am very weary. *Mon Dieu, mon Dieu,*— and is this,
then, the end. . . ."

She rested heavily on Karen's shoulder in rising. "Forgive
me," she said, leaning her head against hers, "forgive me, beloved one. I have done harm where I meant to make a safer
happiness. Forgive me, too, for my bitter words. I should
not have spoken as I did. My child knows that it is a hot and
passionate heart."

Karen, in silence, turned her face to her guardian's breast.

"And do not," said Madame von Marwitz, speaking with
infinite tenderness, while she stroked the bent head, " judge your
husband too hardly because of this. He gives what love he can;
as he knows love. It is as my child said; he does not understand. It is not given to some to understand. He has lived in
a narrow world. Do not judge him hardly, Karen; it is for
the wiser, stronger, more loving soul to lift the smaller towards

the light. He can still give my child happiness. In that trust I find my strength."

They went down the passage together. Gregory came to the drawing-room door. He would have spoken, have questioned, but, shrinking from him and against Karen, as if from an intolerable searing, Madame von Marwitz hastened past him. He heard the front door open and the last silent pause of farewell on the threshold.

Louise scuttled by past him to her mistress's vacated rooms. She did not see him and he heard that she muttered under her breath: *"Ah! par exemple! C'est trop fort, ma parole d'honneur!"*

As Karen came back from the door he went to meet her.

"Karen," he said, "will you come and talk with me, now?"

She put aside his hand. "I cannot talk. Do not come to me," she said. "I must think." And going into their room she shut the door.

CHAPTER XXVI

THE telephone sounded while Gregory next morning ate his solitary breakfast, and the voice of Mrs. Forrester, disembodied of all but its gravity, asked him, if he would, to come and see her immediately.

Gregory asked if Madame von Marwitz were with her. He was not willing, after the final affront that she had put upon him, to encounter Madame von Marwitz again in circumstances where he might seem to be justifying himself. But, with a deeper drop, the disembodied voice informed him that Madame von Marwitz, ten minutes before, had driven to the station on her way to Cornwall. "You will understand, I think, Gregory," said Mrs. Forrester, "that it is hardly possible for her to face in London, as yet, the situation that you have made for her."

Gregory, to this, replied, shortly, that he would come to her at once, reserving his comments on the imputed blame.

He had passed an almost sleepless night, lying in his little dressing-room bed where, by a tacit agreement, never explicitly recognized, he had slept, now, for so many nights. Cold fears, shaped at last in definite forms, stood round him and bade him see the truth. His wife did not love him. From the beginning he had been as nothing to her compared with her guardian. The pale, hard light of her eyes as she had said to him that afternoon, "Speak!" seemed to light the darkness with bitter revelations. He knew that he was what would be called, sentimentally, a broken-hearted man; but it seemed that the process of breaking had been gradual; so that now, when his heart lay in pieces, his main feeling was not of sharp pain but of dull fatigue, not of tragic night, but of a grey commonplace from which all sunlight had slowly ebbed away.

He found Mrs. Forrester in her morning-room among loudly singing canaries and pots of jonquils; and as he shook hands with

253

her he saw that this old friend, so old and so accustomed that she was like a part of his life, was embarrassed. The wrinkles on her withered, but oddly juvenile, face seemed to have shifted to a pattern of perplexity and pained resolution. He was not embarrassed, though he was beaten and done in a way Mrs. Forrester could not guess at; yet he felt an awkwardness.

They had known each other for a life-time, he and Mrs. Forrester, but they were not intimate; and how intimate they would have to become if they were to discuss with anything like frankness the causes and consequences of Madame von Marwitz's conduct! A gloomy indifference settled on Gregory as he realized that her dear friend's conduct was the one factor in the causes and consequences that Mrs. Forrester would not be able to appraise at its true significance.

She shook his hand, and seating herself at a little table and slightly tapping it with her fingers, "Now, my dear Gregory," she said, "will you, please, tell me why you have acted like this?"

"Isn't my case prejudged?" Gregory asked, reconstructing the scene that must have taken place last night when Madame von Marwitz had appeared before her friend.

"No, Gregory; it is not," Mrs. Forrester returned with some terseness, for she felt his remark to be unbecoming. "I hope to have some sort of explanation from you."

"I'm quite ready to explain; but it's hardly possible that my explanation will satisfy you," said Gregory. "You spoke, just now, when you called me up, of a situation and said I'd made it. My explanation can only consist in saying that I didn't make it; that Madame von Marwitz made it; that she came to us in order to make it and then to fix the odium of it on me."

Already Mrs. Forrester had flushed. She looked hard at the pot of jonquils near her. "You really believe that?"

"I do. She can't forgive me for not liking her," said Gregory.

"And you don't like her. You own to it."

"I don't like her. I own to it," Gregory replied with a certain frosty relief. It was like taking off damp, threadbare garments that had chilled one for a long time and facing the winter wind, naked, but invigorated. "I dislike her very much."

"May I ask why?" Mrs. Forrester inquired, with careful courtesy.

"I distrust her," said Gregory. "I think she's dangerous, and tyrannous, and unscrupulous. I think that she's devoured by egotism. I'm sorry. But if you ask me why, I can only tell you."

Mrs. Forrester sat silent for a moment, and then, the flush on her delicate old cheek deepening, she murmured: "It is worse, far worse, than Mercedes told me. Even Mercedes did n't suspect this. Gregory,— I must ask you another question: Do you really imagine that you and your cruel thoughts of her would be of the slightest consequence to Mercedes Okraska, if you had not married the child for whose happiness she holds herself responsible?"

"Of course not. She would n't give me another thought, if I were n't there, in her path; I am in her path, and she feels that I don't like her, and she has n't been able to let me alone."

"She has not let you alone because she hoped to make your marriage secure in the only way in which security was possible for you and Karen. What happiness could she see for Karen's future if she were to have cut herself apart from her life; dropped you, and Karen with you? That, doubtless, would have been the easy thing to do. There is indeed no reason why women like Mercedes Okraska, women with the world at their feet, should trouble to think of the young men they may chance to meet, whose exacting moral sense they don't satisfy. I am glad you see that," said Mrs. Forrester, tapping her table.

"It would have been far kinder to have dropped Karen than deliberately to set to work, as she has done, to ruin her happiness. She has n't been able to keep her hands off it. She could n't stand it — a happiness she had n't given; a happiness for which gratitude was n't due to her."

"Gregory, Gregory," Mrs. Forrester raised her eyes to him now; "you are frank with me, very frank; and I must be frank with you. There is more than dislike here, and distrust, and morbid prejudice. There is jealousy. Hints of it have come to me; I've tried to put them aside; I've tried to believe, as my poor Mercedes did, that, by degrees, you would adjust yourself to the claims on Karen's life, and be generous and understanding, even when you had no spontaneous sympathy to give. But it is all quite clear to me now. You can't accept the fact of your wife's relation to Mercedes. You can't accept the fact of a devotion not wholly directed towards yourself. I've known you since boyhood, Gregory, and I've always had regard and fondness for you; but this is a serious breach between us. You seem to me more wrong and arrogant than I could trust myself to say. And you have behaved cruelly to a woman for whom my feeling is more than mere friendship. In many ways my feeling for Mercedes Okraska is one of reverence. She is one of the great people of the world. To know her has been a possession, a privilege. Anyone might be proud to know such a woman. And when I think of what you have now said of her to me — when I think of how I saw her — here — last night, — broken — crushed,— after so many sorrows —"

Tears had risen to Mrs. Forrester's eyes. She turned her head aside.

"Do you mean," said Gregory after a moment, in which it seemed to him that his grey world preceptibly, if slightly, darkened, "do you mean that I've lost your friendship because of Madame von Marwitz?"

"I don't know, Gregory; I can't tell you," said Mrs. Forrester, not looking at him. "I don't recognize you. As to Karen, I cannot imagine what your position with her can be. How is she to bear it when she knows that it is said that you insulted her guardian's friends and then turned her out of your house?"

"I didn't turn her out," said Gregory; he walked to the window and stared into the street. "She went because that was the most venomous thing she could do. And I didn't insult her friends."

"You said to her that the man she had thought of as a husband for Karen was not a gentleman. You said that you did

not understand how Mercedes could have chosen such a man for
her. You said this with the child standing between you. Oh,
you cannot deny it, Gregory. I have heard in detail what took
place. Mercedes saw that unless she left you Karen's position
was an impossible one. It was to save Karen — and your relation to Karen — that she went."

Gregory, still standing at the window, was silent, and then
asked: "Have you seen Herr Lippheim?"

"No, Gregory," Mrs. Forrester returned, and now with
trenchancy, the concrete case being easier to deal with openly.
"No; I have not seen him; but Mercedes spoke to me about
him last winter, when she hoped for the match, and told me,
moreover, that she was surprised by Karen's refusal, as the child
was much attached to him. I have not seen him; but I know
the type — and intimately. He is a warm-hearted and intelligent musician."

"Your bootmaker may be warm-hearted and intelligent."

"That is petulant — almost an insolent simile, Gregory. It
only reveals, pitifully, your narrowness and prejudice — and,
I will add, your ignorance. Herr Lippheim is an artist; a man
of character and significance. Many of my dearest friends have
been such; hearts of gold; the salt of the world."

"Would you have allowed a daughter of yours, may I ask,
to marry one of these hearts of gold?"

"Certainly; most certainly," said Mrs. Forrester, but with a
haste and heat somewhat suspicious. "If she loved him."

"If he were personally fit, you mean. Herr Lippheim is undoubtedly warm-hearted and, in his own way, intelligent, but
he is as unfit to be Karen's husband as your bootmaker to be
yours."

They had come now, on this lower, easier level, to one of the
points where temper betrays itself as it cannot do on the heights
of contest. Gregory's reiteration of the bootmaker greatly incensed Mrs. Forrester.

"My dear Gregory," she said, "I yield to no one in my appreciation of Karen; owing to the education and opportunities that
Mercedes has given her, she is a charming young woman. But,

17

since we are dealing with facts, the bare, bald, worldly aspects
of things, we must not forget the facts of Karen's parentage
and antecedents. Herr Lippheim is, in these respects, I imagine, altogether her equal. A rising young musician, the friend
and *protégé* of one of the world's great geniuses, and a penniless,
illegitimate girl. Do not let your rancour, your jealousy,
blind you so completely."

Gregory turned from the window at this, smiling a pallid,
frosty smile and Mrs. Forrester was now aware that she had
made him very angry. "I may be narrow," he said, "and
conventional and ignorant; but I'm unconventional and clear-
sighted enough to judge people by their actual, not their market,
value. Of Herr Lippheim I know nothing, except that his
parentage and antecedents have n't made a gentleman, or anything resembling one, of him; while of Karen I know that hers,
unfortunate as they certainly were, have made a lady and a
very perfect one. I don't forgive Madame von Marwitz for a
great many things in regard to her treatment of Karen,"
Gregory went on with growing bitterness, "chief among them
that she has taken her at her market value and allowed her
friends to do the same. I've been able, thank goodness, to rescue
Karen, at all events, from that. Madame von Marwitz can't
carry her about any longer like a badge from some charitable society on her shoulder. No woman who really loved Karen, or
who really appreciated her," Gregory added, falling back on his
concrete fact, "could have thought of Herr Lippheim as a husband for her."

Mrs. Forrester sat looking up at him, and she was genuinely
aghast.

"You are incredible to me, Gregory," she said. "You set
your one year of devotion to Karen against Mercedes's life-time,
and you presume to discredit hers."

"Yes. I do. I don't believe in her devotion to Karen."

"Do you realize that your attitude may mean a complete
rupture between Karen and her guardian?"

"No such luck; I'm afraid!" said Gregory with a grim laugh.
"My only hope is that it may mean a complete rupture be-

tween Madame von Marwitz and me. It goes without saying, feeling as I do, that, if it would n't break Karen's heart, I 'd do my best to prevent Madame von Marwitz from ever seeing her again."

There was a little silence and then Mrs. Forrester got up sharply.

"Very well, Gregory," she said. "That will do."

"Are you going to shake hands with me?" he asked, still with the grim smile.

"Yes. I will shake hands with you, Gregory," Mrs. Forrester replied. "Because, in spite of everything, I am fond of you. But you must not come here again. Not now."

"Never any more, do you really mean?"

"Not until you are less wickedly blind."

"I 'm sorry," said Gregory. "It 's never any more then, I 'm afraid."

He was very sorry. He knew that as he walked away.

CHAPTER XXVII

MRS. FORRESTER remained among her canaries and jonquils, thinking. She was seriously perturbed. She was, as she had said, fond of Gregory, but she was fonder, far, of Mercedes von Marwitz, whom Gregory had caused to suffer and whom he would, evidently, cause to suffer still more.

She controlled the impulse to telephone to Eleanor Scrotton and consult with her; a vague instinct of loyalty towards Gregory restrained her from that. Eleanor would, in a day or two, hear from Cornwall and what she would hear could not be so bad as what Mrs. Forrester herself could tell her. After thinking for the rest of the morning, Mrs. Forrester decided to go and see Karen. She was not very fond of Karen. She had always been inclined to think that Mercedes exaggerated the significance of the girl's devotion, and Gregory's exaggeration, now, of her general significance — explicable as it might be in an infatuated young husband — disposed her the less kindly towards her. She felt that Karen had been clumsy, dull, in the whole affair. She felt that, at bottom, she was somewhat responsible for it. How had Gregory been able, living with Karen, to have formed such an insensate conception of Mercedes? The girl was stupid, acquiescent; she had shown no tact, no skill, no clarifying courage. Mrs. Forrester determined to show them all — to talk to Karen.

She drove to St. James's at four o'clock that afternoon and Barker told her that Mrs. Jardine was in the drawing-room. Visitors, evidently, were with her, and it affected Mrs. Forrester very unpleasantly, as Barker led her along the passage, to hear rich harmonies of music filling the flat. She had expected to be perhaps ushered into a darkened bedroom; to administer comfort and sympathy to a shattered creature before administering reproof and counsel. But Karen not only was up; she was not alone. The strains were those of chamber-music, and a half-perplexed delight mingled with Mrs. Forrester's displeasure as she recognized the heavenly melodies of Schumann's Pianoforte Quintet. The performers were in the third movement.

Karen rose, as Barker announced her, from the side of a stout lady at the piano, and Mrs. Forrester, nodding, her finger at her lips, dropped into a chair and listened.

The stout lady at the piano had a pale, fat, pear-shaped face, her grizzled hair parted above it and twisted to a large outstanding knob behind. She wore eyeglasses and peered through them at her music with intelligent intensity and profound humility. The violin was played by an enormous young man with red hair, and the viola, second violin and 'cello by three young women, all of the black-and-tan Semitic type.

Mrs. Forrester was too much preoccupied with her wonder to listen as she would have wished to, but by the time the end of the movement was come she had realized that they played extremely well.

Karen came forward in the interval. She was undoubtedly pale and heavy-eyed; but in her little dress of dark blue silk, with her narrow lawn ruffles and locket and shining hair, she showed none of the desperate signs appropriate to her circumstances nor any embarrassment at the incongruous situation in which Mrs. Forrester found her.

"This is Frau Lippheim, Mrs. Forrester," she said. "And these are Fräulein Lotta and Minna and Elizabeth, and this is Herr Franz. I think you have often heard Tante speak of our friends."

Her ears buzzing with the name of Lippheim since the night before, Mrs. Forrester was aware that she showed confusion, also that for a brief, sharp instant, while her eyes rested on Herr Franz, a pang of perverse sympathy for Gregory, in a certain aspect of his wickedness, disintegrated her state of mind. He was singular looking indeed, this untidy young man, whose ill-kept clothes had a look of insecurity, like arrested avalanches on a mountain. "No, I can feel for Gregory somewhat in this," Mrs. Forrester said to herself.

"We are having some music, you see," said Karen. "Herr Lippheim promised me yesterday that they would all come and play to me. Can you stay and listen for a little while? They must go before tea, for they have a rehearsal for their concert," she added, as though to let Mrs. Forrester know that she was not unconscious of the matter that must have brought her.

There was really no reason why she shouldn't stay. She could not very well ask to have the Lippheims and their instruments turned out. Moreover she was very fond of the Quintet. Mrs. Forrester said that she would be glad to stay.

When they went on to the fourth movement, and while she listened, giving her mind to the music, Mrs. Forrester's disintegration slowly recomposed itself. It was not only that the music was heavenly and that they played so well. She liked these people; they were the sort of people she had always liked. She forgot Herr Franz's uncouth and mountainous aspect. His great head leaning sideways, his eyes half closed, with the musician's look of mingled voluptuous rapture and cold, grave, listening intellect, he had a certain majesty. The mother, too, all devout concentration, was an artist of the right sort; the girls had the gentle benignity that comes of sincere self-dedication. They pleased Mrs. Forrester greatly and, as she listened, her severity towards Gregory shaped itself anew and more forcibly. Narrow, blind, bigoted young man. And it was amusing to think, as a comment on his fierce consciousness of Herr Lippheim's unfitness, that here Herr Lippheim was, admitted to the very heart of Karen's sorrow. It was inconceivable that anyone but very near and dear friends should have been tolerated by her to-day. Karen, too, after her fashion, was an artist. The music, no doubt, was helpful to her. Soft thoughts of her great, lacerated friend, speeding now towards her solitudes, filled Mrs. Forrester's eyes more than once with tears.

They finished and Frau Lippheim, rubbing her hands with her handkerchief, stood smiling near-sightedly, while Mrs. Forrester expressed her great pleasure and asked all the Lippheims to come and see her. She planned already a musical. Karen's face showed a pale beam of gladness.

"And now, my dear child," said Mrs. Forrester, when the Lippheims had departed and she and Karen were alone and seated side by side on the sofa, "we must talk. I have come, of course you know, to talk about this miserable affair." She put her hand on Karen's; but already something in the girl's demeanour renewed her first displeasure. She looked heavy, she looked phlegmatic; there was no response, no softness in her glance.

"You have perhaps a message to me, Mrs. Forrester, from Tante," she said.

"No, Karen, no," Mrs. Forrester with irrepressible severity returned. "I have no message for you. Any message, I think should come from your husband and not from your guardian."

Karen sat silent, her eyes moving away from her visitor's face and fixing themselves on the wall above her head.

The impulse that had brought Mrs. Forrester was suffering alterations.

Gregory had revealed the case to her as worse than she had supposed; Karen emphasized the revelation. And what of Mercedes between these two young egoists? "I must ask you, Karen," she said, "whether you realise how Gregory has behaved, to the woman to whom you, and he, owe so much?"

Karen continued to look fixedly at the wall and after a moment of deliberation replied: "Tante did not speak rightly to Gregory, Mrs. Forrester. She lost her temper very much. You know that Tante can lose her temper."

Mrs. Forrester, at this, almost lost hers. "You surprise me, Karen. Your husband had spoken insultingly of her friends — and yours — to her. Why attempt to shield him? I heard the whole story, in detail, from your guardian, you must remember."

Again Karen withdrew into a considering silence; but, though her face remained impassive, Mrs. Forrester observed that a slight flush rose to her cheeks.

"Gregory did not intend Tante to overhear what he said," she produced at last. "It was said to me — and I had questioned him — not to her. Tante came in by chance. It is not likely, Mrs. Forrester, that my version would differ in any way from hers."

"You mustn't take offence at what I say, Karen," Mrs. Forrester spoke with more severity; "your version does differ. To my astonishment you seem actually to defend your husband."

"Yes; from what is not true: that is not to differ from Tante as to what took place." Karen brought her eyes to Mrs. Forrester's.

"From what is not true. Very well. You will not deny that he so intensely dislikes your guardian and has shown it so plainly to her that she has had to leave you. You will not deny that, Karen?"

"No. I will not deny that," Karen replied.

"My poor child — it is true, and it is only a small part of the truth. I don't know what Gregory has said to you in private, but even Mercedes had not prepared me for what he said to me this morning."

"What did he say to you this morning, Mrs. Forrester?"

"He believes her to be a bad woman, Karen; do you realise that; has he told you that; can you bear it? Dangerous, un-scrupulous, tyrannous, devoured by egotism, were the words he used of her. I shall not forget them. He accused her of hy-pocrisy in her feeling for you. He hoped that you might never see her again. It is terrible, Karen. Terrible. It puts us all — all of us who love Mercedes, and you through her, into the most impossible position."

Karen sat, her head erect, her eyes downcast, with a rigidity of expression almost torpid.

"Do you see the position he puts us in, Karen?" Mrs. Forrester went on with insistence. "Have you had the matter out with Gregory? Did you realise its gravity? I must really beg you to answer me."

"I have not yet spoken with my husband," said Karen, in a chill, lifeless tone.

"But you will? You cannot let it pass?"

"No, Mrs. Forrester. I will not let it pass."

"You will insist that he shall make a full apology to Mercedes?"

"Is he to apologise to her for hating her?" Karen at this asked suddenly.

"For hating her? What do you mean?" Mrs. Forrester was taken aback.

"If he is to apologise," said Karen, in a still colder, still more lifeless voice, "it must be for something that can be changed. How can he apologise to her for hating her if he continues to hate her?"

"He can apologise for having spoken insultingly to her."

"He has not done that. It was Tante who overheard what she was not intended to hear. And it was Tante who spoke with violence."

"It amazes me to hear you put it on her shoulders, Karen. He can apologise, then, for what he has said to me," said Mrs. Forrester with indignation. "You will not deny that what he said of her to me was insulting."

"He is to tell her that he has said those words and then apologise, Mrs. Forrester? Oh, no; you do not think what you say."

"Really, my dear Karen, you have a most singular fashion of speaking to a person three times your age!" Mrs. Forrester exclaimed, the more incensed for the confusion of thought into which the girl's persistence threw her. "The long and short of it is that he must make it possible for Mercedes to meet him, with decency, in the future."

"But I do not know how that can be," said Karen, rising as Mrs. Forrester rose; "I do not know how Tante, now, can see him. If he thinks these things and does not say them, there may be pretence; but if he says them, to Tante's friends, how can there be pretence?"

There was no appeal in her voice. She put the facts, so evident to herself, before her visitor and asked her to look at them. Mrs. Forrester was suddenly aware that her advice might have been somewhat hasty. She also felt suddenly as though, on a reconnoitring march down a rough but open path, she found herself merging in the gloomy mysteries of a forest. There were hidden things in Karen's voice.

" Well, well," she said, taking the girl's hand and casting about in her mind for a retreat; " that's to see it as hopeless, is n't it, and we don't want to do that, do we? We want to bring Gregory to reason, and you are the person best fitted to do that. We want to clear up these dreadful ideas he has got into his head, heaven knows how. And no one but you can do it. No one in the world, my dear Karen, is more fitted than you to make him understand what our wonderful Tante really is. There is the trouble, Karen," said Mrs. Forrester, finding now the original clue with which she had started on her expedition; " he should n't have been able, living with you, seeing your devotion, seeing from your life, as you must have told him of it, what it was founded on, he should n't have been able to form such a monstrous conception of our great, dear one. You have been in fault there, my dear, you see it now, I am sure. At the first hint you should have made things clear to him. I know that it is hard for a young wife to oppose the man she loves; but love must n't make us cowardly," Mrs. Forrester murmured on more cheerfully as they moved down the passage, " and Gregory will only love you more wisely and deeply if he is made to recognize, once for all, that you will not sacrifice your guardian to please him."

They were now at the door and Karen had not said a word.

" Well, good-bye, my dear," said Mrs. Forrester. Oddly she did not feel able to urge more strongly upon Karen that she should not sacrifice her guardian to her husband. " I hope I 've made things clearer by coming. It was better that you should realize just what your guardian's friends felt — and would feel — about it, was n't it?" Karen still made no reply and on the threshold Mrs. Forrester paused to add, with some urgency: " It was right, you see that, don't you, Karen, that you should know what Gregory is really feeling?"

" Yes," Karen now assented. " It is better that I should know that."

CHAPTER XXVIII

GREGORY when he came in that evening thought at first, with a pang of fear, that Karen had gone out. It was time for dressing and she was not in their room. In the drawing-room it was dark; he stood in the door-way for a moment and looked about it, sad and tired and troubled, wondering if Karen had gone to Mrs. Forrester's, wondering whether, in her grave displeasure with him, she had even followed her guardian. And then, from beside him, came her voice. "I am here, Gregory. I have been waiting for you."

His relief was so intense that, turning up the lights, seeing her sitting there on a little sofa near the door, he bent involuntarily over her to kiss her.

But her hand put him away.

"No; I must speak to you," she said.

Gregory straightened himself, compressing his lips.

Karen had evidently not thought of changing. She wore her dark-blue silk dress. She had, indeed, been sitting there since Mrs. Forrester went. He looked about the room, noting, with dull wonder, the grouped chairs, and open piano. "You have had people here?"

"Yes. The Lippheims came and played to me. I would have written to them and told them not to come; but I forgot. And Mrs. Forrester has been here."

"Quite a reception," said Gregory. He walked to the window and looked out. "Well," he said, not turning to his wife, "what have you to say to me, Karen?" His tone was dry and even ironic.

"Mrs. Forrester came to tell me," said Karen, "that you had seen her this morning."

"Yes. Well?"

"And she told me," Karen went on, "that you had a great

267

deal to say to her about my guardian — things that you have never dared to say to me."

He turned to her now and her eyes from across the room fixed themselves upon him.

"I will say them to you if you like," said Gregory, after a moment. He leaned against the side of the window and folded his arms. And he examined his wife with, apparently, the cold attention that he would have given to a strange witness in the box. And indeed she was strange to him. Over his aching and dispossessed heart he steeled himself in an impartial scrutiny.

"It is true, then," said Karen, "that you believe her tyrannous and dangerous and unscrupulous, and that you think her devoured by egotism, and hypocritical in her feeling for me, and that you hope that I may never see her again?"

She catalogued the morning's declarations accurately, like the witness giving unimpeachable testimony. But it was rather absurd to see her as the witness, when, so unmistakably, she considered herself the judge and him the criminal in the dock. There was relief in pleading guilty to everything. "Yes: it's perfectly true," he said.

She looked at him and he could discover no emotion on her face.

"Why did you not tell me this when you asked me to marry you?" she questioned.

"Oh — I wasn't so sure of it then," said Gregory. "And I loved you and hoped it would never come out. I didn't want to give you pain. That's why I never dared tell you, as you put it."

"You wanted to marry me and you knew that if you told me the truth I would not marry you; that is the reason you did not dare," said Karen.

"Well, there's probably truth in that," Gregory assented, smiling; "I'm afraid I was an infatuated creature, perhaps a dishonest one. I can't expect you to make allowances for my condition, I know."

She lowered her eyes and sat for so long in silence that pres-

ently, rather ashamed of the bitterness of his last words, he went
on in a kinder tone: "I know that I can never make you understand. You have your infatuation and it blinds you.
You've been blind to the way in which, from the very beginning, she has tracked me down. You've been blind to the fact
that the thing that has moved her hasn't been love for you but
spite, malicious spite, against me for not giving her the sort
of admiration she's accustomed to. If I've come to hate her
— I didn't in the least at first, of course — it's only fair to
say that she hates me ten times worse. I only asked that she
should let me alone."

"And let me alone," said Karen, who had listened without
a movement.

"Oh no," Gregory said, "that's not at all true. You surely
will be fair enough to own that it's not; that I did everything
I could to give you both complete liberty."

"As when you applauded and upheld Betty for her insolent
interference; as when you complained to me of my guardian
because she asked that I should have a wider life; as when you
hoped to have Mrs. Talcott here so that my guardian might be
kept out."

"Did she suggest that?"

"She showed it to me. I had not seen it even then. Do
you deny it?"

"No; I don't suppose I can, though it was nothing so definite. But I certainly hoped that Madame von Marwitz would
not come here."

"And yet you can tell me that you have not tried to come
between us."

"Yes; I can. I never tried to come between you. I tried
to keep away. It's been she, as I say, who has tracked me
down. That was what I was afraid of if she came here; that
she'd force me to show my dislike. Can you deny, Karen, I ask
you this, that from the beginning she has made capital to you
out of my dislike, and pointed it out to you?"

"I will not discuss that with you," said Karen; "I know
that you can twist all her words and actions."

"I don't want to do that. I can see a certain justice in her malice. It was hard for her, of course, to find that you'd married a man she didn't take to and who didn't take to her; but why couldn't she have left it at that?"

"It couldn't be left at that. It wasn't only that," said Karen. "If she had liked you, you would never have liked her; and if you had liked her she would have liked you."

The steadiness of her voice as she thus placed the heart of the matter before him brought him a certain relief. Perhaps, in spite of his cold realizations and the death of all illusion as to Karen's love for him, they could really, now, come to an understanding, an accepted compromise. His heart ached and would go on aching until time had blunted its hurts, and a compromise was all he had to hope for. He had nothing to expect from Karen but acceptance of fact and faithful domesticity. But, after all the uncertainties and turmoils, this bitter peace had its balms. He took up her last words.

"Ah, well, she'd have liked my liking," he analysed it. "I don't know that she'd have liked me;—unless I could have managed to give her actual worship, as you and her friends do. But I'm not going to say anything more against her. She has forced the truth from me, and now we may bury it. You shall see her, of course, whenever you want to. But I hope that I shall never have to speak of her to you again."

The talk seemed to have been brought to an end. Karen had risen and Barker, entering at the moment, announced dinner.

"By Jove, is it as late as that," Gregory muttered, nodding to him. He turned to Karen when Barker was gone and, the pink electric lights falling upon her face, he saw as he had not seen before how grey and sunken it was. She had made no movement towards the door.

"Gregory," she said, fixing her eyes upon him, and he then saw that he had misinterpreted her quiet, "I tell you that these things are not true. They are not true. Will you believe me?"

"What things?" he asked. But he was temporizing. He saw that the end had not come.

"The things you believe of Tante. That she is a heartless woman, using those who love her — feeding on their love. I say it is not true. Will you believe me?"

She stood on the other side of the room, her arms hanging at her sides, her hands hanging open, all her being concentrated in the ultimate demand of her compelling gaze.

"Karen," he said, "I know that she must be lovable; I know, of course, that she has power, and charm, and tenderness. I think I can understand why you feel for her as you do. But I don't think that there is any chance that I shall change my opinion of her; not for anything you say. I believe that she takes you in completely."

Karen gazed at him. "You will still believe that she is tyrannous, and dangerous, and false, whatever I may say?"

"Yes, Karen. I know it sounds horrible to you. You must try to forgive me for it. We won't speak of it again; I promise you."

She turned from him, looking before her at the Bouddha, but not as if she saw it. "We shall never speak of it again," she said. "I am going to leave you, Gregory."

For a moment he stared at her. Then he smiled. "You mustn't punish me for telling you the truth, Karen, by silly threats."

"I do not punish you. You have done rightly to tell me the truth. But I cannot live with a man who believes these things."

She still gazed at the Bouddha and again Gregory stared at her. His face hardened. "Don't be absurd, Karen. You cannot mean what you say."

"I am going to-night. Now," said Karen.

"Going? Where?"

"To Cornwall, back to my guardian. She will take care of me again. I will not live with you."

"If you really mean what you say," said Gregory, after a moment, "you are telling me that you don't love me. I've suspected it for some time."

"I feel as if that were true," said Karen, looking now down

upon the ground. "I think I have no more love for you. I find you a petty man." It was impossible to hope that she was speaking recklessly or passionately. She had come to the conclusion with deliberation; she had been thinking of it since last night. She was willing to cast him off because he could not love where she loved. How deeply the roots of hope still knotted themselves in him he was now to realize. He felt his heart and mind rock with the reverberation of the shattering, the pulverizing explosion, and he saw his life lying in a wilderness of dust about him.

Yet the words he found were not the words of his despair. "Even if you feel like this, Karen," he said, "there is no necessity for behaving like a lunatic. Go and stay with your guardian, by all means, and whenever you like. Start to-morrow morning. Spend most of your time with her. I shall not put the smallest difficulty in your way. But — if only for your own sake — have some common-sense and keep up appearances. You must remain my wife in name and the mistress of my house."

"Thank you, you mean to be kind, I know," said Karen, who had not looked at him since her declaration; "But I am not a conventional woman and I do not wish to live with a man who is no longer my husband. I do not wish to keep up appearances. I do not wish it to be said — by those who know my guardian and what she has done for me and been to me — that I keep up the appearance of regard for a man who hates her. I made a mistake in marrying you; you allowed me to make it. Now, as far as I can, I undo it by leaving you. Perhaps," she added, "you could divorce me. That would set you free."

The remark in its childishness, callousness, and considerateness struck him as one of the most revealing she had made. He laughed icily. "Our laws only allow of divorce for one cause and I advise you not to seek freedom for yourself — or for me — by disgracing yourself. It's not worth it. The conventions you scorn have their solid value."

She had now turned her head and was looking at him. "I think you are insulting me," she said.

For the first time he observed a trembling in her voice and

interpreted it as anger. It gave him a hurting satisfaction to
have made her angry. She had appalled and shattered him.

"I am not insulting you, I am warning you, Karen," he said.
"A woman who can behave as you are behaving is capable of
acts of criminal folly. You don't believe in convention, and in
your guardian's world you will meet many men who don't."

"What do you mean by criminal folly?"

"I mean living with a man you're not married to."

He had simply and sincerely forgotten something. Karen's
face grew ashen.

"You mean that my mother was a criminal?"

Even at this moment of his despair Gregory was horribly
sorry. Yet the memory that she recalled brought a deeper fear
for her future. He had spoken with irony of her suggestion
about divorce and freedom. But did not her very blood, as well
as her environment, give him reason to emphasise his warning?

"I didn't mean that. I wasn't thinking of that," he said,
"as you must know. And to be criminally foolish is a very different thing from being a criminal. But I'm convinced that to
break social laws — and these laws about men and women have
deeper than merely social sanctions — to break them, I'm convinced, can bring no happiness. I feel about your mother, and
what she did — I say it with all reverence — that she was as
mistaken as she was unfortunate. And I beg of you, Karen,
never to follow her example."

"It is not for you to speak of her!" Karen said, not moving
from her place but uttering the words with a still and sudden
passion that he had never heard from her. "It is not for you
to preach sermons to me on the text of my mother's misfortunes.
I do not call them misfortunes — nor did she. I do not accept
your laws, and she was not afraid of them. How dare you call
her unfortunate? She lost nothing that she valued and she
gained great happiness, and gave it, for she was happy with
my father. It was a truer marriage than any I have known.
She was more married than you or I have ever been or could
ever have been; for there was deep love between them, and

18

trust and understanding. Do not speak to me of her. I forbid it."

She turned to the door. Gregory sprang to her side and seized her wrist. "Karen! Where are you going? Wait till to-morrow!" he exclaimed, fear for her actual safety surmounting every other feeling.

She stood still under his hand and looked at him with her still passion of repudiation. "I will not wait. I shall go to-night to Frau Lippheim. And to-morrow I shall go to Cornwall. I shall tell Mrs. Barker to pack my clothes and send them to me there."

"You have no money."

"Frau Lippheim will lend me money. My guardian will take care of me. It is not for you to have any thought for me."

He dropped her arm. "Very well. Go then," he said.

He turned from her. He heard that she paused, the knob of the door in her hand. "Good-bye," she then said.

Again it was, inconceivably, the mingled childishness, callousness and considerateness. That, at the moment, she could think of the formality, suffocated him. "Good-bye," he replied, not looking round.

The door opened and closed. He heard her swift feet passing down the passage to their room.

She was not reckless. She needed her hat and coat at least. Quiet, rational determination was in all her actions.

Yet, as he waited to hear her come out again, a hope that he knew to be chimerical rose in him. She would, perhaps, return, throw herself in his arms and, weeping, say that she loved him and could not leave him. Gregory's heart beat quickly.

But when he heard her footsteps again they were not returning. They passed along to the kitchen; she was speaking to Mrs. Barker — Gregory had a shoot of surface thought for Mrs. Barker's astonishment; they entered the hall again, the hall door closed behind them.

Gregory stood looking at the Bouddha. The tears kept mounting to his throat and eyes and, furiously, he choked them back. He did not see the Bouddha.

But, suddenly becoming aware of the bland contemplative gaze of the great bronze image, his eyes fixed themselves on it.

He had known it from the first to be an enemy. Its presage was fulfilled. The tidal wave had broken over his life.

PART II

CHAPTER XXIX

KAREN sat in her corner of the railway carriage looking out at familiar scenery.

Reading and the spring-tide beauties of the Thames valley had gone by in the morning. Then, after the attendant had passed along the corridor announcing lunch, and those who were lunching had followed him in single file, had come the lonely majesty of the Somerset downs, lying like great headlands along the plain, a vast sky of rippled blue and silver above them. They had passed Plymouth where she had always used to look down from the high bridges and wonder over the lives of the midshipmen on the training-ships, and now they were winding through wooded Cornish valleys.

Karen had looked out of her window all day. She had not read, though kind Frau Lippheim had put the latest *tendenz-roman,* paper-bound, into the little basket, which was also stocked with stout beef-sandwiches, a bottle of milk, and the packet of chocolate and bun in paper bag that Franz had added to it at the station.

Poor Franz. He and his mother had come to see her off and they had both wept as the train moved away, and strange indeed it must have been for them to see the Karen Jardine who, only yesterday, had been, apparently, so happy, and so secure in her new life, carried back to the old; a wife who had left her husband.

Karen had slept little the night before, and kind Franz must have slept less; for he had given her his meagre bedroom and spent the night on the narrowest, hardest, most slippery of sofas in the sitting-room of the Bayswater lodging-house where Karen had found the Lippheims very cheaply, very grimly, not to say greasily, installed. It was no wonder that Franz's eyes had been so heavy, his face so puffed and pale that morning; and his tears had given the last touch of desolation to his countenance.

Karen herself had not wept, either at the parting or at the meeting of the night before. She had told them, with no explanations at all, that she had left her husband and was going back to her guardian, and the Lippheims had asked no questions.

It might have been possible that Franz, as he sat at the table, his fingers run through his hair, clutching his head while he and his mother listened to her, was not so dazed and lost as was Frau Lippheim, who had not seen Gregory. Franz might have his vague perceptions. "*Ach! Ach!*" he had ejaculated once or twice while she spoke.

And Frau Lippheim had only said: "*Liebes Kind! Liebes, armes Kind!*"

She was, after all, going back to the great Tante and they felt, no doubt, that no grief could be ultimate which had that compensatory refuge.

She was going back to Tante. As the valleys, in their deepened shadows, streamed past her, Karen remembered that it had hardly been at all of Tante that she had thought while the long hours passed and her eyes observed the flying hills and fields. Perhaps she had thought of nothing. The heavy feeling, as of a stone resting on her heart, of doom, defeat and bitterness, could hardly have been defined as thought. She had thought and thought and thought during these last dreadful days; every mental cog had been adjusted, every wheel had turned; she had held herself together as never before in all her life, in order to give thought every chance. For was n't that to give him every chance? and was n't that, above all, to give herself any chance that might still be left her?

And now the machinery seemed to lie wrecked. There was not an ember of hope left with which to kindle its activity. How

much hope there must have been to have made it work so firmly
and so furiously during these last days! how much, she had n't
known until her husband had come in last night, and, at last,
spoken openly.

Even Mrs. Forrester's revelations, though they had paralyzed
her, had not put out the fires. She had still hoped that he could
deny, explain, recant, own that he had been hasty, perhaps;
perhaps mistaken; give her some loophole. She could have
understood — oh, to a degree almost abject — his point of view.
Mrs. Forrester had accused her of that. And Tante had accused
her of it, too. But no; it had been slowly to freeze to stillness
to hear his clear cold utterance of shameful words, see the
folly of his arrogance and his complacency, realise, in his glacial
look and glib, ironic smile, that he was blind to what he was
destroying in her. For he could not have torn her heart to shreds
and then stood bland, unaware of what he had done, had he loved
her. Her young spirit, unversed in irony, drank in the bitter
draught of disillusion. They had never loved each other; or,
worse, far worse, they had loved and love was this puny thing
that a blow could kill. His love for her was dead.

She still trembled when the ultimate realization surged over
her, looking fixedly out of the window lest she should weep
aloud.

She had only one travelling companion, an old woman who got
out at Plymouth. Karen had found her curiously repulsive
and that was one reason why she had kept her eyes fixed on the
landscape. She had been afraid that the old woman would talk
to her, perhaps offer her refreshments, or sympathy; for she was
a kind old woman, with bland eyes and a moist warm face and
two oily curls hanging forward from her old-fashioned bonnet
upon her shoulders. She was stout, dressed in tight black cash-
mere, and she sat with her knees apart and her hands, gloved
in grey thread gloves, lying on them. She held a handkerchief
rolled into a ball, and from time to time, as if furtively, she
would raise this handkerchief to her brow and wipe it. And
all the time, Karen felt, she looked mildly and humbly at her
and seemed to divine her distress.

Karen was thankful when she got out. She had been ashamed of her antipathy.

Bodmin Road was now passed and the early spring sunset shone over the tree-tops in the valleys below. Karen leaned her head back and closed her eyes. She was suddenly aware of her great fatigue, and when they reached Gwinear Road she found that she had been dozing.

The fresh, chill air, as she walked along the platform, waiting for the change of trains, revived her. She had not been able to eat her beef sandwiches and the thought that so much of Frau Lippheim's good food should be wasted troubled her; she was glad to find a little wandering fox-terrier who ate the meat eagerly. She herself, sitting beside the dog, nibbled at Franz's chocolate. She had had nothing on her journey but the milk and part of the bun which Franz had given her.

Now she was in the little local train and the bleak Cornish country, nearing the coast, spread before her eyes like a map of her future life. She began to think of the future, and of Tante.

She had not sent word to Tante that she was coming. She felt that it would be easiest to appear before her in silence and Tante would understand. There need be no explanations.

She imagined that Tante would find it best that she should live, permanently now, in Cornwall with Mrs. Talcott. It could hardly be convenient for her to take about with her a wife who had left her husband. Karen quite realized that her status must be a very different one from that of the unshadowed young girl.

And it would be strange to take up the old life again and to look back from it at the months of life with Gregory — that mirage of happiness receding as if to a blur of light seen over a stretch of desert. Still with her quiet and unrevealing young face turned towards the evening landscape, Karen felt as if she had grown very old and were looking back, after a life-time without Gregory, at the mirage. How faint and far it would seem to be when she was really old — like a nebulous star trembling on the horizon. But it would never grow invisible; she would never forget it; oh never; nor the dreadful pain of loss.

To the very end of life, she was sure of it, she would keep the pang of the shining memory.

When they reached Helston, dusk had fallen. She found a carriage that would drive her the twelve miles to the coast. It was a quiet, grey evening and as they jolted slowly along the dusty roads and climbed the steep hills at a snail's pace, she leaned back too tired to feel anything any longer. And now they were out upon the moors where the gorse was breaking into flowers; and now, over the sea, she saw at last the great beacon of the Lizard lighthouse sweeping the country with its vast, desolate, yet benignant beam.

They reached the long road and the stile where, a year before, she had met Gregory. Here was the hedge of fuchsia; here the tamarisks on their high bank; here the entrance to Les Solitudes. The steeply pitched grey roofs rose before her, and the white walls with their squares of orange light glimmered among the trees.

She alighted, paid the man, and rang.

A maid, unknown to her, came to the door and showed surprise at seeing her there with her bag.

Yes; Madame von Marwitz was within. Karen had entered with the asking. "Whom shall I announce, Madam?" the maid inquired.

Karen looked at her vaguely. "She is in the music-room? I do not need to be announced. That will go to my room." She put down the bag and crossed the hall.

She was not aware of feeling any emotion; yet a sob had taken her by the throat and tears had risen to her eyes; she opened them widely as she entered the dusky room, presenting a strange face.

Madame von Marwitz rose from a distant sofa.

In her astonishment, she stood still for a moment; then, like a great, white, widely-winged moth, she came forward, rapidly, yet with hesitant, reconnoitring pauses, her eyes on the girl who stood in the doorway looking blindly towards her.

"Karen!" she exclaimed sharply. "What brings you here?"

"I have come back to you, Tante," said Karen.

Tante stood before her, not taking her into her arms, not taking her hands.

"Come back to me? What do you mean?"

"I have left Gregory," said Karen. She was bewildered now. What had happened? She did not know; but it was something that made it impossible to throw herself in Tante's arms and weep.

Then she saw that another person was with them. A man was seated on the distant sofa. He rose, wandering slowly down the room, and revealed himself in the dim light that came from the evening sky and sea as Mr. Claude Drew. Pausing at some little distance he fixed his eyes on Karen, and in the midst of all the impressions, striking like chill, moulding blows on the melted iron of her mood, she was aware of these large, dark eyes of Mr. Drew's and of their intent curiosity.

The predominant impression, however, was of a changed aspect in everything, and as Tante, now holding her hands, still stood silent, also looking at her with intent curiosity, the impression vaguely and terribly shaped itself for her as a piercing question: Was Tante not glad to have her back?

There came from Tante in another moment a more accustomed note.

"You have left your husband — because of me — my poor child?"

Karen nodded. Mr. Drew's presence made speech impossible.

"He made it too difficult for you?"

Karen nodded again.

"And you have come back to me." Madame von Marwitz summed it up rather than inquired. And then, after another pause, she folded Karen in her arms.

The piercing question seemed answered. Yet Karen could not now have wept. A dry, hard desolation filled her. "May I go to my room, Tante?"

"Yes, my child. Go to your room. You will find Tallie. Tallie is in the house, I think — or did I send her in to Helston? — no, that was for to-morrow." She held Karen's hand at a stretch of her arm while she seemed, with difficulty still, to collect her thoughts. "But I will come with you myself. Yes; that is best. Wait here, Claude." This to the silent, dusky figure behind them.

"Do not let me be a trouble." Karen controlled the trembling of her voice. "I know my way."

"No trouble, my child; no trouble. Or none that I am not glad to take."

Tante had her now on the stair — her arm around her shoulders. "You will find us at sixes and sevens; a household hastily organized, but Tallie, directed by wires, has done wonders. So. My poor Karen. You have left him. For good? Or is it only to punish him that you come to me?"

"I have left him for good."

"So," Madame von Marwitz repeated.

With all the veils and fluctuations, one thing was growing clear to Karen. Tante might be glad to have her back; but she was confused, trying to think swiftly, to adjust her thoughts. They were in Karen's little room overlooking the trees at the corner of the house. It was dismantled; a bare dressing-table, the ewer upturned in the basin, the bed and its piled bedding covered with a sheet. Madame von Marwitz sat down on the bed and drew Karen beside her.

"But is not that to punish him too much?"

"It is not to punish him. I cannot live with him any longer."

"I see; I see;" said Madame von Marwitz, with a certain briskness, as though, still, to give herself time to think. "It might have been wiser to wait — to wait for a little. I would have written to you. We could have consulted. It is serious, you know, my Karen, very serious, to leave one's husband. I went away so that this should not come to you."

"I could not wait. I could not stay with him any longer," said Karen heavily.

"There is more, you mean. You had words? He hates me more than you thought?"

Karen paused, and then assented: "Yes; more than I thought."

Above the girl's head, which she held pressed down on her
shoulder, Madame von Marwitz pondered for some moments.
" Alas ! " she then uttered in a deep voice. And, Karen saying
nothing, she repeated on a yet more melancholy note : " Alas ! "

Karen now raised herself from Tante's shoulder ; but, at the
gesture of withdrawal, Madame von Marwitz caught her close
again and embraced her. " I feared it," she said. " I saw it.
I hoped to hide it by my flight. My poor child ! My beloved
Karen ! "

They held each other for some silent moments. Then Madame
von Marwitz rose. " You are weary, my Karen ; you must rest ;
is it not so ? I will send Tallie to you. You will see Tallie —
she is a perfection of discretion ; you do not shrink from Tallie.
And you need tell her nothing ; she will not question you.
Between ourselves ; is it not so ? Yes ; that is best. For the
present. I will come again, later — I have guests, a guest, you
see. Rest here, my Karen." She moved towards the door.

Karen looked after her. An intolerable fear pressed on her.
She could not bear, in her physical weakness, to be left alone with
it. " Tante ! " she exclaimed.

Madame von Marwitz turned. " My child ? "

" Tante — you are glad to have me back ? "

Her pride broke in a sob. She hid her face in her hands.

Madame von Marwitz returned to the bed.

" Glad, my child ? " she said. " For all the sorrow that it
means ? and to know that I am the cause ? How can I be glad
for my child's unhappiness ? "

She spoke with a touch of severity, as though in Karen's tears
she felt an unexpressed accusation.

" Not for that," Karen spoke with difficulty. " But to have
me with you again. It will not be a trouble ? "

There was a little silence and then, her severity passing to
melancholy reproof, Madame von Marwitz said : " Did we not,
long since, speak of this, Karen ? Have you forgotten ? Can
you so wound me once again ? Only my child's grief can excuse
her. It is a sorrow to see your life in ruins ; I had hoped before
I died to see it joyous and secure. It is a sorrow to know that

you have maimed yourself; that you are tied to an unworthy
man. But how could it be a trouble to me to have you with me?
It is a consolation — my only consolation in this calamity. With
me you shall find peace and happiness again."

She laid her hand on Karen's head. Karen put her hand to
her lips.

"There. That is well," said Madame von Marwitz with a
sigh, bending to kiss her. "That is my child. Tante is sad
at heart. It is a heavy blow. But her child is welcome."

When she had gone Karen lay, her face in the billows of the
bed, while she fixed her thoughts on Tante's last words.

They became a sing-song monotone. "Tante is sad at heart.
But her child is welcome. It is a heavy blow. But her child is
welcome."

After the anguish there was a certain ease. She rested in the
given reassurance. Yet the sing-song monotone oppressed her.

She felt presently that her hat, wrenched to one side, and still
fixed to her hair by its pins, was hurting her. She unfastened it
and dropped it to the floor. She felt too tired to do more just
then.

Soon after this the door opened and Mrs. Talcott appeared
carrying a candle, a can of hot water, towels and sheets.

Karen drew herself up, murmuring some vague words of welcome, and Mrs. Talcott, after setting the candle on the dressing-
table and the hot water in the basin, remarked: "Just you lie
down again, Karen, and let me wash your face for you. You
must be pretty tired and dirty after that long journey."

But Karen put her feet to the ground. They just sustained
her. "Thank you, Mrs. Talcott. I will do it," she said.

She bent over the water, and, while she washed, Mrs. Talcott,
with deliberate skill, made up the bed. Karen sank in a chair.

"You poor thing," said Mrs. Talcott, turning to her as she
smoothed down the sheet; "Why you're green. Sit right there
and I'll undress you. Yes; you're only fit to be put to bed."

She spoke with mild authority, and Karen, under her hands,
relapsed to childhood.

"This all the baggage you've brought?" Mrs. Talcott inquired, finding a nightdress in Karen's dressing-case. She expressed no surprise when Karen said that it was all, passed the nightdress over her head and, when she had lain down, tucked the bed-clothes round her.

"Now what you want is a hot-water bottle and some dinner. I guess you 're hungry. Did you have any lunch on the train?"

"I 've had some chocolate and a bun and some milk, oh yes, I had enough," said Karen faintly, raising her hand to her forehead; "but I must be hungry; for my head aches so badly. How kind you are, Mrs. Talcott."

"You lie right there and I 'll bring you some dinner." Mrs. Talcott was swiftly tidying the room.

"But what of yours, Mrs. Talcott? Is n't it your dinner-time?"

"I 've had my supper. I have supper early these days."

Karen dimly reflected, when she was gone, that this was an innovation. Whoever Madame von Marwitz's guests, Mrs. Talcott had, until now, always made an *acte de présence* at every meal. She was tired and not feeling well enough after her illness, she thought.

Mrs. Talcott soon returned with a tray on which were set out hot *consommée* and chicken and salad, a peach beside them. Hot-house fruit was never wanting when Madame von Marwitz was at Les Solitudes.

"Lie back. I 'll feed it to you," said Mrs. Talcott. "It 's good and strong. You know Adolphe can make as good a *consommée* as anybody, if he 's a mind to."

"Is Adolphe here?" Karen asked as she swallowed the spoonfuls.

"Yes, I sent for Adolphe to Paris a week ago," said Mrs. Talcott. "Mercedes wrote that she 'd soon be coming with friends and wanted him. He 'd just taken a situation, but he dropped it. Her new motor 's here, too, down from London. The chauffeur seems a mighty nice man, a sight nicer than Hammond." Hammond had been Madame von Marwitz's recent coachman. Mrs. Talcott talked on mildly while she fed Karen who, in the whirl of trivial thoughts, turning and turning like

midges over a deep pool, questioned herself, with a vague wonder that she was too tired to follow: "Did Tante say anything
to me about coming to Cornwall?"

Mrs. Talcott, meanwhile, as Madame von Marwitz had prophe-
sied, asked no questions.

"Now you have a good long sleep," she said, when she rose to
go. "That's what you need."

She needed it very much. The midges turned more and more
slowly, then sank into the pool; mist enveloped everything, and
darkness.

CHAPTER XXX

KAREN was waked next morning by the familiar sound of the *Wohltemperirtes Clavier*.

Tante was at work in the music-room and was playing the prelude in D flat, a special favourite of Karen's.

She lay and listened with a curious, cautious pleasure, like that with which, half awake, one may guide a charming dream, knowing it to be a dream. There was so much waiting to be remembered; so much waiting to be thought. Tante's beautiful notes, rising to her like the bubbles of a spring through clear water, seemed to encircle her, ringing her in from the wider consciousness.

While she listened she looked out at the branches of young leaves, softly stirring against the morning sky. There was her wall-paper, with the little pink flower creeping up it. She was in her own little bed. Tante was practising. How sweet, how safe, it was. A drowsy peace filled her. It was slowly that memory, lapping in, like the sinister, dark waters of a flood under doors and through crevices, made its way into her mind, obliterating peace, at first, rather than revealing pain. There was a fear formless and featureless; and there was loss, dreadful loss. And as the sense of loss grew upon her, consciousness grew more vivid, bringing its visions.

This hour of awakening. Gregory's eyes smiling at her, not cold, not hard eyes then. His hand stretched out to hers; their morning kiss. Tears suddenly streamed down her face.

It was impossible to hide them from Mrs. Talcott, who came in carrying a breakfast tray; but Karen checked them, and dried her eyes.

Mrs. Talcott set the tray down on the little table near the bed.

"Is it late, Mrs. Talcott?" Karen asked.

288

"It's just nine; Mercedes is up early so as to get some work in before she goes out motoring."

"She is going motoring?"

"Yes, she and Mr. Drew are going off for the day." Mrs. Talcott adjusted Karen's pillow.

"But I shall see Tante before she goes?" It was the formless, featureless fear that came closer.

"My, yes! You'll see her all right," said Mrs. Talcott. "She was asking after you the first thing and hoped you'd stay in bed till lunch. Now you eat your breakfast right away like a good girl."

Karen tried to eat her breakfast like a good girl and the sound of the *Wohltemperirtes Clavier* seemed again to encircle and sustain her.

"How'd you sleep, honey?" Mrs. Talcott inquired. The term hardly expressed endearment, yet it was such an unusual one from Mrs. Talcott that Karen could only surmise that her tears had touched the old woman.

"Very, very well," she said.

"How'd you like me to bring up some mending I've got to do and sit by you till Mercedes comes?" Mrs. Talcott pursued.

"Oh, please do, Mrs. Talcott," said Karen. She felt that she would like to have Mrs. Talcott there with her very much. She would probably cry unless Mrs. Talcott stayed with her, and she did not want Tante to find her crying.

So Mrs. Talcott brought her basket of mending and sat by the window, sewing in silence for the most part, but exchanging with Karen now and then a quiet remark about the state of the garden and how the plants were doing.

At eleven the sound of the piano ceased and soon after the stately tread of Madame von Marwitz was heard outside. Mrs. Talcott, saying that she would come back later on, gathered up her mending as she appeared. She was dressed for motoring, with a long white cloak lined with white fur and her head bound in nun-like fashion with a white coif and veil. Beautiful she looked, and sad, and gentle; a succouring Madonna; and Karen's heart rose up to her. It clung to her and prayed; and the realisation of her own need, her own dependence, was a new thing. She had never before felt dependence on Tante as anything but proud and glad. To pray to her now that she should never belie her loveliness, to cling to that faith in her without which all her life would be a thing distorted and unrecognisable, was not pride or gladness and seemed to be the other side of fear. Yet so gentle were the eyes, so tender the smile and the firm clasp of the hands taking hers, while Tante murmured, stooping to kiss her: "Good morning to my child," that the prayer seemed answered, the faith approved.

If Madame von Marwitz had been taken by surprise the night before, if she had had to give herself time to think, she had now, it was evident, done her thinking. The result was this warmly cherishing tenderness.

"Ah," she said, still stooping over Karen, while she put back her hair, "it is good to have my child back again, mine — quite mine — once more."

"I have slept so well, Tante," said Karen. She was able to smile up at her.

Madame von Marwitz looked about the room. "And now it is to gather the dear old life closely about her again. Gardening, and reading; and quiet times with Tante and Tallie. Though, for the moment, I must be much with my guest; I am helping him with his work. He has talent, yes; it is a strange and complicated nature. You did not expect to find him here?"

Karen held Tante's hand and her gaze was innocent of surmise. Mr. Drew had never entered her thoughts. "No. Yes. No, Tante. He came with you?"

"Yes, he came with me," said Madame von Marwitz. "I had promised him that he should see Les Solitudes one day. I was glad to find an occupation for my thoughts in helping him. I told him that if he were free he might join me. It is good, in great sorrow, to think of others. Now it is, for the young man and for me, our work. Work, work; we must all work, *ma chérie*. It is our only clue in the darkness of life; our only nourishment in the desert places." Again she looked about the room. "You came without boxes?"

"Yes, Mrs. Barker is to send them to me."

"Ah, yes. When," said Madame von Marwitz, in a lower voice, "did you leave? Yesterday morning?"

"No, Tante. The night before."

"The night before? So? And where did you spend the night? With Mrs. Forrester? With Scrotton? I have not yet written to Scrotton."

"No. I went to the Lippheims."

"The Lippheims? So?"

"The others, Tante, would have talked to me; and questioned me. I could not have borne that. The Lippheims were so kind."

"I can believe it. They have hearts of gold, those Lippheims. They would cut themselves in four to help one. And the good Lise? How is she? I am sorry to have missed Lise."

"And she was, oh, so sorry to have missed you, Tante. She is well, I think, though tired; she is always tired, you remember. She has too much to do."

"Indeed, yes; poor Lise. She might have been an artist of the first rank if she had not given herself over to the making of children. Why did she not stop at Franz and Lotta and Minna? That would have given her the quartette,"— Madame von Marwitz smiled — she was in a mildly merry mood. "But on they go — four, five, six, seven, eight — how many are there — *bon Dieu!* of how many am I the god-mother? One grows bewildered. It is almost a rat's family. Lise is not unlike a white mother-rat, with the small round eye and the fat body."

"Oh — not a rat, Tante," Karen protested, a little pained.

"A rabbit, you think? And a rabbit, too, is prolific. No; for the rabbit has not the sharpness, not the pointed nose, the anxious, eager look — is not so the mother, indeed. Rat it is, my Karen; and rat with a golden heart. How do you find Tallie? She has been with you all the morning? You have not talked with Tallie of our calamities?"

" Oh, no, Tante."

" She is a wise person, Tallie; wise, silent, discreet. And I find her looking well; but very, very well; this air preserves her. And how old is Tallie now?" she mused.

Though she talked so sweetly there was, Karen felt it now, a perfunctoriness in Tante's remarks. She was, for all the play of her nimble fancy, preoccupied, and the sound of the motor-horn below seemed a signal for release. "Tallie is, *mon Dieu,*" she computed, rising —" she was twenty-three when I was born — and I am nearly fifty "— Madame von Marwitz was as far above cowardly reticences about her age as a timeless goddess —" Tallie is actually seventy-two. Well, I must be off, *ma chérie.* We have a long trip to make to-day. We go to Fowey. He wishes to see Fowey. I pray the weather may continue fine. You will be with us this evening? You will get up? You will come to dinner?"

She paused at the mantelpiece to adjust her veil, and Karen, in the glass, saw that her eyes were fixed on hers with a certain intentness.

" Yes, I will get up this morning, Tante," she said. " I will help Mrs. Talcott with the garden. But dinner? Mrs. Talcott says that she has supper now. Shall I not have my supper with her? Perhaps she would like that?"

" That would perhaps be well," said Madame von Marwitz. " That is perhaps well thought." Still she paused and still, in the glass, she fixed cogitating eyes on Karen. She turned, then, abruptly. " But no; I do not think so. On second thoughts I do not think so. You will dine with us. Tallie is quite happy alone. She is pleased with the early supper. I shall see you, then, this evening."

A slight irritation lay on her brows; but she leaned with all her tenderness to kiss Karen, murmuring, " *Adieu, mon enfant.*"

When the sound of the motor had died away Karen got up, dressed and went downstairs.

The music-room, its windows open to the sea, was full of the signs of occupancy.

The great piano stood open. Karen went to it and, standing over it, played softly the dearly loved opening notes of the prelude in D flat.

She practised, always, on the upright piano in the morning-room; but when Tante was at home and left the grand piano open she often played on that. It was a privilege rarely to be resisted and to-day she sat down and played the prelude through, still very softly. Then, covering the keys, she shut the lid and looked more carefully about the room.

Flowers and books were everywhere. Mrs. Talcott arranged flowers beautifully; Karen recognized her skilful hand in the tall branches of budding green standing high in a corner, the glasses of violets, the bowls of anemones and the flat dishes of Italian earthenware filled with primroses.

On a table lay a pile of manuscript; she knew Mr. Drew's small, thick handwriting. A square silver box for cigarettes stood near by; it was marked with Mr. Drew's initials in Tante's hand. How kind she was to that young man; but Tante had always been lavish with those of whom she was fond.

Out on the verandah the vine-tendrils were already green against the sky, and on a lower terrace she saw Mrs. Talcott at work, as usual, among the borders. Mrs. Talcott then, had not yet gone to Helston and she would not be alone and she was glad of that. In the little cupboard near the pantry she found a pair of old gardening gloves and her own old gardening hat. The day was peaceful and balmy; all was as it had always been, except herself.

She worked all the morning in the garden and walked in the afternoon on the cliffs with Victor. Victor had come down with Tante.

Mrs. Talcott had adjourned the trip to Helston; so they had tea together. Her boxes had not yet come and when it was time to dress for dinner she had nothing to change to but the little white silk with the flat blue bows upon it, the dress in which Gregory had first seen her. She had left it behind her when she married and found it now hanging in a cupboard in her room.

The horn of the returning motor did not sound until she was dressed and on going down she had the music-room to herself for nearly half an hour. Then Mr. Drew appeared.

The tall white lamps with their white shades had been brought in, but the light from the windows mingled a pale azure with the gold. Mr. Drew, Karen reflected, looked in the dual illumination like a portrait by Besnard. He had, certainly, an unusual and an interesting face, and it pleased her to verify and emphasize this fact; for, accustomed as she was to watching Tante's preoccupations with interesting people, she could not quite accustom herself to her preoccupation with Mr. Drew. To account for it he must be so very interesting.

She was not embarrassed by conjectures as to what, after her entry of last night, Mr. Drew might be thinking about her. It occurred to her no more than in the past to imagine that anybody attached to Tante could spare thought to her. And as in the past, despite all the inner desolation, it was easy to assume to this guest of Tante's the attitude so habitual to her of the attendant in the temple, the attendant who, rising from his seat at the door, comes forward tranquilly to greet the worshipper and entertain him with quiet comment until the goddess shall descend.

" Did you have a nice drive? " she inquired. " The weather has been beautiful."

Mr. Drew, coming up to her as she stood in the open window, looked at her with his impenetrable, melancholy eyes, smiling at her a little.

There was no tastelessness in his gaze, nothing that suggested a recollection of what he had heard or seen last night; yet Karen was made vaguely aware from his look that she had acquired some sort of significance for him.

" Yes, it 's been nice," he said. " I 'm very fond of motoring. I 'd like to spend my days in a motor — always going faster and faster; and then drop down in a blissful torpor at night. Madame von Marwitz was so kind and made the chauffeur go very fast."

Karen was somewhat disturbed by this suggestion. " I am

sure that she, too, would like going very fast. I hope you will
not tempt her."

"Oh, but I 'm afraid I do," Mr. Drew confessed. "What is
the good of a motor unless you go too fast in it? A motor has
no meaning unless it 's a method of intoxication."

Karen received the remark with inattention. She looked out
over the sea, preoccupied with the thought of Tante's reckless-
ness. "I do not think that going so fast can be good for her
music," she said.

"Oh, but yes," Mr. Drew assured her, "nothing is so good for
art as intoxication. Art is rooted in intoxication. It 's all a
question of how to get it."

"But with motoring you only get torpor, you say," Karen
remarked. And, going on with her own train of thoughts, "So
much shaking will be bad, perhaps, for the muscles. And there
is always the danger to consider. I hope she will not go too
fast. She is too important a person to take risks." There was
no suggestion that Mr. Drew should not take them.

"Don't you like going fast? Don't you like taking risks?
Don't you like intoxication?" Mr. Drew inquired, and his eyes
travelled from the blue bows on her breast to the blue bows on
her elbow-sleeves.

"I have never been intoxicated," said Karen calmly — she was
quite accustomed to all manner of fantastic visitors in the temple
—"I do not think that I should like it. And I prefer walking
to any kind of driving. No, I do not like risks."

"Ah yes, I can see that. Yes, that 's altogether in character,"
said Mr. Drew. He turned, then, as Madame von Marwitz came
in, but remained standing in the window while Karen went
forward to greet her guardian. Madame von Marwitz, as she
took her hands and kissed her, looked over Karen's shoulder at
Mr. Drew.

"Why did you not come to my room, *chérie?*" she asked. "I
had hoped to see you alone before I came down."

"I thought you might be tired and perhaps resting, Tante,"
said Karen, who had, indeed, paused before her guardian's door
on her way down, and then passed on with a certain sense of

shyness; she did not want in any way to force herself on Tante.

"But you know that I like to have you with me when I am tired," Madame von Marwitz returned. "And I am not tired: no: it has been a day of wings."

She walked down the long room, her arm around Karen, with a buoyancy of tread and demeanour in which, however, Karen, so deep an adept in her moods discovered excitement rather than gaiety. "Has it been a good day for my child?" she questioned; "a happy, peaceful day? Yes? You have been much with Tallie? I told Tallie that she must postpone the trip to Helston so that she might stay with you." Tante on the sofa encircled her and looked brightly at her; yet her eye swerved to the window where Mr. Drew remained looking at a paper.

Karen said that she had been gardening and walking.

"Good; bravo!" said Tante, and then, in a lower voice: "No news, I suppose?"

"No; oh no. That could not be, Tante," said Karen, with a startled look, and Tante went on quickly: "But no; I see. It could not be. And it has, then, been a happy day for my Karen. What is it you read, Claude?"

Karen's sense of slight perplexity in regard to Tante's interest in Mr. Drew was deepened when she called him Claude, and her tone now, half vexed, half light, was perplexing.

"Some silly things that are being said in the House," Mr. Drew returned, going on reading.

"What things?" said Tante sharply.

"Oh, you wouldn't expect me to read a stupid debate to you," said Mr. Drew, lifting his eyes with a smile.

Dinner was announced and they went in, Tante keeping her arm around Karen's shoulders and sweeping ahead with an effect of unawareness as to her other guest. She had, perhaps, a little lost her temper with him; and his manner was, Karen reflected, by no means assiduous. At the table, however, Tante showed herself suave and sweet.

One reason why things seemed a little strange, Karen further reflected, was that Mrs. Talcott came no longer to dinner; and she was vaguely sorry for this.

CHAPTER XXXI

KAREN'S boxes arrived next day, neatly packed by Mrs. Barker. And not only her clothes were in them. She had left behind her the jewel-box with the pearl necklace that Gregory had given her, the pearl and sapphire ring, the old enamel brooch and clasp and chain, his presents all. The box was kept locked, and in a cupboard of which Gregory had the key; so that he must have given it to Mrs. Barker. The photographs, too, from their room, not those of him, but those of Tante; of her father; and a half a dozen little porcelain and silver trinkets from the drawing-room, presents and purchases particularly hers.

It was right, quite right, that he should send them. She knew it. It was right that he should accept their parting as final. Yet that he should so accurately select and send to her everything that could remind him of her seemed to roll the stone before the tomb.

She looked at the necklace, the ring, all the pretty things, and shut the box. Impossible that she should keep them yet impossible to send them back as if in a bandying of rebuffs. She would wait for some years to pass and then they should be returned without comment.

And the clothes, all these dear clothes of her married life; every dress and hat was associated with Gregory. She could never wear them again. And it felt, not so much that she was locking them away, as that Gregory had locked her out into darkness and loneliness. She took up the round of the days. She practised; she gardened, she walked and read. Of Tante she saw little.

She was accustomed to seeing little of Tante, even when Tante was there; quite accustomed to Tante's preoccupations. Yet, through the fog of her own unhappiness, it came to her, like an object dimly perceived, that in this preoccupation of Tante's there was a difference. It showed itself in a high-pitched restlessness, verging now and again on irritation — not with her, Karen, but with Mr. Drew. To Karen she was brightly, punctually tender, yet it was a tenderness that held her away rather than drew her near.

Karen did not need to be put aside. She had always known how to efface herself; she needed no atonement for the so apparent fact that Tante wanted to be left alone with Mr. Drew as much as possible. The difficulty in leaving her came with perceiving that though Tante wanted her to go she did not want to seem to want it.

She caressed Karen; she addressed her talk to her; she kept her; yet, under the smile of the eyes, there was an intentness that Karen could interpret. It devolved upon her to find the excuse, the necessity, for withdrawal. Mrs. Talcott, in the morning-room, was a solution. Karen could go to her almost directly after dinner, as soon as coffee had been served; for on the first occasion when she rose, saying that she would have her coffee with Mrs. Talcott, Tante said with some sharpness — after a hesitation: "No; you will have your coffee here. Tallie does not have coffee." Groping her way, Karen seemed to touch strange forms. Tante cared so much about this young man; so much that it was almost as if she would be willing to abandon her dignity for him. It was more than the indulgent, indolent interest, wholly Olympian, that she had so often seen her bestow. She really cared. And the strangeness for Karen was in part made up of pain for Tante; for it almost seemed that Tante cared more than Mr. Drew did. Karen had seen so many men care for Tante; so many who were, obviously, in love with her; but she had seen Tante always throned high above the prostrate adorers, idly kind; holding out a hand, perhaps, for them to kiss; smiling, from time to time, if they, fortunately, pleased her; but never, oh never, stepping down towards them.

It seemed to her now that she had seen Tante stepping down. It was only a step; she could never become the suppliant, the pursuing goddess; and, as if with her hand still laid on the arm of her throne, she kept all her air of high command.

But had she kept its power? Mr. Drew's demeanour reminded Karen sometimes of a cat's. Before the glance and voice of authority he would, metaphorically, pace away; pausing to blink up at some object that attracted his attention or to interest himself in the furbishing of flank or chest. At a hint of anger or coercion, he would tranquilly disappear. Tante, controlling indignation, was left to stare after him and to regain the throne as best she might, and at these moments Karen felt that Tante's eye turned on her, gauging her power of interpretation, ready, did she not feign the right degree of unconsciousness, to wreak on her something of the controlled emotion. The fear that had come on the night of her arrival pressed closely on Karen then, but, more closely still, the pain for Tante. Tante's clear dignity was blurred; her image, in its rebuffed and ineffectual autocracy, became hovering, uncertain, piteous. And, in seeing and feeling all these things, as if with a lacerated sensitiveness, Karen was aware that, in this last week of her life, she had grown much older. She felt herself in some ways older than her guardian.

It was on the morning of her seventh day at Les Solitudes that she met Mr. Drew walking early in the garden.

The sea was glittering blue and gold; the air was melancholy in its sweetness; birds whistled.

Karen examined Mr. Drew as he approached her along the sunny upper terrace.

With his dense, dark eyes, delicate face and golden hair, his white clothes and loose black tie, she was able to recognize in him an object that might charm and even subjugate. To Karen he seemed but one among the many strange young men she had seen surrounding Tante; yet this morning, clearly, and for the first time, she saw why he subjugated Tante and why she resented her subjugation. There was more in him than mere pose and peculiarity; he had some power; the power of the cat: he was sincerely indifferent to anything that did not attract him. And at the same time he was unimportant; insignificant in all but his sincerity. He was not a great writer; Tante could never make a great writer out of him. And he was, when all was said and done, but one among many strange young men.

"Good morning," he said. He doffed his hat. He turned and walked beside her. They were in full view of the house. "I hoped that I might find you. Let us go up to the flagged garden," he suggested; "the sea is glittering like a million scimitars. One has a better view up there."

"But it is not so warm," said Karen. "I am walking here to be in the sun."

Mr. Drew had also been walking there to be in the sun; but they were in full view of the house and he was aware of a hand at Madame von Marwitz's window-curtain. He continued, however, to walk beside Karen up and down the terrace.

"I think of you," he said, "as a person always in the sun. You suggest glaciers and fields of snow and meadows full of flowers — the sun pouring down on all of them. I always imagine Apollo as a Norse God. Are you really a Norwegian?"

Karen was, as we have said, accustomed to young men who talked in a fantastic manner. She answered placidly: "Yes. I am half Norwegian."

"Your name, then, is really yours? — your untamed, yet intimate, name. It is like a wild bird that feeds out of one's hand."

"Yes; it is really mine. It is quite a common name in Norway."

"Wild birds are common," Mr. Drew observed, smiling softly.

He found her literalness charming. He was finding her altogether charming. From the moment that she had appeared at the door in the dusk, with her white, blind, searching face, she had begun to interest him. She was stupid and delightful; a limpid and indomitable young creature who, in a clash of loyalties, had chosen, without a hesitation, to leave the obvious one. Also she was married yet unawakened, and this, to Mr. Drew, was a pre-eminently charming combination. The question of the awakened and the unawakened, of the human attitude to passion, preoccupied him, practically, more than any other. His art dealt mainly in themes of emotion as an end in itself.

The possibilities of passion in Madame von Marwitz, as artist
and genius, had strongly attracted him. He had genuinely been
in love with Madame von Marwitz. But the mere woman, as
she more and more helplessly revealed herself, was beginning to
oppress and bore him.

He had amused himself, of late, by imaging his relation to
her in the fable of the sun and the traveller. Her beams from
their high, sublime solitudes had filled him with delight and
exhilaration. Then the radiance had concentrated itself, had
begun to follow him — rather in the manner of stage sunlight
— very unflaggingly. He had wished for intervals of shade.
He had been aware, even during his long absence in America,
of sultriness brooding over him, and now, at these close quarters, he had begun to throw off his cloak of allegiance. She
bored him. It was n't good enough. She pretended to be sublime and far; but she was n't sublime and far; she was near
and watchful and exacting; as watchful and exacting as a mistress and as haughty as a Diana. She was not, and had, evidently, no intention of being, his mistress, and for the mere
pleasure of adoring her Mr. Drew found the price too high
to pay. He did not care to proffer, indefinitely, a reverent passion, and he did not like people, when he showed his weariness,
to lose their tempers with him. Already Madame von Marwitz had lost hers. He did not forget what she looked like
nor what she said on these occasions. She had mentioned the
large-mouthed children at Wimbledon — facts that he preferred
to forget as much as possible — and he did not know that he
forgave her. There was a tranquil malice in realizing that as
Madame von Marwitz became more and more displeasing to
him, Mrs. Jardine, more and more, became pleasing. A new
savour had come into his life since her appearance and he had
determined to postpone a final rupture with his great friend
and remain on for some time longer at Les Solitudes. He
wondered if it would be possible to awaken Mrs. Jardine.

"Have n't I heard you practising, once or twice lately?" he
asked her now, as they turned at the end of the terrace and
walked back.

"Yes," said Karen; "I practise every morning."

"I 'd no idea you played, too."

"It is hardly a case of 'too', is it," Karen said, mildly amused.

"I don't know. Perhaps it is. One may look at a Memling after a Michael Angelo, you know. I wish you 'd play to me."

"I am no Memling, I assure you."

"You can't, until I hear you. Do play to me. Brahms; a little Brahms."

"I have practised no Brahms for a long time. I find him too difficult."

"I heard you doing a Bach prelude yesterday; play that."

"Certainly, if you wish it, I will play it to you," said Karen, "though I do not think that you will much enjoy it."

Mrs. Talcott was in the morning-room over accounts; so Karen went with the young man into the music-room and opened the grand piano there.

She then played her prelude, delicately, carefully, composedly. She knew Mr. Drew to be musicianly; she did not mind playing to him.

More and more, Mr. Drew reflected, looking down at her, she reminded him of flower-brimmed, inaccessible mountain-slopes. He must discover some method of ascent; for the music brought her no nearer; he was aware, indeed, that it removed her. She quite forgot him as she played.

The last bars had been reached when the door opened suddenly and Madame von Marwitz appeared.

She had come in haste — that was evident — and a mingled fatigue and excitement was on her face. Her white cheeks had soft, sodden depressions and under her eyes were little pinches in the skin, as though hot fingers had nipped her there. She looked almost old, and she smiled a determined, adjusted smile, with heavy eyes. "*Tiens, tiens,*" she said, and, turning elaborately, she shut the door.

Karen finished her bars and rose.

"This is a new departure," said Madame von Marwitz. She came swiftly to them, her loose lace sleeves flowing back from

her bare arms. "I do not like my piano touched, you know,
Karen, unless permission is given. No matter, no matter, my
child. Let it not occur again, that is all. You have not found
the right balance of that phrase," she stooped and reiterated
with emphasis a fragment of the prelude. "And now I will
begin my work, if you please. Tallie waits for you, I think,
in the garden, and would be glad of your help. Tallie grows
old. It does not do to forget her."

"Am I to go into the garden, too?" Mr. Drew inquired, as
Madame von Marwitz seated herself and ran her fingers over
the keys. "I thought we were to motor this morning."

"We will motor when I have done my work. Go into the
garden, by all means, if you wish to."

"May I come into the garden with you? May I help you
there?" Mr. Drew serenely drawled, addressing Karen, who,
with a curious, concentrated look, stood gazing at her guardian.

She turned her eyes on him and her glance put him far, far
away, like an object scarcely perceived. "I am not going
into the garden," she said. "Mrs. Talcott is working in the
morning-room and does not need me yet."

"Ah. She is in the morning-room," Madame von Marwitz
murmured, still not raising her eyes, and still running loud and
soft scales up and down. Karen left the room.

As the door closed upon her, Madame von Marwitz, with a
singular effect of control, began to weave a spider's-web of intricate, nearly impalpable, sound. "Go, if you please," she said
to Mr. Drew.

He stood beside her, placid. "Why are you angry?" he
asked.

"I am not pleased that my rules should be broken. Karen
has many privileges. She must learn not to take, always, the
extra inch when the ell is so gladly granted."

He leaned on the piano. Her controlled face, bent with absorption above the lacey pattern of sound that she evoked, interested him.

"When you are angry and harness your anger to your art like

this, you become singularly beautiful," he remarked. He felt it; and, after all, if he were to remain at Les Solitudes and attempt to scale those Alpine slopes he must keep on good terms with Madame von Marwitz.

"So," was her only reply. Yet her eyes softened.

He raised the lace wing of her sleeve and kissed it, keeping it in his hand.

"No foolishness if you please," said Madame von Marwitz. "Of what have you and Karen been talking?"

"I can't get her to talk," said Mr. Drew. "But I like to hear her play."

"She plays with right feeling," said Madame von Marwitz. "She is not a child to express herself in speech. Her music reveals her more truly."

"*Nur wo du bist sei alles, immer kindlich*," Mr. Drew mused. "That is what she makes me think of." With anybody of Madame von Marwitz's intelligence, frankness was far more likely to allay suspicion than guile. And for very pride now she was forced to seem reassured. "Yes. That is so," she said. And she continued to play.

CHAPTER XXXII

KAREN meanwhile made her way to the cliff-path and, seating herself on a grassy slope, she clasped her knees with her hands and gazed out over the sea. She was thinking hard of something, and trying to think only of that. It was true, the permission had been that she was to play on the grand-piano when it was left open. There had been no rule set; it had not been said that she was not to play at other times and indeed, on many occasions, she had played unrebuked, before Tante came down. But the thing to remember now, with all her power, was that, technically, Tante had been right. To hold fast to that thought was to beat away a fear that hovered about her, like a horrible bird of prey. She sat there for a long time, and she became aware at last that though she held so tightly to her thought, it had, as it were, become something lifeless, inefficacious, and that fear had invaded her. Tante had been unkind, unjust, unloving.

It was as though, in taking refuge with Tante, she had leaped from a great height, seeing security beneath, and as though, alighting, she slipped and stumbled on a sloping surface with no foothold anywhere. Since she came, there had been only this sliding, sliding, and now it seemed to be down to unseen depths. For this was more and worse than the first fear of her coming. Tante had been unkind, and she so loved Mr. Drew that she forgot herself when he bestowed his least attention elsewhere.

Karen rose to her feet suddenly, aware that she was trembling.

She looked over the sea and the bright day was dreadful to her. Where was she and what was she, and what was Tante, if this fear were true? Not even on that far day of childhood when she had lost herself in the forest had such a horror of loneliness filled her. She was a lost, an unwanted creature.

She turned from the unanswering immensities and ran down the cliff-path towards Les Solitudes. She could not be alone. To think these things was to feel herself drowning in fear.

Emerging from the higher trees she caught sight below her of Mrs. Talcott's old straw hat moving among the borders; and, in the midst of the emptiness, the sight was strength and hope. The whole world seemed to narrow to Mrs. Talcott. She was secure and real. She was a spar to be clung to. The nightmare would reveal itself as illusion if she kept near Mrs. Talcott. She ran down to her.

Mrs. Talcott was slaying slugs. She had placed pieces of orange-peel around cherished young plants to attract the depredators and she held a jar of soot; into the soot the slugs were dropped as she discovered them.

The sight of her was like a draught of water to parching lips. Reality slowly grew round Karen once more. Tante had been hasty, even unkind; but she was piteous, absorbed in this great devotion; and Tante loved her.

She walked beside Mrs. Talcott and helped her with the slugs.

"Been out for a walk, Karen?" Mrs. Talcott inquired. They had reached the end of the border and moved on to a higher one.

"Only to the cliff," said Karen.

"You look kind of tired," Mrs. Talcott remarked, and Karen owned that she felt tired. "It's so warm to-day," she said.

"Yes; it's real hot. Let's walk under the trees." Mrs. Talcott took out her handkerchief and wiped her large, saffron-coloured forehead.

They walked slowly in the thin shadow of the young foliage.

"You're staying on for a while, aren't you?" Mrs. Talcott inquired presently. She had as yet asked Karen no question and Karen felt that something in her own demeanour had caused this one.

"For more than a while," she said. "I am not going away again." In the sound of the words she found a curious reassurance. Was it not her home, Les Solitudes?

Mrs. Talcott said nothing for some moments, stooping to nip a drooping leaf from a plant they passed. Then she questioned further: "Is Mr. Jardine coming down here?"

"I have left my husband," said Karen.

For some moments, Mrs. Talcott, again, said nothing, but she no longer had an eye for the plants. Neither did she look at Karen; her gaze was fixed before her. "Is that so," was at last her comment.

The phrase might have expressed amazement, commiseration or protest; its sound remained ambiguous. They had come to a rustic bench. "Let's sit down for a while," she said; "I'm not as young as I was."

They sat down, the old woman heavily, and she drew a sigh of relief. Looking at her Karen saw that she, too, was very tired. And she, too — was it not strange that to-day she should see it for the first time? — was very lonely. A sudden pity, profound and almost passionate, filled her for Mrs. Talcott.

"You'll not mind having me here — for all the time now — again, will you?" she asked, smiling a little, with determination, for she did not wish Mrs. Talcott to guess what she had seen.

"No," said Mrs. Talcott, continuing to gaze before her, and shaking her head. "No, I'll be glad of that. We get on real well together, I think." And, after another moment of silence, she went on in the same contemplative tone: "I used to quarrel pretty bad with my husband when I was first married, Karen. He was the nicest, mildest kind of man, as loving as could be. But I guess most young things find it hard to get used to each other all at once. It ain't easy, married life; at least not at the beginning. You expect such a high standard of each other and everything seems to hurt. After a while you get so discouraged, perhaps, finding it isn't like what you expected, that you commence to think you don't care any more and it was all a mistake. I guess every young wife thinks that in the first year, and it makes you feel mighty sick. Why, if marriage didn't tie people up so tight, most of 'em would fly apart in the first year and think they just hated each other,

and that's why it's such a good thing that they're tied so
tight. Why I remember once the only thing that seemed to
keep me back was thinking how Homer — Homer was my
husband's name, Homer G. Talcott — sort of snorted when
he laughed. I was awful mad with him and it seemed as if
he'd behaved so mean and misunderstood me so that I'd got
to go; but when I thought of that sort of childish snort he'd
give sometimes, I felt I couldn't leave him. It's mighty queer,
human nature, and the teeny things that seem to decide your
mind for you; I guess they're not as teeny as they seem. But
those hurt feelings are almost always a mistake — I'm pretty
sure of it. Any two people find it hard to live together and
get used to each other; it don't make any difference how much
in love they are."

There was no urgency in Mrs. Talcott's voice and no pathos of
retrospect. Its contemplative placidity might have been invit-
ing another sad and wise old woman to recognize these facts
of life with her.

Karen's mood, while she listened to her, was hardening to the
iron of her final realization, the realization that had divided her
and Gregory. "It is n't so with us, Mrs. Talcott," she said.
"He has shown himself a man I cannot live with. None of
our feelings are the same. All my sacred things he despises."

"Mercedes, you mean?" Mrs. Talcott suggested after a moment's silence.

"Yes. And more." Karen could not name her mother.

Mrs. Talcott sat silent.

"Has Tante not told you why I was here?" Karen presently
asked.

"No," said Mrs. Talcott. "I have n't had a real talk with
Mercedes since she got back. Her mind is pretty well taken up
with this young man."

To this Karen, glancing at Mrs. Talcott in a slight bewilderment, was able to say nothing, and Mrs. Talcott pursued, resuming her former tone: "There's another upsetting thing
about marriage, Karen, and that is that you can't expect your
families to feel about each other like you feel. It is n't in

nature that they should, and that's one of the things that
young married people can't make up their minds to. Now
Mr. Jardine isn't the sort of young man to care about many
people; few and far between they are, I should infer, and Mercedes ain't one of them. Mercedes wouldn't appeal to him one
mite. I saw that as plain as could be from the first."

"He should have told me so," said Karen, with her rocky
face and voice.

"Well, he didn't tell you he found her attractive, did he?"

"No. But though I saw that there was blindness, I thought
it was because he did not know her. I thought that when he
knew her he would care for her. And I could forgive his not
caring. I could forgive so much. But it is worse, far worse
than that. He accuses Tante of dreadful things. It is hatred
that he feels for her. He has confessed it." The colour had
risen to Karen's cheeks and burned there as she spoke.

"Well now!" Mrs. Talcott imperturbably ejaculated.

"You can see that I could not live with a man who hated
Tante," said Karen.

"What sort of things for instance?" Mrs. Talcott took up her
former statement.

"How can I tell you, Mrs. Talcott. It burns me to think of
them. Hypocrisy in her feeling for me; selfishness and tyranny
and deceit. It is terrible. In his eyes she is a malignant
woman."

"Tch! Tch!" Mrs. Talcott made an indeterminate cluck
with her tongue.

"I struggled not to see," said Karen, and her voice took on a
sombre energy, "and Tante struggled, too, for me. She, too,
saw from the very first what it might mean. She asked me, on
the very first day that they met, Mrs. Talcott, when she came
back, she asked me to try and make him like her. She was so
sweet, so magnanimous," her voice trembled. Oh the deep
relief, so deep that it seemed to cut like a knife — of remembering, pressing to her, what Tante had done for her, endured
for her! "So sweet, so magnanimous, Mrs. Talcott. She did
all that she could — and so did I — to give him time. For it

was not that I lacked love for my husband. No. I loved him. More, even more, than I loved Tante. There was perhaps the wrong. I was perhaps cowardly, for his sake. I would not see. And it was all useless. It grew worse and worse. He was not rude to her. It was not that. It was worse. He was so care- ful — oh I see it now — not to put himself in the wrong. He tried, instead, to put her in the wrong. He misread every word and look. He sneered — oh, I saw it, and shut my eyes — at her little foibles and weaknesses; why should she not have them as well as other people, Mrs. Talcott? And he was blind — blind — blind," Karen's voice trembled more violently, " to all the rest. So that it had to end," she went on in broken sentences. " Tante went because she could bear it no longer. And because she saw that I could bear it no longer. She hoped, by leaving me, to save my happiness. But that could not be. Mrs. Talcott, even then I might have tried to go on living with that chasm — between Tante and my husband — in my life; but I learned the whole truth as even I had n't seen it; as even she had n't seen it. Mrs. Forrester came to me, Mrs. Talcott, and told me what Gregory had said to her of Tante. He believes her a malignant woman," said Karen, re- peating her former words and rising as she spoke. " And to me he did not deny it. Everything, then, was finished for us. We saw that we did not love each other any longer."

· She stood before Mrs. Talcott in the path, her hands hanging at her sides, her eyes fixed on the wall above Mrs. Talcott's head.

Mrs. Talcott did not rise. She sat silent, looking up at Karen, and so for some moments they said nothing, while in the spring sunshine about them the birds whistled and an early white butterfly dipped and fluttered by.

" I feel mighty tired, Karen," Mrs. Talcott then said. Her eyelid with the white mole twitched over her eye, the lines of her large, firm old mouth were relaxed. Karen's eyes went to her and pity filled her.

" It is my miserable story," she said. " I am so sorry."

" Yes, I feel mighty tired," Mrs. Talcott repeated, looking

away and out at the sea. "It's discouraging. I thought you were fixed up all safe and happy for life."

"Dear Mrs. Talcott," said Karen, earnestly.

"I don't like to see things that ought to turn out right turning out wrong," Mrs. Talcott continued, "and I've seen a sight too many of them in my life. Things turning out wrong that were meant to go right. Things spoiled. Poeple, nice, good people, like you and Mr. Jardine, all upset and miserable. I've seen worse things, too," Mrs. Talcott slowly rose as she spoke. "Yes, I've seen about as bad things happen as can happen, and it's always been when Mercedes is about."

She stood still beside Karen, her bleak, intense old gaze fixed on the sea.

Karen thought that she had misheard her last words. "When Tante is about?" she repeated. "You mean that dreadful things happen to her? That is one of the worst parts of it now, Mrs. Talcott — only that I am so selfish that I do not think of it enough — to know that I have added to Tante's troubles."

"No." Mrs. Talcott now said, and with a curious mildness and firmness. "No, that ain't what I mean. Mercedes has had a sight of trouble. I don't deny it, but that ain't what I mean. She makes trouble. She makes it for herself and she makes it for other people. There's always trouble going, of some sort or other, when Mercedes is about."

"I don't understand you, Mrs. Talcott," said Karen. An uncanny feeling had crept over her while the old woman spoke. It was as if, helplessly, she were listening to a sleep-walker who, in tranced unconsciousness, spoke forth mildly the hidden thought of his waking life.

"No, you don't understand, yet," said Mrs. Talcott. "Perhape it's fair that you don't. Perhaps she can't help it. She was born so, I guess." Mrs. Talcott turned and walked towards the house.

The panic of the cliff was rising in Karen again. Mrs. Talcott was worse than the cliff and the unanswering immensities. She walked beside her, trying to control her terror.

"You mean, I think," she said, "that Tante is a tragic person and people who love her must suffer because of all that she has had to suffer."

"Yes, she's tragic all right," said Mrs. Talcott. "She's had about as bad a time as they make 'em — off and on. But she spoils things. And it makes me tired to see it going on. I've had too much of it," said Mrs. Talcott, "and if this can't come right — this between you and your nice young husband — I don't feel like I could get over it somehow." Leaning on Karen's arm with both hands she had paused and looked intently down at the path.

"But Mrs. Talcott," Karen's voice trembled; it was incredible, yet one was forced by Mrs. Talcott's whole demeanour to ask the question without indignation —" you speak as if you were blaming Tante for something. You do not blame her, do you?"

Mrs. Talcott still paused and still looked down, as if deeply pondering. "I've done a lot of thinking about that very point, Karen," she said. "And I don't know as I've made up my mind yet. It's a mighty intricate question. Perhaps we've all got only so much will-power and when most of it is ladled out into one thing there's nothing left to ladle out into the others. That's the way I try, sometimes, to figure it out to myself. Mercedes has got a powerful sight of will-power; but look at all she's got to use up in her piano-playing. There she is, working up to the last notch all the time, taking it out of herself, getting all wrought up. Well, to live so as you won't be spoiling things for other people needs about as much will-power as piano-playing, I guess, when you're as big a person as Mercedes and want as many things. And if you ain't got any will-power left you just do the easiest thing; you just take what you've a mind to; you just let yourself go in every other way to make up for the one way you held yourself in. That's how it is, perhaps."

"But Mrs. Talcott," said Karen in a low voice, "all this — about me and my husband — has come because Tante has thought too much of us and too little of herself. It would have been much easier for her to let us alone and not try and make

Gregory like her. I do not recognise her in what you are saying. You are saying dreadful things."

"Well, dreadful things have happened, I guess," said Mrs. Talcott. "I want you to go back to your nice husband, Karen."

"No; no. Never. I can never go back to him," said Karen, walking on.

"Because he hates Mercedes?"

"Not only that. No. He is not what I thought. Do not ask me, Mrs. Talcott. We do not love each other any longer. It is over."

"Well, I won't say anything about it, then," said Mrs. Talcott, who, walking beside her, kept her hand on her arm. "Only I liked Mr. Jardine. I took to him right off, and I don't take to people so easy. And I take to you, Karen, more than you know, I guess. And I'll lay my bottom dollar there's some mistake between you and him, and that Mercedes is the reason of it."

They had reached the house.

"But wait," said Karen, turning to her. She laid both her hands on the old woman's arm while she steadied her voice to speak this last thought. "Wait. You are so kind to me, Mrs. Talcott; but you have made everything strange — and dreadful. I must ask you — one question, Mrs. Talcott. You have been with Tante all her life. No one knows her as you do. Tell me, Mrs. Talcott. You love Tante?"

They faced each other at the top of the steps, on the verandah. And the young eyes plunged deep into the old eyes, passionately searching.

For a moment Mrs. Talcott did not reply. When she did speak, it was decisively as if, while recognising Karen's right to ask, Karen must recognise that the answer must suffice. "I'd be pretty badly off if I did n't love Mercedes. She's all I've got in the world."

CHAPTER XXXIII

THE sound of the motor, whirring skilfully among the lanes, was heard at six, and shortly after Madame von Marwitz's return Mrs. Talcott knocked at her door.

Madame von Marwitz was lying on the sofa. Louise had removed her wraps and dress and was drawing off her shoes. Her eyes were closed. She seemed weary.

"I'll see to Madame," said Mrs. Talcott with her air of composed and unassuming authority. It was somewhat the air of an old nurse, sure of her prerogatives in the nursery.

Louise went and Mrs. Talcott took off the other shoe and fetched the white silk *mules*.

Madame von Marwitz had only opened her eye for a glimmer of recognition, but as Mrs. Talcott adjusted a *mule,* she tipped it off and muttered gloomily: "Stockings, please. I want fresh stockings."

There was oddity — as Mrs. Talcott found, and came back, with a pair of white silk stockings — in the sight of the opulent, middle-aged figure on the sofa, childishly stretching out first one large bare leg and then the other to be clothed; and it might have aroused in Mrs. Talcott a vista of memories ending with the picture of a child in the same attitude, a child as idle and as autocratic.

"Thank you, Tallie," Madame von Marwitz said, wearily but kindly, when the stockings were changed.

Mrs. Talcott drew a chair in front of the sofa, seated herself and clasped her hands at her waist. "I've come for a talk, Mercedes," she said.

Madame von Marwitz now was sleepily observing her.

"A talk! *Bon Dieu!* But I have been talking all day long!"

She yawned, putting a folded arm under her head so that,

slightly raising it, she could look at Mrs. Talcott more comfortably. "What do you want to talk about?" she inquired.

Mrs. Talcott's eyes, with their melancholy, immovable gaze, rested upon her. "About Karen and her husband," she said. "I gathered from some talk I had with Karen to-day that you let her think you came away from London simply and solely because you'd had a quarrel with Mr. Jardine."

Madame von Marwitz lay as if arrested by these words for some moments of an almost lethargic interchange, and then in an impatient voice she returned: "What business is it of Karen's, pray, if I didn't leave London simply and solely on account of my quarrel with her husband? I had found it intolerable to be under his roof and I took the first opportunity for leaving it. The opportunity happened to coincide with my arrangements for coming here. What has that to do with Karen?"

"It has to do with her, Mercedes, because the child believes you were thinking about her when, as a matter of fact, you weren't thinking about her or about anyone but this young man you've gotten so taken up with. Karen believes you care for her something in the same way she does for you, and it's a sin and a shame, Mercedes," Mrs. Talcott spoke with no vehemence at all of tone or look, but with decision, "a sin and a shame to let that child ruin her life because of you."

Again Madame von Marwitz, now turning her eyes on the ceiling, seemed to reflect dispassionately. "I never conceived it possible that she would leave him," she then said. "I found him insufferable and I saw that unless I went Karen also would come to see him as insufferable. To spare the poor child this I came away. And I was amazed when she appeared here. Amazed and distressed," said Madame von Marwitz. And after another moment she took up: "As for him, he has what he deserves."

Mrs. Talcott eyed her. "And what do you deserve, I'd like to know, for going meddling with those poor happy young things? Why couldn't you let them alone? Karen's been a bother to you for years. Why couldn't you be satisfied at having her nicely fixed up and let her tend to her own potato-patch while you tended to yours? You can't make me believe that it was n't your fault — the whole thing — right from the beginning. I know you too well, Mercedes."

Again Madame von Marwitz lay, surprisingly still and surprisingly unresentful. It was as if, placidly, she were willing to be undressed, body or soul, by her old nurse and guardian. But after a moment, and with sudden indignation, she took up one of Mrs. Talcott's sentences.

"A bother to me? I am very fond of Karen. I am devoted to Karen. I should much like to know what right you have to intimate that my feeling for her is n't sincere. My life proves the contrary. As for saying that it is my fault, that is merely your habit. Everything is always my fault with you."

"It always has been, as far as I 've been able to keep an eye on your tracks," Mrs. Talcott remarked.

"Well, this is not. I deny it. I absolutely," said Madame von Marwitz, and now with some excitement, "deny it. Did I not give her to him? Did I not go to them with tenderest solicitude and strive to make possible between him and me some relation of bare good fellowship? Did I not curb my spirit, and it is a proud and impatient one, as you know, to endure, lest she should see it, his veiled insolence and hostility? Oh! when I think of what I have borne with from that young man, I marvel at my own forbearance. I have nothing to reproach myself with, Tallie; nothing; and if his life is ruined I can say, with my hand on my heart,"— Madame von Marwitz laid it there —"that he alone is to blame for it. A more odious, arrogant, ignorant being," she added, "I have never encountered. Karen is well rid of him."

Mrs. Talcott remained unmoved. "You don't like him because he don't like you and that's about all you 've got against him, I reckon, if the truth were known," she said. "You can make yourself see it all like that if you 've a mind to, but you can't make me; I know you too well, Mercedes. You were mad at him because he did n't admire you like you 're used to being admired, and you went to work pinching and picking here

and there, pretending it was all on Karen's account, but really
so as you could get even with him. You could n't stand their
being happy all off by themselves without you. Why I can see
it all as plain and clear as if I 'd been there right along. Just
think of your telling that poor deluded child that you wanted
her to make her husband like you. That was a nice way, was n't
it, for setting her heart at rest about you and him. If you
did n't like him and saw he did n't like you, why did n't you keep
your mouth shut? That 's all you had to do, and keep out of
their way all you could. If you 'd been a stupid woman there
might have been some excuse for you, but you ain't a stupid
woman, and you know precious well what you 're about all the
time. I don't say you intended to blow up the whole concern
like you 've done; but you wanted to get even with Mr. Jardine
and show him that Karen cared as much for you as she did for
him, and you did n't mind two straws what happened to Karen
while you were doing it."

Madame von Marwitz had listened, turning on her back and
with her eyes still on the ceiling, and the calm of her face might
have been that of indifference or meditation. But now, after a
moment of receptive silence, indignation again seemed to seize
her. "It 's false!" she exclaimed.

"No it ain't false, Mercedes, and you know it ain't," said
Mrs. Talcott gloomily.

"False, and absolutely false!" Madame von Marwitz repeated. "How could I keep my mouth shut — as you delicately put it — when I saw that Karen saw? How keep my
mouth shut without warping her relation to me? I spoke to
her with lightest, most tender understanding, so that she should
know that my heart was with her while never dreaming of the
chasms that I saw in her happiness. It was he who forced me
to an open declaration and he who forced me to leave; for how
was happiness possible for Karen if I remained with them?
No. He hated me, and was devoured by jealousy of Karen's
love for me."

"I guess if it comes to jealousy you 've got enough for two in
any situation. It don't do for you to talk to me about jealousy,

Mercedes," Mrs. Talcott returned, " I 've seen too much of you.
You can't persuade me it was n't your fault, not if you were to
talk till the cows come home. I don't deny but what it was
pretty hard for you to see that Mr. Jardine did n't admire you.
I make allowances for that; but my gracious me," said Mrs.
Talcott with melancholy emphasis, " was that any reason for a
big middle-aged woman like you behaving like a spiteful child?
Was it any reason for your setting to work to spoil Karen's life?
No, Mercedes, you 've done about as mean a thing as any I 've
seen you up to and what I want to know now is what you 're
going to do about it."

"Do about it?" Madame von Marwitz wrathfully repeated.
"What more can I do? I open my house and my heart to the
child. I take her back. I mend the life that he has broken.
What more do you expect of me?"

" Don't talk that sort of stage talk to me, Mercedes. What I
want you to do is to make it possible so as he can get her back."

"He is welcome to get her back if he can. I shall not stand
in his way. It would be a profound relief to me were he to get
her back."

" I can see that well enough. But how 'll you help standing in
his way? The only thing you could do to get out of his way
would be to help Karen to be quit of you. Make her see that
you 're just as bad as he thinks you. I guess if you told her
some things about yourself she 'd begin to see that her husband was n't so far wrong about you."

"*Par exemple!*" said Madame von Marwitz with a short
laugh. She raised herself to give her pillow a blow and turning on her side and contemplating more directly her ancient
monitress she said, " I sometimes wonder what I keep you here
for."

" I do, too, sometimes," said Mrs. Talcott, " and I make it out
that you need me."

" I make it out," Madame von Marwitz repeated the phrase
with a noble dignity of manner, " that I am too kind of heart,
too aware of what I owe you in gratitude, to resent, as I have

every right to do, the license you allow yourself in speaking to
me."

"Yes; you'll always get plain speaking from me, Mercedes,"
Mrs. Talcott remarked, "just as long as you have anything to
do with me."

"Indeed I shall. I am but too well aware of the fact," said
Madame von Marwitz, "and I only tolerate it because of our
life-long tie."

"You'll go on tolerating it, I guess, Mercedes. You'd feel
mighty queer, I expect, if the one person in the world who knew
you through and through and had stood by you through everything wasn't there to fall back on."

"I deny that you know me through and through," Madame
von Marwitz declared, but with a drop from her high manner;
sulkily rather than with conviction. "You have always seen
me with the eye of a lizard." Her simile amused her and she
suddenly laughed. "You have somewhat the vision of a lizard,
Tallie. You scrutinize the cracks and the fissures, but of the
mountain itself you are unaware. I have cracks and fissures,
no doubt, like all the rest of our sad humanity; but, *bon Dieu!*
— I am a mountain, and you, Tallie," she went on, laughing
softly, "are a lizard on the mountain. As for Mr. Jardine, he
is a mole. But if you think that Karen will be happier bur-
rowing underground with him than here with me, I will do my
best. Yes;" she reflected; "I will write to Mrs. Forrester.
She shall see the mole and tell him that when he sends me
an apology I send him Karen. It is a wild thing to leave one's
husband like this. I will make her see it."

"Now you see here, Mercedes," said Mrs. Talcott, rising and
fixing an acute gaze upon her, "don't you go and make things
worse than they are. Don't you go interfering between Karen
and her husband. The first move's got to come from them. I
don't trust you round the corner where your vanity comes in, and
I guess what you've got in your mind now is that you'd like to
make it out to your friends how you've tried to reconcile Karen
and her husband after he's treated you so bad. If you want to

tell Karen that he was right in all the things he believed about you and that this is n't the first time by a long shot that you've wrecked people with your jealousy, and that he loves her ten times more than you do, that's a different thing, and I'll stand by you through it. But I won't have you meddling any more with those two poor young things, so you may as well take it in right here."

Madame von Marwitz's good humour fell away. "And for you, may I ask you kindly to mind your own business?" she demanded.

"I'll make this affair of Karen's my business if you ain't real careful, Mercedes," said Mrs. Talcott, standing solid and thick and black, in the centre of the room. "Yes, you'd better go slow and sure or you'll find there are some things I can't put up with. This affair of Karen has made me feel pretty sick, I can tell you. I've seen you do a sight of mean things in your life, but I don't know as I've seen you do a meaner. I guess," Mrs. Talcott continued, turning her eyes on the evening sea outside, "it would make your friends sit up — all these folks who admire you so much — if they could know a thing or two you've done."

"Leave the room," said Madame von Marwitz, now raising herself on her elbow and pointing to the door. "Leave the room at once. I refuse to lie here and be threatened and insulted and brow-beaten by you. Out of my sight."

Mrs. Talcott looked at the sea for a moment longer, in no provocative manner, but rather as if she had hardly heard the words addressed to her; and then she looked at Mercedes, who, still raised on her elbow, still held her arm very effectively outstretched. This, too, was no doubt a scene to which she was fully accustomed.

"All right," she said, "I'm going." She moved towards the door. At the door she halted, turned and faced Madame von Marwitz again. "But don't you forget, Mercedes Okraska," she said, "that I'll make it my affair if you ain't careful."

CHAPTER XXXIV.

KAREN, during the two or three days that followed her strange conversation with Mrs. Talcott, felt that while she pitied and cared for Mrs. Talcott as she had never yet pitied and cared for her, she was also afraid of her. Mrs. Talcott had spoken no further word and her eyes rested on her with no more than their customary steadiness; but Karen knew that there were many words she could speak. What were they? What was it that Mrs. Talcott knew? What secrets were they that she carried about in her lonely, ancient heart?

Mrs. Talcott loomed before her like a veiled figure of destiny bearing an urn within which lay the ashes of dead hopes. Mrs. Talcott's eyes looked at her above the urn. It was always with them. When they gardened together it was as if Mrs. Talcott set it down on the ground between them and as if she took it up again with a sigh of fatigue — it was heavy — when they turned to go. Karen felt herself tremble as she scrutinized the funereal shape. There was no refuge with Mrs. Talcott. Mrs. Talcott holding her urn was worse than the lonely fears.

And, for those two or three days of balmy, melancholy spring, the lonely fears did not press so closely. They wheeled far away against the blue. Tante was kinder to her and was more aware of her. She almost seemed a little ashamed of the scene with the piano. She spoke to Karen of it, flushing a little, explaining that she had slept badly and that Karen's rendering of the Bach had made her nervous, emphasizing, too, the rule, new in its explicitness, that the grand piano was only to be played on by Karen when it was left open. "You did not understand. But it is well to understand rules, is it not, my child?" said Madame von Marwitz. "And this one, I know, you will not transgress again."

Karen said that she understood. She had something of her

rocky manner in receiving these implicit apologies and commands, yet her guardian could see an almost sick relief rising in her jaded young eyes.

Other things were different. Tante seemed now to wish very constantly to have her there when Mr. Drew was with her. She made much of her to Mr. Drew. She called his attention to her skill in gardening, to her directness of speech, to her individuality of taste in dress. These expositions made Karen uncomfortable, yet they seemed an expression of Tante's desire to make amends. And Mr. Drew, with his vague, impenetrable regard, helped her to bear them. It was as if, a clumsy child, she were continually pushed forward by a fond, tactless mother, and as if, mildly shaking her hand, the guest before whom she was displayed showed her, by kind, inattentive eyes, that he was paying very little attention to her. Mr. Drew put her at her ease and Tante embarrassed her. She became, even, a little grateful to Mr. Drew. But now, aware of this strange bond, it was more difficult to talk to him when they were alone and when, once or twice, he met her in the garden or house, she made always an excuse to leave him. She and Mr. Drew could have nothing to say to each other when Tante was not there.

One evening, returning to Les Solitudes after a walk along the cliffs, Karen found that tea was over, as she had intended that it should be, Tante and Mr. Drew not yet come in from their motoring, and Mrs. Talcott safely busied in the garden. There was not one of them with whom she could be happily alone, and she was glad to find the morning-room empty. Mrs. Talcott had left the kettle boiling for her on the tea-table and the small tea-pot, which they used in their usual *tête-à-tête*, ready, and Karen made herself a cup.

She was tired. She sat down, when she had had her tea, near the window and looked out over the ranged white flowers growing in their low white pots on the window-seat, at the pale sea and sky. She sat quietly, her cheek on one hand, the other in her lap, and from time to time a great involuntary sigh lifted her breast. It seemed nearer peace than fear, this mood of immeasurable, pale sorrow. It folded her round like the twilight falling outside.

The room was dim when she heard the sound of the returning motor and she sat on, believing that here she would be undisturbed. Tante rarely came to the morning-room. But it was Tante who presently appeared, wearing still her motoring cloak and veil, the nun-like veil bound round her head. Karen thought, as she rose, and looked at her, that she was like one of the ghost-like white flowers. And there was no joy for her in seeing her. She seemed to be part of the sadness.

She turned and closed the door with some elaboration, and as she came nearer Karen recognized in her eyes the piteous look of quelled watchfulness.

"You are sitting here, alone, my child?" she said, laying her hand, but for a moment only, on Karen's shoulder. Karen had resumed her seat, and Tante moved away at once to take up a vase of flowers from the mantelpiece, smell the flowers, and set it back. "Where is Tallie?"

"Still in the garden, I think. I worked with her this morning and before tea. Since tea I have had a walk."

"Where did you walk?" Madame von Marwitz inquired, moving now over to the upright piano and bending to examine in the dusk the music that stood on it. Karen described her route.

"But it is lonely, very lonely, for you, is it not?" Tante murmured after a moment's silence. Karen said nothing and she went on, "And it will be still more lonely if, as I think probable, I must leave you here before long. I shall be going; perhaps to Italy."

A sensation of oppression that she could not have analyzed passed over Karen. Why was Tante going to Italy? Why must she leave Les Solitudes? Her mind could not rest on the supposition that her own presence drove Tante forth, that the broken *tête-à-tête* was to be resumed under less disturbing circumstances. She could not ask Tante if Mr. Drew was to be in Italy; yet this was the question that pressed on her heart.

"Oh, but I am very used to Les Solitudes," she said.

"Used to it. Yes. Too used to it," said Madame von Marwitz, seating herself now near Karen, her eyes still moving
about the room. "But it is not right, it is not fitting, that
you should spend your youth here. That was not the destiny
I had hoped for you. I came here to find you, Karen, so that
I might talk to you." Her fingers slightly tapped her chair-
arm. "We must talk. We must see what is to be done."

"Do you mean about me, Tante?" Karen asked after a
moment. The look of the ghostly room and of the white, enfolded figure seated before her with its restless eyes seemed part
of the chill that Tante's words brought.

"About you. Yes. About who else, *parbleu!*" said Madame
von Marwitz with a slight laugh, her eyes shifting about the
room; and with a change of tone she added: "I have it on my
heart — your situation — day and night. Something must be
done and I am prepared to do it."

"To do what?" asked Karen. Her voice, too, had changed,
but not, as Madame von Marwitz's, to a greater sweetness.

"Well, to save it — the situation; to help you." Madame von
Marwitz's ear was quick to catch the change. "And I have
come, my Karen, to consult with you. It is a matter, many
would say, for my pride to consider; but I will not count my
pride. Your happiness, your dignity, your future are the
things that weigh with me. I am prostrated, made ill, by the
miserable affair; you see it, you see that I am not myself. I
cannot sleep. It haunts me — you and your broken life. And
what I have to propose," Tante looked down at her tapping
fingers while she spoke, "is that I offer myself as intermediary.
Your husband will not take the first step forward. So be it.
I will take it. I will write to Mrs. Forrester. I will tell her
that if your husband will but offer me the formal word of
apology I will myself induce you to return to him. What do
you say, my Karen? Oh, to me, as you know, the forms are
indifferent; it is of you and your dignity that I think. I know
you; without that apology from him to me you could not contemplate a reconciliation. But he has now had his lesson,
your young man, and when he knows that, through me, you

would hold out the olive-branch, he will, I predict, spring to
grasp it. After all, he is in love with you and has had time
to find it out; and even if he were not, his mere man's pride
must writhe to see himself abandoned. And you, too, have had
your lesson, my poor Karen, and have seen that romance is a
treacherous sand to build one's life upon. Dignity, fitness, one's
rightful place in life have their claims. You are one, as I
told you, to work out your destiny in the world, not in the
wilderness. What do you say, Karen? I would not write without consulting you. *Hein!* What is it?"

Karen had risen, and Madame von Marwitz's eyelashes fluttered a little in looking up at her.

"I will never forgive you, I will never forgive you," said
Karen in a harsh voice, "if you speak of this again."

"What is this that you say to me, Karen?" Madame von
Marwitz, too, rose.

"Never speak to me of this again," said Karen.

In the darkening room they looked at each other as they had
never in all their lives looked before. They were equals in
maturity of demand.

For a strange moment sheer fury struggled with subtler emotions in Madame von Marwitz's face, and then self-pity, overpowering, engulfing all else. "And is this the return you make
me for my love?" she cried. Her voice broke in desperate
sobs and long-pent misery found relief. She sank into her
chair.

"I asked for no reconciliation," said Karen. "I left him
and we knew that we were parting forever. There is no love
between us. Have you no understanding at all, and no thought
of my pride?"

It was woman addressing woman. The child Karen was
gone.

"Your pride?" Madame von Marwitz repeated in her sobs.
"And what of mine? Was it not for you, stony-hearted girl?
Is it not your happiness I seek? If I have been mistaken in my
hopes for you, is that a reason for turning upon me like a
serpent!"

Karen had walked to the long window that opened to the verandah and looked out, pressing her forehead to the pane. "You must forgive me if I was unkind. What you said burned me."

"Ah, it is well for you to speak of burnings!" Madame von Marwitz sobbed, aware that Karen's wrath was quelled. "I am scorched by all of you! by all of you!" she repeated incoherently. "All the burdens fall upon me and, in reward, I am spurned and spat upon by those I seek to serve!"

"I am sorry, Tante. It was what you said. That you should think it possible."

"Sorry! Sorry! It is easy to say that you are sorry when you have rolled me in the dust of your insults and your ingratitude!" Yet the sobs were quieter.

"Let us say, then, that it has been misunderstanding," said Karen. She still stood in the window, but as she spoke the words she drew back suddenly. She had found herself looking into Mr. Drew's eyes. His face, gazing in oddly upon her, was at the other side of the pane, and' in the apparition, its suddenness, its pallor, rising from the dusk, there was something almost horrible.

"Who is that?" came Tante's voice, as Karen drew away. She had turned in her chair.

It seemed to Karen, then, that the room was filled with the whirring wings of wild emotions, caught and crushed together. Tante had sprung up and came with long, swift strides to the window. She, too, pressed her face against the pane. "Ah! It is Claude," she said, in a hushed strange voice, "and he did not see that I was here. What does he mean by looking in like that?" she spoke now angrily, drying her eyes as she spoke. She threw open the window. "Claude. Come here."

Mr. Drew, whose face seemed to have sunk, like a drowned face, back into dark water, returned to the threshold and paused, arrested by his friend's wretched aspect. "Come in. Enter," said Madame von Marwitz, with a withering stateliness of utterance. "You have the manner of a spy. Did you think that Karen and I were quarrelling?"

"I couldn't think that," said Mr. Drew, stepping into the room, "for I didn't see that you were here."

"We have had a misunderstanding," said Madame von Marwitz. "No more. And now we understand again. Is it not so, my Karen? You are going?"

"I think I will go to my room," said Karen, who looked at neither Madame von Marwitz nor Mr. Drew. "You will not mind if I do not come to dinner to-night."

"Certainly not. No. Do as you please. You are tired. I see it. And I, too, am tired." She followed Karen to the door, murmuring: *"Sans rancune, n'est-ce-pas?"*

"Yes, Tante."

As the door closed upon Karen, Madame von Marwitz turned to Mr. Drew.

"If you wish to see her, why not seek her openly? Who makes it difficult for you to approach her?" Her voice had the sharpness of splintering ice.

"Why, no one, *ma chère*," said Mr. Drew. "I wasn't seeking her."

"No? And what did it mean, then, your face pressed close to hers, there at the window?"

"It meant that I couldn't see who it was who stood there. Just as I can hardly now see more than that you are unhappy. What is the matter, my dear and beautiful friend?" His voice was solicitous.

Madame von Marwitz dropped again into her chair and leaning forward, her hands hanging clasped between her knees, she again wept. "The matter is the old one," she sobbed. "Ingratitude! Ingratitude on every hand! My crime now has been that I have sought — at the sacrifice of my own pride — to bring a reconciliation between that stubborn child and her husband, and for my reward she overwhelms me with abuse!"

"Tell me about it," said Mr. Drew, seating himself beside her and, unreproved, taking her hand.

CHAPTER XXXV

KAREN did not go to her room. She was afraid that Mrs. Talcott would come to her there. She asked the cook for a few sandwiches and going to one of the lower terraces she found a seat there and sat down. She felt ill. Her mind was sore and vague. She sat leaning her head on her hand, as she had sat in the morning-room, her eyes closed, and did not try to think.

She had escaped something — mercifully. Yes, the supreme humiliation that Tante had prepared for her was frustrated. And she had been strangely hard and harsh to Tante and in return Tante had been piteous yet unmoving. Her heart was dulled towards Tante. She felt that she saw her from a great distance.

The moon had risen and was shining brightly when she at last got up and climbed the winding paths up to the house.

A definite thought, after the hours that she had sat there, had at last risen through the dull waters of her mind. Why should Tante go away? Why should not she herself go? There need be no affront to Tante, no alienation. But, for a time, at least, would it not be well to prove to Tante that she could be something more than a problem and a burden? Could she not go to the Lippheims in Germany and teach English and French and Italian there — she knew them all — and make a little money, and, when Tante wanted her again to come to Les Solitudes, come as an independent person?

It was a curious thought. It contradicted the assumptions upon which her life was founded; for was she not Tante's child and Tante's home her home? So curious it was that she contemplated it like an intricate weapon laid in her hand, its oddity concealing its significance.

She turned the weapon over. She might be Tante's child and

328

Tante's home might be hers; yet a child could gain its own bread, could it not? What was there to pierce and shatter in the thought that it would be well for her to gain her bread? "Tante has worked for me too long," she said to herself. She was not pierced or shattered. Something very strange was in her hand, but she was only reasonable.

She had stood still, in the midst of her swift climbing towards the house, to think it all out clearly, and it was as she stood there that she saw the light of a cigarette approaching her. It was Mr. Drew and he had seen her. Karen was aware of a deep stirring of displeasure and weariness. "But, please," he said, as, slightly bowing her head, and murmuring, "Goodnight," she passed him; "I want — I very particularly want — to see you." He turned to walk beside her, tossing away his cigarette. "There is something I particularly want to say."

His tone was grave and kind and urgent. It reproached her impatient impulse. He might have come with a message from Tante.

"Where is my guardian?" she asked.

"She has gone to bed. She has a horrible headache, poor thing," said Mr. Drew, who was leading her through the little copse of trees and along the upper paths. "Here, shall we sit down here? You are not cold?"

They were in the flagged garden. Karen, vaguely expectant, sat down on the rustic bench and Mr. Drew sat beside her. The moonlight shone through the trees and fell fantastically on the young man's face and figure and on Karen, sitting upright, her little shawl of white knitted wool drawn closely about her shoulders and enfolding her arms. "Not for long, please," she said. "It is growing late and although I am not cold I am tired. What have you to say, Mr. Drew?"

He had so much to say and it was, so obviously, his opportunity, his complete opportunity at last, that, before the exquisite and perilous task of awakening this creature of flowers and glaciers, Mr. Drew collected his resources with something of the skill and composure of an artist preparing canvas and palette. He must begin delicately and discreetly, and then he must be sudden and decisive.

"I want to make you feel, in the first place, if I can," he said, leaning forward to look into her face and observing with satisfaction that she made no movement of withdrawal as he came a litile nearer in so doing, "that I 'm your friend. Can I, do you think, succeed in making you feel that? " His experience had told him that it really did n't matter so much what one said. To come near was the point, and to look deeply. "I 've had so few chances of showing you how much your friend I am."

"Thank you," said Karen. "You are kind." She did not say that he would succeed in making her feel him a friend.

"We have been talking about you, talking a great deal, since you left us, your guardian and I," Mr. Drew continued, and he looked at the one of Karen's hands that was visible, emerging from the shawl to clasp her elbow, the left hand with its wedding-ring, "and ludicrous as it may seem to you, I can't but feel that I understand you a great deal better than she does. She still thinks of you as a child — a child whose little problems can be solved by facile solutions. Forgive me, I know it may sound fatuous to you, but I see what she does not see, that you are a suffering woman, and that for some problems there are no solutions." His eyes now came back to hers and found them fixed on him with a wide astonished gaze.

"Has my guardian asked you to say anything to me? " she said.

"No, not exactly that," said Mr. Drew, a little disconcerted by her tone and look, while at the same time he was marvelling at the greater and greater beauty he found in the impassive moonlit face — how had he been so unconscionably stupid as not to see for so long how beautiful she was! —"No, she certainly has n't asked me to say anything to you. She is going away, you know, to Italy; it 's a sudden decision and she 's been telling me about it. I can't go with her. I don't think it a good plan. I can stay on here, but I can't go to Italy. Perhaps she 'll give it up. She did n't find me altogether sympathetic and I 'm afraid we 've had something of a disagreement. I am sure you 've seen since

you 've been here that if your guardian does n't understand you
she does n't understand me, either."

"But I cannot speak of my guardian to you," said Karen.
She had kept her eyes steadily upon him waiting to hear what
he might have to say, but now the thought of Tante in her rejected queenliness broke insufferably upon her making her sick
with pity. This man did not love Tante. She rose as she spoke.

"Do not speak of her to me," she said.

"But we will not speak of her. I do not wish to speak of her,"
said Mr. Drew, also rising, a stress of excitement and anxiety
making itself felt in his soft, sibilant, hurried tones; "I understand every exquisite loyalty that hedges your path. And I 'm
hedged, too; you see that. Wait, wait — please listen. We
won't speak of her. What I want to speak of is you. I want
to ask you to make use of me. I want to ask you to trust me.
You love her, but how can you depend on her? She is a child,
an undisciplined, capricious child, and she is displeased with you,
seriously displeased. Who is there in the world you can depend
on? You are unutterably alone. And I ask you to turn to me."

Her frosty scrutiny disconcerted him. He had not touched her
in the least.

"These are things you cannot say to me," she said. "There
is nothing that you can do for me. I only know you as my
guardian's friend; you forgot that, I think, when you brought
me here." She turned from him.

"Oh, but you do not understand! I have made you angry!
Oh, please, Mrs. Jardine;" his voice rose to sharp distress. He
caught her hand with a supplicating yet determined grasp.
"You can't understand. You are so inconceivably unaware. It
is because of you; all because of you. Have n't you really seen
or understood? She can't forgive you because I love you. I
love you, you adorable child. I have only stayed on and borne
with her because of you!"

His passion flamed before her frozen face. And as, for a trans-
fixed moment of stupor, she stood still, held by him, he read into
her stillness the pause of the woman to whom the apple of the
tree of life is proffered, amazed, afraid, yet thrilled through all

her being, tempted by the very suddenness, incapable of swift repudiation. He threw his arms around her, taking, in a draught of delight, the impression of silvery, glacial loveliness that sent dancing stars of metaphor streaming in his head, and pressed his lips to her cheek.

It was but one moment of attainment. The thrust that drove him from her was that, indeed, of the strong young goddess, implacable and outraged. Yet even as he read his deep miscalculation in her aspect he felt that the moment had been worth it. Not many men, not even many poets, could say that they had held, in such a scene, on such a night, an unwilling goddess to their breast.

She did not speak. Her eyes did not pause to wither. They passed over him. He had an image of the goddess wheeling to mount some chariot of the sky as, with no indignity of haste, she turned from him. She turned. And in the path, in the entrance to the flagged garden, Tante stood confronting them.

She stood before them in the moonlight with a majesty at once magnificent and ludicrous. She had come swiftly, borne on the wings of a devouring suspicion, and she maintained for a long moment her Medusa stare of horror. Then, it was the ugliest thing that Karen had ever seen, the mask broke. Hatred, fury, malice, blind, atavistic passions distorted her face. It was to fall from one nightmare to another and a worse; for Tante seized her by the shoulders and shook and shook and shook her, till the blood sprang and rang in her ears and eyeballs, and her teeth chattered together, and her hair, loosened by the great jerks, fell down upon her shoulders and about her face. And while she shook her, Tante snarled — seeming to crush the words between her grinding teeth, " Ah! *perfide! perfide! perfide!* "

From behind, other hands grasped Karen's shoulders. Mr. Drew grappled with Tante for possession of her.

" Leave me — with my guardian," she gathered her broken breath to say. She repeated it and Mr. Drew. invisible to her, replied, " I can't. She 'll tear you to pieces."

" Ah! You have still to hear from me — vile seducer﹗ Madame von Marwitz cried, addressing the young man over

Karen's shoulder. "Do you dare dispute my right to save her from you — foul serpent! Leave us! Does she not tell you to leave us?"

"I'll see her safely out of your hands before I leave her," said Mr. Drew. "How dare you speak of perfidy when you saw her repulse me? You'd have found it easier to forgive, no doubt, if she had n't."

These insolent words, hurled at it, convulsed the livid face that fronted Karen. And suddenly, holding Karen's shoulders and leaning forward, Madame von Marwitz broke into tears, horrible tears — in all her life Karen had never pitied her as she pitied her then — sobbing with raking breaths: "No, no; it is too much. Have I not loved him with a saintly love, seeking to uplift what would draw me down? Has he not loved me? Has he not sought to be my lover? And he can spit upon me in the dust!" She raised her head. "Did you believe me blind, infatuated? Did you think by your tricks and pretences to evade me? Did I not see, from the moment that she came, that your false heart had turned from me?" Her eyes came back to Karen's face and fury again seized her. "And as for you, ungrateful girl — perfidious, yes, and insolent one — you deserve to be denounced to the world. Oh, we understand those retreats. What more alluring to the man who pursues than the woman who flees? What more inflaming than the pose of white, idiotic innocence? You did not know. You did not understand —" fiercely, in a mincing voice, she mimicked a supposed exculpation. "You are so young, so ignorant of life — so *immer kindlich!* Ah!" she laughed, half strangled, "until the man seizes you in his arms you are quite unaware — but quite, quite unaware — of what he seeks from you. Little fool! And more than fool. Have I not seen your wiles? From day to day have I not watched you? Now it is the piano. You must play him your favourite little piece; so small; you have so little talent; but you will do your best. Now the chance meeting in the garden; you are so fond of flowers; you so love the open air, the sea, the wandering on the cliffs; such a free, wild creature you are. And now we have the frustrated *rendezvous* of this evening;

he should find you dreaming, among your flowers, in the dusk.
The pretty picture. And no, you want no dinner; you will
go to your own room. But you are not to be found in your own
room. Oh, no; it is again the garden; the moon; the sea and
solitude that you seek! Be silent!" this was almost shouted at
Claude Drew, who broke in with savage denials. "Do you think
still to impose on me — you traitor? — No," her eyes burned on
Karen's face. "No; you are wiser. You do not speak. You
know that the time for insolence has passed. What! You take
refuge with me here. You fly from your husband and throw
yourself on my hands and say to me," — again she assumed the
mincing tones —"Yes, here I am again. Continue, pray, to
work for me; continue, pray, to clothe and feed and lodge me;
continue to share your life with me and all of rich and wide
and brilliant it can offer; continue, in a word, to hold me high
— but very high — above the gutter from which I came — and
I take you, I receive you in my arms, I shelter you from malicious tongues, I humble myself in seeking to mend your shattered life; and for my reward you steal from me the heart of
the one creature in the world I loved — the one — the only
one! Until you came he was mine. Until you came he yearned
for me — only for me. Oh, my heart is broken! broken!
broken!" She leaned forward, wildly sobbing, and raising herself she shook the girl with all her force, crying: "Out of
my sight! Be off! Let me see no more of you!" Covering
her face with her hands, she reeled back, and Karen fled
down the path, hearing a clamour of sobs and outcries behind
her.

She fled along the cliff-path and an incomparable horror was
in her soul. Her life had been struck from her. It seemed a
ghost that ran, watched by the moon, among the trees.

On the open cliff-path it was very light. The sky was without a cloud. The sea lay like a vast cloth of silk, diapered in
silver.

Karen ran to where the path led to a rocky verge.

From here, in daylight, one looked down into a vast hollow
in the coast and saw at the bottom, far beneath, a stony beach,

always sad, and set with rocks. To-night the enormous cup was brimmed with blackness.

Karen, pausing and leaning forward, resting on her hands, stared across the appalling gulf of inky dark, and down into the nothingness.

Horror had driven her to the spot, and horror, like a presence, rose from the void, and beckoned her down to oblivion. Why not? Why not? The question of despair seemed, like a vast pendulum, to swing her to and fro between the sky and the blackness, so that, blind and deaf and dumb, she felt only the horror, and her own pulse of life suspended over annihilation. And while her fingers clutched tightly at the rock, the thought of Gregory's face, as it had loved her, dimly, like a far beacon, flashed before her. Their love was dead. He did not love her. But they had loved. She moved back, trembling. She did not want to die. She lay down with her face to the ground on the grassy cliff.

When she raised herself it was as if after a long slumber. She was immensely weary, with leaden limbs. Horror was spent; but a dull oppression urged her up and on. There was something that she must never see again; something that would open before her again the black abyss of nothingness; something like the moon, that once had lived, but was now a ghost, white, ghastly, glittering. She must go. At once. And, as if far away, a tiny picture rose before her of some little German town, where she might earn a living and be hidden and forgotten.

But first she must see Mrs. Talcott. She must say good-bye to Mrs. Talcott. There was nothing now that Mrs. Talcott could show her.

She went back softly and carefully, pausing to listen, pushing through unused, overgrown paths and among thickets of gorse and stunted Cornish elms. In the garden all was still; the dreadful clamour had ceased. By the back way she stole up to her room.

A form rose to meet her as she opened the door. Mrs. Talcott had been waiting for her. Taking her hand, Mrs. Talcott drew her in and closed the door.

CHAPTER XXXVI

MRS. TALCOTT sat down on the bed and Karen knelt before her with her head in her lap. The old woman's hand passed quietly over her hair while she wept, and the homely gentleness, like the simplicity of milk to famished lips, flowed into her horror-haunted mind.

She tried to tell Mrs. Talcott what had happened. "She does not love me, Mrs. Talcott. She has turned me out. Tante has told me to go."

"I've seen her," said Mrs. Talcott, stroking on. "I was just going out to look for you if you did n't come in. Did she tear your hair down like this? It's all undone."

"It was when she shook me, Mrs. Talcott. She found me with Mr. Drew. He had kissed me. I could not help it. She knew that I could not help it. She knows that I am not a bad woman."

"You must n't take Mercedes at her word when she's in a state like that, Karen. She's in an awful state. She's parted from that young man."

"And I am going, Mrs. Talcott."

"Well, I've wanted you to go, from the first. Now you've found her out, this ain't any place for you. You can't go hanging on for all your life, like I've done."

"But Mrs. Talcott — what does it mean? What have I found out? What is Tante?" Karen sobbed. "For all these years so beautiful — so beautiful — to me, and suddenly to become my enemy — someone I do not know."

"You never got in her way before. She's got no mercy, Mercedes has n't, if you get in her way. Where'd you thought of going, Karen?"

"To Frau Lippheim. She is still in London, I think. I

336

could join her there. You could lend me a little money, Mrs.
Talcott. Enough to take me to London."

Mrs. Talcott was silent for a moment. " Come up here, on the
bed, Karen," she then said. " Here, wrap this cloak around you;
you 're awful cold. That 's right. Now I want you to sit quiet
while I explain things to you the best I can. I 've made up my
mind to do it. Mercedes will be in her right mind to-morrow
and frantic to get hold of you again and get you to forgive her.
Oh, I know her. And I don't want her to get hold of you again.
I want you to be quit of her. I want you to see, as clear as day,
how your husband was right about Mercedes, all along."

" Oh, do not speak of him —" Karen moaned, covering her
face as she sat on the bed beside Mrs. Talcott.

" I ain't going to speak about him. I 'm going to tell you
about me and Mercedes," said Mrs. Talcott. " I 'm going to
explain Mercedes. And I 'm going way back to the very beginning to do it."

" Explain it to me. What is she? Has it all been false —
all her loveliness ? "

" I don't know about false," said Mrs. Talcott. " Mercedes
ain't all bad; not by a long shot. She feels good sometimes, like
most folks, when it ain't too much trouble. You know how it
began, Karen. You know how I 'm a sort of connection of Mercedes's mother and I 've told you about Dolores. The prettiest
creature you ever set eyes on. Meredes looks like her; only it
was a softer face than Mercedes's with great, big black eyes.
I can see her now, walking round the galleries of that lovely
house in New Orleans with a big white camellia in her black hair
and a white muslin dress, standing out round her — like they
wore then; singing — singing — so young and happy — it almost breaks my heart to think about her. I 've told you about
Mercedes's father, too, Pavelek Okraski, and how he came out
to New Orleans and gave lessons to Dolores Bastida and made
love to her on the sly and got her to run away with him —
poor silly thing. When I think it all over I seem to piece things
out and see how Mercedes came to be what she is. Her mother
was just as sweet and loving as she could be, but scatter-brained

22

and hot-tempered. And Pavelek was a mighty mean man and
a mighty bad man, too, a queer, tricky, sly sort of man; but
geniusy, with very attractive manners. Mercedes has got his
eyes and his way of laughing; she shows her teeth just like he
used to do when he laughed. Well, he took Dolores off to
Poland and spent all her money as fast as he could get it, and
then Señor Bastida and the two boys — nice, hot-tempered boys
they were and perfect pictures — all got killed in a vendetta
they had with another family in Louisiana, and poor Señora
Bastida got sick and died and all the family fortunes went to
pieces and there was no more home and no more money either,
for Dolores. She just lost everything straight off.

"She sent for me then. Her baby was coming and Pavelek
had gone off and she did n't know where he was and she was
about distracted. I'd been married before she ran away with
Pavelek, but Homer only lived four years and I was a widow
then. I had folks left still in Maine; but no one very near
and there was n't anybody I seemed to take to so much as I
always had to Dolores. You may say she had a sort of fasci-
nation for me. So I sold out what I had and came. My, what
a queer journey that was. I don't know how I got to Cracow.
I only spoke English and travelling was n't what it is nowadays.
But I got there somehow and found that poor child. She was
the wretchedest creature you ever set eyes on; thin as thin;
and all haggard and wild. Pavelek neglected her and ran after
other women and drank, and when he got drunk and she used
to fly out at him — for she was as hot-tempered as she could
be — he used to beat her. Yes; that man used to beat Dolores."
A note of profound and enduring anger was in Mrs. Talcott's
voice.

"He came back after I got there. I guess he thought I'd
brought some money, and he came in drunk one day and tried to
hit her before me. He did n't ever try it again after that. I
just got up and struck him with all my might and main right
in the face and he fell down and hurt his head pretty bad and
Dolores began to shriek and said I'd killed her husband; but
he did n't try it again. He was sort of scared of me, I guess.

No: I ain't forgiven Pavelek Okraski yet and I reckon I never shall. I don't seem to want to forgive him, neither in this world nor the next — if there is a next," Mrs. Talcott commented.

"Well, the time for the baby came and on the day Mercedes was born the Austrians bombarded Cracow; it was in '48. I took Dolores down to the cellar and all day long we heard the shells bursting, and the people screeching. And that was the time Mercedes came into the world. Dolores most died, but she got through. But afterwards I could n't get proper care for her, or food either. She just pined off and died five months after the baby came. Pavelek most went off his head. He was always fond of her in his own mean way, and I guess he suffered considerable when she died. He went off, saying he 'd send some money for me and the baby, but precious little of it did I ever see. I made some by sewing and giving lessons in English — I reckon some of those young Poles got queer ways of speaking from me, I was never what you 'd call a polished speaker — and I scraped on. Time and time again we were near starving. My! that little garret room, and that big church — Panna Marya they called it — where I 'd go and sit with the baby when the services were on to see if I could keep warm in the crowd! And the big fire in '50, when I carried the baby out in a field with lots of other people and slept out. It lasted for ten days that fire.

"It seems like a dream sometimes, all that time," Mrs. Talcott mused, and the distant sorrow of her voice was like the blowing of a winter wind. "It seems like a dream to think I got through with the child alive, and that my sweet, pretty little Dolores went under. There 's some things that don't bear thinking about. Well, I kept that baby warm and I kept it fat, and it got to be the prettiest, proudest thing you ever set eyes on. She might have been a queen from the very beginning. And as for Pavelek, she just ruled him from the time she began to have any sense. It was mighty queer to see that man, who had behaved so bad to her mother, cringing before that child. He doted on her, and she did n't care a button for him. It used to make me feel almost sorry for Pavelek, sometimes.

She'd look at him, when he tried to please her and amuse her, like he was a performing dog. It kept Pavelek in order, I can tell you, and made things easier for me. She'd just say she wanted things and if she did n't get them straight off she'd go into a black rage, and he'd be scared out of his life and go and work and get 'em for her. And then she began to show she was a prodigy. Pavelek taught her the violin first and then the piano and when he realized she was a genius he most went off his head with pride. Why that man — the selfishest, laziest creature by nature — worked himself to skin and bone so that she should have the best lessons and everything she needed. We both held our noses to the grindstone just as tight as ever we could, and Mercedes was brought up pretty well, I think, considering.

"She gave that first concert in Warsaw — we'd moved to Warsaw — and then Pavelek seemed to go to pieces. He just drank himself to death. Well, after that, rich relations of Mercedes's turned up — cousins of the Bastidas', who lived in Paris. They had n't lifted a finger to help Dolores, or me with the baby after Dolores died; but they remembered about us now Mercedes was famous and made us come to live with them in Paris and said they had first claim on Mercedes. I did n't take to the Bastidas. But I stayed on because of Mercedes. I got to be a sort of nurse for her, you may say. Well, as she got older, and prettier and prettier, and everyone just crazy about her, I saw she did n't have much use for me. I did n't judge her too hard; but I began to see through her then. She'd behaved mighty bad to me again and again, she used to fly at me and bite me and tear my hair, when she was a child, if I thwarted her; but I always believed she really loved me; perhaps she did, as much as she can. But after these rich folks turned up and her life got so bright and easy she just seemed to forget all about me. So I went home.

"I stayed home for four or five years and then Mercedes sent for me. She used to write now and then to her 'Dearest Tallie' as she always called me, and I'd heard all about how she'd come out in Paris and Vienna as a great pianist, and how she'd quarrelled with her relations and how she'd run away with a

young English painter and got married to him.   It was an awful
silly match, and they'd all opposed it; but it pleased me somehow.   I thought it showed that Mercedes was soft-hearted like
her mother, and unworldly.   Well, she wrote that she was miserable and that her husband was a fiend and broke her heart and
that she hated all her relations and they'd all behaved like
serpents to her — Mercedes is always running across serpents
— and how I was the only true friend she had and the only
one who understood her, and how she longed for her dear Tallie.
So I sold out again — I'd just started a sort of little farm near
the old place in Maine, raising chickens and making jam —
and came over again.   I don't know what it is about Mercedes,
but she gets a hold over you.   And guess I always felt like she
was my own baby.   I had a baby, but it died when it was born.
Well, she was living in Paris then and they had a fine flat and
a big studio, and when Mercedes got into a passion with her
husband she'd take a knife and slash up his canvases.   She
quarrelled with him day and night, and I was n't long with them
before I saw that it was all her fault and that he was a weak,
harmless sort of young creature — he had yellow hair, longish,
and used to wear a black velvet cap and paint sort of dismal
pictures of girls with long necks and wild sort of eyes — but
that the truth was she was sick of him and wanted to marry
the Baron von Marwitz.

"You can commence to get hold of the story now, Karen.
You remember the Baron.   A sad, stately man he was, as cultured and intellectual as could be and going in the best society.
Mercedes had found pretty quick that there was n't much fun
in being married to a yellow-haired boy who lived on the money
she made and was n't a mite in society.   And the Baron was
just crazy over her in his dignified, reverential way.   Poor fellow!" said Mrs. Talcott pausing in a retrospect over this vanished figure, "Poor fellow!   I guess he came to rue the day
he ever set eyes on her.   Well, Mercedes made out to him how
terrible her life was and how she was tied to a dissipated, worth-
less man who lived on her and was unfaithful to her.   And it's
true that Baldwin Tanner behaved as he should n't; but he was a

weak creature and she'd disillusionized him so and made him so miserable that he just got reckless. And he'd never asked any more than to live in a garret with her and adore her, and paint his lanky people and eat bread and cheese; he told me so, poor boy; he just used to lay his head down on my lap and cry like a baby sometimes. But Mercedes made it out that she was a victim and he was a serpent; and she believed it, too; that's the power of her; she's just determined to be in the right always. So at last she made it all out. She couldn't divorce Baldwin, being a Catholic; but she made it out that she wasn't really married to him. It appears he didn't get baptized by his folks; they hadn't believed in baptizing; they were free-thinkers. And the Baron got his powerful friends to help and they all set to work at the Pope, and they got him to fix it up, and Mercedes's marriage was annulled and she was free to marry again. That's what was in her mind in sending for me, you see; she'd quarrelled with her folks and she wanted a steady respectable person who knew all about her to stand by her and chaperon her while she was getting rid of Baldwin. Mercedes has always been pretty careful about her reputation; she's hardly ever taken any risks.

"Well, she was free and she married the Baron, and poor Baldwin got a nice young English girl to marry him, and she reformed him, and they're alive and happy to this day, and I guess he paints pretty poor pictures. And it makes Mercedes awful mad to hear about how happy they are; she has a sort of idea, I imagine, that Baldwin didn't have any right to get married again. I've always had a good deal of satisfaction over Baldwin," said Mrs. Talcott. "It's queer to realize that Mercedes was once just plain Mrs. Baldwin Tanner, ain't it? It was a silly match and no mistake. Well, it took two or three years to work it all out, and Mercedes was twenty-five when she married the Baron. I didn't see much of them for a while. They put me around in their houses to look after things and be there when Mercedes wanted me. She'd found out she couldn't get along without me in those two or three years. Mercedes was the most beautiful creature alive at that time, I

do believe, and all Europe was wild about her. She and the
Baron went about and she gave concerts, and it was just a
triumphal tour. But after a spell I began to see that things
were n't going smooth. Mercedes is the sort of person who 's
never satisfied with what she 's got. And the Baron was beginning to find her out. My! I used to be sorry for that man.
I 'll never forget his white, sick face the first time she flew out
at him and made one of her scenes. ' *Emprisonné ma jeunesse,' "*
Mrs. Talcott quoted with a heavy accent. " That 's what she
said he 'd done to her. He was twenty years older than Mercedes, the Baron. Mercedes always liked to have men who were
in love with her hanging about, and that 's what the trouble
was over. The more they cared the worse she treated them,
and the Baron was a very dignified man and did n't like having
them around. And she was dreadful jealous of him, too, and
used to fly out at him if he so much as looked at another
woman; in her way I guess he was the person Mercedes cared for
most in all her life; she respected him, too, and she knew he
was as clever as she was and more so, and as for him, in spite
of everything, he always stayed in love with her. They used to
have reconciliations, and when he 'd look at her sort of scornful
and loving and sad all together, it would make her go all to
pieces. She 'd throw herself in his arms and cry and cry. No,
she ain't all bad, Mercedes. And she thought she could make
things all right with him after she 'd let herself go; she depended on his caring for her so much and being sorry for her.
But I saw well enough as the years went on that he got more and
more depressed. He was a depressed man by nature, I reckon,
and he read a sight of philosophy of the gloomy kind — that
writer Schopenhauer was a favourite of his, I recollect, and
Mercedes thought a sight of him, too — and after ten years or so
of Mercedes I expect the Baron was pretty sick of life.

" Well, you came. You thought it was Mercedes who was so
good to you, and it was in a way. But it was poor Ernst who
really cared. He took to you the moment he set eyes on you,
and he 'd liked your father. And he wanted to have you to live
with them and be their adopted daughter and inherit their

money when they died. It had always been a grief to him that
Mercedes would n't have any children. She just had a horror
of having children, and he had to give up any hope of it.
Well, the moment Mercedes realized how he cared for you she
got jealous and they had a scene over you right off, in that
hotel at Fontainebleau. She took on like her heart would break
and put it that she could n't bear to have any one with them for
good, she loved him so. It was true in a way. I did n't count
of course. He looked at her, sick and scornful and loving, and
he gave way. That was why you were put to school. She
tried to make up by being awful nice to you when you came
for your holidays now and then; but she never liked having
you round much and Ernst saw it and never showed how much
he cared for you. But he did care. You had a real friend in
him, Karen. Well, after that came the worst thing Mercedes
ever did." Mrs. Talcott paused, gazing before her in the dimly
lighted room. "Poor things! Poor Mercedes! It nearly
killed her. She 's never been the same since. And it was all
her fault and she knows it and that 's why she 's afraid. That 's
why," she added in a lower voice, "you 're sorry for her and
put up with everything, because you know she 's a miserable
woman and it would n't do for her to be alone.

"A young man turned up. His name don't matter now,
poor fellow. He was just a clever all-over-the-place young
man like so many of them, thinking they know more about
everything than God Almighty; — like this young man in a way,
only not a bad young man like him; — and downright sick with
love of Mercedes. He followed her about all over Europe and
went to every concert she gave and laid himself out to please
her in all the ways he could. And he had a great charm of
manner — he was a Russian and very high-bred — and he sort
of fascinated her, and she liked it all, I can tell you. Her
youth was beginning to go, and the Baron was mighty gloomy,
and she just basked in this young man's love, and pretty soon
she began to think she was in love with him — perhaps she was
— and had never loved before, and she certainly worked herself
up to suffer considerably. Well, the Baron saw it. He saw

she did n't treat him the way she 'd treated the others; she was kind of humble and tender and distracted all the time. The Baron saw it all, but she never noticed that he was getting gloomier and gloomier. I sometimes wonder if things might have been different if he 'd been willing to confide in me some. It does folks a sight of good if there 's someone they can tell things to. But the Baron was very reserved and never said a word. And at last she burst out with a dreadful scene. You were with them; yes, it was that summer at Felsenschloss; but you did n't know anything about it of course. I was pretty much in the thick of it all, as far as Mercedes went, and I tried to make her see reason and told her she was a sinful woman to treat her husband so; but I could n't hold her back. She broke out at him one day and told him he was like a jailor to her, and that he suffocated her talent and that he hung on her like a vampire and sucked her youth, and that she loved the other man. I can see her now, rushing up and down that long saloon on that afternoon, with the white blinds drawn down and the sun filtering through them, snatching with her hands at her dress and waving her arms up and down in the air. And the Baron sat on a sofa leaning on his elbow with his hand up over his eyes and watched her under it. And he did n't say one word. When she fell down on another sofa and cried and cried, he got up and looked at her for a moment; but it was n't the scornful, loving look; it was a queer, dark, dead way. And he just went out. And we never saw him alive again.

"You know the rest, Karen. You found him. But no one knows why he did it, no one but you and me. He put an end to himself, because he could n't stand it any longer, and to set her free. They called it suicidal mania and the doctors said he must have had melancholia for years. But I shan't ever forget his face when he went out, and no more will Mercedes. After he was gone she thought she 'd never cared for anything in the world but him. She never saw that young man again. She wrote him a letter and laid the blame on him, and said he 'd tried to take her from her adored husband and that she 'd never

forgive him and loathed the thought of him, and that he had
made her the most wretched of women, and he went and blew his
brains out and that was the end of him. I had considerable
difficulty in getting hold of that letter. It was on him when he
killed himself. But I managed to talk over the police and hush
it up. Mercedes gave me plenty of money to manage with. I
don't know what she thinks about that poor fellow; she's never
named his name since that day. And she went on like a mad
thing for two years or more. You remember about that, Karen.
She said she'd never play the piano again or see anybody and
wanted to go and be a nun. But she had a friend who was a
prioress of a convent, and she advised her not to. I guess poor
Mercedes wouldn't have stayed long in a convent. And the
reason she was nice to you was because the Baron had been fond
of you and she wanted to make up all she could for that dreadful
thing in her life. She had you to come and live with her. You
didn't interfere with anything any longer and it sort of soothed
her to think it was what he'd have liked. She's fond of you,
too. She wouldn't have put up with you for so long if she
hadn't been. She'd have found some excuse for being quit of
you. But as for loving you, Karen child, like you thought she
did, or like you love her, why it's pitiful. I used to wonder
how long it would be before you found her out."

Karen's face was hidden; she had rested it upon her hands,
leaning forward, her elbows on her knees, and she had not
moved while Mrs. Talcott told her story. Now, as Mrs. Talcott
sat silent, she stirred slightly.

"Tante! Tante!" she muttered. "My beautiful!"

Mrs. Talcott did not reply to this for some moments; then she
laid her hand on Karen's shoulder. "That's it," she said.
"She's beautiful and it most kills us to find out how cruel and
bad she can be. But I guess we can't judge people like Mercedes, Karen. When you go through life like a mowing-ma-
chine and see everyone flatten out before you, you must get
kind of exalted ideas about yourself. If anything happens
that makes a hitch, or if anybody don't flatten out, why it
must seem to you as if they were wrong in some way, doing

you an injury. That's the way it is with Mercedes. She don't
mean to be cruel, she don't mean to be bad; but she's a mowing-
machine and if you get in her way she'll cut you up fine and
leave you behind. And the thing for you to do, Karen, is to
get out of her way as quick as you can."

"Yes, I am going," said Karen.

Again Mrs. Talcott sat silent. "I'd like to talk to you about
that, Karen," she then said. "I want to ask you to give up
going to Frau Lippheim. There ain't any sense in that. It's
a poor plan. What you ought to do, Karen, is to go right back
to your nice young husband."

Karen, who sat on as if crushed beyond the point where
anything could crush her further, shook her head. "Do not
ask me that, Mrs. Talcott," she said. "I can never go back to
him."

"But, Karen, I guess you've got to own now that he was
right and you were wrong in that quarrel of yours. I guess
you'll have to own that it must have made him pretty sick to see
her putting him in the wrong with you all the time and spoiling
everything; and there's no one on earth can do that better than
Mercedes."

"I see it all," said Karen. "But that does not change what
happened between Gregory and me. He does not love me. I
I saw it plainly. If he had me back it would only be because he
cares for conventions. He said cruel things to me."

"I guess you said cruel things to him, Karen."

Karen shook her head slightly, with weariness rather than impatience.

"No, for he saw that it was my loyalty to her — my love of
her — that he was wounding. And he never understood. He
never helped me. I can never go back to him, for he does not
love me."

"Now, see here, Karen," said Mrs. Talcott, after a pause, "you
just let me work it out. You'll have a good sleep and to-morrow morning I'll see you off, before Mercedes is up, to a nice
little farm near here that I know about — just a little way by
train — and there you'll stay, nice and quiet, and I'll not let

Mercedes know where you are. And I'll write to Mr. Jardine and tell him just what's happened and what you meant to do, and that you want to go to Frau Lippheim; and you mark my words, Karen, that nice young husband of yours'll be here quicker than you can say Jack Robinson."

Karen had dropped her hands and was looking at her old friend intently. "Mrs. Talcott, you do not understand," she said. "You cannot write to him. Have I not told you that he does not love me?"

"Shucks!" said Mrs. Talcott. "He'll love you fast enough now that Mercedes is out of the way."

"But, Mrs. Talcott," said Karen, rising and looking down at the old woman, whose face, in the dim light, had assumed to her reeling mind an aspect of dangerous infatuation —"I do not think you know what you are saying. What do I want of a man who only loves me when I cease to love my guardian?"

"Well, say you give up love, then," Mrs. Talcott persisted, and a panic seized Karen as she heard the unmoved tones. "Say you don't love him and he don't love you. You can have conventions, then — he wants that you say, and so can you — and a good home and a nice husband who won't treat you bad in any way. That's better than batting about the world all by yourself, Karen; you take my word for it. And you can take my word for it, too, that if you behave sensible and do as I say, you'll find out that all this is just a miserable mistake and that he loves you just as much as ever. Now, see here," Mrs. Talcott, also, had risen, and stood in her habitual attitude, resting heavily on one hip, "you're not fit to talk and I'm not going to worry you any more. You go to sleep and we'll see about what to do to-morrow. You go right to sleep, Karen," she patted the girl's shoulder.

The panic was deepening in Karen. She saw guile on Mrs. Talcott's storm-beaten and immutable face; and she heard specious reassurance in her voice. Mrs. Talcott was dangerous. She had set her heart on this last desire of her passionless, impersonal life and had determined that she and Gregory should come together again. It was this desire that had unsealed her

lips: she would never relinquish it. She might write to Gregory;
she might appeal to him and put before him the desperate plight
in which his wife was placed. And he might come. What were
a wife's powers if she was homeless and penniless, and a husband
claimed her? Karen did not know; but panic breathed upon
her, and she felt that she must fly. She, too, could use guile.
"Yes," she said. "I will go to sleep. And to-morrow we will
talk. But what you hope cannot be. Good-night, Mrs. Talcott."

"Good-night, child," said Mrs. Talcott.

They had joined hands and the strangeness of this farewell,
the knowledge that she might never see Mrs. Talcott again, and
that she was leaving her to a life empty of all that she had believed it to contain, rose up in Karen so strongly that it blotted
out for a moment her own terror.

"You have been so good to me," she said, in a trembling
voice. "Never shall I forget what you have done for me, Mrs.
Talcott. May I kiss you good-night?"

They had never kissed.

Mrs. Talcott's eyes blinked rapidly, and a curious contortion
puckered her mouth and chin. Karen thought that she was
going to cry and her own eyes filled with tears.

But Mrs. Talcott in another moment had mastered her
emotion, or, more probably, it could find no outlet. The silent,
stoic years had sealed the fount of weeping. Only that dry contortion of her face spoke of her deep feeling. Karen put her
arms around her and they kissed each other.

"Good-night, child," Mrs. Talcott then said in a muffled voice,
and disengaging herself she went out quickly.

Karen stood listening to the sound of her footsteps passing
down the corridor. They went down the little flight of stairs
that led to another side of the house and faded away. All was
still.

She did not pause or hesitate. She did not seem to think.
Swiftly and accurately she found her walking-shoes and put them
on, her hat and cloak; her purse with its half-crown, its sixpence
and its few coppers. Swiftly she laid together a change of underwear and took from her dressing-table its few toilet appur-

tenances.   She paused then, looking at the ornaments of her girl-hood.   She must have money.   She must sell something; yet all these her guardian had given her.

No; not all.   Her little gold watch ticked peacefully, lying on the table beside her bed as it had lain beside her for so many years; her beautiful little watch, treasured by her since the distant birthday when Onkel Ernst had given it.   ·

She clutched it tightly in her hand and it seemed to her, as she had once said to Gregory, that the iron drove deep into her heart and turned up not only dark forgotten things but dark and dreadful things never seen before.

She leaned against the table, putting the hand that held Onkel Ernst's watch to her eyes, and his agony became part of her own.   How he had suffered.   And the other man, the young, forgotten Russian.   Mrs. Talcott's story became real to her as it had not yet been.   It entered her; it filled her past; it linked itself with everything that she had been and done and believed. And the iron drove down deeper, until of her heart there seemed only to be left a deep black hole.

CHAPTER XXXVII

M RS. TALCOTT had a broken night and it was like a continuation of some difficult and troubled dream when she heard the voice of Mercedes saying to her: "Tallie, Tallie, wake up. Tallie, will you wake! *Bon Dieu!* how she sleeps!"

The voice of Mercedes when she had heard it last had been the voice of passion and desperation, but its tone was changed this morning; it was fretful, feverishly irritable, rather than frantic.

Mrs. Talcott opened her eyes and sat up in bed. She wore a Jaeger nightgown and her head, with its white hair coiled at the top, was curiously unaltered by its informal setting.

"What do you mean by coming waking me up like this after the night you've given me," she demanded, fully awakened now. "Go right straight away or I'll put you out."

"Don't be a fool, Tallie," said Madame von Marwitz, who, in a silken dressing-gown and with her hair unbound, had an appearance at once childish and damaged. "Where is Karen? I've been to her room and she is not there. The door downstairs is unbolted. Is she gone out to walk so early?"

Mrs. Talcott sat still and upright in her bed. "What time is it?" she asked.

"It is seven. I have been awake since dawn. Do you imagine that I have had a pleasant night?"

Mrs. Talcott did not answer this query. She sprang out of bed.

"Perhaps she's gone to meet the bus at the cross-roads. But I told her I was going to take her. Tell Burton to come round with the car as quick as he can. I'll go after her and see that she's all right. Why, the child hasn't got any money," Mrs. Talcott muttered, deftly drawing on her clothes beneath her nightgown which she held by the edge of the neck between her teeth.

351

Madame von Marwitz listened to her impeded utterance frowning.

"The bus? What do you mean? Why is she meeting the bus?"

"To take her to London where she's going to the Lipp-heims," said Mrs. Talcott, casting aside the nightgown and re-vealing herself in chemise and petticoat. "You go and order that car, Mercedes," she added, as she buckled together her sturdy, widely-waisted stays. "This ain't no time for talk."

Madame von Marwitz looked at her for another moment and then rang the bell. She put her head outside the door to await the housemaid and, as this person made some delay, shouted in a loud voice: "Handcock! Jane! Louise! Where are you? *Fainéantes!*" she stamped her foot, and, as the housemaid ap-peared, running; "Burton," she commanded. "The car. At once. And tell Louise to bring me my tea-gown, my shoes and stockings, my fur cloak, at once; but at once; make haste!"

"What are you up to, Mercedes?" Mrs. Talcott inquired, as Madame von Marwitz thrust her aside from the dressing-table and began to wind up her hair before the mirror.

"I am getting ready to go with you, *parbleu!*" Madame von Marwitz replied. "Is that you, Louise? Come in. You have the things? Put on my shoes and stockings; quickly; *mais dépêchez-vous donc!* The tea-gown — yes, over this — over it I say! So. Now bring me a motor-veil and gloves. I shall do thus."

Mrs. Talcott, while Louise with an air of profoundest gloom arrayed her mistress, kept silence, but when Louise had gone in search of the motor-veil she remarked in a low but imperative voice: "You'll get out at the road-side and wait for me, that's what you'll do. I won't have you along when I meet Karen. She could n't bear the sight of you."

"Peace!" Madame von Marwitz commanded, adjusting the sash of her tea-gown. "I shall see Karen. The deplorable mis-understanding of last night shall be set right. Her behaviour has been undignified and underhanded; but I misunderstood her, and, pierced to the heart by the treachery of a man I trusted, I

spoke wildly, without thought. Karen will understand. I know
my Karen."

It was not the moment for dispute. Louise had re-entered
with the veil and Madame von Marwitz bound it about her head,
standing before the mirror, and gazing at herself, fixedly and
unseeingly, with dark eyes set in purpled orbits. She turned
then and swept from the room and Mrs. Talcott, pinning on her
hat as she went, followed her.

Not until they were speeding through the fresh, chill air, did
Mrs. Talcott speak. Madame von Marwitz, leaning to one side
of the open car, scanned the stretch of road before them,
melancholy and monotonous under the pale morning sky, and
Mrs. Talcott, moving round determinedly in her corner, faced
her.

" I want to tell you, right now, Mercedes," said Mrs. Talcott,
"that Karen's done with you. There's no use in your coming,
for you'll never get her back. I've told her all about you, Mercedes; — yes, I ain't afraid of you and you know it; — I told
her. I made up my mind to it last night after I'd seen you
and heard all your shameful story and how you'd treated her.
I made up my mind that you should n't get hold of her again,
not if I could help it. The time had come to tell that child that
her husband was right all along and that you ain't a woman to
be trusted. She'd seen for herself what you could do, and I
made a sure thing of it. I've held my tongue for all my life,
but I spoke out last night. I want her to be quit of you for
good. I want her to go back to her husband. Yes, Mercedes;
I've burst up the whole concern."

Madame von Marwitz, her hand holding tightly the side of
the car and her eyes like large, dark stones in her white face,
was sitting upright and was staring at her. She could not
speak and Mrs. Talcott went on.

" She knows all about you now; about you and Baldwin
Tanner and you and Ernst, and about that pitiful young Russian. She knows how you treated them. She knows how it
was n't you but Ernst who was her real friend, and how you
did n't want her to live with you. She knows that you're a

23

mighty unfortunate creature and a mighty dangerous one; and what I advise you to do, Mercedes, is to get out here and go right home. Karen won't ever come back to you again, I'm as sure of it as I'm sure my name's Hannah Talcott."

They sped, with softly singing speed, through the chill morning air. The hard, tight, dark eyeballs still fixed themselves on the old woman almost lifelessly, and still she sat grasping the side of the car. She had the look of a creature shot through the heart and maintaining the poise and pride of its startled and arrested life. Mechanical forces rather than volition seemed to sustain her.

"Say, Mercedes, will you get out?" Mrs. Talcott repeated. And the rigid figure then moved its head slightly in negation.

They reached the cross-roads where a few carts and an ancient fly stood waiting for the arrival of the omnibus that plied between the Lizard and Helston. Karen was nowhere to be seen.

"Perhaps she went across the fields and got into the bus at the Lizard," said Mrs. Talcott. "We'll wait and see, and if she isn't in the bus we'll go on to Helston. Perhaps she's walking."

Madame von Marwitz continued to say nothing, and in a moment they heard behind them the clashing and creaking of the omnibus. It drew up at the halt and Karen was not in it.

"To Helston," said Mrs. Talcott, standing up to speak to the chauffeur.

They sped on before the omnibus had resumed its journey.

Tints of azure and purple crept over the moors; the whitening sky showed rifts of blue; it was a beautiful morning. Mrs. Talcott, keeping a keen eye on the surrounding country, became aware presently that Mercedes had turned her gaze upon her and was examining her.

She looked round.

There was no anger, no resentment, even, on the pallid face. It seemed engaged, rather, in a deep perplexity — that of a child struck down by the hand that, till then, had cherished it. It brooded in sick wonder on Mrs. Talcott, and Mrs. Talcott looked

back with her ancient, weary eyes. Madame von Marwitz broke
the silence. She spoke in a toneless voice. " Tallie — how
could you? " she said. " Oh, Tallie — how could you have told
her? "

" Mercedes," said Mrs. Talcott, gently but implacably, " I had
to. It was right to make sure you should n't get hold of her
again. She had to go, and she had to go for good. If you want
me to go, too, I will, but it 's only fair to tell you that I never
felt much sorrier for you than I do at this minute."

" There have been tragedies in my life," Madame von Marwitz went on in the low, dulled voice. " I have been a passion-
tossed woman. Yes, I have not been guiltless. But how could
you cut out my heart with all its scars and show it to my
child? "

" It was right to do it, Mercedes, so as you should n't ruin
her life. She 's not your child, and you 've shown her she 's not.
A mother don't behave so to her child, however off her head she
goes."

" I was mad last night." The tears ran slowly down Madame
von Marwitz's cheeks. " I can tell that to Karen. I can explain. I can throw myself on her mercy. I loved him and my
heart was broken. One is not responsible. It is the animal,
wounded to death, that shrieks and tears at the spear it feels
entering its flesh."

" I 'm awful sorry for you, Mercedes," said Mrs. Talcott.

And now, hiding her face in her hands and leaning back in
her cushions, Madame von Marwitz began to weep with the soft
reiterated sobbing of a miserable child. " I have no one left.
I am alone," she sobbed. " Even you have turned against
me."

" No, I have n't turned against you," said Mrs. Talcott.
" I 'm here." And presently, while Mercedes wept, Mrs. Talcott took her hand and held it.

They reached Helston and climbed the steep, stony road to
the station. There was no sign of Karen. Mrs. Talcott got out
and made inquiries. She might have gone to London by the

train that left at dawn; but no one had noticed such a young lady. Mrs. Talcott came back to the car with her fruitless story.

Mercedes, by this time, had dried her eyes and was regaining, apparently, her more normal energies. "Not here? Not seen? Not heard of?" she repeated. "But where is she then?"

Mrs. Talcott stood at the door of the car and looked at her charge. "Well, I'm afraid she made off in the night, straight away, after I'd talked to her."

"Made off in the night?" A dark colour suddenly suffused Madame von Marwitz's face.

"Yes, that's it, I reckon. I must have said something to scare her about her going back to her husband. Perhaps she thought I'd bring him down without her knowing, and perhaps she wasn't far wrong. I'm afraid I've played the fool. She thought I'd round on her in some way and so she just lit out."

Madame von Marwitz stared at her. The expression of her face had entirely altered; there was no trace of the dazed and wretched child. Dark forces lit her eyes and the relaxed lines of her lips tightened.

"Get in," she commanded. "Tell him to drive back, and get in." And when Mrs. Talcott had taken her place beside her she went on in a low, concentrated voice: "Is it not possible that she has joined that vile seducer?"

Mrs. Talcott eyed her with the fixity of a lion-tamer. Their moment of instinctive closeness had passed. "Now see here, Mercedes," she said; "I advise you to be careful what you say."

"Careful! I am half mad! Between you all you will drive me mad!" said Madame von Marwitz with intensity of fury. "You fill Karen's mind with lies about my past — oh, there are two sides to every story! she shall hear my side! — you drive her forth with your threats to hand her over to the man she loathes, and she takes refuge — where else? — with that miscreant. Why not? Where else had she to go? You say that she had no money. We call now at the hotel. If he is gone, and if within the day we do not hear that she is with Lise, we will send at once for detectives."

"You'd better control yourself, Mercedes," said Mrs. Talcott. "If Karen ain't found it'll be a mighty ugly story for you to face up to, and if she's found it won't be all plain sailing for you either; you've got to pay the price for what you've done. But if it gets round that you drove her out and then spread scandal about her, you'll do for yourself — just keep your mind on that if you can."

"Scandal! What scandal shall I spread? If he disappears and she with him, will the facts not shriek aloud? If she is found she will be found by me. I will wire at once to Lise."

"We'll wire to Lise and we'll wire to Mr. Jardine, that's what we'll do. Karen may have changed her mind. She may have felt shy of telling me she had. She may have come to see that he's the thing she's got to hang on to. What I hope for is that if she ain't in London already with him, she's hiding somewhere about here and has sent for him herself."

"Ah, I understand your hope; it is of a piece with all your treachery," said Madame von Marwitz in a voice suffocated by conflicting angers. "If she is with her husband he, too, will hear the story — the false, garbled story of my crimes. He is my enemy, you know it; my malignant enemy; you know that he will spread this affair broadcast. And you can rejoice in this! You are glad for my disgrace and ruin!" Tears again streamed from her eyes.

"Don't take on so, Mercedes," said Mrs. Talcott. "If Karen's with her husband all they're likely to be thinking about is that he was right and has got her back again. Karen's bound to tell him something about what happened, and you can depend upon Karen for saying as little as she can. But if you imagine that you're going to be let off from being found out by that young man, you're letting yourself in for a big disappointment, and you can take my word for it. It's because he's right about you that Karen'll go back to him."

Madame von Marwitz turned her head away and fixed her eyes on the landscape.

They reached the little village near Les Solitudes, and at the little hotel, with its drowsy, out-of-season air, Mrs. Talcott descended, leaving Mercedes proudly seated in the car, indifferent to the possible gaze from above of her faithless devotee. Mrs. Talcott returned with the information that Mr. Drew was upstairs and not yet awake. "Go up. Go up to him," said the tormented woman, after a moment of realized relief or disappointment — who can say? "He may have seen her. He may have given her money for her journey. They may have arranged to meet later."

Mrs. Talcott again disappeared and she only returned after some ten minutes. "Home," she then said to Burton, climbing heavily into the car. "Yes, there he was, sleeping as peaceful as a dormouse in his silk pyjamas," she remarked. "I startled him some, I reckon, when I waked him up. No, he don't know anything about her. Wanted to jump up and look for her when I told him she was missing. Keep still, Mercedes — what do you mean by bouncing about like that — folks can see you. I talked to him pretty short and sharp, that young man, and I told him the best thing he could do now was to pack his grip-sack and clear out. He's going right away and he promised to send me a telegram from London to-night. He can catch the second train."

Madame von Marwitz leaned back. She closed her eyes. The car had climbed to the entrance of Les Solitudes and the fuchsia hedge was passing on each side. Mrs. Talcott, looking at her companion, saw that she had either actually fainted or was simulating a very realistic fainting-fit. Mercedes often had fainting-fits at moments of crisis; but she was a robust woman, and Mrs. Talcott had no reason to believe that any of them had been genuine. She did not believe that this one was genuine, yet she had to own, looking at the leaden eyelids and ashen face, that Mercedes had been through enough in the last twelve hours to break down a stronger person. And it was appropriate that she should return to her desolate home in a prostrate condition.

Mrs. Talcott, as often before, played her part. The maids were summoned; they supported Madame von Marwitz's body;

Burton took her shoulders and Mrs. Talcott her feet. So the afflicted woman was carried into the house and upstairs and laid upon her bed.

Mrs. Talcott then went and sent telegrams to Frau Lippheim and to Gregory Jardine. She asked them to let her know if Karen arrived in London during the day. She had her answers that evening. That from Gregory ran—"Not seen or heard of Karen. What has happened? Write by return. Or shall I come to you?" The other was from the Lippheims' landlady and said that the Lippheims had returned to Germany four days before and that no one had arrived to see them.

The evening post had gone. Mrs. Talcott went out and answered Gregory by wire: "Writing to-morrow morning. We think Karen is in London. Stay where you are."

CHAPTER XXXVIII

MRS. TALCOTT went early to Madame von Marwitz's room
next morning, as soon, in fact, as she had seen her break-
fast-tray carried away. She had shown Mercedes her telegrams the evening before, and Mercedes, lying on her bed where
she had passed the day in heavy slumbers, had muttered, "Let
me sleep. The post is gone. We can do nothing more till to-
morrow." Like a wounded creature she was regaining strength
and wholeness in oblivion. When Mrs. Talcott had gone softly
into her room at bed-time, she had found her soundly sleeping.

But the fumes and torpors of grief and pain were this morning
dispersed. Mercedes sat at the desk in her bedroom attired in
a *robe-de-chambre,* and rapidly and feverishly wrote.

"I'm glad to see you're feeling better, Mercedes," said Mrs.
Talcott, closing the door and coming to her side. "We've got a
lot to talk over this morning. I guess we'll have to send for
those detectives. What are you writing there?"

Madame von Marwitz, whose face had the sodden, slumbrous
look that follows long repose, drew the paper quickly to one side
and replied: "You may mind your affairs and leave me to mind
my own. I write to my friend. I write to Mrs. Forrester."

"You hand me that letter, Mercedes," said Mrs. Talcott, in a
mild but singularly determined tone, and after a moment Madame von Marwitz did hand it to her.

Mrs. Talcott perused the first page. Then she lifted her eyes
to her companion, who, averting hers with a sullen look, fixed
them on the sea outside. It was raining and the sea was leaden.

"Now just you listen to me, Mercedes Okraska," said Mrs.
Talcott, heavily emphasizing her words and leaning the hand that
held the letter on the writing-table, "I'll go straight up to
London and tell the whole story to Mr. Jardine and Mrs. Forrester — the same as I told it to Karen with all that's hap-

pened here besides — I will as sure as my name's Hannah Talcott — if you write one word of that shameful idea to your
friends. Lay down that pen."

Madame von Marwitz did not lay it down, but she turned in
her chair and confronted her accuser, though with averted eyes.
" You say ' shameful.' I say, yes; shameful, and true. She has
not gone to her husband. She has not gone to the Lippheims.
I believe that he has joined her. I believe that it was arranged.
I believe that she is with him now."

" You can't look me in the eye and say you believe it, Mercedes," said Mrs. Talcott.

Madame von Marwitz looked her in the eye, sombrely, and she
then varied her former statement. " He has pursued her. He
has found her. He will try to keep her. He is a depraved and
dangerous man."

" We'll let him alone. We're done with him for good and all,
I guess. My point is this: don't you write any lies to your
friends thinking that you're going to whiten yourself by blackening Karen. I'm speaking the sober truth when I say I'll go
straight off to London and tell Mr. Jardine and Mrs. Forrester
the whole story, unless you write a letter, right now, as you sit
here, that I can pass."

Again averting her eyes, Madame von Marwitz clutched her
pen in rigid fingers and sat silent.

" It is blackmail! Tyranny! " she ejaculated presently.

" All right. Call it any name you like. But my advice to
you, Mercedes, is to pull yourself together and see this thing
straight for your own sake. I know what's the matter with you,
you pitiful, silly thing; it's this young man; it makes you behave like a distracted creature. But don't you see as plain as
can be that what Karen's probably done is to go to London and
that Mr. Jardine'll find her in a day or two. Now when those
two young people come together again, what kind of a story will
Karen tell her husband about you — what'll he think of you —
what'll your friends think of you — if they all find out that in
addition to behaving like a wild-cat to that poor child because
you were fairly daft with jealousy, and driving her away — oh,

yes you did, Mercedes, it don't do any good to deny it now —
if in addition to all that they find out that you've been trying
to save your face by blackening her character? Why, they'll
think you're the meanest skunk that ever walked on two legs;
and they'll be about right. Whereas, Mercedes," Mrs. Talcott
had been standing square and erect for some time in front of her
companion, and now, as her tone became more argumentative and
persuasive, she allowed her tired old body to sag and rest heavily
on one hip —"whereas if you write a nice, kind, loving, self-
reproachful letter, all full of your dreadful anxiety and affection
— why, if Karen ever sees it it'll soften her towards you perhaps; and it'll make all your friends sorry for you, too, and
inclined to hush things up if Mr. Drew spreads the story around
— won't it, Mercedes?"— Madame von Marwitz had turned
in her chair and was staring before her with a deeply thoughtful
eye.—"Why, it's as plain as can be, Mercedes, that that's your
line."

"True," Madame von Marwitz now said. "True." Her
voice was deep and almost solemn. "You are right. Yes; you
are right, Tallie."

She leaned her forehead on her hand, shading her eyes as she
pondered. "A letter of noble admission; of sorrow; of love.
Ah! you recall me to my better self. It will touch her, Tallie; it
is bound to touch her, is it not? She cannot feel the bitterness
she now feels if she reads such a letter; is not that so, Tallie?"

"That's so. You've got it," said Mrs. Talcott.

Madame von Marwitz, however, continued to lean on her desk
and to shade her eyes, and some moments of silence passed thus.
Then, as she leaned, the abjectness of her own position seemed
suddenly borne in upon her. She pushed back her chair and
clutching the edge of the desk with both hands, gave a low cry.

Mrs. Talcott looked at her, inquiring, but unmoved.

"Oh — it is easy for you — standing there — watching my
humiliation — making your terms!" Madame von Marwitz exclaimed in bitter, trembling tones. "You see me in the dust,
— and it is you who strike me there. I am to drag myself —
with precautions — apologies — to that child's feet — that waif!

— that bastard! — that thing I picked up and made! I am to
be glad because I may hope to move her to mercy! Ah! — it
is too much! too much! I curse the day that I saw her! I
had a presentiment — I remember it now — as I saw her standing there in the forest with her foolish face. I felt in my inmost
soul that she was to bring me sorrow. She takes him from me!
She puts me to shame before the world! And I am to implore
her to take pity on me!"

She had extended her clenched hand in speaking and now
struck it violently on the desk. The silver blotter, the candle-
sticks, the pen-tray and ink-stand leaped in their places and the
ink, splashing up, spattered her white silk robe.

"There now," said Mrs. Talcott, eyeing her impassively,
"you've gone and spoiled your nice dress."

"Damn the dress!" said Madame von Marwitz. Leaning her
elbows on the desk and her face on her hands, she wept; the tears
trickled between her fingers.

But in a very little while the storm passed. She straightened
herself, found her lace-edged handkerchief and dried her eyes
and cheeks; then, taking a long breath, she drew forward a
pad of paper.

"I am a fool, am I not, Tallie," she remarked. "And you are
wise; a traitor, yet wise. I will do as you say. Wait there and
you shall see."

Mrs. Talcott now subsided heavily into a chair and for some
fifteen minutes there was no sound but the scratching of Madame von Marwitz's pen and the deep sighs that from time to
time she heaved.

Then: "So: will that do?" she asked, leaning back with
the deepest of the sighs and handing the pages to Mrs. Talcott.

Her dark, cold eyes, all clouded with weeping, had a singularly
childlike expression as she thus passed on her letter for inspec-
tion. And — as when she had stretched out her legs for Mrs.
Talcott to put on her stockings — one saw beyond the instinctively confiding gesture a long series of scenes reaching back
to childhood, scenes where, in crises, her own craft and violence
and unscrupulous resource having undone her, she had fallen

back in fundamental dependence on the one stable and inalienable figure in her life.

Mrs. Talcott read:

"My Friend — Dearest and best Beloved,— I am in the straits of a terrible grief.— I am blind with weeping, dazed from a sleepless night and a day of anguish.— My child, my Karen, is gone and, oh my friend, I am in part to blame.— I am hot of blood, quick of tongue, as you know, and you know that Karen is haughty, resentful, unwilling to brook reproof even from me. But I do not attempt to exonerate myself. I will open my heart to you and my friend will read aright and interpret the broken words. You know that I cared for Claude Drew; you guessed perhaps how strong was the hold upon me of the frail, ambiguous, yet so intelligent modern spirit. It was to feel the Spring blossom once more on my frosty branches when this young life fell at my knees and seemed to find in me its source and goal. Mine was a sacred love and pain mingled with my maternal tenderness when he revealed himself to me as seeking from me the lesser things of love, the things I could not give, that elemental soil of sense and passion without which a man's devotion so strangely withers,— I could give him water from the wells and light from the air; I could not give him earth. My friend, he was here when Karen came, and, already I had seen it, his love was passing from me. Her youth, her guilelessness, her courage and the loyalty of her return to me, aroused his curiosity, his indolent and — you will remember — his unsatisfied, passion. I saw at once, and I saw danger. I knew him to be a man believing in neither good nor evil, seeking only beauty and the satisfaction of desire. Not once — but twice, thrice, did I warn Karen, and she resented my warnings. She is a creature profoundly pure and profoundly simple and her stubborn spirit rests in security upon its own assurances. She resented my warnings and she repulsed my attempts to lead and guard her. Another difference had also come between us. I hoped to effect a reconciliation between her and her husband; I suggested to Karen that I should write to you and offer myself

as an intermediary; I could not bear to see her young life ruined
for my sake. Karen was not kind to me; the thought of her
husband is intolerable to her and she turned upon me with
bitterness. I was hurt and I told her so. She brought me to
tears. My friend, it was late on the night of that day — the
night before last — that I found her with Claude Drew in the
garden; and found her in his arms. Do not misunderstand;
she had not returned his love; she repulsed him as I came upon
them; but I, in my consternation, my anger, my dismay,
snatched her from him and spoke to them both with passionate
reproof. I sent Karen to the house and remained behind to
deal with the creature who had so betrayed my trust. He is
now my avowed enemy. So be it. I do not see him again.

"At dawn, after a sleepless night, I went to Karen's room to
take her in my arms and to ask her pardon for my harsh words.
She was gone. Gone, my friend. Tallie tells me that she believed me to have said that unless she could obey me I must
forbid her to remain under my roof. These were not my words;
but she had misunderstood and had fiercely resented my displeasure. She told Tallie that she would go to the Lippheims,
— for them, as I have told you, she has a deep affection. Tallie
urged upon her that she should communicate with her husband,
let him know what had happened, return to him — even if it
were to blacken me in his eyes — and would to God that it had
been so! — But she repulsed the suggestion with bitterness. It
must also have filled her with terror lest we should ourselves
make some further attempt to bring about a reconciliation; for
it was in the night, and immediately after her talk with Tallie,
that she went, although she and Tallie had arranged that she
was to go to the Lippheims next day.

"We have wired to the Lippheims and find that they have left
England. And we have wired to Mr. Jardine, and she is not
with him. She may be on her way to Germany; she may be
concealed in the country near here; she may be in London.
Unless we have news of her to-morrow I send for a detective.
Oh, to hold her in my arms! I am crushed to the earth with

sorrow and remorse. Show this letter to her husband. I have
no thought of pride.

"Your devoted and unhappy Mercedes."

Mrs. Talcott read and remained for some moments reflecting
after she had read. "Well, I suppose that's got to do," she
commented, "though I don't call it a satisfactory letter.
You've fixed it up real smart, but it's a long way off the truth."

Madame von Marwitz, while Mrs. Talcott read, had been putting back the disordered strands of her hair, adjusting her laces,
and dabbing vaguely with her handkerchief at the splashes of
ink that disfigured the front of her dress — thereby ruining the
handkerchief; she looked up sharply now.

"I deny that it is a long way off the truth."

"A long way off," Mrs. Talcott repeated colourlessly; "but
I guess it'll have to do. I'm willing you should make the best
story out for yourself you can to your friends, so long as Karen
knows the truth and so long as you don't spread scandal about
her. Now I'll write to Mr. Jardine."

Madame von Marwitz's eyes were still fixed sharply on her
and a sudden suspicion leapt to them. "Here then!" she exclaimed. "You write in my presence as I have done in yours.
And we go to the village together that I may see you post the
self-same letter. I have had enough of betrayals!"

Mrs. Talcott allowed a grim smile to touch her lips. "My,
but you're silly, Mercedes," she said. "Get up, then, and let me
sit there. I'd just as leave I'm sure. You know I'm determined that Karen shall go back to her husband and that I'm going to do all I can so as she shall. So there's nothing I want
to hide."

She took up the pen and Madame von Marwitz leaned over her
shoulder and read as she wrote:

"Dear Mr. Jardine,— Mercedes and Karen have had a disagreement and Karen took it very hard and has made off, we
don't know where. Go round to Mrs. Forrester and see what
Mercedes has got to say about it. Karen will tell you her side

when you see her.   She feels very bad about you yet; and thinks
things are over between you; but you hang on, Mr. Jardine, and
it'll all come right.   You'd better find out whether Karen's
called at the Lippheims' and get a detective and try and trace her
out.   If she's with them in Germany I advise you to go right
over and see her.— Yours sincerely,

" Hannah Talcott."

Mrs. Talcott, as she finished, heard that the breathing of Mercedes, close upon her, had become heavier.   She did not look at
her.   She knew what Mercedes was feeling, and dreading; and
that Mercedes was helpless.

" There's no reason under the sun why Handcock should n't
take these letters as usual," she remarked; " but if you're set on
it that you're being betrayed, put on your shoes and dress and
we'll walk down and mail them together."

CHAPTER XXXIX

IT was on the second morning after this that the letters were brought in to Madame von Marwitz while she and Mrs. Talcott sat in the music-room together.

The two days had told upon them both. The face of Mercedes was like a beautiful fruit, rain-sodden and gnawed at the heart by a worm. Mrs. Talcott's was more bleached, more desolate, more austere.

The one letter that Handcock brought to Mrs. Talcott was from Gregory Jardine:

"Dear Mrs. Talcott," it said, "Thank you for your kind note. I am very unhappy and only a little less unhappy than when Karen left me. One cause of our estrangement is, perhaps, removed; but the fact borne in upon me at the time of that parting was that, while she was everything in life to me, she hardly knew the meaning of the words love and marriage. I need not tell you that I will do all in my power to induce her to return to me, and all in my power to win her heart. It was useless to make any attempt at reconciliation while her guardian stood between us. I cannot pretend that I feel more kindly towards Madame von Marwitz now; rather the reverse. It is plain to me that she has treated Karen shamefully. You must forgive me for my frankness.— Sincerely yours,

"Gregory Jardine."

Mrs. Talcott when she looked up from this letter saw that Mercedes was absorbed in hers. Her expression had stiffened as she read, and when she had finished the hand holding it dropped to her side. She sat looking down in a dark contemplation.

Mrs. Talcott asked no question. United in the practical exigencies of their search for Karen, united in their indestructible relation of respective dependence and stability, which the last catastrophe had hardly touched — for Mercedes had accepted her betrayal with a singular passivity, as if it had been a force of nature that had overtaken her — there was yet a whole new region of distrust between them. She and Mercedes, as Mrs. Talcott cheerlessly imaged it, were like a constable and his captive adrift, by a curious turn of fortune, on the waters of a sudden inundation. Together they baled out water and worked at the oar, but both were aware that when the present peril was past a sentence had still to be carried out on one of them. Mercedes could not evade her punishment. If Karen were found Gregory Jardine must come to know that her guardian had, literally, driven her from her home. In that case it rested with Gregory's sense of mercy whether Mercedes should be exposed to the world or not. And after reading Gregory's letter Mrs. Talcott reflected that there was not much to hope of mercy from him. So she showed a tactful consideration of her companion's state of nerves by pressing her no further than was necessary.

On this occasion, however, there was no need for pressure; Mercedes, in her dismal plight, turned to her with the latest development of it.

" Ah," she said, while she still continued to gaze down fixedly, " this it is to have true friends. This is human loyalty. It is well."

" What's the matter, Mercedes? " Mrs. Talcott asked, as she was evidently invited to do.

" Read if you will," said Madame von Marwitz. She held out the letter which Mrs. Talcott rose to take.

It was from Mrs. Forrester and was full of sympathy for her afflicted friend, and full of sympathy for foolish, headstrong little Karen. The mingled sympathies rang strangely. She avowed self-reproach. She was afraid that she had precipitated the rupture between Karen and her husband, not quite, perhaps, understanding the facts. She had seen Gregory, she was very sorry for him. She was, apparently, sorry for everyone; except

24

of course, Mr. Drew, the villain of the piece; but of Mr. Drew and of Mercedes's sacred love for him, she made no mention. Mrs. Forrester was fond, but she was wary. She had received, evidently, her dim thrust of disillusion. Mercedes had blamed herself and Mrs. Forrester did not deny that Mercedes must be to blame.

"Yes; she's feeling pretty sick," Mrs. Talcott commented when she had read. "The trouble is that anybody who knows how much Karen loved you knows that she would n't have made off like that without you'd treated her ugly. That'll be the trouble with most of your friends, I reckon. Who's your other letter from?"

Madame von Marwitz roused herself from her state of contemplation. She opened the second letter saying, tersely: "Scrotton."

"She ain't likely to take sides with Karen," Mrs. Talcott observed, inserting her hand once more in the stocking she was darning, these homely occupations having for the last few days been brought into the music-room, since Mercedes would not be left alone. "She was always just as jealous of Karen as could be."

She proceeded to darn and Madame von Marwitz to read, and as she read a dark flush mounted to her face. Clenching her hand on Miss Scrotton's letter, she brought it down heavily on the back of the chair she sat in. Then, without speaking, she got up, tossed the letter to Mrs. Talcott, and began to pace the room, setting the furniture that she encountered out of her way with vindictive violence.

"My Darling, Darling Mercedes," Miss Scrotton wrote, "This is too terrible. Shall I come to you at once? I thought this morning after I had seen Mrs. Forrester and read your heart-breaking letter that I would start to-day; but let me hear from you; you may be coming up to town. If you stay in Cornwall, Mercedes, you must not be alone; you must not; and I am, as you know, devoted heart and soul. If all the world turned against you, Mercedes, I should keep my faith in you. I need

hardly tell you what is being said. Claude Drew is in London
and though, naturally, he does not dare face your friends with
his story, rumours are abroad. Betty Jardine does not know
him, but already she has heard; I met her only a few hours ago
and the miserable little creature was full of malicious satisfaction. The story that she has heard — and believes — and that
London will believe — is the crude, gross one that facts, so dis-
astrously, have lent colour to; you, in a fit of furious jealousy,
driving Karen away. My poor, great, suffering friend, I need
not tell you that I understand. Your letter rings true to me
in every line, and is but too magnanimous.— Oh Mercedes! —
had you but listened to my warnings about that wretched man.
Do you remember that I told you that you were scattering your
pearls before swine? And your exculpation of Karen did not
convince me as it seemed to do Mrs. Forrester. A really guileless woman is not found — late at night — in a man's arms.
I cannot forget Karen's origins. There must be in her the element of reckless passion. Mr. Drew is spreading a highly
idealised account of her and says that to see you together was
to see Antigone in the clutches of Clytemnestra. There is some
satisfaction in knowing that the miserable man is quite distracted
and is haunted by the idea that Karen may have committed
suicide. Betty Jardine says that in that case you and he would
have to appear at the inquest.— Oh, my poor Mercedes! — But
I feel sure that this is impossible. Temper, not tragedy, drove
Karen from you and it was on her part a dastardly action. I
am seeing everybody that I can; they shall have my version.
The Duchess is in the country; I have wired to her that I will go
to her at once if you do not send for me; it is important that she
should have the facts as I see them before these abominable
rumours reach her. Dear Mrs. Forrester means, I am sure, to
do loyally; you may count upon her to listen to no scandal; but
its breath alarms and chills her: she does not interpret your
letter as I do.

" Good-bye, my dear one. Wire to me please, at once.
                Ever and always *ton Eleanor devouée.*"

"Well," Mrs. Talcott commented warily, folding the letter and glancing at Madame von Marwitz; "she don't let any grass grow under her feet, does she? Do you want her down?"

"Want her! Why should I want her! The insufferable fool!" cried Madame von Marwitz still striding to and fro with tigerish regularity. "Does she think me, too, a fool, to be taken in by her grimaces of loyalty when it is as apparent as the day that delight is her chief emotion. Here is her opportunity — *parbleu!* — At last! I am in the dust — and if also in the dock so much the better. She will stand by me when others fall away. She will defend the prostrate Titaness from the vultures that prey upon her and gain at last the significance she has, for so long, so eagerly and so fruitlessly pursued. Ah! — *par exemple!* Let her come to me expecting gratitude. I will spurn her from me like a dog!" Madame von Marwitz, varying her course, struck a chair aside as she spoke.

"Well, I should n't fly out at her if I was you," said Mrs. Talcott. "She's as silly as they make 'em, I allow, but it's all to the good if her silliness keeps her sticking to you through thick and thin. It's just as well to have someone around to drive off the vultures, even if it's only a scarecrow — and Miss Scrotton is better than that. She's a pretty brainy woman, for all her silliness, and she's pretty fond of you, too, only you have n't treated her as well as she thinks you ought to have, and it makes her feel kind of spry and cheerful to see that her time's come to show you what a fine fellow she is. Most folks are like that, I guess," Mrs. Talcott mused, returning to her stocking, "they don't suffer so powerful over their friends' misfortunes if it gives them a chance of showing what fine fellows they are."

"Friends!" Madame von Marwitz repeated with scorching emphasis. "Friends! Truly I have proved them, these friends of mine. Cowards and traitors all, or crouching hounds. I am to be left, I perceive, with the Scrotton as my sole companion." But now she paused in her course, struck by a belated memory. "You had a letter. You have heard from the husband."

"Yes, I have," said Mrs. Talcott, "and you may as well see it."

She drew forth Gregory's letter from under the heap of darning appliances on her lap.

Madame von Marwitz snatched it from her and read it, once rapidly, once slowly; and then, absorbed again in dark meditations, she stood holding it, her eyes fixed on the ground.

"He ain't as violent as might be expected, is he?" Mrs. Talcott suggested. Distrust was abroad in the air between her and Mercedes; she offered the fact of Gregory's temperateness as one that might mitigate some anticipations.

"He is as insolent as might be expected," said Madame von Marwitz. She flung the letter back to Mrs. Talcott, resuming her pacing, with a bitter laugh. "And to think," she said presently, "that I hoped — but truly hoped — with all my heart — to reconcile them! To think that I offered myself to Karen as an intermediary. It was true — yes, literally true — what I told Mrs. Forrester — that I spoke to Karen of it — with all love and gentleness and that she turned upon me like a tigress."

"And you 'll recollect," said Mrs. Talcott, "that I told you to keep your hands off them and that you 'd made enough mischief as it was. Why I guess you did hope she 'd go back. You wanted to get rid of Karen and to have that young man to yourself; that 's the truth, but you did n't tell that to Mrs. Forrester."

"I deny it," said Madame von Marwitz; but mechanically; her thoughts were elsewhere. She still paced.

"Well," said Mrs. Talcott, "you 'd better send that telegram to Miss Scrotton, telling her not to come, or you 'll have her down here as soon as she 's seen the Duchess."

"Send it; send it at once," said Madame von Marwitz. "Tell her that I do not need her. Tell her that I will write." The force of her fury had passed; counsels of discretion were making themselves felt. "Go at once and send it."

She paused again as Mrs. Talcott rose. "If Karen is not found within three days, Tallie, I go to London. I believe that she is in London."

Mrs. Talcott faced her. "If she 's in London she 'll be found as soon by Mr. Jardine as by you."

"Yes; that may be," said Mercedes, and discretion, now, had evidently the mastery; "but Karen will not refuse to see me. I must see her. I must implore her forgiveness. You would not oppose that, would you, Tallie?"

"No, I'd not oppose your asking her to forgive you," Mrs. Talcott conceded, "when she's got back to her husband. Only I advise you to stay where you are till you hear she's found."

"I will do as you say, Tallie," said Madame von Marwitz meekly. She went to the piano, and seating herself began to play the *Wohltemperirtes Clavier.*

CHAPTER XL

SIX days had passed since Karen's disappearance. The country had been searched; London, still, was being examined, and the papers were beginning to break into portraits of the missing girl. Karen became remote, non-existent, more than dead, it seemed, when her face, like that of some heroine of a newspaper novelette, gazed at one from the breakfast-table. The first time that this happened, Madame von Marwitz, flinging the sheet from her, had burst into a violent storm of weeping.

She sat, on the afternoon of the sixth day, in a sunny corner of the lower terrace and turned the leaves of a book with a listless hand. She was to be alone till dinner-time; Tallie had gone in to Helston by bus, and she had the air of one who feels solitude at once an oppression and a relief. She read little, raising her eyes to gazè unseeingly over the blue expanses stretched beneath her or to look down as vaguely into the eyes of Victor, who lay at her feet. The restless spirit of the house had reached Victor. He lay with his head on his extended paws in an attitude of quiescence; but his ears were pricked to watchfulness, his eyes, as he turned them now and again up to his mistress, were troubled. Aware of his glance, on one occasion, Madame von Marwitz stooped and caressed his head, murmuring: "*Nous sommes des infortunés, hein, mon chien.*" Her voice was profoundly sad. Victor understood her. Slightly thudding his tail he gave a soft responsive groan; and it was then, while she still leaned to him and still caressed his head, that shrill, emphatic voices struck on Madame von Marwitz's ear.

The gravelled nook where she sat, her garden chair, with its adjusted cushions, set against a wall, was linked by ascending paths and terraces to the cliff-path, and this again, though only through a way overgrown with gorse and bramble, to the public

375

coast-guards' path along the cliff-top. The white stones that marked the way for the coast-guards made a wide *détour* behind Madame von Marwitz's property and this nearer egress to the cliff was guarded by a large placard warning off trespassers. Yet, looking in the direction of the voices, Madame von Marwitz, to her astonishment, saw that three ladies, braving the interdict, were actually marching down in single file upon her.

One was elderly and two were young; they wore travelling dress, and, as she gazed at them in chill displeasure, the features of the first became dimly familiar to her. Where, she could not have said, yet she had seen that neat, grey head before, that box-like hat with its depending veil, that firmly corseted, matronly form, with its silver-set pouch, suggesting, typical of the travelling American lady as it was, a marsupial species. She did not know where she had seen this lady; but she was a travelling American; she accosted one in determined tones, and, at some time in the past, she had waylaid and inconvenienced her. Madame von Marwitz, as the three trooped down upon her, did not rise. She pointed to the lower terrace. "This is private property," she said, and her aspect might well have turned the unwary visitors, Acteon-like, into stags, "I must ask you to leave it at once. You see the small door in the garden wall below; it is unlocked and it leads to the village. Good-day to you."

But, with a singularly bright and puckered look, the look of a surf-bather, who measures with swift eye the height of the rolling breaker and plunges therein, the elderly lady addressed her with extraordinary volubility.

"Baroness, you don't remember us — but we 've met before, we have a mutual friend: — Mrs. General Tollman of St. Paul's, Minnesota.— Allow me to introduce myself again: — Mrs. Slifer — Mrs. Hamilton K. Slifer: — my girls, Maude and Beatrice. We had the privilege of making your acquaintance over a year ago, Baroness, at the station in London, just before you sailed, and we had some talks on the steamer to that perfectly charming woman, Miss Scrotton. I hope she 's well. We 're over again this year, you see; we pine for dear old England and come just as often as we can. We feel we belong here more than over there sometimes, I'm afraid,"— Mrs. Slifer laughed swiftly and deprecatingly.—"My girls are so often taken for English girls, the Burne-Jones type you know. We've got friends staying at Mullion, so we thought we'd just drop down on Cornwall for a little tour after we landed at Southampton, and we drove over this afternoon and came down by the cliff — we are just crazy about your scenery, Baroness — it's just the right setting for you — we've been saying so all day — to have a peek at the house we've heard so much about; and we don't want to disturb you, but it's the greatest possible pleasure, Baroness, to have this beautiful glimpse of you — with your splendid dog — how d'ye do, Victor — why I do believe he remembers me; we petted him so much at the station when your niece was holding him. We saw Mrs. Jardine the other day, Baroness — such a pleasant surprise that was, too — only we're sorry to see she's so delicate. The New Forest will be just the place for her. We stayed there three days after landing, because my Beatrice here was very sea-sick and I wanted her to have a little rest. We were simply crazy over it. I do hope Mrs. Jardine's getting better."

All this had been delivered with such speed, such an air of decision and purpose, that Madame von Marwitz, who had risen in her bewildered indignation and stood, her book beneath her arm, her white cloak caught about her, had found no opportunity to check the torrent of speech, and as these last words came as swiftly and as casually as the rest she could hardly, for a moment, collect her faculties.

"My niece? Mrs. Jardine?" she repeated, with a wild, wan utterance. "What do you say of her?"

It was at this moment that Miss Beatrice began, in the background, to adjust her camera. She told her mother and sister afterwards that she seemed to feel it in her bones that something was doing.

Mrs. Slifer, emerging from her breaker in triumph, struck out, blinking and smiling affably. "We heard all about the wedding in America," she said, "and we thought we might call upon her

in London and see that splendid temple you'd given her — we
heard all about that, too.   I never saw a picture of him, but I
knew her in a minute, naturally, though she did look so pulled
down.   Why, Baroness — what's the matter!"

Madame von Marwitz had suddenly clutched Mrs. Slifer's arm
with an almost appalling violence of mien and gesture.

"What is the matter?" Madame von Marwitz repeated, shaking Mrs. Slifer's arm.   "Do you know what you are saying?
My niece has been lost for a week!   The whole country is searching for her!   Where have you seen her?   When was it?   Answer me at once!"

"Why Baroness, by all means, but you need n't shake my head
off," said Mrs. Slifer, not without dignity, raising her free hand
to straighten her hat.   "We've never heard a word about it.
Why this is perfectly providential.— Baroness — I must ask you
not to go on shaking me like that.   I've got a very delicate
stomach and the least thing upsets my digestion."

"*Justes cieux!*" Madame von Marwitz cried, dropping Mrs.
Slifer's arm and raising her hands to her head, while, in the
background, Miss Beatrice's kodak gave a click —"Will the
woman drive me mad!   Karen!   My child!   Where is she!"

"Why, we saw her at the station at Brockenhurst — in the
New Forest — did n't we Maude," said Mrs. Slifer, "and it must
have been — now let me see —" poor Mrs. Slifer collected her
wits, a bent forefinger at her lips.   "To-day's Thursday and
we got to Mullion yesterday — and we stopped at Winchester
for a day and night on our way to the New Forest, it was on
Saturday last of course.   We'd been having a drive about that
part of the forest and we were taking the train and they had
just come and we saw them on the opposite platform.   He was
just helping her out of the train and we did n't have any time
to go round and speak to them —"

"They!" Madame von Marwitz nearly shouted.   "She was
with a man!   Last Saturday!   Who was it?   Describe him to
me!   Was he slender — with fair hair — dark eyes — the air
of a poet?"   She panted.   And her aspect was so singular

that Miss Beatrice, startled out of her professional readiness,
failed to snap it.

"Why no," said Mrs. Slifer, keeping her clue.   "I should n't
say a poetical looking man, should you, Maude?   A fleshy man
— very big and fleshy, and he was taking such good care of her
and looked so kind of tender and worried that I concluded he
was her husband.   She looked like a very sick woman, Baroness."

"Fleshy?" Madame von Marwitz repeated, and the word, in
her moan, was almost graceful.   "Fleshy, you say?   An old
man?   A stout old man?" she held her hands distractedly
pressed to her head.   "What stout old man does Karen know?
Is it a stranger she has met?"

"No, he was n't old.   This was a young man, Baroness.   He
had — now let me see — his hair was sort of red — I remember
noticing his hair; and he wore knee-pants and a soft hat with a
feather in it and was very high coloured."

"*Bon Dieu!*" Madame von Marwitz gasped.   She had again,
while Mrs. Slifer spoke, seized her by the arm as though afraid
that she might escape her and she now gazed with a fixed gaze
above Mrs. Slifer's head and through the absorbed Maude and
Beatrice.   "Red hair? — A large young man? — Was he clean
shaven?   Did he wear eyeglasses?   Had he the face of a musician?   Did he look like an Englishman — an English gentleman?"

Mrs. Slifer, nodding earnest assent to the first questions,
shook her head at the latter.   "No, he did n't.   What I said to
Maude and Beatrice was that Mr. Jardine looked more German
than English.   He looked just like a German student, Baroness."

"Franz Lippheim!" cried Madame von Marwitz.   She sank
back upon the seat from which she had risen, putting a hand
before her eyes.

Victor, at her knees, laid a paw upon her lap and whined an
interrogative sympathy.   The three American ladies gathered
near and gazed in silence upon the great woman, and Beatrice,
carefully adjusting her camera, again took a snap.   The picture
of Madame von Marwitz, with her hand before her eyes, her

anxious dog at her knees, found its way into the American press and illustrated touchingly the story of the lost adopted child. Madame von Marwitz was not sorry when, among a batch of press-cuttings, she came across the photograph and saw that her most genuine emotion had been thus made public.

She looked up at last, and the dizziness of untried and perilous freedom was in her eyes; but curious, now, of other objects, they took in, weighed and measured the little group before her; power grew in them, an upwelling of force and strategy.

She smiled upon the Slifers and she rose.

"You have done me an immeasurable service," she said, and as she spoke she took Mrs. Slifer's hand with a noble dignity. "You have lifted me from despair. It is blessed news that you bring. My child is safe with a good, a talented man; one for whom I have the deepest affection. And in the New Forest — at Brockenhurst — on Saturday. Ah, I shall soon have her in my arms."

Still holding Mrs. Slifer's hand she led them up the terraces and towards the house. "The poor child is ill, distraught. She had parted from her husband — fled from him. Ah, it has been a miserable affair, that marriage. But now, all will be well. *Bon Dieu!* what joy! What peace of heart you have brought me! I shall be with her to-morrow. I start at once. And you, my good friends, let me hear your plans. Let me be of service to you. Come with me for the last stage of your journey. I will not part with you willingly."

"It's all simply too wonderful, Baroness," Mrs. Slifer gasped, as she skipped along on her short legs beside the goddess-like stride of the great woman, who held her — who held her very tightly. "We were just going to drift along up to Tintagel and then work up to London, taking in all the cathedrals we could on our way."

"And you will change your route in order to give me the pleasure of your company. You will forfeit Tintagel: is it not so?" Madame von Marwitz smiled divinely. "You will come with me in my car to Truro where we take the train and I will drop you to-night at the feet of a cathedral. So. Your luggage

is at Mullion? That is simple. We wire to your friends to
pack and send it on at once. Leave it to me. You are in my
hands. It is a kindness that you will do me. I need you, Mrs.
Slifer," she pressed the lady's arm. "My old friend, who lives
with me, has left me for the day, and, moreover, she is too
old to travel. I must not be alone. I need you. It is a kindness that you will do me. Now you will wait for me here and
tea will be brought to you. I shall keep you waiting but for a
few moments."

It was to be lifted on the back of a genie. She had wafted
them up, along the garden paths, across the verandah, into the
serenity and spaciousness and dim whites and greens and silvers
of the great music-room, with a backward gaze that had, in all
its sweetness, something of hypnotic force and fixity.

She left them with the Sargent portrait looking down at
them and the room in its strangeness and beauty seemed part
of the spell she laid upon them. The Slifers, herded together
in the middle of it, gazed about them half awe-struck and spoke
almost in whispers.

"Why, girls," said Mrs. Slifer, who was the first to find words,
"this is the most thrilling thing I ever came across."

"You've pulled it off this time, mother, and no mistake,"
said Maude, glancing somewhat furtively up at the Sargent.
"Do look at that perfectly lovely dress she has on in that
picture. Did you ever see such pearls; and the eyes seem to
follow you, don't they?"

"The poor, distracted thing just clings to us," said Mrs.
Slifer. "I shouldn't wonder if she was as lonely as could be."

"All the same," Beatrice, the doubting Thomas of the group,
now commented, "I don't think however excited she was she
ought to have shaken you like that, mother." Beatrice had examined the appurtenances of the great room with a touch of
nonchalance. It was she whom Gregory had seen at the station,
seated on the pile of luggage.

"That's petty of you, Bee," said Mrs. Slifer gravely. "Real
small and petty. It's a great soul at white heat we've been
looking at."

Handcock at this point brought in tea, and after she had placed the tray and disposed the plates of cake and bread-and-butter and left the Slifers alone again, Mrs. Slifer went on under her breath, seating herself to pour out the tea. "And do look at this teapot, girls; is n't it too cute for words. My! What will the Jones say when they hear about this! They'd give their eye-teeth to be with us now."

The Slifers, indeed, were never to forget their adventure. It was to be impressed upon their minds not only by its supreme enviableness but by its supreme discomfort. It was almost five when, like three Ganymedes uplifted by the talons of a fierce, bright bird, they soared with Madame von Marwitz towards Truro, and at Truro, in spite of a reckless speed which desperately dishevelled their hair and hats, they arrived too late to catch the 6.40 train for Exeter.

Madame von Marwitz strode majestically along the platform, her white cloak trailing in the dust, called for station-masters, demanded special trains, fixed haughty, uncomprehending eyes upon the officials who informed her that she could not possibly get a train until ten, resigned herself, with sundry exclamations of indignation and stamps of the foot, to the tedious wait, sailed into the refreshment room only to sail out again, mounted the car not yet dismissed, bore the Slifers to a hotel where they had a dinner over which she murmured at intervals *" Bon Dieu, est-ce-donc possible!"* and then, in the chill, dark evening, toured about in the adjacent country until ten, when Burton was sent back to Les Solitudes and when they all got into the train for Exeter.

She had never in all her life travelled alone before. She hardly knew how to procure her ticket, and her helplessness in regard to box and dressing-case was so apparent that Mrs. Slifer saw to the one and Maude carried the other, together with the fur-lined coat when this was thrown aside.

The hours that they passed with her in the train were the strangest that the Slifers had ever passed. They were chilled, they were sleepy, they were utterly exhausted; but they kept

their eyes fixed on the perplexing, resplendent object that up-
bore them.

Beatrice, it is true, showed by degrees, a slight sulkiness.
She had not liked it when, at Truro, Madame von Marwitz
had supervised their wires to the Jones, and she liked it less
when Madame von Marwitz explained to them in the train
that she relied upon them not to let the Jones — or anybody
for the present — know anything about Mrs. Jardine. Something in Madame von Marwitz's low-toned and richly murmured
confidences as she told Maude and Mrs. Slifer that it was important for Mrs. Jardine's peace of mind, and for her very
sanity, that her dreaded husband should not hear of her where-
abouts, made Beatrice, as she expressed it to herself, "tired."

She looked out of the window while her mother and sister
murmured, "Why certainly, Baroness; why yes; we perfectly
understand," leaning forward in the illuminated carriage like
docile conspirators.

After this Madame von Marwitz said that she would try to
sleep; but, propped in her corner, she complained so piteously
of discomfort that Mrs. Slifer and Maude finally divested
themselves of their jackets and contrived a pillow for her out
of them. They assured her that they were not cold and Madame
von Marwitz, reclining now at full length, murmured *"Mille
remerciements."* Soon she fell asleep and Mrs. Slifer and
Maude, very cold and very unresentful, sat and watched her
slumbers. From time to time she softly snored. She was very
comfortable in her fur-lined cloak.

It was one o'clock when they reached Exeter and drove, dazed
and numbed, to a hotel. Here Madame von Marwitz further
availed herself of the services of Maude and Mrs. Slifer, for she
was incapable of unpacking her box and dressing-case. Mrs.
Slifer maided her while Maude, with difficulty at the late hour,
procured her hot water, bouillon and toast. Beatrice meanwhile, callously avowing her unworthiness, said that she was
"dead tired" and went to bed.

Madame von Marwitz bade Mrs. Slifer and Maude the kindest

good-night, smiling dimly at them over her bed-room candle-
stick as she ushered them to the door. " So," she said; " I
leave you to your cathedral."

When the Slifers arose next day, late, for they were very
weary, they found that Madame von Marwitz had departed by
an early train.

.   .   .   .

Meanwhile, at Les Solitudes, old Mrs. Talcott turned from
side to side all night, sleepless. Her heart was heavy with
anxiety.

Karen was found and to-morrow Mercedes would be with her;
she had sent for Mercedes, so the note pinned to Mrs. Talcott's
dressing-table had informed her, and Mercedes would write.

What had happened? Who were the unknown ladies who had
appeared from no one knew where during her absence at Helston
and departed with Mercedes for Truro?

" Something's wrong. Something's wrong," Mrs. Talcott
muttered to herself during the long hours. " I don't believe
she's sent for Mercedes — not unless she's gone crazy."

At dawn she fell at last into an uneasy sleep. She dreamed
that she and Mercedes were walking in the streets of Cracow,
and Mercedes was a little child. She jumped beside Mrs.
Talcott, holding her by the hand. The scene was innocent, yet
the presage of disaster filled it with a strange horror. Mrs.
Talcott woke bathed in sweat.

" I'll get an answer to my telegram this morning," she said
to herself. She had telegraphed to Gregory last night, at once:
" Karen is found. Mercedes has gone to her. That's all I
know yet."

She clung to the thought of Gregory's answer. Perhaps he,
too, had news. But she had no answer to her telegram. The
post, instead, brought her a letter from Gregory that had been
written the morning before.

" Dear Mrs. Talcott," it ran. " Karen is found. The detectives discovered that Mr. Franz Lippheim had not gone to
Germany with his family. They traced him to an inn in the

New Forest. Karen is with him and has taken his name. May I ask you, if possible, to keep this fact from her guardian for the present.— Yours sincerely,

"Gregory Jardine."

When Mrs. Talcott had read this she felt herself overcome by a sudden sickness and trembling. She had not yet well recovered from her illness of the Spring. She crept upstairs to her room and went to bed.

CHAPTER XLI

I T seemed to Karen, after hours had passed, that she had ceased to be tired and that her body, wafted by an involuntary rhythm, was as light as thistle-down on the wind.

She had crossed the Goonhilly Downs where the moonlight, spreading far and wide with vast unearthly brightness, filled all the vision with immensities of space and brought memories of strains from Schubert's symphonies, silver monotonies of never-ending sound.

She had plunged down winding roads, blackly shadowed by their hedgerow trees, passing sometimes a cottage that slept between its clumps of fuchsia and veronica. She had climbed bare hill-sides where abandoned mines or quarries had left desolate mementoes that looked in the moonlight like ancient tombs and catacombs.

Horror lay behind her at Les Solitudes, a long, low cloud on the horizon to which she had turned her back. The misery that had overpowered and made her one with its dread realities lay beneath her feet. She was lifted above it in a strange, disembodied enfranchisement all the night, and the steady blowing of the wind, the leagues of silver, the mighty sky with its far, high priestess, were part of an ecstasy of sadness, impersonal, serene, hallucinated, like that of the music that accompanied the rhythm of her feet.

The night was almost over and dawn was coming, when, on a long uphill road, she felt her heart flag and her footsteps stagger.

The moon still rode sharp and high, but its light seemed concentrated in its own glittering disk and the world was visible in an uncanny darkness that was not dark. The magic of the night had vanished and the beat of vast, winding melodies melted

from Karen's mind leaving her dry and brittle and empty,
like a shell from which the tides have drawn away.

She knew what she had still tu do. At the top of the road
she was to turn and cut across fields to a headland above Falmouth — from which a path she knew led to the town. She
had not gone to Helston, but had taken this cross-country way
to Falmouth because she knew that at any hour of the night
she might be missed and followed and captured. They would
not think of Falmouth; they would not dream that she could
walk so far. In the town she would pawn Onkel Ernst's watch
and take the early train to London and by evening she would be
with Frau Lippheim. So she had seen it all, in flashes, last
night.

But now, toiling up the interminable road, clots of darkness
floating before her eyes, cold sweats standing on her forehead,
the sense of her exhaustion crushed down upon her. She tried
to fix her thoughts on the trivial memories and forecasts that
danced in her mind. The odd blinking of Mrs. Talcott's eyelid
as she had told her story; the pattern of the breakfast set that
she and Gregory had used — ah, no! — not that! she must not
fix that memory! — the roofs and chimneys of some little German town where she was to find a refuge; for though it was to
join the Lippheims that she fled, she did not see her life as led
with theirs. Leaning upon these pictures as if upon a staff she
held, she reached the hill-top. Her head now seemed to dance
like a balloon, buffeted by the great throbs of her blood. She
trailed with leaden feet across the fields. In the last high meadow
she paused and looked down at the bend of the great bay under
the pallid sky and at the town lying like a scattering of shells
along its edge. How distant it was. How like a mirage.

A little tree was beside her and its leaves in the uncanny light
looked like crisp black metal. The sea was grey. The sunrise
was still far off. Karen sank beneath the tree and leaned her
head against it. What should she do if she were unable to
walk on? There was still time — hours and hours of time —
till the train left Falmouth; but how was she to reach Falmouth?
Fears rolled in upon her like dark breakers, heaping them-

selves one upon the other, stealthy, swift, not to be escaped.
She saw the horrible kindness in Mrs. Talcott's eyes, relegated,
not relinquished. She saw herself pursued, entrapped, confronted by Gregory, equally entrapped, forced by her need,
her helplessness, to come to her and coldly determined — as
she had seen him on that dreadful evening of their parting —
to do his duty by her, to make her and to keep her safe, and
his own dignity secure. To see him again, to strive against
him again, weaponless, now, without refuge, and revealed to
herself and to him as a creature whose whole life had been
founded on illusion, to strive not only against his ironic authority but, worst of all, against a longing, unavowed, unlooked
at, a longing that crippled and unstrung her, and that ran
under everything like a hidden river under granite hills —
she would die, she felt, rather than endure it.

She had closed her eyes as she leaned her head against the
tree and when she opened them she saw that the leaves of the
tree had turned from black to green and that the grass was
green and the sea and sky faintly blue. Above her head the
long, carved ripples of the morning cirri flushed with a heavenly
pink and there came from a thicket of a little wood the first
soft whistle of a wakened bird. Another came and then another, and suddenly the air was full of an almost jangling
sweetness. Karen felt herself trembling. Shudders ran over
her. She was ravished to life, yet without the answering power
of life. Her longing, her loneliness, her fear, were part of the
intolerable loveliness and they pierced her through and through.

She struggled to her feet, holding the tree in her clasp, and,
after the galvanised effort, she closed her eyes again, and again
leaned her head upon the bark.

Then it was that she heard footsteps, sudden footsteps, near.
For a moment a paralysis of fear held down her eyelids. " *Ach
Gott!* " she heard. And opening her eyes, she saw Franz Lipp-
heim before her.

Franz Lippheim was dressed, very strangely dressed, in tweeds
and knicker-bockers and wore a soft round hat with a quill in
it — the oddest of hats — and had a knapsack on his back.

The colours of the coming day were caricatured in his ruddy face and red-gold hair, his bright green stockings and bright red tie. He was Germanic, flagrant, incredible, and a Perseus, an undreamed of, God-sent Perseus.

"*Ach Gott!* Can it be so!" he was saying, as he approached her, walking softly as though in fear of dispersing a vision.

And as, not speaking, still clasping her tree, she held out her hand to him, he saw the extremity of her exhaustion and put his arm around her.

She did not faint; she kept her consciousness of the blue sky and the cirri — golden now — and even of Franz's tie and eyeglasses, glistening golden in the rising sun-light; but he had lowered her gently to the ground, kneeling beside her, and was supporting her shoulders and putting brandy to her lips. After a little while he made her drink some milk and then she could speak to him.

She must speak and she must tell him that she had left her guardian. She must speak of Tante. But what to say of her? The shame and pity that had gone with her for days laid their fingers on her lips as she thought of Tante and of why she had left her. Her mind groped for some availing substitute.

"Franz," she said, "you must help me. I have left Tante. You will not question me. There is a breach between us; she has been unkind to me. I can never see her again." And now with clearer thought she found a sufficient truth. "She has not understood about me and my husband. She has tried to make me go back to him; and I have fled from her because I was afraid that she would send for him. She is not as fond of me as I thought she was, Franz, and I was a burden to her when I came. Franz, will you take me to London, to your mother? I am going with you all to Germany. I am going to earn my living there."

"*Du lieber Gott!*" Herr Lippheim ejaculated. He stared at Karen in consternation. "Our great lady — our great Tante — has been unkind to you? Is it then possible, Karen?"

"Yes, Franz; you must believe me. You must not question me."

"Trust me, my Karen," said Herr Lippheim now; "do not fear. It shall be as you say. But I cannot take you to the Mütterchen in London, for she is not there. They have gone back to Germany, Karen, and it is to Germany that we must go."

"Can you take me there, Franz, at once? I have no money; but I am going to pawn this watch that Onkel Ernst gave me."

"That is all simple, my Karen. I have money. I took with me the money for my tour; I was on a walking-tour, do you see, and reached Falmouth last night and had but started now to pay my respects at Les Solitudes. I wished to see you, Karen, and to see if you were well. But it is very far to your village. How have you come so far, at night?"

"I walked. I have walked all night. I am so tired, Franz. So tired. I do not know how I shall go any further." She closed her eyes; her head rested against his shoulder.

Franz Lippheim looked down at her with an infinite compassion and gentleness. "It will all be well, my Karen; do not fear," he said. "The train does not go from Falmouth for three hours still. We will take it then and go to Southampton and sail for Germany to-night. And for now, you will drink this milk — so, yes; that is well; — and eat this chocolate; — you cannot; it will be for later then. And you will lie still with my cloak around you, so; and you will sleep. And I will sit beside you and you will have no troubled thoughts. You are with your friends, my Karen." While he spoke he had wrapped her round and laid her head softly on a folded garment that he drew from his knapsack; and in a few moments he saw that she slept, the profound sleep of complete exhaustion.

Franz Lippheim sat above her, not daring to light his pipe for fear of waking her. He watched the glory of the sunrise. It was perhaps the most wonderful hour in Franz's life.

Phrases of splendid music passed through his mind, mingling with the sound of the sea. No personal pain and no personal hope was in his heart. He was uplifted, translated, with the beauty of the hour and its significance.

Karen needed him. Karen was to come to them. He was

to see her henceforward in his life. He was to guard and help her. He was her friend. The splendour and the peace of the golden sky and golden sea were the angels of a great initiation. Nothing could henceforth be as it had been. His brain stirred with exquisite intuitions, finding form for them in the loved music that, henceforth, he would play as he had never before played it. And when he looked from the sea and sky down at the sleeping face beside him, wasted and drawn and piteous in its repose, large tears rose in his eyes and flowed down his cheeks, and the sadness was more beautiful than any joy that he had known.

What she had suffered! — the dear one. What they must help her to forget! To her, also, the hour would send it angels: she would wake to a new life.

He turned his eyes again to the rising sun, and his heart silently chanted its love and pride and sadness in the phrases of Beethoven, of Schubert and of Brahms, and from time to time, softly, he muttered to himself, this stout young German Jew with the red neck-tie and the strange round hat: *" Süsses Kind! Unglückliches Kind! Oh — der schöne Tag!"*

CHAPTER XLII

MADAME VON MARWITZ looked out from her fly at the ugly little wayside inn with its narrow lawn and its bands of early flowers. Trees rose round it, the moors of the forest stretched before. It was remote and very silent.

Here it was, she had learned at the station, some miles away, that the German lady and gentleman were staying, and the lady was said to be very ill. Madame von Marwitz's glance, as it rested upon the goal of her journey, had in it the look of vast, constructive power, as when, for the first time, it rested on a new piece of music, realized it, mastered it, possessed it, actual, in her mind, before her fingers gave it to the world. So, now, she realized and mastered and possessed the scene that was to be enacted.

She got out of the fly and told the man to carry in her box and dressing-case and then to wait. She opened the little gate, and as she did so, glancing up, she saw Franz Lippheim standing looking out at her from a ground-floor window. His gaze was stark in its astonishment. She returned it with a solemn smile. In another moment she had put the landlady aside with benign authority and was in the little sitting-room. " My Franz ! " she exclaimed in German. " Thank God ! " She threw her arms around his neck and burst into sobs.

Franz, holding a pipe extended in his hand, stood for a moment in silence his eyes still staring their innocent dismay over her shoulder. Then he said : " How have you come here, *gnädige Frau?* "

" Come, Franz ! " Madame von Marwitz echoed, weeping : " Have I not been seeking my child for the last six days ! Love such as mine is a torch that lights one's path ! Come ! Yes ; I am come. I have found her ! She is safe, and with my Franz ! "

"But Karen is ill, very ill indeed," said Franz, speaking with some difficulty, locked as he was in the great woman's arms. "The doctor feared for her life three days ago. She has been delirious. And it is you, *gnädige Frau,* whom she fears; — you and her husband."

Madame von Marwitz leaned back her head to draw her hand across her eyes, clearing them of tears.

"But do I not know it, Franz?" she said, smiling a trembling smile at him. "Do I not know it? I have been in fault; yes; and I will make confession to you. But — oh! — my child has punished me too cruelly. To leave me without a word! At night! It was the terror of her husband that drove her to it, Franz. Yes; it has been a delirium of terror. She was ill when she went from me."

She had released him now, though keeping his hands in hers, and she still held them as they sat down at the centre table in the little room, he on one side, she on the other, she leaning to him across it; and she read in his face his deep discomfort.

"But you see, *gnädige Frau,*" Franz again took up his theme; "she believes that you wish to send her back to him; she has said it; she could not trust you. And so she fled from you. And I have promised to take care of her. I am to take her to my mother in Germany as soon as she can travel. We were on our way to Southampton and would have been, days since, with the Mütterchen, if in the train Karen had not become so ill — so very ill. It was a fever that grew on her, and delirium. I did not know what was best to do. And I remembered this little inn where the Mütterchen and we four stayed some years ago, when we came first to England. The landlady was very good; and so I thought of her and brought Karen here. But when she is better I must take her to Germany, *gnädige Frau.* I have promised it."

While Franz thus spoke a new steadiness had come to Madame von Marwitz's eyes. They dilated singularly, and with them her nostrils, as though she drew a deep new breath of realisation. It was as if Franz had let down a barrier; pointed out a way.

There was no confession to be made to Franz. Karen had spared her.

She looked at him, looked and looked, and she shook her head with infinite gentleness. "But Franz," she said, "I do not wish her to go back to her husband. I was in fault, yes, grave fault, to urge it upon her; but Karen's terror was her mistake, her delirium. It was for my sake that she had left him, Franz, because to me he had shown insolence and insult;— for your sake, too, Franz, for he tried to part her from all her friends and of you he spoke with an unworthy jealousy. But though my heart bled that Karen should be tied to such a man, I knew him to be not a bad man; hard, narrow, but in his narrowness upright, and fond, I truly believed it, of his wife. And I could not let her break her marriage — do you not see, Franz,— if it were for my sake. I could not see her young life ruined in its dawn. I wished to write to my good friend Mrs. Forrester — who is also Karen's friend, and his, and I offered myself as intermediary, as intercessor from him to Karen, if need be. Was it so black, my fault? For it was this that Karen resented so cruelly, Franz. Our Karen can be harsh and quick, you know that, Franz. But no! Can she — can you, believe for one moment that I would now have her return to him, if, indeed, it were any longer possible? No, Franz; no; no; no; Karen shall never see that man again. Only over my dead body should he pass to her. I swear it, not only to you, but to myself. And Franz, dear Franz, what I think of now is you, and your love and loyalty to my Karen. You have saved her; you have saved me; it is life you bring — a new life, Franz," and smiling upon him, her cheeks still wet with tears, she softly sang Tristan's phrase to Kurvenal: *" Holder! Treuer! — wie soll dir Tristan danken!"*

Her joy, her ecstasy of gratitude, shone upon him. She was the tutelary goddess of his family. Trust, for himself and for his loved Karen, went out to her and took refuge beneath the great wings she spread. And as she held his hands and smiled upon him he told her in his earnest, honest German, all that had happened to him and Karen; of his walking-tour; and of the meeting on the Falmouth headland at dawn; and of their journey here. "And one thing, *gnädige Frau*," he said, "that troubled me, but that will now be well, since you are come to us, is that I have told them here that Karen is my wife. See you, *gnädige Frau,* the good landlady knows us all and knows that Lotta, Minna and Elizabeth are the only daughters that the Mütterchen has — besides the little ones. I remembered that the Mütterchen had told her this; she talked much with her; it was but three years ago, *gnädige Frau;* it was not time enough for a very little one to grow up; so I could not say that Karen was my sister; and I have to be much with her; I sit beside her all through the night — for she is afraid to be alone, the *armes Kind;* and the good landlady and the maid must sleep. So it seemed to me that it was right to tell them that Karen was my wife. You think so, too, *nicht wahr, gnädige Frau?*"

Madame von Marwitz had listened, her deeply smiling eyes following, understanding all; and as the last phase of the story came they deepened to only a greater sweetness. They showed no surprise. A content almost blissful shone on Franz Lipp-heim.

"It is well, Franz," she said. "Yes, you have done rightly. All is well; more well than you yet perhaps see. Karen is safe, and Karen shall be free. What has happened is God-sent. The situation is in our hands."

For a further moment, silent and weighty, she gazed at him and then she added: "There need be no fear for you and Karen. I will face all pain and difficulty for you both. You are to marry Karen, Franz."

The shuttle that held the great gold thread of her plan was thrown. She saw the pattern stretch firm and fair before her. Silently and sweetly, with the intentness of a sibyl who pours and holds forth a deep potion, she smiled at him across the table.

Franz, who all this time had been leaning on his arms, his hands in hers, his eyes, through their enlarging pince-nez, fixed on her, did not move for some moments after the astounding statement reached him. His stillness and his look of arrested stupor suggested, indeed, a large blue-bottle slung securely in the subtle threads of a spider's web and reduced to torpid acquiescence by the spider's stealthy ministrations. He gazed with mildness, almost with blandness, upon the enchantress, as if some prodigy of nature overtopping all human power of comment had taken place before him. Then in a small, feeble voice he said: "*Wass meinen Sie, gnädige Frau?*"

"Dear, dear Franz," Madame von Marwitz murmured, pressing his hands with maternal solicitude, and thus giving him more time to adjust himself to his situation. "It is not as strange as your humility finds it. And it is now inevitable. You do not I think realize the position in which you and Karen are placed. I am not the only witness; the landlady, the doctor, the maid, and who knows who else,— all will testify that you have been here with Karen as your wife, that you have been with her day and night. Do not imagine that Mr. Jardine has sought to take Karen back or would try to. He has made no movement to get her back. He has most completely acquiesced in their estrangement. And when he hears that she has fled with you, that she has passed here, for a week almost, as your wife, he will be delighted — but delighted, with all his anger against you — to seize the opportunity for divorcing her and setting himself free."

But while she spoke Franz's large and ruddy face had paled. He had drawn his hands from hers though she tried to retain them. He rose from his chair. "But, *gnädige Frau,*" he said, "that is not right. No; that is wrong. He may not divorce Karen."

"How will you prevent him from divorcing her, Franz?" Madame von Marwitz returned, holding him with her eye, while, in great agitation, he passed his hand repeatedly over his forehead and hair. "You have been seen. I have been told by those who had seen you that you and Karen were here. Already Karen's husband must know it. And if you could prevent it, would you wish to, Franz? Would you wish, if you could, to bind her to this man for life? Try to think clearly, my friend.

It is Karen's happiness that hangs in the balance. It is upon
that that we must fix our eyes. My faith forbids divorce; but
I am not *dévote,* and Karen is not of my faith, nor is her
husband, nor are you. I take my stand beside Karen. I say
that one so young, so blameless, so unfortunate, shall not have
her life wrecked by one mistake. With me as your champion
you and Karen can afford to snap your fingers at the world's
gross verdict. Karen will be with me. I will take her abroad.
I will cherish her as never child was cherished. We make no
defence. In less than a year the case is over. Then you will
come for Karen and you will be married from my house. I
will give Karen a large dot; she shall want for nothing in her
life. And you and she will live in Germany, with your friends
and your great music, and your babies, Franz. What I had
hoped for two years ago shall come to pass and this bad dream
shall be forgotten."

Franz, looking dazedly about him while she spoke, now
dropped heavily on his chair and joining his hands before his
eyes leaned his head upon them. He muttered broken ejacula-
tions. *"Ach Gott! Unbegreiflich!* Such happiness is not to
think on! You are kind, kind, *gnädige Frau.* You believe that
all is for the best. But Karen — *gnädige Frau,* our little
Karen! She does not love me. How could she be happy with
me? Never for one moment have I hoped. It was against
my wish that the Mütterchen wrote to you that time two years
ago. No; always I saw it; she had kindness only for me and
friendliness; but no love; never any love. And it will be to
smirch our Karen's name, *gnädige Frau.* It will be to accept
disgrace for her. We must defend her from this accusation,
for it is not true. Ah, *gnädige Frau,* you are powerful in the
world. Can you not make it known that it is untrue, that
Karen did not come to me?"

He leaned his forehead on his clasped hands, protesting, ap-
pealing, expostulating, and Madame von Marwitz, leaning
slightly back in her chair, resting her cheek against her finger,
scrutinized his bent head with a change of expression. Intently, almost fiercely, with half-closed lids, she examined

Franz's crisp upstanding hair, the thick rims of his ruddy ears, the thick fingers with their square and rather dirty nails and the large turquoise that adorned one of them. Cogitation, self-control and fierce determination were in her gaze; then it veiled itself again in gentleness and, with a steady and insistent patience, she said: "You are astray, my friend, much astray, and very ignorant. Look with me at fact, and then say, if you can, that we can make it known that it is untrue. You are known to be in love with Karen; you are known to have asked me for her hand. Karen makes a marriage that is unhappy; it is known that she is not happy with her husband. Did you not yourself see that all was not well with them? It has been known for long. You arrive in London; Karen sees you again; next day she flies from Mr. Jardine and takes refuge with you at your lodgings. Yes, you will say, but your mother, your sisters, too, were there. Yes, the world will answer, and she came to me to wait till they were gone and you free to join her. In a fortnight's time she seizes a pretext for leaving me — I speak of what the world will say Franz — and meets you. Will the world, will Karen's husband, believe that it was by chance? She is found hidden with you here, those who see you come to me; it is so I find you, and she is here bearing your name. Come, my friend, it is no question of saving Karen from smirches; the world will say that it is your duty as an honourable man to marry Karen. Better that she should be known as your wife than as your abandoned mistress. So speaks the world, Franz. And though we know that it speaks falsely we have no power to undeceive it. But now, mark me, my friend; I have no wish to undeceive it. I do not see the story, told even in these terms, as disgraceful; I do not see my Karen smirched. I am not one who weighs the human heart and its needs in the measures of convention. Bravely and in truth, Karen frees herself. So be it. You say that she does not love you. I say, Franz, how do you know that? I say that if she does not love you yet, she will love you; and I add, Franz, for the full ease of your conscience, that if Karen, when she is free, does not wish to marry you, then — it is very simple

—she remains with me and does not marry. But what I ask of you now is bravery and discretion, for our Karen's sake. She must be freed; in your heart you know that it is well that Karen should be freed. In your heart you know that Karen must not be bound till death to this man she loathes and dreads and will never see again. If not you, Franz, is it not possible that Karen may love another man one day? But it is you that she will love; nay, it is you she loves. I know my Karen's heart. Tell me, Franz, am I not right in what I say?"

For some time now Franz had been looking at her and her voice grew more tender and more soft as she saw that he found no word of protest. He sat upright, still, at intervals, running his fingers through his hair, breathing deeply, near tears, yet arrested and appeased. And hope, beautiful, strange hope, linking itself to the intuitions of the dawn when he had sat above Karen's sleep, stole into his heart. Why could it not be true? Why should not Karen come to love him? She would be with him, free, knowing how deep and tender was his love for her, and that it made no claim. Would not her heart answer his one day? And as if guessing at his thoughts Madame von Marwitz added, the dimness of tears in her own eyes: "See, my Franz, let it be in this wise. I bring Karen to your mother in a few days; she will be strong enough for travel in a few days, is it not so? She will then be with you and yours in Germany, and I watching over you. So you will see her from day to day? So you will gently mend the torn young heart and come to read it. And you may trust a wise old woman, Franz, when I prophesy to you that Karen's heart will turn and grow to yours. You may trust one wise in hearts when she tells you that Karen is to be your loving wife."

She rose, and the sincerity of her voice was unfeigned. She was moved, deeply moved, by the beauty of the pattern she wove. She was deeply convinced by her own creation.

Franz, too, got up, stumbling.

"And now, Franz," she said, "we say *au revoir*. I have come and it is not seemly that you remain here longer. You go to Germany to make ready for us and I write to your mother to-day. Ah!—the dear Lise! Her heart will rejoice! Where is your room, Franz, and where is Karen's?"

There were three doors in the little sitting-room. She had entered from the passage by one. She looked now towards the others.

Franz opened one, it showed a flight of stairs. "Karen's room is up those stairs," he said, closing it very softly. "And mine is here, next this one where we are. We are very quiet, you see, and shut in to ourselves. There is no other way to Karen's room but this, and her room is at the back, so that no disturbance reaches her. I think that she still sleeps, *gnädige Frau;* we must not wake her if she sleeps. I will take you to her as soon as she is awake."

Madame von Marwitz, with her unchanging smile, was pressing him towards the door of his own room.

"I will wait. I will wait until she wakes, Franz. Your luggage? It is here? I will help you to pack, my Franz."

She had drawn him into his room, her arm passed into his, and, even while she spoke, she pointed out the few effects scattered here and there. And, with his torpid look of a creature hypnotized, Franz obeyed her, taking from her hands the worn brush, the shaving appliances, the socks and book and nightshirt.

When all were laid together in his knapsack and he had drawn the straps, he turned to her, still with the dazzled gaze. "But this may wait," he said, "until I have said good-bye to Karen."

Madame von Marwitz looked at him with an almost musing sweetness. She had the aspect of a conjuror who, with a last light puff of breath or touch of a magic finger, puts forth the final resource of a stupefying dexterity. So delicately, so softly, with a calm that knew no doubt or hesitation, she shook her head. "No; no farewells, now, my Franz. That would not be well. That would agitate her. She could not listen to all our story. She could not understand. Later, when she is in my arms, at peace, I will tell her all and that you are gone to wait for us, and give her your adieu."

He gazed at the conjuror. "But, *gnädige Frau,* may I not

say good-bye to Karen? Together we could tell her. It will be strange to her to wake and find that I am gone."

Her arm was passed in his again. She was leading him through the sitting-room. And she repeated with no change of voice: "No, my Franz. I know these illnesses. A little agitation is very bad. You will write to her daily. She shall have your letters, every day. You promise me — but I need not ask it of our Franz — to write. In three days, or in four, we will be with you."

She had got him out of his room, out of the sitting-room, into the passage. The cab still waited, the cabman dozed on his box in the spring sunlight. Before the landlady Madame von Marwitz embraced Franz and kissed and blessed him. She kept an arm round him till she had him at the cab-door. She almost lifted him in.

"You will tell Karen — that you did not find it right — that I should say good-bye to her," he stammered.

And with a last long pressure of the hand she said: "I will tell her, Franz. We will talk much of you, Karen and I. Trust me, I am with you both. In my hands you are safe."

The cab rolled away and Franz's face, from under the round hat and the quill, looked back at the triumphant conjuror, dulled and dazed rather than elated, by the spectacle of her inconceivable skill.

CHAPTER XLIII

KAREN lay sleeping in the little room above. She had slept so much since they had carried her, Franz, and the two women with kind faces, into this little room; deep draughts of sleep, as though her exhausted nature could never rest enough. Fever still drowsed in her blood and a haze of half delirious visions often accompanied her waking. They seemed to gather round her now, as, in confused and painful dreams, she rose from the depths towards consciousness again. Dimly she heard the sound of voices and her dream wove them into images of fear and sorrow.

She was running along the cliff-top. She had run for miles and it was night and beside her yawned the black gulfs of the cliff-edge. And from far below, in the darkness, she heard a voice wailing as if from some creature lost upon the rocky beach. It was Gregory in some great peril. Pity and fear beat upon her like black wings as she ran, and whether it was to escape him or to succour him she did not know.

Then from the waking world came distinctly the sound of rolling wheels, and opening her eyes she looked out upon her room, its low uneven ceiling, its coloured print of Queen Victoria over the mantelpiece, its text above the washhand-stand and chest of drawers. On the little table beside her bed Onkel Ernst's watch ticked softly. The window was open and a tree rustled outside. And through these small, familiar sounds she still heard the rolling of retreating wheels. The terror of her dream fastened upon this sound until another seemed to strike, like a soft, stealthy blow, upon her consciousness.

Footsteps were mounting the stairs to her room. Not Franz's footsteps, nor the doctor's, nor the landlady's, nor Annie the housemaid's. She knew all these.

Who was it then who mounted, softly rustling, towards her?

The terror of the dream vanished in a tense, frozen panic of actuality.

She wished to scream, and could not; she wished to leap up and fly, but there was no way of escape. It was Tante who came, slowly, softly, rustling in silken fabrics; the very scent of her garments seemed wafted before her, and Karen's heart stopped in its heavy beating as the door handle gently turned and Tante stood within the room.

Karen looked at her and Madame von Marwitz looked back, and Madame von Marwitz's face was almost as white as the death-like face on the pillow. She said no word, nor did Karen, and in the long stillness delirium again flickered through Karen's brain, and Tante, standing there, became a nightmare presence, dead, gazing, immutable. Then she moved again, and the slow, soft moving was more dreadful than the stillness, and coming forward Tante fell on her knees beside the bed and hid her face in the bedclothes.

Karen gave a strange hoarse cry. She heard herself crying, and the sound of her own voice seemed to waken her again to reality: "Franz! Franz! Franz!"

Madame von Marwitz was weeping; her large white shoulders shook with sobs. "Karen," she said, "forgive me! Karen, it is I. Forgive me!"

"Franz!" Karen repeated, turning her head away on the pillow.

"Karen, you know me?" said Madame von Marwitz. She had lifted her head and she gazed through her tears at the strange, changed, yet so intimately known, profile. It was as if Karen were the more herself, reduced to the bare elements of personality; rocky, wasted, alienated. "Do not kill me, my child," she sobbed, "Listen to me, Karen! I have come to explain all, and to implore for your forgiveness." She possessed herself of one of the hot, emaciated hands. Karen drew it away, but she turned her head towards her.

Tante's tears, her words and attitude of abjection, dispersed the nightmare horror. She understood that Tante had come not as a ghastly wraith; not as a pursuing fury; but as a suppliant.

Her eyes rested on her guardian and their gaze, now, was like cold, calm daylight. "Why are you here?" she asked.

Madame von Marwitz's sobs, at this, broke forth more violently. "You remember our parting, my child! You remember my mad and shameful words! How could I not come!" she articulated brokenly. "Oh, I have sought you in terror, in unspeakable longing! My child — it was a madness. Did you not see it? I went to you at dawn that day to kneel before you, as I kneel now, and to implore your pardon. And you were gone! Oh, Karen — you will listen to me now!"

"You need not tell me," said Karen. "I understand."

"Ah, no: ah, no:" said Madame von Marwitz, laying her supplicating hand on the sleeve of Karen's nightdress. "You do not understand. How could you — young and cold and flawless — understand my heart, my wild, stained heart, Karen, my fierce and desolate and broken heart. You are air and water; I am earth and fire; how could you understand my darkness and my rage?" She spoke, sobbing, with a sincerity dreadful and irrefragable, as if she stripped herself and showed a body scarred and burning. With all the forces of her nature she threw herself on Karen's pity, tearing from herself, with a humility far above pride and shame, the glamour that had held Karen's heart to hers. Deep instinct guided her spontaneity. Her glamour, now, must consist in having none; her nobility must consist in abasement, her greatness in being piteous.

"Listen to me, Karen," she sobbed, "The world knows but one side of me — you have known but one side; — even Tallie, who knows so much, who understands so much — does not know the other — the dark and tortured soul. I am not a good woman, Karen, the blood that flows in my veins is tainted, ambiguous. I have sinned. I have been savage and dastardly; but it has always been in a madness when I could not seize my better self: flames seem to sweep me on. Listen, Karen, you are so strong, so calm, how could you dream of what a woman's last wild passion can be, a woman whose whole soul is passion? Love! it is all that I have craved. Love! love! all my inner life has been enmeshed in it — in craving, in seek-

ing, in destroying. It is like a curse upon me, Karen. You
will not understand; yet that love of love, is it not so with all
us wretched women; do we not long, always, all of us, for the
great flame to which we may surrender, the flame that will ap-
pease and exalt us, annihilate us, yet give us life in its suprem-
acy? So I have always longed; and not grossly; mine has
never been the sensual passion; it has been beauty and the heights
of life that I have sought. And my curse has been that for me
has come no appeasement, no exaltation, but only, always, a
dark smouldering of joylessness. With my own hand I broke
the great and sacred devotion that blessed my life, because I was
thus cursed. Jealousy, the craving for a more complete possession, for the ecstasy I had not found, blind forces in my blood,
drove me on to the destruction of that precious thing. I wrecked
myself, I killed him. Oh, Karen, you know of whom I speak."
Convulsively, the blackness of her memories assailing her in their
old forms of horror, Madame von Marwitz sobbed, burying her
face in the bed-clothes, her hand forgetting to clutch at Karen's
sleeve. She lifted her face and the tears streamed from under
her closed lids. " Let me not think of it or I shall go mad.
How could I, having known that devotion, sink to the place
where you have seen me? Be pitiful. He needed me so much
— I believed. My youth was fading; I was growing old. Soon
the time was to come when no man's heart would turn to me.
Be pitiful. You do not know what it is to look without and see
life slowly growing dark and look within and see only sinister
memories. It came to me like late sunlight — like cool, sweet
water — his love. I believed in it. I loved him. Oh —" she
sobbed, " how I loved him, Karen! How my heart was torn
with sick jealousy when I saw that his had turned from me to
you. I loved you, Karen, yet I hated you. Open your generous
heart to me, my child; do not spurn me from you. Understand how it may be that one can strike at the thing one loves.
I knew myself in the grasp of an evil passion, but I could not
tear it from me. I even feared, with a savage fear that seemed
to eat into my brain, that you responded to his love. Oh, Karen,
it was not I who spoke those shameful words, when I found

you with him, but a creature maddened with pain and jealousy, who for days had fought against her madness and knew when she spoke that she was mad. When I had sent him from me, when he was gone from my life, and I knew that all was over, the evil fury passed from my brain like a mist. I knew myself again. I saw again the sweet and sacred places of my life. I saw you, Karen. Oh, my child," again the pleading hand trembled on Karen's sleeve, " it has not all been misplaced, your love for me; not all illusion. I am still the woman who has loved you through so many years. You will not let one hour of frenzy efface our happy years together?"

The words, the sobbing questions that waited for no answer, the wailing supplications, had been poured forth in one great upwelling. Through the tears that streamed she had seen Karen's face in blurred glimpses, lying in profile to her on its pillow. Now, when all had been said and her mind was empty, waiting, she passed her hand over her eyes, clearing them of tears, and fixed them on Karen.

And silence followed. So long a silence that wonder came. Had she understood? Was she half unconscious? Had all the long appeal been wasted?

But Karen at last spoke and the words, in their calm, seemed to the listening woman to pass like a cold wind over buds and tendrils of reviving life, blighting them.

" I am sorry for you," said Karen. " And I understand."

Madame von Marwitz stared at her for another silent moment. " Yes," she then said, " you are sorry for me. You understand. It is my child's great heart. And you forgive me, Karen?"

Again came silence; then, restlessly turning her head as if the effort to think pained her, Karen said, " What do you mean by forgiveness?"

" I mean pity, Karen," said Madame von Marwitz. " And compassion, and tenderness. To be forgiven is to be taken back."

" Taken back?" Karen repeated. " But I do not feel that I love you any longer." She spoke in a dull, calm voice.

Madame von Marwitz remained kneeling for some moments

longer. Then a dark flush mounted to her face. She became aware that her knees were stiff with kneeling and her cheeks salt with tears. Her head ached and a feeling of nausea made her giddy. She rose and looked about her with dim eyes.

A small wooden chair stood against the wall at a little distance from the bed. She went to it and sank down upon it, and leaning her head upon her hand she wept softly to herself. Her desolation was extreme.

Karen listened to her for a long time, and without any emotion. Now that the horror had passed, her only feeling was one of sorrow and oppression. She was very sorry for the weeping woman; but she wished that she would go away. And her mind at last wandered from the thought of Tante. "Where is Franz?" she asked.

The fount of Madame von Marwitz's tears was exhausted. She dried her eyes and cheeks. She blew her nose. She gathered together her thoughts. "Karen," she said, "I will not speak of myself. You say that you do not love me. I can only pray that my love for you may in time win you to me again. Never again, I know it, can I stand before you, untarnished, as I stood before; but I will trust my child's deep heart as strength once more comes to her. Pity will grow to love. I will love you; that will be enough. But I have come to you not only as a mother to her child. I have come to you as a friend to whom your welfare is of the first importance. I have much to say to you, Karen."

Madame von Marwitz rose. She went to the washhand-stand and bathed her face. The triumph that she had held in her hand seemed melting through her fingers; but, thinking rapidly and deeply, she drew the scattered threads of the plan together once more, faced her peril and computed her resources.

The still face on the pillow was unchanged, its eyes still calmly closed. She could not attempt to take the hand of this alien Karen, nor even to touch her sleeve. She went back to her chair.

"Karen," she said, "if you cannot love me, you can still think of me as your friend and counsellor. I am glad to hear you

speak of our Franz. That lights my way. I have had much
talk with our good and faithful Franz. Together we have faced
all that there is of difficult and sad to face. My child shall
be spared all that could trouble her. Franz and I are beside
you through it all. Your husband, Karen, is to divorce you
because of Franz. You are to be set free, my child."

A strange thing happened then. If Madame von Marwitz had
plunged a dagger into Karen's heart, the change that transformed her deathly face could hardly have been more violent.
It was as if all the amazed and desperate life fled to her eyes
and lips and cheeks. Colour flooded her. Her eyes opened and
shone. Her lips parted, trembled, uttered a loud cry. She
turned her head and looked at her guardian. Her dream was
with her. What was that loud cry for help, hers or his?

Madame von Marwitz looked back and her face, too, was
changed. Realizations, till then evaded, flashed over it as
though from Karen's it caught the bright up-flaming of the
truth. Fear followed, darkening it. Karen's truth threatened
the whole fabric of the plan, threatened her life in all that
it held of value. Resentment for a moment convulsed it. Then,
with a steady mastery, yet the glance, sunken, sickened, of one
who holds off disabling pity while he presses out a fluttering
life beneath his hand, she said: "Yes, my child. Your wild
adventure is known. You have been here for days and nights
with this young man who loves you and he has given you his
name. Your husband seizes the opportunity to free himself.
Can you not rejoice, Karen, that it is to set you free also? It
is of that only that I have thought. I have rejoiced for you.
And I have told Franz that I will stand by you and by him
so that no breath of shame or difficulty shall touch you. In
me you have the staunchest friend."

Madame von Marwitz, while she addressed these remarks to
the strange, vivid face that stared at her with wide and shining
eyes, was aware of a sense of nausea and giddiness so acute that
she feared she might succumb to sickness. She put her hand
before her eyes, reflecting that she must have some food if she
were to think clearly. She sat thus for some moments, strug-

gling against the invading weakness. When she looked up
again, the flame whose up-leaping had so arrested her, which
had, to be just, so horrified her, was fallen to ashes.

Karen's eyes were closed. A bitter composure, like that sometimes seen on the face of the dead, folded her lips.

Madame von Marwitz, suddenly afraid, rose and went to her
and stooped over her. And, for a dreadful moment, she did not
know whether it was with fear or hope that she scanned the
deathly face. Abysses of horror seemed to fall within her as she
thus bent over Karen and wondered whether she had died.

It had been a foolish fear. The child had not even fainted.
Madame von Marwitz's breath came back to her, almost in a
sob, as, not opening her eyes, Karen repeated her former question: "Where is Franz?"

"He will be back soon; Franz will soon be here," said Madame
von Marwitz gently and soothingly.

"I must see him," said Karen.

"You shall. You shall see him, my Karen," said Madame
von Marwitz. "You are with those who love you. Have no
fear. Franz is of my mind in this matter, Karen. You will not
wish to defend yourself against your husband's suit, is it not
so? Defence, I fear, my Karen, would be useless. The chain of
evidence against you is complete. But even if it were not, if
there were defence to make, you would not wish to sue to your
husband to take you back?"

Karen still with closed eyes, turned her head away on the pillow. "Let him be free," she said. "He knows that I wished
him to be free. When I left him I told him that I hoped to
set him free. Let him believe that I have done so."

Madame von Marwitz still leaned above her and, as when
Franz had imparted the unlooked-for tidings of Karen's
reticence, so now her eyes dilated with a deepened hope.

"You told him so, Karen?" she repeated gently, after a
moment.

"Yes," said Karen, "I told him so. I shall make no defence.
Will you go now? I am tired. And will you send Franz to me
when he comes back?"

"Yes, my child; yes," said Madame von Marwitz. "It is well. I will be below. I will watch over you." She raised herself at last. "There is nothing that I can do for you, my Karen?"

"Nothing," said Karen. Her voice, too, seemed sinking into ashes.

Madame von Marwitz opened the door to the dark little staircase and closed it. In the cloaking darkness she paused and leaned against the wall. *"Bon Dieu!"* she murmured to herself *"Bon Dieu!"*

She felt sick. She wished to sleep. But she could not sleep yet. She must eat and restore her strength. And she had letters to write; a letter to Mrs. Forrester, a letter to Frau Lippheim, and a note to Tallie. It was as if she had thrown her shuttle across a vast loom that, drawing her after the thread she held, enmeshed her now with all the others in its moving web. She no longer wove; she was being woven into the pattern. Even if she would she could not extricate herself.

The thought of this overmastering destiny sustained and fortified her. She went on down the stairs and into the little sitting-room.

CHAPTER XLIV

THE days that passed after her arrival at the inn were to live in Madame von Marwitz's memory as a glare of intolerable anxiety, obliterating all details in its heat and urgency. She might, during the hours when she knelt supplicating beside Karen's bed, have been imaged as a furnace and Karen as a corpse lying in it, strangely unconsumed, passive and unresponsive. There was no cruelty in Karen's coldness, no unkindness even. Pity and comprehension were there; but they were rocks against which Madame von Marwitz dashed herself in vain.

When she would slip from her kneeling position and lie grovelling and groaning on the ground, Karen sometimes would say: "Please get up. Please don't cry," in a tone of distress. But when the question, repeated in every key, came: "Karen, will you not love me again?" Karen's answer was a helpless silence.

Schooling the fury of her eagerness, and in another mood, Madame von Marwitz, after long cogitations in the little sitting-room, would mount to point out to Karen that to persist in her refusal to marry Franz, when she was freed, would be to disgrace herself and him, and to this Karen monotonously and immovably would reply that she would not marry Franz.

Madame von Marwitz had not been able to keep from her beyond the evening of the first day that Franz had gone. " To Germany, my Karen, where he will wait for you." Karen's eyes had dwelt widely, but dully, on her when she made this announcement and she had spoken no word; nor had she made any comment on Madame von Marwitz's further explanations.

"He felt it right to go at once, now that I had come, and bring no further scandal on your head. He would not have you waked to say good-bye."

411

Karen lay silent, but the impassive bitterness deepened on her lips. When Franz's first letter to Karen arrived Madame von Marwitz opened, read and destroyed it. It revealed too plainly, in its ingenuous solicitude and sorrow, the coercion under which Franz had departed. Yes; the plan was there and they were all enmeshed in it; but what was to happen if Karen would not marry Franz? How could that be made to match the story she had now written to Mrs. Forrester? And what was to happen if Karen refused to come with her? It would not do, Madame von Marwitz saw that clearly, for an alienated Karen to be taken to the Lippheims'. Comparisons and disclosures would ensue that would send the loom, with a mighty whirr, weaving rapidly in an opposite direction to that of the plan. Franz, in Germany, must be pacified, and Karen be carried off to some lovely, lonely spot until the husband's suit was safely won. It was not fatal to the plan that Karen should be supposed, finally, to refuse to marry Franz; that might be mitigated, explained away when the time came; but a loveless Karen at large in the world was a figure only less terrifying than a Karen reunited to her husband. She felt as if she had drawn herself up from the bottom of the well where Karen's flight had precipitated her and as if, breathing the air, seeing the light of the happy world, she swung in a circle, clutching her wet rope, horrible depths below her and no helping hand put out to draw her to the brink.

Gregory's letter in answer to the letter she had sent to Mrs. Forrester, with the request that he should be informed of its contents, came on the second morning. It fortified her. There was no questioning; no doubt. He formally assured her that he would at once take steps to set Karen free.

"Ah, he does not love her, that is evident," said Madame von Marwitz to herself, and with a sense of quieted pulses. The letter was shown to Karen.

Mrs. Forrester's note was not quite reassuring. It, also, accepted her story; but its dismay constituted a lack of sympathy, even, Madame von Marwitz felt, a reproach.

She wrote of Gregory's broken heart. She lamented the breach that had come between him and Karen and made this disaster possible.

Miss Scrotton's pæan was what it inevitably would be. From Tallie came no word, and this implied that Tallie, too, was convinced, though Tallie, no doubt, was furious, and would, as usual, lay the blame on her.

Danger, however, lurked in Tallie's direction, and until she was safely out of England with Karen she should not feel herself secure. Pertinaciously and blandly she insisted to the doctor that Frau Lippheim was now quite well enough to make a short sea voyage. She would secure the best of yachts and the best of trained nurses, and a little voyage would be the very thing for her. The doctor was recalcitrant, and Madame von Marwitz was in terror lest, during the moments they spent by her bedside, Karen should burst forth in a sudden appeal to him.

A change for the worse, very much for the worse, had, he said, come over his patient. He was troubled and perplexed. "Has anything happened to disturb her?" he asked in the little sitting-room, and something in his chill manner reminded her unpleasantly of Gregory Jardine;—"her husband's sudden departure?"

Madame von Marwitz felt it advisable, then, to take the doctor into her confidence. He grew graver as she spoke. He looked at her with eyes more scrutinizing, more troubled and more perplexed. But, reluctantly, he saw her point. The unfortunate young woman upstairs, a fugitive from her husband, must be spared the shock of a possible brutal encounter. Perhaps, in a day or two, it might be possible to move her. She could be taken in her bed to Southampton and carried on board the yacht.

Madame von Marwitz wired at once and secured the yacht.

It was after this interview with the doctor, after the sending of the wire, that she mounted the staircase to Karen's room with the most difficult part of her task still before her. She had as yet not openly broached to Karen the question of what the immediate future should be. She approached it now by a circuitous way, seating herself near Karen's bed and unfolding and handing

to her a letter she had that morning received from Franz. It
was a letter she could show. Franz was in Germany.

" The dear Franz. The good Franz," Madame von Marwitz
mused, when Karen had finished and her weak hand dropped with
the letter to the sheet. " No woman had ever a truer friend than
Franz. You see how he writes, Karen. He will never trouble
you with his hopes."

" No; Franz will never trouble me," said Karen.

" Poor Franz," Madame von Marwitz repeated. " He will be
seen by the world as a man who refuses to marry his mistress
when she is freed."

" I am not his mistress," said Karen, who, for all her apathy,
could show at moments a disconcerting vehemence.

" You will be thought so, my child."

" Not by him," said Karen.

" No; not by him," Madame von Marwitz assented with
melancholy.

" Not by his mother and sisters," said Karen. " And not by
Mrs. Talcott."

" Nor by me, my Karen," said Madame von Marwitz with a
more profound gloom.

" No; not by you. No one who knows me will think so,"
said Karen.

Madame von Marwitz paused after this for a few moments.
Experience had taught her that to abandon herself to her grief
was not the way to move Karen. When she spoke again it was
in a firm, calm voice.

" Listen, my Karen," she said. " I see that you are fixed in
this resolve and I will plead with you no further. I will weary
you no more. Remember only, in fairness, that it is for your
sake that I have pleaded. You will be divorced; so be it. And
you will not marry Franz. But after this Karen? and until
this ? "

Karen lay silent for a moment and then turned her head restlessly away.

" Why do you ask me? How can I tell ? " she said. " I wish

to go to Frau Lippheim. When I am well again I wish to work
and make my living."

"But, my Karen," said Madame von Marwitz with great
gentleness, " do you not see that for you to go to Franz's mother
now, in her joy and belief in you, is a cruelty? Later on, yes ;
you could then perhaps go to her, though it will be at any time,
with this scandal behind you, to place our poor Lise, our poor
Franz, in an ambiguous position indeed. But now, Karen?
While the case is going on? Your husband says, you remember, that he starts proceedings at once."

Karen lay still. And suddenly the tears ran down her cheeks.
"Why cannot I see Franz?" she said. "Why do you ask me
questions that I cannot answer? How do I know what I shall
do?" She sobbed, quick, dry, alarming sobs.

"Karen — my Karen," Madame von Marwitz murmured, " do
not weep, my dear one. You exhaust yourself. Do not speak so
harshly to me, Karen. Will you let me think for you? See, my
child, I accept all. I ask for nothing. You do not forgive me
— oh, not truely — you do not love me. Our old life is dead.
I have killed it with my own hand. I see it all, Karen. And
I accept my doom. But even so, can you not be merciful to
me and let me help you now? Do not break my heart, my child.
Do not crush me down into the dust. Come with me. I will
take you to quiet and beautiful shores. I will trouble you in
nothing. There will be no more pleading; no more urgency.
You shall do as it pleases you in all things, and I will ask only
to watch over you. Let me do this until you are free and can
choose your own life. Do not tell me that you hate me so much
that you will not do this for me."

Her voice was weighted with its longing, its humility, its
tenderness. The sound of it seemed to beat its way to Karen
through mists that lay about her as Tante's cries and tears had
not done. A sharper thrust of pity pierced her. "I do not
hate you," she said. "You must not think that. I understand
and I am very sorry. But I do not love you. I shall not love
you again. And how could I come with you? You said — what

did you say that night?" She put her hand before her eyes
in the effort of memory. "That I was ungrateful; — that you
fed and clothed me; — that I took all and gave nothing. And
other, worse things; you said them to me. How can that be
again? How could I come with a person who said those things
to me?"

"Oh — but — my child —" Madame von Marwitz's voice
trembled in its hope and fear, though she restrained herself from
rising and bending to the girl: "did I not make you believe me
when I told you that I was mad? Do you not know that the vile
words were the weapons I took up against you in my madness?
That you gave nothing, Karen? When you are my only stay in
life, the only thing near me in the world — you and Tallie — the
thing that I have thought of as mine — as if you were my child.
And if you came to me now you would give still more. If it is
known that you will not return — that you will not forgive me
and come with me — I am disgraced, my child. All the world
will believe that I have been cruel to you. All the world will
believe that you hate me and that hatred is all that I have deserved from you."

Karen again had put her hand to her head. "What do you
mean?" she questioned faintly. "Will it help you if I come
with you?"

Madame von Marwitz steadied her voice that now shook with
rising sobs. "If you will not come I am ruined."

"You ask to have me to come — though I do not love you?"

"I ask you to come — on any terms, my Karen. And because
I love you; because you will always be the thing dearest in the
world to me."

"I could go to Frau Lippheim, if you would help to send me
to her," said Karen, still holding her hand to her head; "I
could, I am sure, explain to her and to Franz so that they would
not blame me. But people must not think that I hate you."

"No; no?" Madame von Marwitz hardly breathed.

"They must not think that; for it is not true. I do not love
you, but I have no hatred for you," said Karen.

"You will come then, Karen?"

Still with her eyes hidden the girl hesitated as if bewildered by the pressure of new realisations. "You would leave me much alone? You would not talk to me? I should be quiet?"

"Oh, my Karen — quiet — quiet —" Madame von Marwitz was now sobbing. "You will send for me if you feel that you can see me; unless you send I do not obtrude myself on you. You will have an attendant of your own. All shall be as you wish."

"And when I am free I may choose my own life?"

"Free! free! the world before you! all that I have at your feet, to spurn or stoop to!" Tante moaned incoherently.

"When will it be — that we must go?" Karen then, more faintly, asked. Madame von Marwitz had risen to her feet. In her ecstasy of gladness she could have clapped her hands above her head and danced. And the strong control she put upon herself gave to her face almost the grimace of a child that masters its weeping. She was drawn from her well. She stood upon firm ground. "In two days, my child, if you are strong enough. In two days we will set sail."

"In two days," Karen repeated. And, dully, she repeated again; "I come with you in two days."

Madame von Marwitz now noticed that tears ran from under the hand. These tears of Karen's alarmed her. She had not wept at all before to-day.

"My child is worn and tired. She would rest. Is it not so? Shall I leave her?" she leaned above the girl to ask.

"Yes; I am tired," said Karen.

And leaning there, above the hidden face, above the heart wrung with its secret agony, in all her ecstasy and profound relief, Madame von Marwitz knew one of the bitterest moments of her life. She had gained safety. But what was her loss, her irreparable loss? In the dark little staircase she leaned, as on the day of her coming, against the wall, and murmured, as she had murmured then: *"Bon Dieu! Bon Dieu!"* But the words were broken by the sobs that, now uncontrollably, shook her as she stumbled on in the darkness.

CHAPTER XLV

SOME years had passed since Mrs. Talcott had been in London, and it seemed to her, coming up from her solitudes, noisier, more crowded, more oppressive than when she had seen it last. She had a jaded yet an acute eye for its various aspects, as she drove from Paddington towards St. James's, and a distaste, born of her many years of life in cities, took more definite shape in her, even while the excitement of the movement and uproar accompanied not inappropriately the strong impulses that moved her valorous soul.

Mrs. Talcott wore a small, round, black straw hat trimmed with a black bow. It was the shape that she had worn for years; it was unaffected by the weather and indifferent to the shifting of fashion. Her neck-gear was the one invariable with her in the day-time; a collar of lawn turned down over a black silk stock. About her shoulders was a black cloth cape. Sitting there in her hansom, she looked very old, and she looked also very national and typical; the adventurous, indomitable old girl of America, bent on seeing all that there was to see, emerged for the first time in her life from her provinces, and carrying, it might have been, a Baedeker under her arm.

It was many years since Mrs. Talcott had passed beyond the need of Baedekers, and her provinces were a distant memory; yet she, too, was engaged, like the old American girl, in the final adventure of her life. She did not know, as she drove along in her hansom with her shabby little box on the roof, whether she were ever to see Les Solitudes again.

"Carry it right up," she said to the porter at the mansions in St. James's when she arrived there. "I've come for the night, I expect."

The porter had told her that Mr. Jardine had come in. And he looked at Mrs. Talcott curiously.

418

At the door of Gregory's flat Mrs. Talcott encountered a check. Barker, mournful and low-toned as an undertaker, informed her firmly that Mr. Jardine was seeing nobody. He fixed an astonished eye upon Mrs. Talcott's box which was being taken from the lift.

"That 's all right," said Mrs. Talcott. "Mr. Jardine 'll see me. You tell him that Mrs. Talcott is here."

She had walked past Barker into the hall and her box was placed beside her.

Barker was very much disconcerted, yet he felt Mrs. Talcott to be a person of weight. He ushered her into the drawing-room.

In the late sunlight it was as gay and as crisp as ever, but for the lack of flowers, and the Bouddha still sat presiding in his golden niche.

"Mr. Jardine is in the smoking-room, Madam," said Barker, and, gauging still further the peculiar significance of this guest whose name he now recovered as one familiar to him on letters, he added in a low voice: "He has not used this room since Mrs. Jardine left us."

"Is that so?" said Mrs. Talcott gravely. "Well, you go and bring him here right away."

Mrs. Talcott stood in the centre of the room when Barker had gone and gazed at the Bouddha. And again her figure strongly suggested that of the sight-seer, unperturbed and adequate amidst strange and alien surroundings. Gregory found her before the Bouddha when he came in. If Mrs. Talcott had been in any doubt as to one of the deep intuitions that had, from the first, sustained her, Gregory's face would have reassured her. It had a look of suffocated grief; it was ravaged; it asked nothing and gave nothing; it was fixed on its one devouring preoccupation.

"How do you do, Mrs. Talcott," he said. They shook hands. His voice was curiously soft.

"I 've come up, you see," said Mrs. Talcott. "I 've come up to see you, Mr. Jardine."

"Yes?" said Gregory gently. He had placed a chair for her but, when she sat down, he remained standing. He did not, it was evident, imagine her errand to be one that would require a prolonged attention from him.

"Mr. Jardine," said Mrs. Talcott, "what was your idea when you first found out about Karen from the detective and asked me not to tell?"

Gregory collected his thoughts, with difficulty. "I don't know that I had any idea," he answered. "I was stunned. I wanted time to think."

"And you hoped it wasn't true, perhaps?"

"No; I hadn't any hope. I knew it was true. Karen had said things to me that made it nothing of a surprise. But perhaps my idea was that she would be sorry for what she had done and write to me, or to you. I think I wanted to give Karen time."

"Well, and then?" Mrs. Talcott asked. "If she had written?"

"Well, then, I'd have gone to her."

"You'd have taken her back?"

"If she would have come, of course," said Gregory, in his voice of wraith-like gentleness.

"You wanted her back if she'd gone off with another man like that and didn't love you any more?"

Gregory was silent for a moment and she saw that her persistence troubled and perplexed him.

"As to love," he said, "Karen was a child in some things. I believe that she would have grown to love me if her guardian hadn't come between us. And it might have been to escape from her guardian as well as with the idea of freeing herself from me that she took refuge with this man. I am convinced that her guardian behaved badly to her. It's rather difficult for me to talk to you, Mrs. Talcott," said Gregory, "though I am grateful for your kindness, because I so inexpressibly detest a person whom you care for."

"Mr. Jardine," said Mrs. Talcott, fixing her eyes upon him, "I want to say something right here, so as there shan't be any mistake about it. You were right about Mercedes, all along; do you take that in? I don't want to say any more about Mer-

cedes than I've got to; I've cut loose from my moorings, but
I guess I do care more about Mercedes than anyone's ever done
who's known her as well as I do.   But you were right about her.
And I'm your friend and I'm Karen's friend, and it pretty
near killed me when all this happened."

Gregory now had taken a chair before her and his eyes, with a
new look, gazed deeply into hers as she went on: "I wouldn't
have accepted what your letter said, not for a minute, if I hadn't
got Mercedes's next thing and if I hadn't seen that Mercedes, for
a wonder, wasn't telling lies.   I was a mighty sick woman, Mr.
Jardine, for a few days; I just seemed to give up.   But then I
got to thinking.   I got to thinking, and the more I thought the
more I couldn't lie there and take it.   I thought about Mercedes,
and what she's capable of; and I thought about you and how I
felt dead sure you loved Karen; and I thought about that poor
child and all she'd gone through; and the long and short of it
was that I felt it in my bones that Mercedes was up to mischief.
Karen sent for her, she said; but I don't believe Karen sent for
her; — I believe she got wind somehow of where Karen was and
lit out before I could stop her; yes, I was away that day, Mr.
Jardine, and when I came back I found that three ladies had
come for Mercedes and she'd made off with them.   It may be
true about Karen; she may have done this wicked thing; but
if she's done it I don't believe it's the way Mercedes says she
has.   And I've worked it out to this: you must see Karen, Mr.
Jardine; you must have it from her own mouth that she loves
Franz and wants to go off with him and marry him before you
give her up."

Gregory's face, as these last words were spoken, showed a delicate stiffening.   "She won't see me," he said.

"Who says so?" asked Mrs. Talcott.

"Don't imagine that I'd have accepted her guardian's word
for it," said Gregory, "but everything Madame von Marwitz has
written has been merely corroborative.   She told us that Karen
was there with this man and I knew it already.   She said that
Karen had begun to look to him as a rescuer from me on the
day she saw him here in London, and what I remembered of that

day bore it out. She said that I should remember that on the
night we parted Karen told me that she would try to set herself
free. Karen has confided in her; it was true. And it's true,
is n't it, that Karen was in terror of falling into my hands. You
can't deny this, can you? Why should I torture Karen and myself by seeing her?" said Gregory. He had averted his eyes as
he spoke.

"But do you want her back, Mr. Jardine?" Mrs. Talcott
had faced his catalogue of evidence immovably.

"Not if she loves this man," said Gregory. "And that's the
final fact. I know Karen; she could n't have done this unless
she loved him. The provocation was n't extreme enough otherwise. She would n't, from sheer generosity, disgrace herself to
free me, especially since she knew that I considered that that
would be to disgrace me, too. No; her guardian's story has all
the marks of truth on it. She loves the man and she had
planned to meet him. And all I've got to do now is to see that
she is free to marry him as soon as possible." He got up as he
spoke and walked up and down the room.

Mrs. Talcott's eye followed him and his despair seemed a fuel
to her faith. "Mr. Jardine," she said, after a moment of silence,
"I'll stake my life on it you're wrong. I know Karen better
than you do; I guess women understand each other better than
a man ever understands them. The bed-rock fact about a woman
is that she'll hide the thing she feels most and she'll say what
she hopes ain't true so as to give the man a chance for con-
vincing her it ain't true. And the blamed foolishness of the
man is that he never does. He just goes off, sick and mournful,
and leaves her to fight it out the best she can. Karen don't
love Franz Lippheim, Mr. Jardine; nothing'll make me believe
she loves him. And nothing'll make me believe but what you
could have got her to stay that time she left you if you'd understood women better. She loves you, Mr. Jardine, though
she may n't know it, and it's on the cards she knows it so well
that she's dead scared of showing it. Because Karen's a wife
through and through; can't you see it in her face? You're
youngish yet, and a man, so I don't feel as angry with you as

you deserve, perhaps, for not understanding better and for letting
Karen get it into her head you did n't love her any more; for
that 's what she believes, Mr. Jardine. And what I 'm as sure
of as that my name 's Hannah Talcott is that she 'll never get
over you. She 's that kind of woman; a rare kind; rocky; she
don't change. And if she 's gone and done this thing, like it appears she has, it is n't in the way Mercedes says; it 's only to
set you free and to get away from the fear of being handed
over to a man who don't love her. For she did n't understand,
either, Mr. Jardine. Women are blamed foolish in their way,
too."

Gregory had stopped in his walk and was standing before Mrs.
Talcott looking down at her; and while Mrs. Talcott fixed the
intense blue of her eyes upon him he became aware of an impression almost physical in its vividness. It was as if Mrs. Talcott
were the most wise, most skilful, most benevolent of doctors who,
by some miraculous modern invention, were pumping blood into
his veins from her own superabundance. It seemed to find its
way along hardened arteries, to creep, to run, to tingle; to spread
with a radiant glow through all his chilled and weary body.
Hope and fear mounted in him suddenly.

He could not have said, after that, exactly what happened, but
he could afterwards recall, brokenly, that he must have shed
tears; for his first distinct recollection was that he was leaning
against the end of the piano and that Mrs. Talcott, who had risen,
was holding him by the hand and saying: "There now, yes,
I guess you 've had a pretty bad time. You hang on, Mr. Jardine, and we 'll get her back yet."

He wanted to put his head on Mrs. Talcott's shoulder and be
held by her to her broad breast for a long time; but, since such
action would have been startlingly uncharacteristic of them both,
he only, when he could speak, thanked her.

"What shall I do, now?" he asked. He was in Mrs. Talcott's
hands. "It 's no good writing to Karen. Madame von Marwitz
will intercept my letter if what you believe is true. Shall we go
down to the New Forest directly? Shall I force my way in on
Karen?"

"That's just what you'll have to do; I don't doubt it," said Mrs. Talcott. "And I'll go with you, to manage Mercedes while you get hold of Karen. And I'm not fit for it till I've had a night's rest, so we'll go down first thing to-morrow, Mr. Jardine. I'm spending the night here so as we can talk it all out to-night. But first I'm going round to Mrs. Forrester's. If I'm right, Mr. Jardine, and there ain't any 'if' about it in my own mind, it's important that people should know what the truth is now, before we go. We don't want to have to seem to work up a story to shield Karen if she comes back to you. I'm going to Mrs. Forrester's and I'm going to that mighty silly woman, Miss Scrotton, and I'll have to tell them a thing or two that'll make them sit up."

"But wait first, you must be so tired. Do have some tea first," Gregory urged, as the indomitable old woman made her way towards the door. "And what can you say to them, after all? We are sure of nothing."

Mrs. Talcott paused with her hand on the door knob. "I'm sure of one thing, and they've got to hear it; and that is that Mercedes treated Karen so bad she had to go. Mercedes isn't going to get let off that. I told her so. I told her I'd come right up and tell her friends about her if she stole a march on me, and that's what she's done. Yes," said Mrs. Talcott, opening the door, "I've cut loose from my moorings and Mercedes's friends have got to hear the truth of that story and I'm going to see that they do right away. Good-bye, Mr. Jardine. I don't want any tea; I'll be back in time for dinner, I guess."

CHAPTER XLVI

PEACE had descended upon the little room where Karen lay, cold, still peace. There were no longer any tears or clamour, no appeals and agonies. Tante was often with her; but she seldom spoke now and Karen had ceased to feel more than a dull discomfort when she came into the room.

Tante smiled at her with the soft, unmurmuring patience of her exile, she tended her carefully, she told her that in a day or two, at furthest, they would be out at sea in the most beautiful of yachts. "All has been chosen for my child," she said. "The nurse meets us at Southampton and we wing our way straight to Sicily."

Karen was willing that anything should be done with her except the one thing. It had surprised her to find how much it meant to Tante that she should consent to go back to her. It had not been difficult to consent, when she understood that that was all that Tante wanted and why she wanted it so much. It was the easier since in her heart she believed that she was dying.

All these days it had been like holding her way through a whirlpool. The foam and uproar of the water had beat upon her fragile bark of life, had twisted it and turned it again and again to the one goal where she would not be. Tante had been the torrent, at once stealthy and impetuous, and the goal where she had wished to drive her had been marriage to Franz. Karen had known no fear of yielding, it would have been impossible to her to yield; yet she had thought sometimes that the bark would crack under the onslaught of the torrent and she be dragged down finally to unconsciousness.

All that torment was over. She seemed to be sliding rapidly and smoothly down a misty river. She could see no banks, no sky; all was white, soft, silent. There was no strength left in her with which to struggle against the thought of death, no strength with which to fear it.

But, as she lay in the little room, her hands folded on her breast, corpse-like already in her placidity, something wailed within her and lamented. And sometimes tears rose slowly and swelled her eyelids and she felt herself a creature coffined and underground, put away and forgotten, though not yet a creature dead. Her heart in the darkness still lived and throbbed. Thoughts of Gregory were with her always, memories of him and of their life together which, now that she had lost him forever, she might cherish. She felt, though she lay so still, that she put out her hands always, in supplication, to Gregory. He would forget her, or remember her only as his disgrace. It seemed to her that if she could feel Gregory lean to her and kiss her forehead in tenderness and reconciliation her breath could sweetly cease.

The day before the departure was come and it was a warm, quiet afternoon. Tante had been with her in the morning, engaged in preparations for the journey. She had brought to show to Karen the exquisite nightgowns and wrappers, of softest wool and silk, that she was to wear on the yacht. The long cloak, too, of silk all lined with swansdown, such a garment as the tenderest, most cherished of mortals should wear. This was for Karen when she lay on deck in the sun. And there was a heavier fur-lined cloak for chilly days and the loveliest of shoes and stockings and scarves. All these things Tante had sent for for Karen, and Karen thanked her, as she displayed them before her, gently and coldly. She felt that Tante was piteous at these moments, but nothing in her was moved towards her. Already she was dead to Tante.

She was alone now, again, and she would not see Tante till tea-time. Tante had asked her if she could sleep and she had said yes. She lay with eyes closed, vaguely aware of the sounds that rose to her from the room beneath, where Tante was engaged with the landlady in arranging the new possessions in boxes, and of the fainter sounds from the road in front of the house. Wheels rolled up and stopped. They often came, during these last days; Tante's purchases were arriving by every post. And the voices below seemed presently to alter in pitch and rhythm, mounting to her in a sonorous murmur, dully rising and falling. Karen listened in indifference.

But suddenly there came another sound and this was sharp and near.

There was only one window in the little room; it was open, and it looked out at the back of the house over a straggling garden set round with trees and shrubberies. The sound was outside the window, below it and approaching it, the strangest sound, scratching, cautious, deliberate.

Karen opened her eyes and fixed them on the window. The tree outside hardly stirred against the blue spring sky. Someone was climbing up to her window.

She felt no fear and little surprise. She wondered, placidly, fixing her eyes upon the patterned square of blue and green. And upon this background, like that of some old Italian picture, there rose the head and shoulders of Mrs. Talcott.

Karen raised herself on her elbow and stared. The river stopped in its gliding; the mists rolled away; the world rocked and swayed and settled firmly into a solid, visible reality; Mrs. Talcott's face and her round black straw hat and her black caped shoulders, hoisting themselves up to the window-sill. Never in her life was she to forget the silhouette on the sky and the branching tree, nor Mrs. Talcott's resolute, large, old, face, nor the gaze that Mrs. Talcott's eyes fixed on her as she came.

Mrs. Talcott put her knee on the window-sill and then struggled for a moment, her foot engaged in the last rung of the ladder; then she turned and stepped down backwards into the room.

Karen, raised on her elbow, was trembling.

"Lay down, honey," said Mrs. Talcott, gently and gravely, as they looked at each other; and, as she came towards the bed, Karen obeyed her and joined her hands together. "Oh, will you come with us?" she breathed. "Will you stay with me? I can live if you stay with me, Mrs. Talcott — dear Mrs. Talcott."

She stretched out her hands to her, and Mrs. Talcott, sitting down on the bed beside her, took her in her arms.

"You're all right, now, honey. I'm not going to leave you," she said, stroking back Karen's hair.

Karen leaned her head against her breast, and closed her eyes.

"Listen, honey," said Mrs. Talcott, who spoke in low, careful tones: "I want to ask you something. Do you love Franz Lippheim? Just answer me quiet and easy now. I'm right here, and you're as safe as safe can be."

Karen, on Mrs. Talcott's breast, shook her head. "Oh, no, Mrs. Talcott; you could not believe that. Why should I love dear Franz?"

"Then it's only so as to set your husband free that you're marrying Franz?" Mrs. Talcott went on in the same even voice.

"But no, Mrs. Talcott," said Karen, "I am not going to marry Franz." And now she lifted her head and looked at Mrs. Talcott. "Why do you ask me that? Who has told you that I am to marry Franz?"

Mrs. Talcott, keeping an arm around her, laid her back on the pillow.

"But, Karen, if you run off like that with Franz and come here and stay as his wife," she said, "and get your husband to divorce you by acting so, it's natural that people should think that you're going to marry the young man, ain't it?"

A burning red had mounted to Karen's wasted cheeks. Her sunken eyes dwelt on Mrs. Talcott with a sort of horror. "It is true," she said. "He may think that; he must think that; because unless he does he cannot divorce me and set himself free, and he must be free, Mrs. Talcott; he has said that he wishes to be free. But I did not run away with Franz. I met him, on the headland, that morning, and he was to take me to his mother, and I was so ill that he brought me here. That was all."

Mrs. Talcott smoothed back her hair. "Take it easy, honey," she said. "There's nothing to worry over one mite. And now I've asked my questions and had my answers, and I've got something to tell. Karen, child, it's all been a pack of lies

that Mercedes has told so as to get hold of you, and so as he
should n't — so 'as your husband should n't, Karen. Listen,
honey: your husband loves you just for all he's worth. I 've
seen him. I went up to him. And he told me how you were
all the world to him, and how, if only you did n't love this young
man and did n't want to be free, he'd do anything to get you
back, and how if you'd done the wicked thing he'd been told
and then gotten sorry, he'd want you back just the same because you were his dear wife, and the one woman he loved. But
he could n't force himself on you if you loved someone else and
hated him. So I just told him that I did n't believe you loved
Franz; and I got him to hope it, too, and we came down together,
Karen, and Mercedes is like a lion at bay downstairs, and she 's
in front of that door that leads up here and swears it 'll kill you
to see us; and I 'd seen the ladder leaning on the wall and I
just nipped out while she was talking, and brought it round to
what I calculated would be your window and climbed up, and
that 's what I 've come to tell you, Karen, that he loves you, and
that he 's downstairs, and that he 's waiting to know whether
you 'll see him."

Mrs. Talcott rose and stood by the bed looking down into
Karen's eyes. "Honey, I can bring him up, can't I?" she
asked.

Karen's eyes looked up at her with an intensity that had
passed beyond joy or appeal. Her life was concentrated in her
gaze.

"You would not lie to me?" she said. "It is not pity? He
loves me?"

"No, I would n't lie to you, dearie," said Mrs. Talcott, with
infinite tenderness; "lies ain't my line. It 's not pity. He
loves you, Karen."

"Bring him," Karen whispered. "I have always loved him.
Don't let me die before he comes."

CHAPTER XLVII

MRS. TALCOTT, as she descended the staircase, heard in the little sitting-room a voice, the voice of Mercedes, speaking on and on, in a deep-toned, continuous roll of vehement demonstration, passionate protest, subtle threat and pleading. Gregory's voice she did not hear. No doubt he stood where she had left him, at the other side of the table, confronting his antagonist.

Mrs. Talcott turned the knob of the door and slightly pushed it. A heavy weight at once was flung against it.

"You shall not come in! You shall not! I forbid it! I will not be disturbed!" cried the voice of Mercedes, who must, in the moment, have guessed that she had been foiled.

"Quit that foolishness," said Mrs. Talcott sternly. She leaned against the door and forced it open, and Mercedes, dishevelled, with eyes that seemed to pant on her like eyes from some dangerous jungle, flung herself once more upon the door and stood with her back against it.

"Mr. Jardine," said Mrs. Talcott, not looking at her recovered captive, "Karen is upstairs and wants to see you. She does n't love Franz Lippheim and she is n't going to marry him. She did n't run away with him; she met him when she 'd run away from her guardian and he was going to take her to his mother, only she got sick and he had to bring her here. She was told that you wanted to divorce her and wanted to be free. She loves you, Mr. Jardine, and she 's waiting up there; only be mighty gentle with her, because she 's been brought to death's door by all that she 's been through."

"I forbid it! I forbid it!" shrieked Madame von Marwitz from her place before the door, spreading her arms across it. "She is mad! She is delirious! The doctor has said so! I have promised Franz that you shall not come to her unless across

430

my dead body. I have sworn it! I keep my promise to
Franz!"

Gregory advanced to the door, eyeing her. "Let me pass," he
said. "Let me go to my wife."

"No! no! and no!" screamed the desperate woman. "You
shall not! It will kill her! You shall be arrested! You wish
to kill a woman who has fled from you! Help! Help!" He
had her by the wrists and her teeth seized his hands. She fought
him with incredible fury.

"Hold on tight, Mr. Jardine," Mrs. Talcott's voice came to
him from below. "There; I've got hold of her ankles. Put
her down."

With a loud, clashing wail through clenched and grinding
teeth, Madame von Marwitz, like a pine-tree uprooted, was laid
upon the floor. Mrs. Talcott knelt at her feet, pinioning them.
She looked along the large white form to Gregory at the other
end, who was holding down Madame von Marwitz's shoulders.
"Go on, Mr. Jardine," she said. "Right up those stairs.
She'll calm down now. I've had her like this before."

Gregory rose, yet paused, torn by his longing, yet fearful of
leaving the old woman with the demoniac creature. But
Madame von Marwitz lay as if in a trance. Her lids were closed.
Her breast rose and fell with heavy, regular breaths.

"Go on, Mr. Jardine," said Mrs. Talcott. So he left them
there.

He went up the little stairs, dark and warm, and smelling —
he was never to forget the smell — of apples and dust, and
entered a small, light room where a window made a square of
blue and green. Beyond it in a narrow bed lay Karen. She did
not move or speak; her eyes were fixed on his; she did not smile.
And as he looked at her Mrs. Talcott's words flashed in his
mind: "Karen's that kind: rocky: she don't change."

But she had changed. She was his as she had never been,
never could have been, if the sinister presence lying there downstairs had not finally revealed itself. He knelt beside her and
she was in his arms and his head was laid in the old sacred way
beside his darling's head. They did not seem to speak to each

other for a long time nor did they look into each other's eyes.
He held her hand and looked at that, and sometimes kissed it
gently. But after words had come and their eyes had dared to
meet in joy, Karen said to him: "And I must tell you of
Franz, Gregory, dear Franz. He is suffering, I know. He, too,
was lied to, and he was sent away without seeing me again.
We will write to Franz at once. And you will care for my
Franz, Gregory?"

"Yes; I will care for your Franz; bless your Franz," said
Gregory, with tears, his lips on her hand.

"He came to me like an angel that morning," Karen said in
her breath of voice; "and he has been like a beautiful mother
to me; he has taken care of me like a mother. It was on the
headland over Falmouth — that he came. Oh, Gregory," she
turned her face to her husband's breast, "the birds were beginning to sing and I thought that I should never see you
again."

CHAPTER XLVIII

WHEN the door had shut behind Gregory, Madame von Marwitz spoke, her eyes still closed:
"Am I now permitted to rise?"

Mrs. Talcott released her ankles and stood up.

"You've made a pretty spectacle of yourself, Mercedes," she remarked as Madame von Marwitz raised herself with extraordinary stateliness. "I've seen you behave like you were a devil before, but I never saw you behave like you were quite such a fool. What made you fight him and bite him like that? What did you expect to gain by it I'd like to know? As if you could keep that strong young man from his wife."

Madame von Marwitz had walked to the small mirror over the mantelpiece and was adjusting her hair. Her face, reflected between a blue and gold shepherd and shepherdess holding cornucopias of dried honesty, was still ashen, but she possessed all her faculties. "This is to kill Karen," she now said. "And yours will be the responsibility."

"Taken," Mrs. Talcott replied, but with no facetiousness.

Several of the large tortoiseshell pins that held Madame von Marwitz's abundant locks were scattered on the floor. She turned and looked for them, stooped and picked them up. Then returning to the mirror she continued, awkwardly, to twist up and fasten her hair. She was unaccustomed to doing her own hair and even the few days without a maid had given her no facility.

Mrs. Talcott watched her for a moment and then remarked: "You're getting it all screwed round to one side, Mercedes. You'd better let me do it for you."

Madame von Marwitz for a moment made no reply. Her eyes fixed upon her own mirrored eyes, she continued to insert the pins with an air of stubborn impassivity; but when

28   433

a large loop fell to her neck she allowed her arms to drop. She sank upon a chair and, still with unflawed stateliness, presented the back of her head to Mrs. Talcott's skilful manipulations. Mrs. Talcott, in silence, wreathed and coiled and pinned and the beautiful head resumed its usual outlines.

When this was accomplished Madame von Marwitz rose. "Thank you," she uttered. She moved towards the door of her room.

"What are you going to do now, Mercedes?" Mrs. Talcott inquired. Her eyes, which deepened and darkened, as if all her years of silent watchfulness opened long vistas in them, were fixed upon Mercedes.

"I am going to pack and return to my home," Madame von Marwitz replied.

"Well," said Mrs. Talcott, "you'll want me to pack for you, I expect."

Madame von Marwitz had opened her door and her hand was on the door-knob. She paused so and again, for a long moment, she made no reply. "Thank you," she then repeated. But she turned and looked at Mrs. Talcott. "You have been a traitor to me," she said after she had contemplated her for some moments, "you, in whom I completely trusted. You have ruined me in the eyes of those I love."

"Yes, I've gone back on you, Mercedes, that's a fact," said Mrs. Talcott.

"You have handed Karen over to bondage," Madame von Marwitz went on. "She and this man are utterly unsuited. I would have freed her and given her to a more worthy mate." Her voice had the dignity of a disinterested and deep regret.

Mrs. Talcott made no reply. The long vistas of her eyes dwelt on Mercedes. After another moment of this mutual contemplation Madame von Marwitz closed the door, though she still kept her hand on the door-knob.

"May I ask what you have been saying of me to Mrs. Forrester, to Mr. Jardine?"

"Well, as to Mr. Jardine, Mercedes," said Mrs. Talcott, "there was no need of saying anything, was there, if I turned

out right in what I told him I suspected. He sees I'm right.
He'd been fed up, along with the rest of them, on lies, and
Karen can help him out with the details if he wants to ask for
them. As for the old lady, I gave her the truth of the story
about Karen running away. I made her see, and see straight,
that your one idea was to keep Karen's husband from getting
her back because you knew that if he did the truth about you
would come out. I let you down as easy as I could and put it
that you were n't responsible exactly for the things you said
when you went off your head in a rage and that you were awful
sorry when you found Karen had taken you at your word and
made off. But that old lady feels mighty sick, Mercedes, and
I allow she'll feel sicker when she's seen Mr. Jardine. As for
Miss Scrotton, I saw her, too, and she's come out strong; you've
got a friend there, Mercedes, sure; she won't believe anything
against her beloved Mercedes," a dry smile touched Mrs. Talcott's grave face as she echoed Miss Scrotton's phraseology,
" until she hears from her own lips what she has to say in explanation of the story. You'll be able to fix her up all right,
Mercedes, and most of the others, too, I expect. I'd advise you
to lie low for a while and let it blow over. People are mighty
glad to be given the chance for forgetting things against anyone like you. It'll simmer down and work out, I expect, to
a bad quarrel you had with Karen that's parted you. And
as for the outside world, why it won't mind a mite what you
do. Why you can murder your grandmother and eat her, I
expect, and the world'll manage to overlook it, if you're a
genius."

" I thank you," said Madame von Marwitz, her hand clasping
and unclasping the door-knob. " I thank you indeed for your
reassurance. I have murdered and eaten my grandmother, but
I am to escape hanging because I am a genius. That is a most
gratifying piece of information. You, personally, I infer, consider that the penalty should be paid, however gifted the
criminal."

" I don't know, Mercedes, I don't know," said Mrs. Talcott
in a voice of profound sadness. " I don't know who deserves

penalties and who don't, if you begin to argue it out to yourself." Mrs. Talcott, who had seated herself at the other side of
the table, laid an arm upon it, looking before her and not at
Mercedes, as she spoke. " You're a bad woman; that ain't to
be denied. You're a bad, dangerous woman, and perhaps what
you've been trying to do now is the worst thing you've ever
done. But I guess I'm way past feeling angry at anything
you do. I guess I'm way past wanting you to get come up with.
I can't make out how to think about a person like you. Maybe
you figured it all out to yourself different from the way it looks.
Maybe you persuaded yourself to believe that Karen would be
better off apart from her husband. I guess that's the way with
most criminals, don't you? They figure things out different
from the way other people do. I expect you can't help it. I
expect you were born so. And I guess you can't change. Some
bad folks seem to manage to get religion and that brings 'em
round; but I expect you ain't that kind."

Madame von Marwitz, while Mrs. Talcott thus shared her
psychological musings with her, was not looking at the old
woman: her eyes were fixed on the floor and she seemed to
consider.

" No," she said presently. " I am not that kind."

She raised her eyes and they met Mrs. Talcott's. " What are
you going to do now? " she asked.

" Well," said Mrs. Talcott, drawing a long sigh of fatigue,
" I've been thinking that over and I guess I'll stay over here.
There ain't any place for me in America now; all my folks are
dead. You know that money my Uncle Adam left me a long
time ago that I bought the annuity with. Well, I've saved
most of that annuity; I'd always intended that Karen should
have what I'd saved when I died. But Karen don't need it
now. It'll buy me a nice little cottage somewhere and I can
settle down and have a garden and chickens and live on what
I've got."

" How much was it, the annuity? " Madame von Marwitz
asked after a moment.

" A hundred and ten pounds a year," said Mrs. Talcott.

"But you cannot live on that," Madame von Marwitz, after another moment, said.

"Why, gracious sakes, of course I can, Mercedes," Mrs. Talcott replied, smiling dimly.

Again there was silence and then Madame von Marwitz said, in a voice a little forced: "You have not got much out of life, have you, Tallie?"

"Well, no; I don't expect you would say as I had," Mrs. Talcott acquiesced, showing a slight surprise.

"You have n't even got me — now — have you," Madame von Marwitz went on, looking down at her door-knob and running her hand slowly round it while she spoke. "Not even the criminal. But that is a gain, you feel, no doubt, rather than a loss."

"No, Mercedes," said Mrs. Talcott mildly; "I don't feel that way. I feel it 's a loss, I guess. You see you 're all the family I 've got left."

"And you," said Madame von Marwitz, still looking down at her knob, "are all the family I have left."

Mrs. Talcott now looked at her. Mercedes did not raise her eyes. Her face was sad and very pale and it had not lost its stateliness. Mrs. Talcott looked at her for what seemed to be a long time and the vistas of her eyes deepened with a new acceptance.

It was without any elation and yet without any regret that she said in her mild voice: "Do you want me to come back with you, Mercedes?"

"Will you?" Madame von Marwitz asked in a low voice.

"Why, yes, of course I 'll come if you want me, Mercedes," said Mrs. Talcott.

Madame von Marwitz now opened her door. "Thank you, Tallie," she said.

"You look pretty tired," Mrs. Talcott, following her into the bedroom, remarked. "You 'd better lie down and take a rest while I do the packing. Let 's clear out as soon as we can."

THE END

There Are Two Sides to Everything—

—including the wrapper which covers every Grosset & Dunlap book. When you feel in the mood for a good romance, refer to the carefully selected list of modern fiction comprising most of the successes by prominent writers of the day which is printed on the back of every Grosset & Dunlap book wrapper.

You will find more than five hundred titles to choose from—books for every mood and every taste and every pocketbook.

Don't forget the other side, but in case the wrapper is lost, write to the publishers for a complete catalog.

www.ingramcontent.com/pod-product-compliance
Lightning Source LLC
Chambersburg PA
CBHW020829030726
47496CB00001B/157